PINUP GIRL

The scene I glimpsed over Titus' shoulder will remain with me through all my nights. A picture-nail in his hand, Jack stared at us in frozen shock from his place by the wall.

Both my eyes and nose, though, drew me away from him to the naked flesh on the bed. Whether she was fair I cannot say, as he had repeatedly slashed her face. Her throat was cut; it gaped at me like a second, speechless mouth. He had gutted her as well.

When we interrupted him, Jack was hanging bits of the woman's flesh on the wall. He waved in invitation to the blood-drenched sheets. "Plenty there for the lot of yez," said he, grinning.

By Harry Turtledove
Published by Ballantine Books:

The Videssos Cycle:
  THE MISPLACED LEGION
  AN EMPEROR FOR THE LEGION
  THE LEGION OF VIDESSOS
  SWORDS OF THE LEGION

NONINTERFERENCE

A WORLD OF DIFFERENCE

KALEIDOSCOPE

KALEIDOSCOPE

Harry Turtledove

A Del Rey Book

BALLANTINE BOOKS • NEW YORK

A Del Rey Book
Published by Ballantine Books

The contents of this work were originally published in the following
magazines: AMAZING STORIES, ANALOG Science Fiction/
Science Fact, DRAGON, FANTASY AND SCIENCE FICTION,
FANTASY BOOK, PLAYBOY, and THE TWILIGHT ZONE.

Grateful acknowledgment is made to Gardner Dozois and Susan
Casper for permission to reprint "Gentlemen of the Shade" by
Harry Turtledove from RIPPER! (Tor.) Copyright © 1988 by Gard-
ner Dozois and Susan Casper.

Library of Congress Catalog Card Number: 89-91550

ISBN 0-345-36477-5

Manufactured in the United States of America

First Edition: April 1990

Cover art by Barclay Shaw

TABLE OF CONTENTS

I've done a whole series of stories set in an alternate world where *Homo erectus* settled the Americas several hundred thousand years ago but the Indians never made it across the Siberian land-bridge (these stories are collected as *A Different Flesh*, Congdon & Weed, 1988). The presence of these subhumans—"sims"—and the Indians' absence would have made a profound difference in the way North and South America were settled by European colonists . . . and the way people looked at our place in nature. I've chosen this particular story because of the issues it raises—and because writing pastiche is so much *fun*.

AND SO TO BED

MAY 4, 1661. *A FINE BRIGHT MORNING. SMALL* beer and radishes for to break my fast, then into London for this day. The shambles on Newgate Street stinking unto heaven, as is usual, but close to it my destination, the sim marketplace. Our servant Jane with too much for one body to do, and whilst I may not afford the hire of another man or maid, two sims shall go far to ease her burthen.

Success also sure to gladden Elizabeth's heart, my wife being ever one to follow the dame Fashion, and sims all the go of late, though monstrous ugly. Them formerly not much seen here, but since the success of our Virginia and Plymouth colonies are much more often fetched to these shores from the wildernesses the said colonies front upon. They are also commenced to be bred on English soil, but no hope there for me, as I do require workers full-grown, not cubs or babes in arms or whatsoever the proper term may be.

The sim-seller a vicious lout, near unhandsome as his wares. No, the truth for the diary: such were a slander on any man, as I saw on his conveying me to the creatures.

Have seen these sims before, surely, but briefly, and in their masters' livery, the which by concealing their nakedness conceals as well much of their brutishness. The males are most of them well made, though lean as rakes from the ocean passage and, I warrant, poor victualing after. But all are so hairy as

1

more to resemble rugs than men, and the same true for the females, hiding such dubious charms as they may possess nigh as well as a smock of linen: nought here, God knows, for Elizabeth's jealousy to light on.

This so were the said females lovely of feature as so many Aphrodites. They are not, nor do the males recall to mind Adonis. In both sexes the brow projects with a shelf of bone, and above it, where men do enjoy a forehead proud in its erectitude, is but an apish slope. The nose broad and low, the mouth wide, the teeth nigh as big as a horse's (though shaped, it is not to be denied, like a man's), the jaw long, deep, and devoid of chin. They stink.

The sim-seller full of compliments on my coming hard on the arrival of the *Gloucester* from Plymouth, him having thereby replenished his stock in trade. Then the price should also be not so dear, says I, and by God it did do my heart good to see the ferret-faced rogue discomfited.

Rogue as he was, though, he dickered with the best, for I paid full a guinea more for the pair of sims than I had looked to, spending in all £11.6s.4d. The coin once passed over (and bitten, for to ensure its verity), the sim-seller signed to those of his chattels I had bought that they were to go with me.

His gestures marvelous quick and clever, and those the sims answered with too. Again, I have seen somewhat of the like before. Whilst coming to understand in time the speech of men, sims are without language of their own, having but a great variety of howls, grunts, and moans. Yet this gesture-speech, which I am told is come from the signs of the deaf, they do readily learn, and often their masters answer back so, to ensure commands being properly grasped.

Am wild to learn it my own self, and shall. Meseems it is in its way a style of tachygraphy or short-hand such as I use to set down these pages. Having devised varying tachygraphic hands for friends and acquaintances, 'twill be amusing taking to a *hand* that is exactly what its name declares.

As I was leaving with my new charges, the sim-seller did bid me lead them by the gibbets on Shooter's Hill, there to see the bodies and members of felons and of sims as have run off from their masters. It wondered me they should have the wit to take the meaning of such display, but he assured me they should. And so, reckoning it good advice if true and no harm if a lie, I chivvied them thither.

A filthy sight I found it, with the miscreants' flesh all shrunk to the bones. But *hoo*! quoth my sims, and looked close upon the corpses of their own kind, which by their hairiness and flat-skulled heads do seem even more bestial dead than when animated with life.

Home then, and Elizabeth as delighted in my success as am I. An excellent dinner of a calf's head boiled with dumplings, and an abundance of buttered ale with sugar and cinnamon, of which in celebration we invited Jane to partake, and she grew right giddy. Bread and leeks for the sims, and water, it being reported they grow undocile on stronger drink.

After much debate, though good-natured, it was decided to style the male Will and the female Peg. Showed them to their pallets down cellar, and they took to them readily enough, as finer than what they were accustomed to.

So to bed, right pleased with myself despite the expense.

May 7. An advantage of having sims present appears that I had not thought on. Both Will and Peg quite excellent ratters, finer than any puss-cat. No need, either, to fling the rats on the dungheap, for they devour them with as much gusto as I should a neat's tongue. They having subsisted on such small deer in the forests of America, I shall not try to break them of the habit, though training them not to bring in their prey when we are at table with guests. The Reverend Mr. Milles quite shocked, but recovering nicely on being plied with wine.

May 8. Peg and Will the both of them enthralled with fire. When the work of them is done of the day, or at evening ere they take their rest, they may be found before the hearth observing the sport of the flames. Now and again one will to the other say *hoo*!—this noise, I find, they utter on seeing that which does interest them, whatsoever it may be.

Now as I thought on it, I minded me reading or hearing, I recall not which, that in their wild unpeopled haunts the sims know the use of fire as they find it set from lightning or other such mischance, but not the art of its making. No wonder then they are Vulcanolaters, reckoning flame more precious than do we gold.

Considering such reflections, I resolved this morning on an experiment, to see what they might do. Rising early for to void my bladder in the pot, I put out the hearthfire, which in any case was gone low through want of fuel. Retired then to put on my dressing gown and, once clad, returned to await developments.

First up from the cellar was Will, and his cry on seeing the flames extinguished heartrending as Romeo's over the body of fair Juliet when I did see that play acted this December past. In a trice comes Peg, whose moaning with Will did rouse my wife, and she much upset at being so rudely wakened.

When the calm in some small measure restored, I bade by signs, in the learning of which I proceed apace, for the sims to sit quietly before the hearth, and with flint and steel restored that which I had earlier destroyed. They both made such outcry as if they had heard sounded the Last Trump.

Then doused I that second fire too, again to much distress from Peg and Will. Elizabeth by this time out of the house in some dudgeon, no doubt to spend money we lack on stuffs of which we have no want.

Set up in the hearth thereupon several small fires of sticks, each with much tinder so as to make it an easy matter to kindle. A brisk striking of flint and steel dropping sparks onto one such produced a merry little blaze, to the accompaniment of much *hoo*ing out of the sims.

And so the nub of it. Shewing Will the steel and flint, I clashed them once more the one upon the other so he might see the sparks engendered thereby. Then pointed to one of the afore-mentioned piles of sticks I had made up, bidding him watch close, as indeed he did. Having made sure of't, I did set that second pile alight.

Again put the fires out, the wailing accompanying the act less than heretofore, for which I was not sorry. Pointed now to a third assemblage of wood and timber, but instead of myself lighting it, I did convey flint and steel to Will, and with signs essayed to bid him play Prometheus.

His hands much scarred and callused, and under their hair knobby-knuckled as an Irishman's. He held at first the imple-ments as if not taking in their purpose, yet the sims making tools of stone, as is widely reported, he could not wholly fail to grasp their utility.

And indeed ere long he did try parroting me. When his first clumsy attempt yielded no result, I thought he would abandon such efforts as beyond his capacity and reserved for men of my sort. But persist he did, and at length was reward with scintillae like unto those I had made. His grin so wide and gleeful I thought it would stretch clear round his head.

Then without need of my further demonstration he set the instruments of fire production over the materials for the blaze.

Him in such excitement as the sparks fell upon the waiting tinder that beneath his breeches rose his member, indeed to such degree as would have made me proud to be its possessor. And Peg was, I think, in such mood as to couple with him on the spot, had I not been present and had not his faculties been directed elsewhere than toward the lectual.

For at his success he cut such capers as had not been out of place upon the stage, were they but a trifle more rhythmical and less unconstrained. Yet of the making of fire, even if by such expedient as the friction of two sticks (which once I was forced by circumstance to attempt, and would try the patience of Job), as of every other salutary art, his race is as utterly ignorant as of the moons of Jupiter but lately found by some Italian with an optic glass.

No brute beast of the field could learn to begin a fire on the technique being shown it, which did Will nigh readily as a man. But despite most diligent instruction, no sim yet has mastered such subtler arts as reading and writing, nor ever will, meseems. Falling in capacity thus between man and animal, the sims do raise a host of conundrums vexing and perplexing. I should pay a pound, or at the least ten shillings, merely to know how such strange fusions came to be.

So to the Admiralty full of such musings, which did occupy my mind, I fear, to the detriment of my proper duties.

May 10. Supper this evening at the Turk's Head, with the other members of the Rota Club. The fare not of the finest, being boiled venison and some few pigeons, all meanly done up. The lamb's wool seemed nought but poor ale, the sugar, nutmeg and meat of roasted apples hardly to be tasted. Miles the landlord down with a quartan fever, but ill served by his staff if such is the result of his absence.

The subject of the Club's discussions for the evening much in accord with my own recent curiosity, to wit, the sims. Cyriack Skinner did maintain them creatures of the Devil, whereupon was he roundly rated by Dr. Croon as having in this contention returned to the pernicious heresy of the Manichees, the learned doctor reserving the power of creation of the Lord alone. Much flinging back and forth of Biblical texts, the which all struck me as being more the exercise of ingenuity of the debaters than bearing on the problem, for in plain fact the Scriptures nowhere mention sims.

When at length the talk did turn to matters more ascertainable, I spoke somewhat of my recent investigation, and right well-received my remarks were, or so I thought. Others with experience of sims with like tales, finding them quick enough on things practic but sadly lacking in any higher faculties. Much jollity at my account of the visible manifestation of Will's excitement, and whispers that his lady or that (the names, to my vexation, I failed to catch) owned her sims for naught but their prowess in matters of the mattress.

Just then came the maid by with coffee for the Club, not of the best, but better, I grant, than the earlier wretched lamb's wool. She a pretty yellow-haired lass called I believe Kate, a wench of perhaps sixteen years, a good-bodied woman not over thick or thin in any place, with a lovely bosom she did display most charmingly as she bent to fill the gentlemen's cups.

Having ever an eye for beauty, such that I reckon little else beside it, I own I did turn my head for to follow this Kate as she went about her duties. Noticing which, Sir William Henry called out, much to the merriment of the Club and to my chagrin, "See how Samuel peeps!" Him no mean droll, and loosed a pretty pun, if at my expense. Good enough, but then at the far end of the table someone, I saw not who, worse luck, thought to cap it by braying like the donkey he must be, "Not half the peeping, I warrant, as at his sims of nights!"

Such mockery clings to a man like pitch, regardless of the truth in't, which in this case is none. Oh, the thing could be done, but the sims so homely 'twould yield no titillation, of that I am practically certain.

May 12. The household being more infected this past week with nits than ever before, resolved to bathe Peg and Will, which also I hoped would curb somewhat their stench. And so it proved, albeit not without more alarums than I had looked for. The sims most loth to enter the tub, which must to them have seemed some instrument of torment. The resulting shrieks and outcry so deafening a neighbor did call out to be assured all was well.

Having done so, I saw no help for it but to go into the tub my own self, notwithstanding my having bathed but two weeks before. I felt, I think more hesitation stripping down before Peg than I should in front of Jane, whom I would simply dismiss from consideration but in how she performed her duties. But I did wonder what Peg made of my body, reckoning it against the hairy forms of her own kind. Hath she the wit to deem mankind superior, or is our smoothness to her as gross and repellent as the peltries of the sims to us? I cannot as yet make shift to enquire.

As may be, my example showing them they should not be harmed, they bathed themselves. A trouble arose I had not foreseen, for the sims being nearly as thickly haired over all their bodies as I upon my head, the rinsing of the soap from their hides less easy than for us, and requiring much water. Lucky I am the well is within fifty paces of my home. And so from admiral of the bath to the Admiralty, hoping henceforward to scratch myself less.

May 13. A pleasant afternoon this day, carried in a coach to see the lions and other beasts in the menagerie. I grant the lions pride of place through custom immemorial, but in truth am more taken with the abnormal creatures fetched back from the New World than those our forefathers have known since the time of Arthur. Nor am I alone in this conceit, for the cages of lion, bear, camel had but few spectators, whilst round those of the American beasts I did find myself compelled to use hands and elbows to make shift to pass through the crowds.

This last not altogether unpleasant, as I chanced to brush against a handsome lass, but when I did enquire if she would take tea with me she said me nay, which did irk me no little, for as I say she was fair to see.

More time for the animals, then, and wondrous strange ever they strike me. The spear-fanged cat is surely the most horridest murderer this shuddering world hath seen, yet there is for him prey worthy of his mettle, what with beavers near big as our bears, wild oxen whose horns are to those of our familiar kine as the spear-fanged cat's teeth to the lion's, and the great hairy elephants which do roam the forests.

Why such prodigies of nature manifest themselves on those distant shores does perplex me most exceedingly, as they are unlike any beasts even in the bestiaries, which as all men know are more flights of fancy than sober fact. Amongst them the sims appear no more than one piece of some great jigsaw, yet no pattern therein is to me apparent; would it were.

Also another new creature in the menagerie, which I had not seen before. At first I thought it a caged sim, but on inspection it did prove an ape, brought back by the Portuguese from Afric lands and styled there, the keeper made so good as to inform me, shimpanse. It flourishes not in England's clime, he did continue, being subject to sickness in the lungs from the cool and damp, but is so interesting as to be displayed whilst living, how-soever long that may prove.

The shimpanse a baser brute than even the sim. It goes on all fours, and its hinder feet more like unto monkeys' than men's, having thereon great toes that grip like thumbs. Also, where a sim's teeth, as I have observed from Will and Peg, are uncommon large, in shape they are like unto a man's, but the shim-panse hath tushes of some savagery, though of course paling alongside those of the spear-fanged cat.

Seeing the keeper a garrulous fellow, I enquired of him further anent this shimpanse. He owned he had himself thought it a sort of sim on its arrival, but sees now more distinguishing points than likenesses: gait and dentition, such as I have herein remarked upon, but also in its habits. From his experience, he has seen it to be ignorant of fire, repeatedly allowing to die a blaze though fuel close at hand. Nor has it the knack of shaping stones to its ends, though it will, he told me, cast them betimes against those who annoy it, once striking one such with force enough to render him some time senseless. Hearing the villain had essayed tormenting the creature with a stick, my sympathies lay all for the shimpanse, wherein its keeper concurred.

And so homewards, thinking on the shimpanse as I rode. Whereas in the lands wherewith men are most familiar it were easy distinguishing men from beasts, the strange places to which our vessels have but lately fetched themselves reveal a stairway ascending the chasm, and climbers on the stairs, some higher, some lower. A pretty image, but why it should be so there and not here does I confess escape me.

May 16. A savage row with Jane today, her having forgotten a change of clothes for my bed. Her defense that I had not so instructed her, the lying minx, for I did plainly make my wishes known the evening previous, which I recollect most distinctly. Yet she did deny it again and again, finally raising my temper to such a pitch that I cursed her right roundly, slapping her face and pulling her nose smartly.

Whereupon did the ungrateful trull lay down her service on the spot. She decamped in a fury of her own, crying that I treated the sims, those very sims which I had bought for to ease her labors, with more kindlier consideration than I had for her own self.

So now we are without a serving-maid, and her a dab hand in the kitchen, her swan pie especially being toothsome. Dined tonight at the Bell, and expect to tomorrow at the Swan on the Hoop, in Fish Street. For Elizabeth no artist over the hearth, nor am I myself. And as for the sims, I should sooner open my veins than indulge of their cuisine, the good Lord only knowing what manner of creatures they in their ignorance should add to a pot.

Now as my blood has somewhat cooled, I must admit a germ of truth in Jane's scolds. I do not beat Will and Peg as a man would servitors of more ordinary stripe. They, being but new come from the wilds, are not inured to't as are our servants, and might well turn on me their master. And being in part of brute kind, their strength does exceed mine, Will's most assuredly and that of Peg perhaps. And so, say I, better safe. No satisfaction to me for the sims on Shooter's Hill gallows, were I not there to see't.

May 20. Today to my lord Sandwich's for supper. This doubly pleasant, in enjoying his fine companionship and saving the cost of a meal, the house being still without maid. The food and drink in excellent style, as to suit my lord. The broiled lobsters very sweet, and the lamprey pie (which for its rarity I but seldom eat of) the best ever I had. Many other fine victuals as well (the tanzy in especial), and the wine all sugared.

Afterwards backgammon, at which I won £5 ere my luck turned. Ended 15s. in my lord's debt, which he did graciously excuse me afterwards, a generosity not looked for but which I did not refuse. Then to crambo, wherein by tagging *and rich* to *Sandwich* I was adjudged winner, the more so for playing on his earlier munificence.

Thereafter nigh a surfeit of good talk, as is custom at my lord's. He mentioning sims, I did relate my own dealings with Peg and Will, to which he listened with much interest. He thinks on buying some for his own household, and unaware I had done so.

Perhaps it was the wine let loose my tongue, for I broached somewhat my disjoint musings on the sims and their place in nature, on the strangeness of the American fauna and much else besides. Lord Sandwich did acquaintance me with a New World beast found in their southerly holdings by the Spaniards, of strange outlandish sort: big as an ox, or nearly, and all covered over with armor of bone like a man wearing chain. I should pay out a shilling or even more for to see't, were one conveyed to London.

Then coffee, and it not watered as so often at an inn, but full and strong. As I and Elizabeth making our departures, Lord Sandwich did bid me join him tomorrow night to hear speak a savant of the Royal Society. It bore, said he, on my prior ramblings, and would say no more, but looked uncommon sly. Even did it not, I should have leaped at the chance.

This written at one of the clock, for so the watchman just now cried out. Too wound up for bed, what with coffee and the morrow's prospect. Elizabeth aslumber, but the sims also awake, and at frolic meseems, from the noises up the stairway.

If they be of human kind, is their fornication *sans* clergy sinful? Another vexing question. By their existence, they do engender naught but disquietude. Nay, strike that. They may in sooth more sims engender, a pun good enough to sleep on, and so to bed.

May 21. All this evening worrying at my thoughts as a dog at a bone. My lord Sandwich knows not what commotion internal he did by his invitation, all kindly meant, set off in me. The speaker this night a spare man, dry as dust, of the very sort I learned so well to loathe when at Cambridge.

Dry as dust! Happy words, which did spring all unbidden from my pen. For of dust the fellow did discourse, if thereby is meant, as commonly, things long dead. He had some men bear in bones but lately found by Swanscombe at a grave-digging. And such bones they were, and teeth (or rather tusks), as to make it all I could do to hold me in my seat. For surely they once graced no less a beast than the hairy elephant whose prototype I saw in menagerie so short a while ago. The double-curving tusks admit of no error, for those of all elephants with which we are anciently familiar form but a single segment of arc.

When, his discourse concluded, he gave leave for questions, I made bold to ask to what he imputed the hairy elephant's being so long vanished from our shores yet thriving in the western lands. To this he confessed himself baffled, as am I, and admiring of his honesty as well.

Before the hairy elephant was known to live, such monstrous bones surely had been reckoned as from beasts perishing in the Flood whereof Scripture speaks. Yet how may that be so, them surviving across a sea wider than any Noah sailed?

Meseems the answer lieth within my grasp, but am balked from setting finger to't. The thwarting fair to drive me mad, worse even, I think, than with a lass who will snatch out a hatpin for to defend her charms against my importuning.

* * *

May 22. Grand oaks from tiny acorns grow! This morning came a great commotion from the kitchen. I rushing in found Will at struggle with a cur dog which had entered, the door being open on account of fine weather, to steal half a flitch of salt bacon. It dodging most nimbly round the sim, snatched up the gammon and fled out again, him pursuing but in vain.

Myself passing vexed, having intended to sup thereon. But Will all downcast on returning, so had not the heart further to punish him. Told him instead, him understanding I fear but little, it were well men not sims dwelt in England, else would wolves prowl the London streets still.

Stood stock still some time thereafter, hearing the greater import behind my jesting speech. Is not the answer to the riddle of the hairy elephant and other exotic beasts existing in the New World but being hereabouts long vanished their having there but sims to hunt them? The sims in their wild haunts wield club and sharpened stone, no more. They are ignorant even of the bow, which from time out of mind has equipt the hunter's armory.

Just as not two centuries past we Englishmen slew on this island the last wolf, so may we not imagine our most remotest grandsires serving likewise the hairy elephant, the spear-fanged cat? They being more cunning than sims and better accoutered, this should not have surpassed their powers. Such beasts would survive in America, then, not through virtue inherent of their own, but by reason of lesser danger to them in the sims than would from mankind come.

Put this budding thought at luncheon today to my lord Sandwich. Him back at me with Marvell to his coy mistress (the most annoyingest sort!), viz., had we but world enough and time, who could reckon the changes as might come to pass? And going on, laughing, to say next will be found dead sims at Swanscombe.

Though meant but as a pleasantry, quoth I, why not? Against true men they could not long have stood, but needs must have given way as round Plymouth and Virginia. Even without battle they must soon have failed, as being less able than mankind to provide for their wants.

There we let it lay, but as I think more on't, the notion admits of broader application. Is't not the same for trout as for men, or for lilacs? Those best suited living reproduce their kind, whilst the trout with twisted tail or bloom without sweet scent die all unmourned leaving no descendants. And each succeeding generation being of the previous survivors constituted, will by such reasoning show some little difference from the one as went before.

Seeing no flaw in this logic, resolve tomorrow to do this from its tachygraphic state, bereft of course of maunderings and privacies, for prospectus to the Royal Society, and mightily wondering whatever they shall make of it.

May 23. Closeted all this day at the Admiralty. Yet did it depend on my diligence alone, I fear me the Fleet should drown. Still, a deal of business finished, as happens when one stays by it. Three quills worn quite out, and my hands all over ink. Also my fine camlet cloak with the gold buttons, which shall mightily vex my wife, poor wretch, unless it may be cleaned. I pray God to make it so, for I do mislike strife at home.

The burning work at last complete, homeward in the twilight. It being washing-day, dined on cold meat. I do confess, felt no small strange stir in my breast on seeing Will taking down the washing before the house. A vision it was, almost, of his kind roaming England long ago, till perishing from want of substance or vying therefor with men. And now they are through the agency of men returned here again, after some great interval of years. Would I knew how many.

The writing of my notions engrossing the whole of the day, had no occasion to air them to Lord Brouncker of the Society, as was my hope. Yet expound I must, or burst. Elizabeth, then, at dinner made audience for me, whether she would or no. My spate at last exhausted, asked for her thoughts on't.

She said only that Holy Writ sufficed on the matter for her, whereat I could but make a sour face. To bed in some anger, and in fear lest the Royal Society prove as close-minded, which God prevent. Did He not purpose man to reason on the world around him, He should have left him witless as the sim.

May 24. To Gresham College this morning, to call on Lord Brouncker. He examined with great care the papers I had done up, his face revealing nought. Felt myself at recitation once more before a professor, a condition whose lack these last years I have not missed. Feared also he might not be able to take in the writing, it being done in such haste some short-hand characters may have replaced the common ones.

Then to my delight he declared he reckoned it deserving of a hearing at the Society's weekly meeting next. Having said so much, he made to dismiss me, himself being much occupied with devising a means whereby to calculate the relation of a circle's circumference to its diameter. I wish him joy of't. I do resolve one day soon, however, to learn the multiplication table, which meseems should be of value at the Admiralty. Repaired there from the college, to do the work I had set by yesterday.

May 26. Watch these days Will and Peg with new eyes. I note for instance them using between themselves our deaf-man's signs, as well as to me and my wife. As well they might, them conveying far more subtler meanings than the bestial howlings and gruntings that are theirs in nature. Thus though they may not devise any such, they own the wit to see its utility.

I wonder would the shimpanse likewise?

A girl came today asking after the vacant maidservant's post, a pretty bit with red hair, white teeth, and fine strong haunches. Thought myself she would serve, but Elizabeth did send her away. Were her looks liker to Peg's, she had I think been hired on the spot. But a quarrel on it not worth the candle, the more so as I have seen fairer.

May 28. This writ near cockcrow, in hot haste, lest any detail of the evening escape my recollection. Myself being a late addition, spoke last, having settled the title "A Proposed Explication of the Survival of Certain Beasts in America and Their Disappearance Hereabouts" on the essay.

The prior speakers addressed one the organs internal of bees and other the appearance of Saturn in the optic glass, both topics which interest me but little. Then called to the podium by Lord Brouncker, all aquiver as a virgin bride. Much wished myself in the company of some old soakers over roast pigeons and dumplings and sack. But a brave front amends for much, and so plunged in straightaway.

Used the remains of the hairy elephant presented here a sennight past as example of a beast vanished from these shores yet across the sea much in evidence. Then on to the deficiencies of sims as hunters, when set beside even the most savagest of men.

Thus far well-received, and even when noting the struggle to live and leave progeny that does go on among each kind and between the several kinds. But the storm broke, as I feared it should and more, on my drawing out the implications therefrom: that of each generation only so many may flourish and breed; and that each succeeding generation, being descended of these survivors alone, differs from that which went before.

My worst and fearfullest nightmare then came true, for up rose shouts of blasphemy. Gave them back what I had told Elizabeth on the use of reason, adding in some heat I had expected such squallings of my wife who is a woman and ignorant, but better from men styling themselves natural philosophers. Did they aim to prove me wrong, let them so by the reason they do profess to cherish. This drew further catcalling but also approbation, which at length prevailed.

Got up then a pompous little manikin, who asked how I dared set myself against God's word insofar as how beasts came to be. On my denying this, he did commence reciting at me from Genesis. When he paused for to draw breath, I asked most mildly of him on which day the Lord did create the sims. Thereupon he stood discomfited, his foolish mouth hanging open, at which I was quite heartened.

Would the next inquisitor had been so easily downed! A Puritan he was, by his somber cloak and somberer bearing. His questions took the same tack as the previous, but not so stupidly. After first enquiring if I believed in God, whereat I truthfully told him aye, he asked did I think Scripture to be the word of God. Again said aye, by now getting and dreading the drift of his argument. And as I feared, he bade me next point him out some place where Scripture was mistaken, ere supplanting it with fancies of mine own.

I knew not how to make answer, and should have in the next moment fled. But up spake to my great surprise Lord Brouncker, reciting from Second Chronicles, the second verse of the fourth chapter, wherein is said of Solomon and his Temple, *Also he made the molten sea of ten cubits from brim to brim, round in compass, and the height thereof was five cubits, and a line of thirty cubits did compass it round about.*

This much perplexed the Puritan and me as well, though I essayed not to show it. Lord Brouncker then proceeded to his explication, to wit that the true compass of a ten-cubit round vessel was not thirty cubits, but above one and thirty, I misremember the exact figure he gave. Those of the Royal Society learned in mathematics did agree he had reason, and urged the Puritan make the experiment for his self with cup, cord, and rule, which were enough for to demonstrate the truth.

I asked if he was answered. Like a gentleman he owned he was, and bowed, and sat, his face full of troubles. Felt with him no small sympathy, for once one error in Scripture is admitted, where shall it end?

The next query was of different sort, a man in periwig enquiring if I did reckon humankind to have arisen by the means I described. Had to reply I did. Our forefathers might be excused for thinking otherwise, them being so widely separate from all other creatures they knew.

But we moderns in our travels round the globe have found the shimpanse, which standeth nigh the flame of reasoned thought; and more important still the sim, in whom the flame does burn, but more feebly than in ourselves. These bridging the gap twixt man and beast meseems do show mankind to be in sooth a part of nature, whose engenderment in some past distant age is to be explained through natural law.

Someone rose to doubt the variation in each sort of living thing being sufficient eventually to permit the rise of new kinds. Pointed out to him the mastiffe, the terrier, and the bloodhound, all of the dog kind, but become distinct through man's choice of mates in each generation. Surely the same might occur in nature, said I. The fellow admitted it was conceivable, and sat.

Then up stood a certain Wilberforce, with whom I have some small acquaintance. He likes me not, nor I him. We know it on both sides, though for civility's sake feigning otherwise. Now he spoke with smirking air, as one sure of the mortal thrust. He did grant my willingness to have a sim as great-grandfather, said he, but was I so willing to claim one as great-grandmother? A deal of laughter rose, which was his purpose, and to make me out a fool.

Had I carried steel, I should have drawn on him. As was, rage sharpened my wit to serve for the smallsword I left at home. Told him it were no shame to have one's great-grandfather a sim, as that sim did use to best advantage the intellect he had. Better that, quoth I, than dissipating the mind on such digressive and misleading quibbles as he raised. If I be in error, then I am; let him shew it by logic and example, not as it were playing to the gallery.

Came clapping from all sides, to my delight and the round dejection of Wilberforce. On seeking further questions, found none. Took my own seat whilst the Fellows of the Society did congratulate me and cry up my essay louder, I thought, than either of the other two. Lord Brouncker acclaimed it as a unifying principle for the whole of the study of life, which made me as proud a man as any in the world, for all the world seemed to smile upon me.

And so to bed.

"Bluff" is based on the fascinating speculations Julian Jaynes put forward in *The Origins of Consciousness in the Breakdown of the Bicameral Mind*. They give rise to my favorite kind of aliens: those who think as well as people but not at all like them.

Not long after "Bluff" appeared in *Analog*, I got a letter from Professor Jaynes. I have to say that I opened the envelope with some trepidation. Much to my relief, I found inside a kind note telling me that he'd liked the story. So I must have done something right.

BLUFF

THE PICTURES FROM THE SURVEY SATELLITES came out of the fax machine one after the other, *chunk*, *chunk*, *chunk*. Ramon Castillo happened to be close by. He took them from the tray, more out of a sense of duty than in the expectation of finding anything interesting. The previous photo runs of the still-unnamed planet below had proven singularly dull.

There hadn't been a good shot of this river-valley system before, though. As he studied the print, his heavy eyebrows lifted like raven's wings. He felt a flush of excitement beneath his coppery skin, and damned himself for a fool. "Wishful thinking," he muttered aloud. Just the same, he slipped the print into the magnifying viewer.

His whoop brought people running from all over the *William Howells*. Helga Stein was first into the fax compartment: a stocky blonde in her late twenties, her normally serious expression now replaced by surprise. "*Mein Gott*, was that you, Ramon?" she exclaimed; Castillo was usually very quiet.

Most of the time he found her intensely annoying; he was a cultural anthropologist and she a psychologist, and their different approaches to problems that touched them both led to frequent arguments. Now, though, he stepped away from the viewer and invited her forward with a courtly sweep of his arm. "You'll see for yourself," he said grandly. He spoke Latin with a facility that left everyone else aboard the *Howells* jealous.

"What am I looking for?" she asked, fiddling with the focus. By then the other members of the survey team were crowding in: physical anthropologist Sybil Hussie and her husband George Davies, who was a biologist (they were married just before up-ship, and George had endured in good spirits all the stale jokes about practicing what he studied); Xing Mei-lin the linguist; and Manolis Zakythinos, whose specialty was geology.

Even Stan Jeffries stuck his head in to see what the fuss was about. "Found the mountain of solid platinum, did you?" the navigator chuckled, seeing Helga peering into the viewer.

She looked up, puzzlement on her face. "What is that in Latin?" she asked; the ship's English-speakers consistently forgot to use the international scholarly tongue. Grumbling, Jeffries repeated himself.

"Ah," she said, distracted enough to be polite instead of freezing him for his heavy-handed wit. "Interpreting such photos is not my area of expertise, you must understand; I leave that to Sybil or Manolis or Ramon who saw this first. But along the banks of this river there are I think cities set in the midst of a network of canals."

Yells like Castillo's ripped from the entire scientific crew. They all scrambled toward the viewer at the same time. "Ouch!" Sybil Hussie said as an elbow caught her in the ribs. "Have a care, there. This is no bloody rugby scrum—and try doing that into Latin, if anybody has a mind to."

At last, grudgingly, they formed a line. "You see?" Castillo said as they examined the print in turn. He was still voluble in his excitement. "Walled towns with major works of architecture at their centers; outlying hamlets; irrigation works that cover the whole floodplain. Judging by the rest of the planet, I would guess that this is its very first civilization, equivalent to Sumer or Egypt back on Earth."

They had known for several days that the world was inhabited, but nothing at a level higher than tiny farming villages had shown up on any earlier pictures—certainly no culture worth contacting. Now, though—

"A chance to really see how a hydraulic civilization functions, instead of guessing from a random selection of 5,000-year-old finds," Ramon said dreamily.

Mei-lin spoke with down-to-earth practicality: "A chance for a new dissertation." Her Latin was not as fluent as his, but had a precision Caesar might have admired.

"Publications," Helga and George Davies said in the same breath. Everyone laughed.

"Maybe enough art objects to make us all rich," Jeffries put in.

Manolis Zakythinos made a small, disgusted noise. All the same, the navigator's words hung in the air. It had happened before, to other incoming survey teams. There was always a premium on new forms of beauty.

Zakythinos slipped out. Thinking he was still annoyed, Ramon started to go after him, but the geologist quickly returned with a bottle of ouzo. "To the crows with the vile excuse for vodka the food unit turns out," he cried, his deep-set brown eyes flashing. "This calls for a true celebration."

"Call the captain," someone said as, amid cheers, they repaired to the galley. Most of them stopped at their cabins for something special; Sybil was carrying a squat green bottle of Tanqueray that she put between bourbon and scotch. Odd, Ramon thought, how her husband favored the American drink while Jeffries, who was from the States, preferred scotch.

Castillo's own contribution came from the hills outside his native Bogotá. He set the joints, rolled with almost compulsive neatness, beside the liquor. Being moderate by nature, he still had most of the kilo he had brought, and had given away a good deal of what was gone.

Given a choice, he would sooner have drunk beer, but space restrictions aboard the *Howells* made taking it impossible. He sighed and fixed himself a gin and tonic.

He was, inevitably and with inevitable fruitlessness, arguing with Helga about what the aliens below would be like when the buzz of conversation around them quieted for a moment. Blinking, Ramon looked up. Captain Katerina Tolmasova stood in the galley doorway.

Always, Ramon thought, she had that way of drawing attention to herself. Part of it lay in her staying in uniform long after the rest of them had relaxed into jeans or coveralls. But she would have worn her authority like a cloak over any clothes, or none.

In any clothes or none, also, she would have drawn male glances. Not even George Davies was immune, in spite of being a contented newlywed. She was tall, slim, dark; not at all the typical Russian. But her nationality showed in her broad, high cheekbones and in her eyes—enormous blue pools in which a man would gladly drown himself.

It still amazed Ramon, and sometimes frightened him a little, that they shared a bed.

She came over to him, smiling. "I am to understand that we have you to thank for this, ah, occasion?" Her voice made a slow music of Latin. It was the only language they had in common; he wondered how many times in the past thousand years it had been used for lovemaking.

Now he shrugged. "It could have been anyone. Whoever saw the pictures first would have recognized what was on them."

"I am glad you did, even so. Making contact is ever so much more interesting than weeks in the endless sameness of hyper-drive, though the instructors at the Astrograd Starship Academy would frown to hear me say so." She paused to sip vodka over ice—not the rough ship's brew, but Stolichnaya from her private hoard, which went down like a warm whisper—then went on, "Also I am glad we have here beings without a high technology. I shall worry less, of nights." The weapons of the *Howells*, of course, were under her control, along with everything else having to do with the safety of the ship.

"I hope," he said, touching her hand, "that I can help keep you from worrying."

"It is a shame romantic speeches have so little to do with life," she said. She sounded a little sad. Seeing the hurt spring into his eyes, she added quickly, "Not that they are not welcome even so. My quarters would be lonely without you tonight, the more so as afterward we will be busy, first I guiding the ship down and then you with this new species. We shall not have much time together then; best enjoy while we may."

Pitkhanas, steward-king of the river-god Tabal for the town of Kussara, awoke with the words of the god ringing in his ears: "See to the dredging of the canals today, lest they be filled with silt!"

King though he was, he scrambled from his bed, throwing aside the light, silky coverlet; disobeying the divine voice was unimaginable. He hardly had a backward glance to spare for the superb form of his favorite wife Azzias.

She muttered a drowsy complaint at being disturbed. "I am sorry," he told her. "Tabal has ordered me to see to the dredging of the canals today, lest they be filled with silt."

"Ah," she said, and went back to sleep.

Slaves hurried forward to dress Pitkhanas, draping him in the gold-shot crimson robe of state, setting the conical crown on his head, and slipping his feet into sandals with silver buckles. As he was being clothed, he breakfasted on a small loaf, a leg of boiled fowl from the night before that would not stay fresh much longer, and a pot of fermented fruit juice.

Tabal spoke to him again as he was eating, echoing the previous command. He felt the beginnings of a headache, as always happened when he did not at once do what the god demanded. He hastily finished his food, wiped his mouth on the sleeve of his robe, and hurried out of the royal bedchamber. Servants scrambled to open doors before him.

The last portal swung wide; he strode out of the palace into the central square of Kussara. The morning breeze from the Til-Barsip river was refreshing, drying the sweat that prickled on him under the long robe.

Close by the palace entrance stood the tomb of his father Zidantas, whose skull topped the monument. Several commoners were laying offerings at the front of the tomb: fruits, bread, cheese. In the short skirts of thin stuff that were their sole garments, they were more comfortable than he. When they saw him, they went down on their knees, touching their heads to the ground.

"Praise to your father, my lord king," one of them quavered, his voice muffled. "He has told me where I misplaced a fine alabaster bowl."

"Good for you, then," Pitkhanas said. Dead no less than alive, his father always had a harsh way of speaking to him.

As now: "I thought you were going to see to the dredging of the canals today," Zidantas snapped.

"So I am," Pitkhanas said mildly, trying to avoid Zidantas's wrath.

"Then do it," his father growled. The old man had been dead for three years or so. At times his voice and manner were beginning to remind the king of Labarnas, his own grandfather and Zidantas's father. Labarnas rarely spoke from the tomb anymore, save to old men and women who remembered him well. Zidantas's presence, though, was as real and pervasive in Kussara as that of Pitkhanas.

Surrounded by his attendants, the king hurried through the town's narrow, winding streets, stepping around or over piles of stinking garbage. The mud-brick housefronts were monotonous, but the two-story buildings provided welcome shade. Despite the breeze, the day was already hot.

Pitkhanas heard people chattering in the courtyards behind the tall blank walls of their homes. A woman's angry screech came from the roof where she and her husband had been sleeping: "Get up, you sot! Are you too sozzled to listen to the gods and work?"

The gods she spoke of were paltry, nattering things, fit for the lower classes: gods of the hearth, of the various crafts, of wayfaring. Pitkhanas had never heard them and did not know all their names; let the priests keep them straight. The great gods of the heavens and earth dealt with him directly, not through such intermediaries.

Kussara's eastern gate was sacred to Ninatta and Kulitta, the god and goddess of the two moons. Their statues stood in a niche above the arch, the stone images fairly bursting with youth. Below them, carts rumbled in and out, their ungreased axles squealing. Sentries paced the wall over the gate. The sun glinted off their bronze spearpoints.

The gate-captain, a scar-seamed veteran named Tushratta, bowed low before Pitkhanas. "How can this one serve you, my lord?"

"Tabal has reminded me that the canals need dredging," the king replied. "Tell some of your soldiers to gather peasants from the fields—three hundred overall will do—and set them to work at it."

"I hear you and obey as I hear and obey the gods," Tushratta said. He touched the alabaster eye-idol that he wore on his belt next to his dagger. They were common all through the Eighteen Cities, as channels to make the voices of the gods easier to understand.

Tushratta bawled the names of several warriors; some came down from the wall, others out of the barracks by the gate. "The canals need dredging," he told them. "Gather peasants from the field—three hundred overall will do—and set them to work at it."

The men dipped their heads, then fanned out into the green fields to do as they had been ordered. The peasants working at their plots knew instinctively what the soldiers were about, and tried to disappear. The warriors routed them out one by one. Soon they gathered the required number, most with hoes or digging-sticks already in their hands.

Pitkhanas gave them their commands, watched them troop off toward the canals in groups of ten or so. They splashed about, deepening the channels so the precious water could flow more freely. The king started to go back to the palace to tend to other business, then wondered whether he should stay awhile to encourage the canal-dredgers.

He paused, irresolute, glanced up at the images of the gods for guidance. Kulitta spoke to him. "Best you remain. Seeing the king as well as hearing his words reminds the worker of his purpose."

"Thank you, mistress, for showing me the proper course," Pitkhanas murmured. He went out to the canals to let the peasants see him at close range. His retinue followed, a slave holding a parasol above his head to shield him from the strong sun.

"His majesty is gracious," Tushratta remarked to one of the king's attendants, a plump little man named Radus-piyama, who was priest to the sky-god Tarhund.

The priest clucked reproachfully. "Did you not hear him answer the goddess? Of course he follows her will."

Kulitta's advice had been good; the work went more swiftly than it would have without Pitkhanas's presence. Now and then a man or two would pause to stretch or have a moment's horse-play, splashing muddy water at each other, but they soon returned to their tasks. "The canals need dredging," one reminded himself in stern tones very like the king's.

Because the goddess had told Pitkhanas to stay and oversee the peasants, he was close by when the sky ship descended. The first of it he knew was a low mutter in the air, like distant thunder—but the day was bright and cloudless. Then Radus-piyama cried out and pointed upward. Pitkhanas's gaze followed the priest's finger.

For a moment he did not see what Radus-piyama had spied, but then his eye caught the silver glint of light. It reminded him of the evening star seen at earliest twilight—but only for an instant, for it moved through the heavens like a stooping bird of prey, growing brighter and (he rubbed his eyes) larger. The noise in the sky became a deep roar that smote the ears. Pitkhanas clapped his hands over them. The sound still came through.

"Ninatta, Kulitta, Tarhund lord of the heavens, tell me the meaning of this portent," Pitkhanas exclaimed. The gods were silent, as if they did not know. The king waited, more afraid than he had ever been in his life.

If he knew fear, raw panic filled his subjects. The peasants toiling in the canals were screaming and shrieking. Some scrambled onto dry land and fled, while others took deep breaths and ducked under the water to hide from the monstrous heavenly apparition.

Even a few members of Pitkhanas's retinue broke and ran.

The soldiers Tushratta had gathered were on the edge of running too, but the gate-captain's angry bellow stopped them: "Hold fast, you cowards! Where are your guts? Stand and protect your king." The command brought most of them back to their places, though a couple kept pelting back toward Kussara.

"Is it a bird, my lord?" Radus-piyama shouted through the thunder. The priest of Tarhund was still at Pitkhanas's side, still pointing to the thing in the sky. It had come close enough to show a pair of stubby wings, though those did not flap.

"Say rather a ship," Tushratta told him. Campaigning had, of necessity, made him a keen observer. "Look there: you can see a row of holes along either side, like the oarports of a big rivership."

"Where are the oars, then?" Radus-piyama asked. Tushratta shrugged, having no more idea than the tubby priest.

"Who would sail a ship through the sky?" Pitkhanas whispered. "The gods?" But they had not spoken to him, nor, as he could see from the fear of the men around him, to anyone else.

The ship, if that was what it was, crushed half a plot of grain beneath it when it touched ground about a hundred paces from the king and his retinue. A gust of warm air blew in their faces. The thunder gradually died. Several of Pitkhanas's attendants— and several of the soldiers—moaned and hid their eyes with their arms, certain their end had come. Had it not been beneath his royal dignity, the king would have done the same.

Tushratta, though, was staring with interest at the marks painted along the sides of the ship below the holes that looked like oarports. "I wonder if that is writing," he said.

"It doesn't look like writing," Radus-piyama protested. All the Eighteen Cities of the Til-Barsip valley used the same script; most of its symbols still bore a strong resemblance to the objects they represented, though rebus-puns and specific grammatical determinants became more subtle and complex generation by generation.

The gate-captain said stubbornly, "There are more ways to write than ours, sir. I've fought against the hill-barbarians, and seen their villages. They use some of our signs for their language, but they have signs of their own, too, ones we don't have in the valley."

"Foreigners," Radus-piyama snorted. "I despise foreigners."

"So do I, but I have had to deal with them," Tushratta said.

Foreigners were dangerous. They worshiped gods different from those of the Eighteen Cities, gods who spoke to them in their own unintelligible tongues. And if they spoke with angry voices, war was sure to follow.

A door swung open in the side of the ship. Pitkhanas felt his hearts pounding in his chest; excitement began to replace fear. Perhaps they were all inside the sky ship, having come to Kussara for some reason of their own. What an honor! Almost everyone heard the gods scores of times each day, but they were rarely seen.

A ramp slid down from the open doorway. The king saw a stir of motion behind it . . . and his hopes of meeting the gods face-to-face were dashed, for the people emerging from the sky ship were the most foreign foreigners he had ever seen.

He wondered if they *were* people. The tallest of them was half a head shorter than the Kussaran average. Instead of blue-gray or green-gray skins, theirs were of earthy shades, rather like dried mud bricks. One was darker than that, and another almost golden. Some had black hair like the folk of the Eighteen Cities and all the other peoples they knew, but the heads of others were topped with brownish-yellow or even orange-red locks. One had hair on his face!

Their gear was an unfamiliar as their persons. They wore trousers of some heavy blue fabric, something like those of the hillmen but tight, not baggy. Despite the heat, they were all in tunics, dyed with colors Pitkhanas had never seen on cloth. They held a variety of curious implements.

"Some of those will be warriors," Tushratta said as the royal party drew nearer.

"How can you tell that?" the king asked. To him the square black box one of them was lifting to his face—no, *her* face; by the breasts it was a woman, though what was a woman doing in the company of voyagers?—was as alien as the long, thin contraptions of wood and metal borne by the hairy-faced stranger and a couple of others.

"The way they carry them, my lord," the gate-captain answered, pointing to the trio with the long things. "And the way they watch us—they have something of the soldier to them."

Once it was pointed out to him, Pitkhanas could also see what Tushratta had noticed. He would never have spotted it for himself, though. "How can you observe so clearly, with the voices of the gods mute?" he said. That awful silence inside his head left him bewildered.

Tushratta shrugged. "I have seen soldiers among us and among the barbarians in the hills, my lord. My eyes tell me how these men are like them. Were the gods speaking, they would say the same, surely."

The golden-skinned stranger, the smallest of them all, descended from the ramp of the sky ship and slowly approached Pitkhanas and his followers. He held his hands out before him. The gesture was plainly peaceful, but not fully reassuring to the king; the foreigners, he saw, had only one thumb on each hand.

A moment later, the breath hissed from his nostrils in anger. "They insult me—it is a woman they send as herald!" This foreigner was so slimly made that only up close did the difference become apparent.

Hearing Pitkhanas's exclamation, one of the soldiers stepped forward to seize the offender. But before he could lay hands on her, she touched a button on her belt and shot into the air, hovering overhead at five times the height of a man.

The soldier, the attendants, the king gaped in astonishment. The sky ship was entirely outside their experience, too alien for them to gauge the power it represented. This, though—"Do not try to injure them again, or they will destroy us all!" Zidantas shouted to Pitkhanas.

"Of course, sire," the king gasped, putting his palms to his temples in relief that his dead father's voice had returned to him. "Do not try to injure them again, or they will destroy us all!" he called to his men, adding, "Abase yourselves, so they can see your repentance."

Heedless of their robes and skirts, his followers went to their knees in the soft mud of the field. Pitkhanas himself bowed from the waist, holding his eyes to the ground.

One of the strangers on the ramp of the sky ship called out something. His voice sounded like any other man's, but the words were meaningless to the king.

A soft touch on his shoulder made him look up. The foreign woman was standing before him, her feet touching the ground once more. She gestured that he should straighten himself. When he had, she bowed in return, as deeply as he had. She pointed to his men and motioned for them to rise too.

"Stand up," he told them.

As they were doing so, the woman went to her knees in the mud herself, careless of her rich, strange clothing. She got up quickly, echoing Pitkhanas's command with a questioning note in her voice.

He corrected her, using the singular verb-form this time instead of the plural. She understood at once, pointing to one man and repeating the singular and then at several and using the plural. He smiled, dipped his head, and spread his arms wide to show that she was right.

It began there.

"May I speak with you, my lord?" Radus-piyama asked.

"Yes," Pitkhanas said, a little wearily. He could feel in his belly what was about to come from the priest. Radus-piyama had been saying the same thing for many days now.

Nor did he surprise the king; with more passion than one would have expected to find in his small, round frame, he burst out, "My lord, I ask you again to expel the dirt-colored foreigners from Kussara. Tarhund has spoken to me once more, urging me to set this task upon you, lest they corrupt Kussara and all the Eighteen Cities."

"The god has given me no such command," Pitkhanas replied, as he had all the previous times Radus-piyama had asked him to get rid of the strangers. "If I hear it from his lips, be sure I shall obey. But until then these people from the far land called Terra are welcome here. They bring many fine gifts and things to trade." His hand went to his belt. The knife that hung there was a present from the Terrajin; it was made from a gray metal that was stronger than the best bronze and held a better edge.

"Come with me to the temple, then," Radus-piyama said. "Perhaps in his own home you will know the god's will more clearly."

Pitkhanas hesitated. Tarhund spoke to him: "Go with my priest to my house in Kussara. If I have further commands for you, you should best hear them there."

"The god bids me go with you to his house in Kussara," the king told Radus-piyama. "If he has further commands for me, I should best hear them there."

Radus-piyama showed his teeth in a delighted grin. "Splendid, my lord! Surely Tarhund will show you the proper course. I had begun to fear that you no longer heard the gods at all, that you had become as deaf to them as the Terrajin are."

Pitkhanas made an angry noise in the back of his throat. "Not agreeing with you, priest, does not leave one accursed. Tushratta, for instance, prospers, yet he is most intimate with the Terrajin of anyone in Kussara."

Radus-piyama had begun to cringe in the face of the king's temper, but at mention of the officer he recovered and gave a contemptuous sneer. "Choose someone else as an example, my lord, not Tushratta. The gods have gradually been forgetting him for years. Why, he told me once that without his eye-idol he rarely hears them. Aye, he is a fit one to associate with the foreigners. He even has to cast the bones to learn what course he should take."

"Well, so do we all, now and then," the king reproved. "They show us the will of the gods."

"Oh, no doubt, my lord," Radus-piyama said. "But no one I know of has to use the bones as often as Tushratta. If the gods spoke to him more, he would have fewer occasions to call on such less certain ways of learning what they wanted of him."

"He is a good soldier," Pitkhanas said stiffly. Radus-piyama, seeing that he could not sway the king on this question, bowed his head in acquiescence. "To the temple, then," Pitkhanas said.

As usual near midday, the central square of Kussara was jammed with people. Potters and smiths traded their wares for grain or beer. Rug-makers displayed their colorful products in the hope of attracting customers wealthy enough to afford them. "Clear, fresh river-water!" a hawker called. "No need to drink it muddy from the canal!" He had two large clay jugs slung over his shoulder on a carrying-pole. Harlots swayed boldly through the crowd. Slaves followed them with their eyes or dozed in whatever shade they could find. More gathered at a small shrine, offering a handful of meal or fruit to its god in exchange for advice.

Pitkhanas also saw a couple of Terrajin in the square. The foreigners still drew stares from peasants new in town and attracted small groups of curious children wherever they went, but most of Kussara had grown used to them in the past year-quarter. Their odd clothes and coloring, the metal boxes they carried that clicked or hummed, were accepted peculiarities now, like the feather-decked turbans of the men from the city of Hurma or the habit the people of the town of Yuzat had of spitting after every sentence.

The Terraj called Kastiyo was haggling with a carpenter over the price of a stool as the king and Radus-piyama came by. "I know wood is valuable because you have to trade to get it," the Terraj was saying, "but surely this silver ring is a good payment." Kastiyo fumbled for words and spoke slowly, but he made himself understood; after tiny Jingmaylin, he probably had the best grasp of Kussara's language.

The carpenter weighed the ring in his hand. "Is it enough?"

"Who—ah, whom—do you ask?" the Terraj said.

"Why, my god, of course: Kadashman, patron of woodworkers. He says the bargain is fair." The carpenter lifted the stool, gave it to Kastiyo, and held out his hand for the ring.

The foreigner passed it to him, but persisted, "How is it you know what the god says?"

"I hear him, naturally, just as I hear you; but you will go away and he is always with me." The carpenter looked as confused as the Terraj. Then he brightened. "Perhaps you do not know Kadashman because you are not a woodworker and he has no cause to speak to you. But surely your own gods talk to you in much the same way."

"I have never heard a god," Kastiyo said soberly. "None of my people has. That is why we is—*are*—so interested in learning more about those of Kussara."

The carpenter's jaw dropped at Kastiyo's admission.

"You see?" Radus-piyama said to Pitkhanas. "Out of their own mouths comes proof of their accursedness."

"They have gods, or a god," the king answered. "I have asked them that."

Radus-piyama laughed. "How could there be only one god? And even if there were, would he not speak to his people?"

To that Pitkhanas had no reply. He and the priest walked in silence to the temple of Tarhund, the Great House, as it was called: after the shrine of Tabal, the tallest and most splendid building in Kussara. The temples towered over the palace of the steward-king, who was merely the gods' servant. The huge rectangular tower of mud-brick rose in ever smaller stages to Tarhund's chamber at the very top.

Together, Pitkhanas and Radus-piyama climbed the temple's 316 steps—one for each day of the year. Under-priests bowed to their chief and to the king, who could see the surprise on their faces at his unscheduled visit.

"Is the god properly robed?" Radus-piyama called when they were nearly at the top.

The door to Tarhund's chambers swung open. A priest whose skin was gray with age emerged, his walk a slow hobble helped by a stick. "That he is, sir," he replied, "and pronounces himself greatly pleased with his new vestments, too."

"Excellent, Millawanda," Radus-piyama said. "Then he will give our king good advice about the Terrajin."

Millawanda's eyesight was beginning to fail, and he had not noticed Pitkhanas standing beside Radus-piyama. The king waved for him not to bother when he started a shaky bow. "Thank you, my lord. Yes, Tarhund has mentioned the foreigners to me. He says—"

"I will hear for myself what he says, thank you," Pitkhanas said. He stepped toward the god's chambers. When Radus-piyama started to follow him, he waved him back; he was still annoyed that the priest had feared Tarhund was not speaking to him anymore.

Tarhund stood in his niche, an awesome figure, taller than a man. Torchlight played off the gold leaf that covered his face, hands, and feet, and off the gold and silver threads running through the thick, rich cloth of his new ankle-length robe. In his left hand he held the solid-gold globe of the sun, in his right black stormclouds.

The king suddenly saw with horror that he had forgotten to bring any offering when the god summoned him. He groveled on his belly before Tarhund as the lowliest of his slaves would have before him. Stripping off his sandals with their silver buckles, he set them on the table in front of the god next to the gifts of food, beer, and incense from the priests. "Accept these from this worm, your servant," he implored.

Tarhund's enormous eyes of polished jet gripped and held him. The god's words echoed in Pitkhanas's ears: "You may speak."

"Thank you, my master." Still on the floor, the king poured out everything that had happened since the coming of the Terrajin. "Are they stronger than you, lord, and your brother and sister gods? When we first met them, their powers and strangeness silenced your voices, and we despaired. You returned as we grew to know them, but now you speak in one way to your priests and in another to me. What shall I do? Shall I destroy the Terrajin, or order them to leave? Or shall I let them go on as they would, seeing that they have done no harm yet? Say on; let me know your will."

The god took so long answering that Pitkhanas trembled and felt his limbs grow weak with fear. If the strangers *were* mightier than the gods—but at last Tarhund replied, though his voice seemed faint and far away, almost a divine mumble: "Let them go on as they would. Seeing that they have done no harm yet, they will keep on behaving well.''

Pitkhanas knocked his forehead against mud-brick. ''I hear and obey, my master.'' He dared another question: ''My lord, how is it that the Terrajin hear no gods of their own?''

Tarhund spoke again, but only in a gabble from which the king could understand nothing. Tears filled his eyes. He asked, ''Is it as Radus-piyama says, that they are accursed?''

''No.'' This time the god's answer came quick, clear, and sharp. ''Accursed men would work evil. They do not. Tell Radus-piyama to judge them by their deeds.''

''Aye, my master.'' Sensing that the divine audience was over, Pitkhanas rose and left Tarhund's chamber. Radus-piyama and Millawanda were waiting expectantly outside. The king said, ''The god has declared to me that the Terrajin are not accursed. Accursed men would work evil. They do not, and they will keep on behaving well. Judge them by their deeds. This is Tarhund's command to me, and mine to you. Hear it always.''

The priests blinked in surprise. But their obedience to the king was as ingrained as their service to Tarhund. ''I hear you and obey as I hear and obey the god,'' Radus-piyama acknowledged, Millawanda following him a moment later.

Satisfied, Pitkhanas started down the long stairway of Tarhund's Great House. Had he conveyed his orders in writing, the priests might somehow have found a way to bend them to their own desires. Now, though, his wishes and Tarhund's would both be ringing in their ears. They would give him no more trouble over the Terrajin.

The tape of Ramon Castillo dickering with the Kussaran woodworker ended. The video screen went dark. Helga Stein lifted her headphones, rubbed her ears. ''Another one,'' she sighed.

''What was that?'' Castillo was still wearing his 'phones, which muffled her words. ''Sorry.'' He took them off quickly.

''It's nothing,'' Helga said wearily. She turned to Mei-lin, who had been going over the tape with them. ''Did I understand that correctly—the native calling on a deity named Kadashman at the decision-point?''

''Oh yes,'' the linguist answered at once. To Ramon she added, ''You do very well with the language. He had no trouble following you at all.''

''Thanks,'' he said; Mei-lin was not one to give praise lightly.

But he had to object, " 'Calling on' isn't quite what happened. He asked a question, got an answer, and acted on it. Look for yourselves."

When he reached to rewind the tape, Helga stopped him. "Don't bother; all of us have seen the like dozens of times already. The local's eyes get far away for a few seconds, or however long it takes, then he comes out of it and does whatever he does. But what does it *mean*?"

" 'Eyes get far away,' " Ramon said. "That's not a bad way to put it, I suppose, but to me it just looks as though the natives are listening."

"To what?" Helga flared, her face going pink. "And if you say 'a god,' I'll brain you with this table."

"It's bolted to the floor," he pointed out.

"Ach!" She snarled a guttural oath that was emphatically not Latin, stormed out of the workroom.

"You should not tease her so, Ramon," Mei-lin said quietly. Trouble rested on her usually calm features.

"I didn't mean to," the cultural anthropologist replied, still taken aback at Helga's outburst. "I simply have a very literal mind. I was going to suggest that if she had to hit me, the stool I bought would serve better."

Mei-lin smiled a dutiful smile. "At least you and Sybil have your stools and other artifacts you can put your hands on to study. All Helga and I can do is examine patterns, and none of the patterns here makes any sense that I can find."

"You shouldn't expect an alien species to think as we do."

"Spare me the tautology," the linguist snapped; her small sarcasm shocked Castillo much more than Helga's losing her temper. "For that matter, I sometimes wonder if these Kussarans think at all."

Ramon was shocked again, for she plainly meant it. "What about this, then?" he said, holding up the stool. It was a fine piece of craftsmanship, the legs beautifully fitted to the seat, the dyed-leather seatcover secured by bronze tacks to the wood below. "What about their walls and temples and houses, their cloth, their fields and canals, their writing, their language?"

"What about their language?" she retorted. "As I said, you've learned it quite well. You tell me how to say 'to think' in Kussaran."

"Why, it's—" Castillo began, and then stopped, his mouth hanging open. *"No sé,"* he admitted, startled back into Spanish, a slip he rarely made.

"I don't know either, or how to say 'to wonder' or 'to doubt' or 'to believe' or any other word that relates to cognition. And any Kussaran who says, 'I feel it in my bones' suffers from arthritis. Your 'literal mind' would make you a wild-eyed dreamer among these people, Ramon. How can they live without reflecting on life? Is it any wonder that Helga and I feel we're eating soup with a fork?"

"No-o," he said slowly. Then he laughed. "Maybe their precious gods do their thinking for them." The laugh was not one of amusement. The problem of the gods vexed him as much as it did Helga. Where she fretted over failing to understand the locals' psychological makeup, he had the feeling he was seeing their cultural patterns only through fog—superficial shapes were clear, but whatever was behind them was hidden in the mist.

Mei-lin failed to find his suggestion even sardonically amusing. "There are no gods. If there were, our instruments would have detected them."

"Telepathy," Ramon probed, hoping to get a rise out of her. She did not take the bait. All she said was, "Assuming it exists (which I don't), telepathy from whom? The bugs we've scattered around show that the king, the ministers, the priests talk to their gods as often as the peasants do—oftener, if anything. There are no secret rulers, Ramon."

"I know." His shoulders sagged a little. "In fact, the Kussarans who hold the fewest one-sided conversations are some of the soldiers and merchants—and everyone else looks down on them on account of it."

"Still, if they were all as interested in us as Tushratta, our job would be ten times easier."

"True enough." The gate-captain spent as much of his time at the *Howells* as his duties allowed. "I wouldn't be surprised if he's around so much because we have no gods at all and give him someone to feel superior to."

"You're getting as cynical as Stan Jeffries," she said, which canceled his pleasure at her earlier compliment. Feeling his face grow hot, he rose and took a hasty leave.

As he passed the galley, he thought there was some god working, and probably a malignant one, for Jeffries himself called, "Hey, Ramon, come sit in for a while. Reiko's engine-watch just started, and we're short-handed."

The inevitable poker game had begun when the *Howells* was still in parking orbit around Terra. Castillo rarely played. Not only were the regulars some of his least favorite people on the ship, they also won money from him with great regularity.

He was about to decline again when he saw Tushratta was one of the players. The Kussarans gambled among themselves with dice, and the soldier was evidently picking up a new game. He looked rather uncomfortable in a Terran chair: it was too small for him and did not quite suit his proportions.

"What does he use to buy chips?" Ramon asked, sitting down across from the native.

João Gomes, one of the engine-room technicians, said a little too quickly, "Oh, we give them to him. He just plays for fun."

Castillo raised an eyebrow. The technician flushed. Jeffries said, "Why fight it, João? He can always ask Tushratta himself. All right, Ramon, he buys it with native goods: pots and bracelets and such. When he wins, we pay off with our own trinkets: a pair of scissors, a pocketknife, a flashlight." He stared defiantly at the anthropologist. "Want to make something of it?"

That sort of dealing was technically against regulations, but Ramon said, "I suppose not, provided I get photos of all the Kussaran artifacts you've gotten from him."

"Naturally," Jeffries agreed. Faces fell all around the table. Castillo hid a smile. Of course the poker players had been planning to hide the small trinkets and sell them for their own profit when they got home. It happened on every expedition that found intelligent natives, one way or another. The anthropologist was also certain he would not see everything.

Tushratta pointed at the deck of cards. "Deal," he said in heavily accented but understandable Latin.

To keep things simple for the beginner, they stuck with five-card stud and one joker. "A good skill game, anyway," Jeffries said. "You can tell where you stand. You play something like seven stud, low in the hole wild, and you don't know whether to shit or go blind."

Ramon lost a little, won a little, lost a little more. He might have done better if he hadn't been paying as much attention to Tushratta as to the cards—or, he told himself with characteristic honesty, he might not. As was to be expected among more experienced players, the native lost, but not too badly. His worst flaw, Castillo thought, was a tendency not to test bluffs—a problem the anthropologist had himself.

When Tushratta ran low on chips, he dug in his pouch and produced a cylinder seal, a beautifully carved piece of alabaster about the size of his little finger designed to be rolled on a mud tablet to show that he had written it. The stake Gomes gave him for it seemed honest.

A couple of hands later, the Kussaran and Jeffries got into an expensive one. Ramon was dealing, but folded after his third card. Everyone else dropped out on the next one, with varied mutters of disgust.

"Last card," the anthropologist said. He tossed them out.

Someone gave a low whistle. Jeffries, grinning, had four diamonds up. A couple of chairs away, Tushratta was sitting behind two pairs: treys and nines.

"Your bet, Tushratta," Ramon said. The Kussaran did, heavily.

"Ah, now we separate the sheep from the goats," Jeffries said, and raised. But the navigator's grin slipped when Tushratta raised back. "Oh, you bastard," he said in English. He shoved in more chips. "Call."

Looking smug, Tushratta showed his hole card: a third nine. "Ouch," Jeffries said. "No wonder you bumped it up, with a full house." Castillo was not sure how much of that Tushratta understood, but the Kussaran knew he had won. He raked in the pot with both hands, started stacking the chips in neat piles of five in front of him.

Jeffries managed a sour grin. "Not that you needed the boat," he said to Tushratta. He turned over his own fifth card. It was a club.

Laughter erupted around the table. "That'll teach you, Stan," Gomes said. "Serves you right."

Tushratta knocked several piles of chips onto the floor. He made no move to pick them up; he was staring at Jeffries's hole card as though he did not believe his eyes. "You had nothing," he said.

The navigator had learned enough Kussaran to follow him. "A pair of sixes, actually."

Tushratta waved that away, as of no importance. He spoke slowly, sounding, Ramon thought, uncertain where his words were leading him: "You saw my two pairs showing. You could not beat them, but you kept betting. Why did you do that?"

"It was a bluff that didn't work," Jeffries answered. The key word came out in Latin. He turned to Castillo for help. "Explain it to him, Ramon; you're smoother with the lingo than I am."

"I'll try," the anthropologist said; he did not know the word for "bluff" either. Circumlocution, then: "You saw Jeffries's four diamonds. He wanted to make you drop by acting as though he had a flush. He did not know you had three nines. If you only had the two pairs that were up, you would lose against a flush, and so you might not bet against it. That was what he wanted—that is what bluff is.''

''But he did not have a flush,'' Tushratta protested, almost in a wail.

''But he seemed to, did he not? Tell me, if you had only had the two pair, what would you have done when he raised?''

Tushratta pressed the heels of his hands against his eyes. He was silent for almost a full minute. At last he said, very low, ''I would have folded.''

Then he did retrieve the chips he had spilled, carefully re-stacked them. ''I have had enough poker for today. What will you give me for these? There are many more here than I had yesterday.''

They settled on a hand-held mirror, three butane lighters, and a hatchet. Ramon suspected the latter would be used on skulls, not timber. For the moment, though, Tushratta was anything but warlike. Still in the brown study that had gripped him since he won the hand from Jeffries, he took up his loot and left, talking to himself.

Castillo did not think he was communing with his mysterious gods; it sounded more like an internal argument. ''But he didn't . . . But he seemed to . . . But he didn't . . . Bluff . . .''

''What's all that about?'' Jeffries asked.

When the anthropologist translated, Gomes chuckled. ''There you go, Stan, corrupting the natives.'' The navigator threw a chip at him.

''I laughed with the rest of them,'' Castillo said as he re-counted the poker game in his cabin that night, ''but looking back, I'm not sure João wasn't absolutely right. Katerina, I'd swear the idea of deceit had never crossed Tushratta's mind.''

Frowning, the captain sat up in bed, her hair spilling softly over her bare shoulders. Her specialty was far removed from Ramon's, but she brought an incisive, highly logical mind to bear on any problem she faced. ''Perhaps he was merely taken aback by a facet of the game that he had not thought of before.''

''It went deeper than that,'' the anthropologist insisted. ''He had to have the whole notion of bluffing defined for him, and it hit him hard. And as for thinking, Mei-lin has me wondering if the Kussarans really do.''

"Really do what? Think? Don't be absurd, Ramon; of course they do. How could they have built this civilization of theirs without thinking?"

Castillo smiled. "Exactly what I said this afternoon." He repeated Mei-lin's argument for Katerina, finished, "As far as I can see, she has a point. Concepts can't exist in a culture without words to express them."

"Just so," the captain agreed. "As Marx said, it is not the consciousness of men that determines their existence, but rather their social existence determines their consciousness."

You and your Marx, Castillo thought fondly. He did not say that aloud, any more than he would have challenged Manolis Zakythinos's Orthodox Christianity. What he did say was, "Here's Kussara in front of us as evidence to the contrary."

"Only because we do not understand it," Katerina said firmly, her secular faith unshakable.

Still, Ramon could not deny the truth in her words, and admitted as much. "Their gods, for instance. We may not be able to see or hear them, but they're real as mud-brick to the Kussarans."

"All primitive peoples talk to their gods," Katerina said.

"But not all of them have gods who answer back," the anthropologist replied, "and the locals certainly listen to theirs. In fact, they—"

His voice trailed away as his mind began working furiously. Suddenly he leaned over and kissed Katerina with a fervor that had nothing to do with lovemaking. He sprang out of bed, hurrying over to the computer terminal at his desk. Katerina exclaimed in surprise and a little indignation. He paid no attention, which was a measure of his excitement.

It took him a while to find the database he needed; it was not one he used often. When at last he did, he could hardly keep his fingers from trembling as he punched in his search commands. He felt like shouting when the readout began flowing across the screen.

Instead, he whispered, "I know, I know."

"You're crazy," Helga Stein said flatly when Ramon finished his presentation at a hastily called meeting the next morning. It was, he thought with a giddiness brought on by lack of sleep, a hell of a thing for a psychologist to say, but then Latin was a blunt language. And glances round the table showed that most of their colleagues agreed with her. Only Mei-lin seemed to be withholding judgment.

"Argue with the evidence, not with me," he said. "As far as I can see, it all points toward the conclusion I've outlined: the Kussarans are not conscious beings."

"Oh, piffle, Ramon," Sybil Hussie said. "My old cat Bill back in Manchester is a conscious being."

Castillo wished he was someplace else; he was too shy to enjoy putting forth a strange idea to a hostile audience. But he was also too stubborn to fold up in the face of mockery. "No, Sybil," he said, "your old Bill, that mangy creature—I've met him, you know—isn't conscious, he's simply aware."

"Well, what is the difference?" Manolis Zakythinos asked.

"Or, better, how do you define consciousness?" George Davies put in.

"With Helga over there waiting to pounce on me, I won't even try. Let her do it."

The psychologist blinked when Ramon tossed the ball to her, rather like a prosecution witness unexpectedly summoned by the defense. Her answer came slowly: "Consciousness is an action, not an essence. It manipulates meanings in a metaphorical space in a way analogous to manipulating real objects in real space. In 'meanings' I include the mental image a conscious being holds of itself. Consciousness operates on whatever the conscious being is thinking about, choosing relevant elements and building patterns from them as experience has taught it. I must agree with Ramon, Sybil: your cat is not a conscious being. It is aware, but it is not aware of itself being aware. If you want a short definition, that is what consciousness is."

Davies was already sputtering protests. "It's bloody incomplete, is what it is. What about thinking? What about learning?"

Reluctantly, Helga said, "One does not have to be conscious to think." That turned a storm of protest against her that dwarfed anything Ramon had faced. She waited for it to end. "I will show you, then. Give me the next number in this sequence: one, four, seven, ten—"

"Thirteen." The response came instantly, from three or four people at once.

"How did you know that?" she asked them. "Were you aware of yourselves reasoning that you had to add three to the last number and then carrying out the addition? Or did you simply recognize the pattern and see what the next element *had* to be?

From the speed with which you answered, I'd guess the latter—and where is the conscious thought there?''

Abrupt silence fell round the conference table. It was, Ramon thought, an introspective sort of silence; the very stuff of consciousness.

George Davies broke it. ''You picked too simple an example, Helga. Give us something more complicated.''

''What about typing, then, or playing a synthesizer? In both of them, the only way to perform well is to suppress your consciousness. The moment you start thinking about what you are doing instead of doing it, you will go wrong.''

That—thoughtful—silence descended once more. When Helga spoke again, she looked first toward Castillo, grudging respect in her eyes. ''You've convinced me of the possibility, at least, Ramon, or rather made me convince myself.''

''I like it,'' Mei-lin said with sudden decision. ''It fits. The total lack of mental imagery in the Kussaran language has been obvious to me for weeks. If the Kussarans are not conscious, they have no need for it.''

''How do they get along without consciousness?'' Davies challenged. ''How can they function?''

''You do yourself, all the time,'' Ramon said. Before the biologist could object, he went on, ''Think of a time when you were walking somewhere deep in a conversation with someone. Haven't you ever looked up and said, 'Oh, we're here,' with no memory of having crossed a street or two or gone by a park? Your consciousness was busy elsewhere, and the rest of your intelligence coped for you. Take away the part that was talking with your friend and you have what the Kussarans are like all the time. They get along just fine on pattern recognition and habit.''

''And what happens when those aren't enough?'' Davies asked, stabbing out a triumphant finger. ''What happens when a Kussaran turns his old familiar corner and the smithy's caught fire and the whole street is burning? What then?''

Castillo licked his lips. He wished the question had not come so soon, or so bluntly. No help for it now, though. He took a deep breath and answered, ''Then his gods tell him what to do.''

He had not known so few people could make so much noise. For a moment he actually wondered if the attack was going to be physical; George Davies and his wife bounced halfway out of their chairs as they showered him with abuse. So did Helga, who shouted, "I was right the first time, Ramon—you *are* crazy." Even Mei-lin was shaking her head.

"Shouldn't you hear me out before you lock me up?" Castillo said tightly, almost shaking with anger.

"Why listen to more drivel?" Sybil Hussie said with a toss of her head.

"No, he is right," Zakythinos said. "Let him back up his claim, if he can. If he can convince such a, ah, skeptical audience, he deserves to be taken seriously."

"Thank you, Manolis." Ramon had himself under tight control again; railing back at them would not help. "Let me start out by saying that what I'm proposing isn't new; the idea was first put forward by Jaynes over a hundred and fifty years ago, back in the 1970s, for ancient Terran civilizations."

Helga rolled her eyes. "*Ach*, that period. Gods from outer space, is it?"

"Nothing like that," Castillo said, adding with some relish, "Jaynes was a psychologist, as a matter of fact."

"And what sort of gods, if I may make so bold as to ask, would a psychologist have?" Sybil said in a tone calculated to put Helga's teeth on edge as well as Ramon's.

The cultural anthropologist, though, had his answer ready: "Auditory and sometimes visual hallucinations, generated by the right side of the brain—the part that deals with patterns and broad perceptions rather than logic and speech. They would not be recognized as hallucinations, you understand; they would be perceived as divine voices. And, operating with the stored-up experience that fit any new or unexpected situation, and tell him what to do. No conscious thought would be involved at all."

"It is drivel—" Sybil began, but her husband was shaking his head.

"I wonder," he said slowly. "Kussaran life is organized neurologically on the same general pattern as Terran; dissection of native corpses and work with domestic animals clearly shows that. There are differences, of course—brain functions, for instance, seem to be arranged fore-and-aft, rather than axially as with us."

"That's your province, of course," Ramon said. If George was arguing on those terms, he had to be considering the idea.

"These 'divine voices,' " Helga said. "They would be related to the voices schizophrenics hear?"

"Very closely," Castillo agreed. "But they would be normal

and universal, not something to be resisted and feared by the vestiges of the conscious mind-pattern. And the threshold for producing them could be much lower than it is in schizophrenics—anything unusual or unfamiliar would touch them off. So could be the sight of an idol; that may be why Kussara is so littered with them.''

Davies sat straighter in his chair, a mannerism he had when he was coming up with an objection he thought telling. ''What possible evolutionary advantage could there be to a way of life based on hallucination?''

''Social control,'' Ramon answered. ''Remember, these aren't conscious beings we're talking about. They cannot visualize a connected series of activities, as we do. The only way for one of them weeding a field, say, to keep at his job all day long without someone standing over him, would be to keep hearing the voice of a chief or king saying over and over, 'Pull them out!' ''

''Hmm,'' was all the biologist said.

''And since the king is part of the system too,'' Helga mused, ''he would hear the voices of whatever high gods his culture had. They would be the only ones with enough authority to direct him.''

''Perhaps of his ancestors also,'' Ramon said. ''Remember that shrine by Pitkhanas's palace—it's a monument to his father, the last king of the city. There are offerings there, as to the gods.''

''So there are.'' The psychologist paused, her eyes going big and round. ''*Lieber Gott!* For such beings, belief in an afterlife would come naturally, and with reason. If a woman still heard, for instance, her mother's voice after her mother had died, would her mother not still be alive for her, in a very real sense of the word?''

''I hadn't even thought of that,'' Ramon whispered.

George Davies remained unconvinced. ''If this style of perception is so wonderful, why aren't we all still blissfully unconscious?''

Castillo gave credit where it was due. ''A remark of Katerina's put me on this track. Work it through. As a society gets increasingly complex, more and more layers of gods get added, to take care of all social levels. Look at Kussara now, with a separate deity for the carpenters and one for every other trade. Eventually, the system breaks down under its own weight.

''Writing helps, too. Writing makes a more complicated society possible, but it also weakens the authority of hallucinations. It's easier to evade a command when it's on a tablet in front of you that can be thrown away than when the king's voice sounds in your ear.

"And finally, the structure is geared to stability. It would have to come apart during war and crisis. What good are the commands of your gods if you're dealing with someone from a different culture, with a different language and strange gods of his own? Their orders would be as likely to get you killed as to save you.

"And in noticing how oddly the foreigners acted, you might account for it through something different inside them. And once you conceived of strangers with interior selves, you might suppose you had one too; the beginning of consciousness itself, maybe."

"There is evidence for that," Mei-lin broke in excitedly. "Remember, Ramon, how you remarked that the Kussarans who talked least with their gods were warriors and traders? They are exactly the ones with the greatest contact with foreigners— they may be on the very edge of becoming conscious beings."

All the anthropologist could do was nod. He felt dazed; the others were running with his hypothesis now in ways he had not imagined. And that, he thought, was as it should be. The concept was too big for any one man to claim it all.

Still sounding sour, George said, "I suppose we can work up experiments to test all this, if it's there." That was fitting too. If the idea had merit, it would come through inquiry unscathed or, better, refined and improved. If not, it did not deserve to survive.

Ramon could hardly wait to find out.

Holding his hands to his ears against the thunder, Pitkhanas watched the sky ship shrink as it rose into the heavens. It was the size of his fist at arm's length . . . the size of a night-flitterer . . . a point of silver light . . . gone.

The king saw how the great weight of the ship had pressed the ground where it had rested down half a forearm's depth. The grain that had been under it, of course, was long dead; the fields around the spot were rank and untended.

The fertility-goddess Yarris addressed Pitkhanas reproachfully. "That is good cropland. Set peasants to restoring its former lushness."

"It shall be done, mistress," he murmured, and relayed the command to his ministers.

His dead father spoke up. "Have warriors out to guard the peasants, to keep the men of Maruwas down the river from raiding as they did when you were a boy. See you to it."

Pitkhanas turned to Tushratta. "Zidantas warns me to have warriors out to guard the peasants, to keep the men of Maruwas down the river from raiding as they did when I was a boy. See you to it."

Tushratta bowed. "I hear you and obey as I hear and obey the gods." The king walked off, never doubting his order would be obeyed.

In fact Tushratta did not hear the gods at all anymore. Their voices had been slowly fading in his ears since his campaigns against the hillmen, but he knew to the day when they had vanished for good. *"Bluff,"* he said under his breath. He used the Terraj word; there was nothing like it in Kussaran.

He missed the gods terribly. He had even beseeched them to return—and how strange a thing was that, for the gods should always be present! Without their counsel, he felt naked and empty in the world.

But he went on. Indeed, he prospered. Perhaps the gods still listened to him, even if they would not speak. In the half-year since they left him, he had risen from gate-captain to warmaster of Kussara—the previous holder of that office having suddenly died. With himself he had brought certain other officers—young men who looked to him for guidance—and the detachments that obeyed them.

He would, he decided, follow Pitkhanas's command after all—but in his own fashion. As leader of the soldiers in the fields he would pick, hmm, Kushukh, who was not loyal to him . . . but who did head the palace guards.

How to get Kushukh to leave his post? *"Bluff,"* Tushratta muttered again. He still used the concept haltingly, like a man trying to speak a foreign language he did not know well. Standing as it were to one side of himself, seeing himself saying or doing one thing but intending another, took an effort that made sweat spring out on his forehead.

He would say . . . would say . . . His fist clenched as the answer came. He would tell Kushukh that Pitkhanas had said no one else could do the job as well. That should suffice.

And then, leading his own picked men, Tushratta would go to the palace and . . . He looked ahead again, to Pitkhanas's corpse being dragged away; to himself wearing the royal robes and enjoying the royal treasures; to lying with Azzias, surely the most magnificent creature the gods ever made. Standing outside himself for those images was easy. He had looked at them many, many times already.

After he had become king, Kushukh would prove no problem; locked in the old ways, he would hear and obey Tushratta just as he heard and obeyed the gods, just as he had heard and obeyed Pitkhanas. Tushratta was less certain of his own backers. He had not explained to them what a *bluff* was, as Kastiyo had for him. But he had repeatedly used the thing-that-seemed-this-but-was-that; he could not have risen half so quickly otherwise. They were quick lads. They might well see what it meant on their own.

If so—if he could never be sure that what one of them told him, what one of them did, was not a *bluff*—how was he to rule? They would not follow his orders merely because it was he who gave them. Must he live all his days in fear? That made him look ahead in a way he did not like, to see himself cowering on the throne he had won.

But why did he have to be the one cowering? If one of his backers tried to move against him and failed (and he would not be such easy meat as Pitkhanas, for he would always be watchful), why not treat that one so harshly that the rest were made afraid? No matter then whether or not they had his commands always ringing in their heads. They would obey anyhow, out of terror.

Would that be enough?

Tushratta could hardly wait to find out.

I've written four novels set in the world of the Empire of Videssos, and I'm working on two more. So far, this is the only piece of short fiction I've done that seemed to fit in that world. It's set a few hundred years before the events in *The Videssos Cycle*, and well to the east of anything that happened there. Like a good deal of what happens in Videssos, it has a real historical model—in this case from the pages of that most accomplished historian, Anna Comnena.

A DIFFICULT UNDERTAKING

ULROR RASKA'S SON STOOD IN THE TOPMOST chamber of the tall watchtower, staring out to sea. Like most Halogai, he was tall and fair. His shining hair hung in a neat braid that reached the small of his back, but there was nothing effeminate about him. His face, hard-featured to begin with, had been battered further by close to half a century of carousing and war. His shoulders were wide as a bear's. Until a few weeks ago, his belly had bulged over his belt. It did not bulge anymore. No one inside the fortress of Sotevag was fat anymore.

Staring out to sea kept Ulror from thinking about the Videssian army that sat outside the walls of the fortress. The sea ran east forever from Sotevag. Looking at it, Ulror could feel free for a while, even if these southern waters were warm and blue, not like the chill, whitecap-flecked Bay of Haloga he had watched so often from the battlements of his own keep.

Of course, in the north the harvest failed one year in three. Even when it did not, there was never enough, nor enough land, not with every family running to three, five, seven sons. And so the Halogai hired on as mercenaries in Videssos and the lesser kingdoms, and manned ships and raided when they saw the chance.

Ulror smacked a big fist into his open palm in frustrated rage. By the gods, this chance had looked so good! With Videssos convulsed as two rival emperors battled, the island of Kalavria, far from the Empire's heartland, should have been easy to seize, to make a place where Halogai could settle freely, could live without fear of starving—it even reminded Ulror of his own district of Namdalen, if one could imagine Namdalen without snow. Chieftains whose clans had hated each other for generations joined in building and crewing the fleet.

The really agonizing thing was that, over much of the island, the men from the far north had managed to establish themselves. And here sat Ulror, under siege. He would not have admitted it to any of his warriors, but he expected Sotevag to fall. If it did, the Videssians would probably mop up the rest of the Halogai, one band at a time.

Damn Kypros Zigabenos anyway!

Kypros Zigabenos stood staring up at the walls of Sotevag, wondering how he was ever going to take the stronghold. His agile mind leapt from one stratagem to another, and unfailingly found flaws in each. From where he stood, the fortress looked impregnable. That was unfortunate, for he was all too likely to lose his head if it held.

An eyebrow quirked in wry amusement. Zigabenos had a long, narrow, mobile face, the kind that made him look younger than his forty-five years. Hardly any gray showed in his dark hair or in the aristocratic fringe of beard tracing the angle of his jaw.

He brushed a speck of lint from the sleeve of his brocaded robe. To wear the rich samite in the field was the mark of a fop, but he did not care. What was the point to civilization, if not the luxuries it made possible?

That they destroyed the opportunity to create such things was to him reason enough to oppose the Halogai. As individuals he valued highly many of the northerners, Ulror not least among them. Certainly Ulror was a better man than the fool and the butcher who each claimed to be rightful Avtokrator of the Videssians.

Both those men had called on him for aid. In a way, he thanked the good god Phos for the arrival of the Halogai. Their attack gave him the perfect excuse to refuse to remove men from Kalavria to take part in internecine strife. He would have done the same, though, if the invaders had not come.

But either the butcher or the fool would be able to rule Videssos, once the internal foe was vanquished. The Empire had survived for close to a thousand years; it had seen bad Emperors before. The eternal bureaucracy, of which Zigabenos was proud to be a part, held Videssos together when leadership faltered.

And that was something the Halogai, were their chieftains the

best leaders in the world—and some came close—could never
do. They knew nothing of the fine art of shearing a flock without
flaying it. Like any barbarians, if they wanted something they
took it, never caring whether the taking ruined in a moment
years of patient labor.

For that Zigabenos would fight them, all the while recognizing and admiring their courage, their steadiness, aye, even their
wit. When Ulror had sensibly decided to stand siege at Sotevag
rather than risk his outnumbered, harried troops in a last desperate battle, Zigabenos had shouted to him up there on the
battlements: "If you're so great a general, come out and fight!"

Ulror had laughed like one of his heathen gods. "If you're so
great a general, Videssian, make me!"

The taunt still rankled. Zigabenos had surrounded the fortress, had even succeeded in cutting it off from the sea. The
Halogai would not escape that way, or gain fresh supplies. But
the storerooms and cisterns of Sotevag were full, thanks in no
small measure to Zigabenos's own exertions the year before.
Now he could not afford to wait and starve Ulror out. While he
sat in front of Sotevag with forces he had scraped together from
all over Kalavria, the northerners could do as they would through
the rest of the island. Yet trying to storm the fortress would be
hellishly expensive in men and materiel.

Damn Ulror Raska's son, anyway!

"They're stirring around down there," said Flosi Wolf's-Pelt,
brushing back from his eyes the thick locks of gray hair that
gave him his sobriquet.

"Aye." Ulror's eyes narrowed in suspicion. Till now, Zigabenos had been content to let hunger do his work for him. Like
many Videssian generals, he played at war as if it were a game
where the object was to win while losing as few pieces as possible. Ulror despised that style of fighting; he craved the hot,
clean certainty of battle.

But there was no denying that what Zigabenos did, he did
very well. He had chivvied Ulror's Halogai halfway across Kalavria, never offering combat unless the odds were all in his
favor. He had even forced Ulror to dance to his tune and go to
earth here like a hunted fox.

So why was he changing his way of doing things, when it had
worked so well for him up to now?

Ulror pondered that as he watched the Videssians deploy.
They moved smartly and in unison, as if they were puppets

animated by Zigabenos's will alone. The Halogai lacked that kind of discipline. Even as the horns called them to their places on the battlements of Sotevag castle, they came out of the great hall in straggling groups of different sizes, getting in each other's way as they went to their assigned sections of the wall.

A single man rode past the palisade the Videssians had thrown up around Sotevag. He came within easy bowshot of the walls, his head bare so the defenders could recognize him. Ulror's lip twisted. Zigabenos might favor a spineless kind of warfare, but he was no coward.

"Your last chance, northerners," the Videssian general called, speaking the Haloga tongue badly but understandably. He did not bellow, as Ulror would have; still, his voice carried. "Surrender the fortress and yield up your commander, and you common soldiers will not be harmed. By Phos I swear it." Zigabenos drew a circle over his breast—the sun sign, symbol of the Videssian god of good. "May Skotos drag me down to hell's ice if I lie."

Ulror and Flosi looked at each other. Zigabenos had offered those same terms at the start of the siege, and been answered with jeers. No commander, though, could be sure how his troops would stand up under privation. . . .

An arrow buried itself in the ground a couple of strides in front of Zigabenos's horse. The beast snorted and sidestepped. The Videssian general, a fine rider, brought it back under control. Even then, he did not retreat. Instead he asked, "Is that your final reply?"

"Aye!" the Halogai yelled, shaking their fists and brandishing weapons in defiance.

"No!" Ulror's great shout overrode the cries of his men. "I have another."

Zigabenos looked his way, suddenly alert. The northern chieftain understood that look, and knew the Videssian thought he was about to turn his coat. Rage ripped through him. "The gods curse you, Zigabenos!" he roared. "The only way you'll get me out of Sotevag is stinking in my coffin!"

His men raised a cheer; the more bravado a Haloga showed in the face of danger, the more his fellows esteemed him. Zigabenos sat impassive until quiet returned. He gave Ulror the Videssian salute, his clenched fist over his heart. "That can be arranged," he said. He wheeled his horse, showing the northerners his back.

Ulror bit his lip. In his own cold-blooded way, Zigabenos had style.

The palisade drew near. The space between Zigabenos's shoulder blades stopped itching. If that had been he in the fortress, no enemy commander who exposed himself would have lived to return to his troops. The Haloga notion of honor struck him as singularly naive.

Yet the trip up to the walls had been worth making. When the northerners once fell into corruption, they wallowed in it. They reminded the Videssian general of a man never exposed to some childhood illness, who would die if he caught it as an adult. His own troops, no more brave or honorable than they had to be, would never sink to the depths of a Haloga who abandoned his code of conduct.

No time for such reverie now, he told himself reproachfully. The trumpeters and fifemen were waiting for his signal. He nodded. As the martial music rang out, his command echoed it: "Forward the palisade!"

Half the Videssian soldiers picked up the stakes and brush surrounding the castle of Sotevag and moved ahead, toward the fortress walls. The rest of the men—the better archers in the army—followed close behind, their bows drawn.

The Halogai began shooting to harass the advance. The range was long and the stuff of the palisade gave some protection. Nevertheless, here and there a man dropped. The dead lay where they had fallen; the wounded were dragged to the rear, where the priests would tend them with healing magic.

Zigabenos gave a quiet order. The musicians sent it to the troops, who halted and began emplacing the palisade once more. "Give them a volley!" the general said. "From now on, they keep their heads down!"

The thrum of hundreds of bowstrings released together was the only pleasant note in the cacophony of war. Arrows hissed toward Sotevag. The Halogai dove for cover. Shouts of fury and screams showed that not all reached it.

One by one, the northerners reappeared, some standing tall and proud, others peering over the top of the battlements. Zigabenos gauged the moment. "Another!" he shouted.

The Halogai vanished again. "Marksmen only, from now on," the general commanded. "If you see a good target, shoot at it. Try not to waste arrows, though."

He had expected a furious answering fire from the besieged

warriors, but it did not come. They were shooting back, but picking their marks as carefully as their foes. That made him want to grind his teeth. Ulror had learned too much, fighting against Videssians. Most of his countrymen would never have thought about saving arrows for a later need.

Zigabenos shook his head in reluctant admiration. He sighed, regretting the need to kill such a man. A race with the restless energy of the Halogai might go far, allied to Videssian canniness. Unfortunately, he knew the first place it would head for: Videssos the city, the great imperial capital. No lesser goal could sate such a folk. And so he would do his duty, and try to make sure it never came into being.

He waved. An aide appeared at his elbow. "Sir?"

"Muster the woodworkers. The time has come to build engines."

"I grow to hate the sounds of carpentry," Ulror said. The Videssian artisans were a quarter-mile away, out of reach of any weapons from inside Sotevag, but there were so many of them and they were chewing up so much timber that the noise of saw, hammer, axe, and adze was always present in the fortress.

"Not I," Flosi Wolf's-Pelt said.

"Eh? Why not?" Ulror looked at his companion in surprise.

"When the building noises stop, they'll be finished. Then they'll start using their toys."

"Oh. Aye." Ulror managed a laugh, as any northerner should in the face of danger, but even he could hear how grim it sounded. Frustrated, he shook his head until his braid switched like a horse's tail. "By the gods, I'd give two thumb's-widths off my prong for a way to strike at those accursed siege engines."

"A sally?" Flosi's eyes lit at the prospect; his hand went to the hilt of his sword.

"No," Ulror said reluctantly. "Look how openly the carpenters are working out there. See the cover off to the flanks? Zigabenos wants to tempt us into the open, so he can slaughter us at his leisure. I'll not give him his triumph so cheap."

Flosi grunted. "There's no honor in such tricks."

"True, but they work all the same." Ulror had lost too many men to ambushes to doubt that. Such tactics were of a piece with the rest of the way the Videssians made war, seeking victory at the least cost to themselves. To counter them, a man had to fight the same way, regardless of how much it went against his grain.

Flosi, though, still wanted to strike a blow at the enemy. "What of using sorcery on their engines?"

That had not occurred to Ulror. Battle magic almost always failed; in the heat of combat, men's emotions flamed strong enough to weaken the bite of spells. Only the most powerful wizards went to war, save as healers or diviners. And the one Haloga with Ulror who knew something of magic, Kolskegg Cheese-Curd, had a better reputation as tosspot than sorcerer.

When Ulror said as much to Flosi, his comrade snorted in disgust. "What do we lose by trying? If you don't aim to fight, why not throw yourself off the wall and have done?"

"I aim to fight," Ulror growled, pointing down into the outer ward, where men chopped logs and filled barrels with earth to build makeshift barriers if the walls should be breached.

"Defense," Flosi said scornfully.

Nettled, Ulror opened his mouth to snarl back, but stopped with his angry words still unspoken. How could he blame Flosi for wanting to hurt the Videssians? He wanted to himself. And who could say? Maybe Kolskegg could take the imperials by surprise. Ulror made for the stairwell, to track down the wizard. Behind him, Flosi nodded in satisfaction.

Kolskegg Cheese-Curd was a big, pockmarked man who, like Ulror, had been fat before the siege of Sotevag began. Now his skin was limp and saggy, like a deflated bladder. Something seemed to have gone out of his spirit, too, when the castle's ale casks ran dry. Living on well-water was torment for him.

His eyes widened in alarm as Ulror explained what he required. "You must be mad!" he burst out. "A hundredth part of such a magic would burn out my brain!"

"No great loss, that," Ulror growled. "How do you have the nerve to call yourself a wizard? What *are* you good for, anyway?"

"My skill at divination is not of the worst." Kolskegg eyed Ulror warily, as if wondering how much trouble that admission would get him into.

"The very thing!" the Haloga chieftain said, slapping him on the back. Kolskegg beamed, until Ulror went on, "Divine me a way to slip out of Zigabenos's clutches."

"But—my art is tyromancy," Kolskegg quavered, "reading the future in the patterns curds make as they separate out in new cheese. Where can I get milk?"

"One of the last two jennies foaled the other day. The colt

went into the stewpot, of course, but we still need the mother for hauling wood and earth. She may not have dried up yet.''

''Ass's milk?'' Kolskegg's lip curled. Even poor sorcerers had standards.

''What better, for you?'' Ulror said brutally. Losing patience, he grabbed Kolskegg by the arm and half-led, half-dragged him down to the ward, where the donkey was dragging a log up to the wall. The beast's ribs showed through its mangy coat; it was plainly on its last legs. It gave a sad bray as Kolskegg squeezed a few squirts of milk into a bowl.

''Butcher it,'' Ulror told his men; if they waited any longer, no meat would be left on those sad bones.

Seeming more confident once he had sniffed and tasted the milk, Kolskegg took Ulror back to his pack, which lay on top of his straw pallet. He rummaged in it until he found a small packet of whitish powder. ''Rennet,'' he explained, ''made from the stomach lining of young calves.''

''Just get on with it,'' Ulror said, faintly revolted.

Kolskegg sat cross-legged in the dry rushes on the floor. He began a low, whining chant, repeating the same phrase over and over. Ulror had seen other wizards act thus, to heighten their concentration. His regard for Kolskegg went up a notch.

He noticed Kolskegg was not blinking. All the sorcerer's attention focused on the chipped earthenware bowl in front of him. Ulror tried to find meaning in the swirling pattern of emerging curds as the rennet coagulated the milk, but saw nothing there he could read.

Kolskegg stiffened. White showed round the irises of his staring blue eyes. ''A coffin!'' he said hoarsely. ''A coffin and the stench of the grave. Only through a death is there escape.'' His eyes rolled up altogether and he slumped over in a faint.

Ulror's lips skinned back from his teeth in a humorless grin. Too well he remembered his roar of defiance to Zigabenos. The gods had a habit of listening to a man when he least wanted them to.

''I wish Skotos would drag that heathen down to the ice of hell now, instead of waiting for him to live out his span of days,'' Kypros Zigabenos said furiously, watching from the Videssian lines as Ulror dashed along the battlements of Sotevag, his blond braid flapping behind him. The barbarian ignored the hail of stones and darts with which the imperials were pounding the fortress. Buoyed by his spirit, the defenders stayed on the walls, shooting back with what they had and rushing to repair the damage from the bombardment.

Then, because he was an honest man—not always an advantage in Videssian service—Zigabenos felt he had to add, "But oh, he is a brave one."

"Sir?" said the servant who fetched him a cup of wine.

"Eh? Nothing." Zigabenos was irritated that anyone should have heard his mumblings. Still, he wished with all his heart for one of the Videssian missiles to dash out Ulror's brains.

Quite simply, the man was too good. Aye, he had let himself be penned here, but only as an alternative to worse. If ever he escaped, he might yet find a way to rally the Halogai and rape Kalavria away from the Empire. He was worth an army to the northerners, just as Zigabenos, without false modesty, assessed his own similar value to Videssos.

He snapped his fingers in happy inspiration. At his shout, a runner came trotting up. He sent the man over to the stone-throwers and ballistae. One by one, the siege engines stopped. Zigabenos took up a white-painted shield—a badge of truce or parley—and walked toward Sotevag's battered walls.

"Ulror!" he called. "Ulror, will you speak with me?"

After a minute or so, the northern chieftain shouted back, "Aye, if you'll talk so my men understand us."

"As you wish," Zigabenos said in the Haloga tongue. Another ploy wasted; he had deliberately used Videssian before to try to make Ulror's warriors doubt their leader. Very well, let them hear: "Come out of the fortress and I will still guarantee all your lives. And I pledge better for you, Ulror: a fine mansion, with a stipend to support a large band of retainers."

"And where will this fine mansion be? Here on the island?"

"You deserve better than this backwater, Ulror. What do you say to a residence at the capital, Videssos the city?"

Ulror was silent so long, Zigabenos's hopes began to rise. At last the northerner asked, "Will you give me a day's leave to think on it?"

"No," Zigabenos said at once. "You'll only use it to strengthen your defenses. Give me your answer."

Ulror boomed laughter. "Oh, how I wish you were a fool. I think I will decline your gracious invitation. With civil war in the Empire, even if by some mischance I reached the capital alive, I'd last about as long as a lobster's green shell when you throw him in the boiling pot."

The Videssian general felt like snarling, but his face never showed it. "You have my personal guarantee of your safety," he said.

"Aye, and that's good as silver so long as I'm on the island, and worth nothing soon as I sail west, since both Emperors hate you for not sending 'em men."

Too good by half, Zigabenos thought. Without another word, he turned and walked away. But Ulror was still in the lobster pot. It remained only to bring him to the boil.

The cat crawled forward, its timber sides and roof covered with green hides to keep them from being burned. Fire arrows streaked from the Videssian archers toward bales of straw the Halogai had hung on the side of the wall to deaden the impact of the battering ram the cat protected. The northerners dumped pails of water and sewage, snuffing out the flames before they took hold.

Then the imperials manhandled their shed up to the base of the wall. The Halogai pelted it with boulders and spears, trying to create rifts in the hide covering through which boiling water and red-hot sand might find their way.

"There!" Ulror cried, pointing, and another stone thudded home. The din was indescribable. Through it all, though, Ulror heard the commands of the Videssian underofficer in the cat, each order delivered as calmly as if on parade.

He could not fathom that kind of courage. The hazards of the field—aye, he had their measure. This siege was harder, but here he had had no good choice. But how men could hold their wits about them advancing turtle-fashion into danger, knowing they would die if their shell was broken, was beyond him.

Like so many Halogai, he scorned the discipline Videssos imposed on her troops; no free man would let himself be used so. Now he saw what such training was worth. His own men, he knew, would have broken under the punishment the imperials were taking. Yet they stolidly labored on.

Rather than hearing the ram strike the wall, Ulror felt it through the soles of his feet. Chains rattled in the cat below as the Videssians drew their great iron-faced log back for another stroke. The wall shook again. Ulror could see the spirit oozing out of his warriors. They had gaily faced the chance of arrow or flying stone, but this methodical pounding stole the manhood from them. He wondered if he could make them fight in the breach. He had no great hope of it.

Just when he was telling himself he should have made what

terms he could with Zigabenos, shrieks replaced the stream of orders coming from the cat. One of the smoking cauldrons the Halogai tipped down on it had found a breach of its own.

When the ram's rhythm missed a beat, the northerners above seemed to realize their doom was not inevitable after all. Ulror bellowed encouragement to them. They redoubled their efforts, working like men possessed.

Three soldiers grunted to lift a huge stone to a crenelation, then shoved it out and down onto the cat. The shed's sloping roof and thick sides had sent other boulders bouncing aside, but this one struck square on the midline. Along with the crash, Ulror heard a metallic snap as a chain holding the ram to the roof of the cat broke. Shouts of pain from the imperials it injured in its fall and curses from the rest were as sweet music in his ears.

Like a wounded animal, the shed began to limp away. Videssian shieldsmen stood at its open front, where the ram had swung. They protected their comrades from the missiles the Halogai rained on them. Whenever one was shot, another took his place. That was bravery Ulror could grasp. Even as he let fly at them, he hoped they would safely reach their own line. Zigabenos, he thought, would want them to fall to the arrows like so many quail. That was sensible, but he did not have the stomach for it.

The Halogai danced with joy as the cat withdrew, their heavy boots clumping on the stone walkways and stairs. "A victory," Flosi Wolf's-Pelt said.

"Aye, or so the lads think, anyway," Ulror answered quietly. "Well, that's worth something of itself, I suppose. It'll take their minds off the stale donkey tripes—the last of them left—and the handful of barley meal they'll be eating tonight."

"We hurt the cat," Flosi protested.

"So we did, and they hurt the wall. Which do you think the easier to repair?"

Flosi grimaced and turned away.

High overhead, a seagull screeched. Ulror envied the bird its freedom. Not too many gulls came near Sotevag anymore. If they did, the Halogai shot them and ate them. Their flesh was tough and salty and tasted strongly of fish, but hungry men did not care. Ulror had stopped asking about the meat that went into the stewpots. He did know he had seen fewer rats lately.

Watching the gull wheel in the sky and glide away was suddenly more than Ulror could bear. He slammed his fist against the stone of the battlement, cursed at the pain. Ignoring Flosi's startled look, he rushed down the stairs and into the outer ward.

Kolskegg Cheese-Curd had been making what looked like a mousetrap out of sticks and leather thongs. He put the contraption aside as his chieftain bore down on him, asked warily, "Is there something I might do for you?"

"Aye, there is." Ulror hauled his reluctant wizard to his feet; his belly might be gone, but he still kept his bull strength. Paying no attention to the protests Kolskegg yammered, he dragged him through the gatehouse into the keep, and on into the chamber he had taken for himself.

The goosefeather mattress had belonged to the Videssian who once commanded here. So did the silk coverlet atop it, now sadly stained. Ulror flopped down on the bed with a sigh of relief, waved Kolskegg to a chair whose delicacy proclaimed it also to be imperial work.

Once Kolskegg had made himself comfortable, Ulror came to the point with his usual directness. "That was a true divination you gave me—that the only way I would leave Sotevag would be in my coffin?"

The wizard licked his lips, but had to answer, "Aye, it was."

To his surprise, his chieftain grunted in satisfaction. "Good. If Zigabenos's priests read the omens, they should learn the same, not so?"

"Aye." Kolskegg had been a warrior long enough to know not to volunteer more than he was asked.

"All right, then," Ulror said. "Give me a spell to turn me to the seeming of a corpse, stench and all, to let me get away. Then when I'm outside, you can take it off, or arrange in the first place for it to last only so long, or whatever you think best." He nodded, pleased at his own ingenuity.

The wizard's face, though, went chalky white. "Have mercy!" he cried. "I am nothing but a miserable diviner. Why do you set me tasks to strain the powers of the greatest adepts? I cannot do this; he who trifles with death in magic courts it."

"You are the only sorcerer I have," Ulror said implacably. "And you will do it."

"I cannot." As a weak man will, Kolskegg sounded querulous in his insistence.

"You will," Ulror told him. "If you do not, Sotevag will surely fall. And if the Videssians take me alive, I will tell them you worked your charms through their dark god Skotos. Once they believe that, you will wish you died fighting. No demon could serve you worse than their inquisitors.''

Kolskegg shivered, for Ulror was right. As dualists, the imperials hated their deity's evil rival and dealt with legendary savagery with anyone who dared revere him. ''You would not—'' the wizard began, and stopped in despair. Ulror would.

The Haloga commander said nothing more. He waited, bending Kolskegg to his will with silence. Under his unwinking stare, the wizard's resolve melted like snow in springtime. ''I will try,'' he said at last, very low. ''Maybe at midnight, a spell I know might serve. It is, after all, only a seeming you seek.''

He spoke more to reassure himself than for any other reason, Ulror judged. That was all right. ''Midnight it is,'' Ulror said briskly. ''I'll see you here then.'' He did not put any special warning in his voice. He had done his job properly, and did not need to.

The wizard returned at the hour he had set, stumbling in the darkness as he approached Ulror's door. Inside, the chieftain had a tallow dip lit. Not many lights burned in Sotevag at night; tallow and olive oil could be eaten, if a man was hungry enough.

Even in the red, flickering light, Kolskegg looked pale. ''I wish I had a beaker of ale,'' he muttered under his breath. He fumbled in his pouch, finally digging out a chain that held a black stone with white veins. ''An onyx,'' he said, hanging it round Ulror's neck. ''The stone for stirring up terrible fantasms.''

''Get on with it,'' Ulror said. He spoke more harshly than he had intended; Kolskegg's nervousness was catching.

The wizard cast a powder into the flame of the tallow dip, which flared a ghastly green. Kolskegg began a slow, rhymeless chant full of assonances. The stone he had set on Ulror's breast grew cold, so he could feel its chill through his tunic. He could also feel the little hairs at the nape of his neck prickling upright.

The chant droned on. Kolskegg began singing faster and faster, as if he wanted to get through the incantation as quickly as he could. In the end, his own fear of what he was doing undid him. His tongue slipped, so that when he meant to intone ''thee,'' ''me'' came out instead.

Had he been wearing the onyx, the spell might have possessed him as he intended it to possess Ulror: as an unpleasant but impermanent illusion. But the Holga chieftain had the magical focus, not his wizard. Before Kolskegg could do more than gasp in horror at his blunder, the transformation struck him.

Ulror gagged on the stench that filled his chamber. He staggered outside and was sick against the wall of the keep. Several of his warriors rushed over, asking if he was all right.

One had the wit to offer a bucket of water. He rinsed his mouth, spat, rinsed again. The sour taste remained. His men began exclaiming over the graveyard reek that followed him into the inner ward.

"You will find a lich—not a fresh one—inside," he told them. "Treat poor Kolskegg with respect; he showed more courage dying at my order than ever he did in life."

As was his privilege, even after midnight, the blue-robed priest burst past Zigabenos's bodyguard and into the tent of the Videssian general. "Sorcery!" he cried, the firelight gleaming from his shaved pate. "Sorcery most foul!"

"Huh?" Zigabenos sat up with a start. He was glad he'd sent the kitchen wench back to her tavern instead of keeping her for the night. He enjoyed his vices, but had learned long since not to flaunt them.

His wits returned with their usual rapidity. "Say what you mean, Bonosos. Are the Halogai assailing us with magic?"

"Eh? No, your illustriousness. But they play at wizardry even so, a wizardry that stinks of Skotos." The priest spat on the ground in rejection of the wicked god, his faith's eternal enemy.

"The conjuration was not aimed against us? You are certain of that?"

"I am," Bonosos said reluctantly. "Yet it was strong, and of a malefic nature. It was not undertaken to curry favor with us."

"I hardly expected it would be," Zigabenos said; he had no intention of letting a priest out-irony him. "Still, so long as they do not send a blast our way, the Halogai are welcome to play at whatever they wish. Maybe it will go awry and eat them up, and save us the trouble."

"May the lord of the great and good mind hear and heed your prayer," Bonosos said, drawing Phos's sun sign on his breast.

Zigabenos did the same; his own piety, though he did not let it interfere with whatever he had to do, ran deep. After a moment he said, "Bonosos, I hope you had a reason for disturbing my rest, other than merely to tell me the Halogai have some fribbling spell afoot."

"Hardly fribbling." Bonosos's glare was wasted; to Zigabenos, he was only a silhouette in the doorway. But there was no mistaking the abhorrence in the priest's voice as he went on, "The conjuration smacked of necromancy."

"Necromancy!" Zigabenos exclaimed, startled. "You must be mistaken."

Bonosos bowed. "Good evening, sir. I tell the truth. If you do not care to hear it, that is none of my affair." He spun on his heel and stalked away.

Stiff-necked old bastard, the Videssian general thought as he settled back under his silk coverlet, and mad as a loon besides. The Halogai inside Sotevag had too many other things to worry about to bother with corpse-raising or anything like it.

Or did they? Zigabenos suddenly remembered Ulror's howl of defiance from the battlements. The northerner must have taken that for prophecy as well as brag. Zigabenos laughed out loud, admiring Ulror's ingenuity in trying to get around his own oath. Unfortunately for the Haloga, he thought, there was no way around it. The northerners fought bravely and, under Ulror's command, resourcefully. Against siege engines, however, bravery and resource only counted for so much. In a week, maybe less, maybe a day or two more, he would be inside Sotevag. And then Ulror's boast would be fulfilled in the most literal way imaginable.

Still chuckling, Zigabenos rolled over and went back to sleep.

After a sleepless night, Ulror stared out to sea, watching the rising sun turn the water to a flaming sheet of molten gold and silver. He regretted Kolskegg's death, and regretted even more that it had been in vain. Now, impaled on his own rash words, he found nothing else to do but face the prospect of dying.

He did not fear death. Few Halogai did; they lived too close to it, both at home and in battle on distant shores. But he bitterly regretted the waste. If only he could get free, rally the Halogai all across Kalavria. In pursuing him, Zigabenos really had concentrated his own forces too much—provided the northerners moved against him in unison. If not, he would go on dealing with them piecemeal, methodical as a cordwainer turning out boots.

Ulror ground his teeth. All he, all any of the Halogai, wanted was a steading big enough for a free man to live on and to pass down to his sons; a good northern woman to wife, with perhaps two or three of these island wenches to keep a bed warm of nights; a chance to enjoy the luxuries the imperials took for granted: wine grown on a man's own holding, a bathtub, wheat bread instead of loaves of rye or oats. If the Empire's god would grant him so much, he might even give worship to Phos along with his own somber deities.

Unless Zigabenos made a mistake, though, none of that would happen. And Zigabenos was not in the habit of making mistakes.

As had happened a few days before, a gull gave its raucous call high over Sotevag. This time the frustration was more than the Haloga chieftain could bear. Without conscious thought, in one smooth motion he reached over his shoulder for an arrow, set it to his bow, and let fly. His rage lent power to the shot. The bird's cry abruptly cut off. It fell with a thud to the dirt of the outer ward. Ulror stared malevolently at the dead gull— miserable, stinking thing, he thought.

"Good shooting," one of his warriors called, ambling over to pick up the bird and carry it off to be cooked.

"Hold!" Ulror shouted suddenly, rushing for a stairway. "That seagull's mine!" The warrior gaped at him, certain he had lost his mind.

An orderly came dashing into the tent, interrupting Zigabenos's breakfast. Paying no attention to the Videssian general's glare, he said breathlessly, "Sir, there's sign of truce over the main gatehouse of Sotevag!"

Zigabenos stood up so quickly that he upset the folding table in front of him. He ignored his valet's squawk of distress and hurried out after the orderly to see this wonder for himself.

It was true. Above the gate, a white shield hung on a spear. "They turned coward at the end," the orderly said, "when they saw what our engines were about to do to them."

"I wonder," Zigabenos said. It was not like Ulror to give in so tamely. What sort of scheme could the Haloga chieftain have come up with? No one had spied him on the walls for several days now. Was he planning a last desperate sally, hoping to slay Zigabenos and throw the Videssian army into confusion?

To forestall that, the general approached the fortress in the midst of a squadron of shieldsmen, enough to get him out of danger no matter what the Halogai tried. When he was within hailing distance, he called, "Well, Ulror? What have you to say to me?"

But it was not Ulror who came to stand by the northerners' truce shield. A raw-boned Haloga with gray hair took that place instead. He stared down at Zigabenos in silence for a long moment, then asked, "Have you honor, imperial?"

Zigabenos shrugged. "If you need the question, would you trust the answer?"

A harsh chuckle. "Summat to that. All right, be it so. You'll do what you promised before, let the rest of us go if we yield you Sotevag and bring out Ulror?"

The Videssian general had all he could do not to cry out for joy. In exchange for Ulror, he was willing, nay eager, to let a few hundred barbarians of no special importance keep their lives. He was too old a hand, however, to let his excitement show. After a suitable pause, he demanded, "Show me Ulror now, so I may see you have him prisoner."

"I cannot," the Haloga said.

Zigabenos turned to leave. "I am not a child, for you to play tricks on."

"He is dead," the northerner replied, and Zigabenos stopped. The northerner went on, "He took a fever a week ago, but fought on with it, as any true man would. He died four nights past. Now that he is gone, we ask ourselves why we must sell our lives dear, and find no answer."

"You need not, of course," Zigabenos said at once. No wonder the Halogai had tried necromancy, he thought. But Ulror was tricksy, and who knew how far he would go to lend versimilitude to a ploy? The Videssian general declared, "I will abide by my terms, save that I add one condition: as each man of yours leaves Sotevag, my wizards will examine him, to be sure he is not Ulror in sorcerous disguise."

The Haloga spokesman spat. "Do what you please. Victors always do. But I have told you you will not find him among them."

They haggled over details for the next hour. Zigabenos was lenient. Why not, with the one great northern chieftain gone and Sotevag about to return to imperial hands?

When noon came, the long-shut fortress gates swung open. As had been agreed, the Halogai came out two by two, in armor and carrying their weapons. They were all skinny, and many wounded. They could not help looking out toward the imperial lines; if Zigabenos wanted to betray them, he could. He did not want to. He expected to fight their countrymen again, and fear of a broken truce would only lead the Halogai to fight to the end from then on.

The Videssian general stood outside the gates with a pair of priests. The blue-robes had anointed their eyes with a paste made from the gall of a male cat and the fat of a pure white hen, an ointment that let them pierce illusion. They examined each emerging northerner, ready to cry out if they spied Ulror behind a veil of magic.

The gray-haired Haloga with whom Zigabenos had dickered came limping out. The general gave him a formal salute. He had developed some respect for this Flosi Wolf's-Pelt, for his spirit, his courage, and his blunt honesty. What sprang from those, though, was easy to anticipate. When the time came, he knew he would beat Flosi. With Ulror he had never been sure.

Flosi looked through him as if he did not exist.

The moment Zigabenos had been waiting for finally came. A dozen Halogai dragged a rough-built coffin behind them on a sledge. "Ulror is inside?" the general asked one of them.

"Aye," the man said.

"Check it," Zigabenos snapped to the priests who flanked him.

They peered at the coffin with their sorcerously enhanced vision. "That is truly Ulror Raska's son within," Bonosos declared.

So Ulror had been a prophet after all, Zigabenos thought, and look what it gained him. Something else occurred to the Videssian general. "Is the rascal dead?"

Bonosos frowned. "A spell to ascertain that will take some little time to prepare, and in any case I mislike touching on death with my sorcery—see how such an unholy effort profited the northerner here. I suggest you make your own examination to satisfy yourself. If he is four days dead, you will know it."

"Something in the air, you mean. Yes, I take your point." Zigabenos chuckled. He added, "Who would expect such plain sense from a priest?" Bonosos's frown turned to scowl. The Videssian general approached the coffin. "Pry up the top of the lid, you," he told one of the northerners.

Shrugging, the Haloga drew his sword and used it to lever up the coffin lid; nails squealed in protest. Through the narrow opening Zigabenos saw Ulror's face, pale and thin and still. The death smell welled out, almost thick enough to slice. "Shut it," Zigabenos said, coughing. He drew Phos' sun-circle on his breast, then saluted the coffin with the same formality he had offered Flosi.

Seeing how exhausted the pallbearers were, Zigabenos said kindly, "If you like, we will bury him for you here."

The Halogai drew themselves up; even in privation, they were proud men. One said, "I thank you, but we care for our own."

"As you wish." Zigabenos waved them on.

When the last northerner had left Sotevag castle, the general sent in a crack platoon to search it from top to bottom. No matter what the priests said, no matter what he had seen and smelled, maybe Ulror had found a way to stay behind and then drop over the walls and escape. Zigabenos did not see how, but he took no chances where Ulror was concerned.

Only when the platoon's lieutenant reported back to him that Sotevag was empty of life did he truly begin to believe he had won.

Hungry, worn, and battered as they were, the Halogai traveled slowly. Still, Kalavria was not a large island; by the end of the second day after they left Sotevag, they were at the end of the central uplands. They camped next to a swift, cool stream.

As the warriors shared the half-ripe fruits and nuts they had gathered on their march and hunters went into the undergrowth after rabbits, Flosi went up to Ulror's coffin. Wrinkling his nose at the stench emanating from it, he pried up the ends of a couple of boards with his dagger.

The coffin shook, as with some internal paroxysm. The boards Flosi had loosened flew up. Ulror scrambled out. The first thing he did was to dive into the water and scrub himself from head to foot with sand from the streambank. When he came splashing out, streaks of the mixture of chalk and grease with which he had smeared his face remained on it, but his natural ruddy color dominated once more.

One of his warriors threw a ragged cloak around him. "Food!" he boomed. "After two days with nothing but three stinking seagulls for company, even the rubbish we were eating back at Sotevag would taste good."

Flosi brought him some of their meager fare. He wolfed it down. One by one, the hunters returned. Fresh meat, even a couple of bites' worth, roasted over an open fire was the most delicious thing he had ever eaten.

His belly was still growling after all the food was gone, but he had grown used to that in Sotevag. He looked around again and again, admiring the stream, the trees, the little clearing in which the Halogai were camped. "Free," he breathed.

"Aye." Flosi still did not seem to believe it. "I thought we were ruined when your magicking with Kolskegg failed."

"And I." Ulror longed for wine, but after a moment he realized triumph was a sweeter, headier brew. He laughed. "We get so used to using sorcery for our ends, we forget what we can do without it. Once I thought of the scheme, my biggest worry was that Zigabenos would attack before the birds got ripe enough to use.''

"A good thing you whitened your face, even so.''

"Oh, indeed. Zigabenos is too canny for me to dare miss a trick against him,'' Ulror said. A swirl of the breeze brought the carrion reek his way. He grimaced. "I was afraid of one other thing, too. He might have noticed something wrong if he'd heard my 'corpse' puking its guts out.''

"So he might.'' Flosi allowed himself a rare smile. He rose and started over to the opened coffin. "The birds have served their purpose. I'll toss them in the creek.''

"Eh? Don't do that,'' Ulror exclaimed.

"Why not? What do you want them for? I wouldn't eat the smelly things if I'd stood siege for years, not a couple of months. Throw 'em away and have done.''

"I have a better plan,'' Ulror said.

"What's that?''

"I'm going to send one back to Zigabenos behind a shield of truce.'' Ulror's eyes glowed with mischief. "I wish I could be there to see his face when he finds out how''—he grinned a huge grin; it felt monstrous good to be able to joke again—"how he's been gulled.''

"Gulled, eh?'' Kypros Zigabenos nodded at the noisome pile of feathers the smirking Haloga herald set before him. He would not give the barbarian the satisfaction of showing he felt anything at all at finding Ulror alive and free. Never in his life, though, had he come so close to dishonoring a truce shield. The northerner would never know by how little he had missed the lash, the thumbscrews, the red-hot bronze needles, and the rest of the ingenious torments the Videssians had devised over the centuries.

But only a vicious fool struck at the bearer of bad news. And so Zigabenos, his heart a cold stone in his breast, poured wine for the Haloga and laughed politely to hear how Ulror had duped him.

"Wait here a moment, if you will,'' he said to the warrior, and stepped out of his tent to speak to one of his guards. The man blinked in surprise, then saluted and hurried away, stringing his bow as he trotted.

Zigabenos returned to his unwelcome guest, refilled the fellow's cup, and went on with the urbane conversation he had briefly interrupted. Behind his smiling mask, he felt desperation building. He had staked too great a part of the imperial forces on Kalavria to finishing Ulror here. The Videssians scattered over the rest of the island were ragtag and bobtail. With his victorious army as a core, they would have sufficed. Now the Halogai would mop up, not he.

And then they would come for him. He wondered how fast his artisans could repair the damage his own engines had done to Sotevag, and what sort of supplies he could bring in. The Halogai were impetuous, impatient. They might not have the staying power to conduct a siege of their own.

But with Ulror leading them, they might.

The sentry with whom Zigabenos had spoken stuck his head into the tent. "I have one, your excellency."

"Very good. Bring it in." The general drew himself up straighter in his chair. Sometimes one won, sometimes one lost; no sane man expected nothing but triumph in his life. But win or lose, style mattered. He prayed the day might never come when he failed to meet misfortune with aplomb.

The bird the Videssian soldier brought in was smaller than the one Ulror had sent, with a deeply forked tail and a black cap. It was still warm. Zigabenos picked it up and ceremoniously offered it to the Haloga. "I hope you will be so kind as to present this to your master, with my compliments."

The northerner looked at him as if he had gone mad. "Just the bird, or shall I say something?"

"The latter." Zigabenos was an imperial, a man of anciently civilized race, and of high blood as well. This grinning blond lout here would never understand, but somehow he felt Ulror might appreciate the spirit in which he sent his message. "Tell him one good tern deserves another."

Sometimes ideas come in pieces. I got the first half of the idea for this one listening to a weather report while driving on the freeway: what if those constantly changing numbers were years instead of degrees? Once I got to a place where I could, I wrote down the notion. That gave me the background against which the story would be presented, but it took me two years to find a story to present. What you're about to read is the result.

THE WEATHER'S FINE

TOM CROWELL GOES INTO THE LITTLE kitchen of his apartment, pulls a Bud out of the refrigerator. To save money, the place is conditioned to only the mid-seventies. He pulls off the ring tab and tosses it into the trash. Then he goes into the living room and turns on the TV news. The couch squeaks as he flops down onto it. Even in the mid-seventies, it isn't new.

As always, the weather is big news, especially in other parts of the country: "The old front sweeping down out of Canada continues to ravage our northern tier of states. It has caused widespread communications breakdowns. Authorities are doing their best to combat them, but problems remain far too widespread for portable generators to be adequate. This film footage, some of the little coming out of the area, is from Milwaukee."

The weatherman disappears from the screen, to be replaced by jerky, grainy black-and-white footage. The streets are tree-lined; horse carts and boxy cars compete for space. The men wear hats, and the women's skirts reach to the ground.

Not for the first time, Tom is glad he lives in southern California, where the weather rarely gets below the fifties. No wonder so many people move here, he thinks.

The weatherman comes back with the local forecast. The weather will be about standard for Los Angeles in April: mostly in the late sixties. Tom decides he won't bother with the conditioner in the car tomorrow. He looks good in long sideburns.

After the news, he stays in front of the TV. No matter where he sets the year conditioner, TV is pretty bad, he thinks. That

65

doesn't stop him from watching it. Finally, he gives up and goes to bed.

He leaves the window down as he drives to work. The Doors, the Stones when they're really the Stones, the Airplane, Creedence—the music coming out of the car radio is better than it will be. The speaker, though, sounds tinny as hell. Trade-offs, Tom thinks.

He feels more businesslike when he gets into the buying office. The boss keeps the conditioner really cranked up. Eighties computer technology makes the expense worthwhile, he claims. Tom doesn't complain, but he does wonder, What price computers when the only links to the upper Midwest are telegraphs and operator-assisted telephones?

He sighs and buckles down to his terminal. It's not his problem. Besides, things could be worse. He remembers the horrible winter when Europe was stuck in the early forties for weeks. He hopes that won't happen again any time soon.

His pants start flapping at the ankles as he trots for his car at quitting time. He grins. He likes bell-bottoms. He remembers he has a cousin with a birthday coming up and decides to go to the mall before he heads home.

Everyone else in the world, it seems, has a cousin with a birthday coming up, too. Tom has to drive around for ten minutes before he can find a parking space. He hikes toward the nearest entrance. "Which isn't any too damn near," he says out loud. Living alone, he has picked up the habit of talking to himself.

Some people are getting up to the entrance, turning around and heading back toward their cars. Tom wonders why until he sees the sign taped to the glass door: SORRY, OUR YEAR CONDITIONER HAS FAILED. PLEASE COME IN ANYHOW. Maybe the people who are leaving really don't have cousins with birthdays coming up. Tom sighs. He does. He pulls the door open and goes in.

Sure enough, the conditioner is down. He doesn't feel the blast of air it ought to be putting out, doesn't hear its almost subliminal hum. The inside of the mall is stuck in the late sixties, same as outside.

Tom smells incense and scented candles. He hasn't been in a shopping center this downyear for a long while. He wonders what he can find for his cousin here-and-now. He smiles a little as he walks past a Jeans West, with its striped pants and Day-

Glo turtlenecks. He doesn't go in. His cousin's taste runs more to cutoffs and T-shirts.

He climbs the stairs. The Pier 1 Imports is a better bet. No matter what the weather is like, they always have all kinds of strange things. The long-hair behind the counter nods at him. "Help you find something, man?"

"Just looking now, thanks."

"No problem. Holler if you need me."

The sitar music coming out of the stereo goes with the rugs from India that are hanging on the walls and the rickety rattan furniture in the center of the store. It's not as good an accompaniment for the shelves of German beer steins or for the silver-and-turquoise jewelry "imported from the Navaho nation." Wrong kind of Indians, Tom thinks.

He picks up a liter stein, hefts it thoughtfully, puts it down. It will do if he can't find anything better. He turns a corner, goes past some cheap flatware from Taiwan, turns another corner and finds himself in front of a display of Greek pottery: modern copies of ancient pieces.

He's seen this kind of thing before, but most of it is crude. This has the unmistakable feel of authenticity to it. The lines of the pots are spare and perfect, the painting elegantly simple. He picks up a pot, turns it over. His cousin doesn't have anything like it, but it goes with everything he does have.

Tom is just turning to thread his way through the maze toward the cash register when a girl comes round the corner. She sees him, rocks back on her heels, then cries. "Tom!" and throws herself into his arms.

"Donna!" he exclaims in surprise. She is a big armful, every bit as tall as his own 5'8", with not a thing missing—she's good to hug.

She tosses her head, a characteristic Donna gesture, to get her long, straight black hair out of her face. Then she kisses him on the mouth. When Tom finally comes up for air, he looks at the familiar gray eyes a couple of inches from his, asks, "Are you here for anything special?"

She grins. "Just to spend money." Very much her kind of answer, he thinks.

"Let me pay for this; then do you want to come home with me?"

Her grin gets wider. "I thought you'd never ask." They link arms and head for the front of the store. She whistles *Side by Side*. Now he is grinning, too.

When he sets the pot on the counter so the clerk can ring it up, Donna exclaims over it. "I didn't even notice it before," she says. "I was too busy looking at you." That makes Tom feel ten feet tall as the long-hair gives him his change.

When they get to the glass door with the sign on it, he holds it open so she can go through. The only thing he can think when he sees what dark, patterned hose and a short skirt do for her legs is, Gilding the lily. Or lilies, he amends—she definitely has two of them. He admires them both.

He opened the passenger door to let her in, then goes around to his own side. He doesn't bother with the year conditioner. He likes the weather fine the way it is. He does keep having to remind himself to pay attention to his driving. Her skirt is even shorter when she's sitting down.

There is a parking space right in front of his building. He slides the car into it. "Sometimes you'd rather be lucky than good," he says.

Donna looks at him. "I think you're pretty good."

His right arm slips around her waist as they climb the stairs to his apartment. When he takes it away so he can get out his keys, she is pressed so tightly against him that he can hardly put his hand in his pocket. He enjoys trying, though. She doesn't seem unhappy, either. If anything, she moves closer to him.

She turns her head and nibbles his ear while he is undoing the deadbolt. After that, he has to try more than once before he can work the regular lock. Finally, the key goes in, turns. He opens the door.

The conditioned air inside blows on him and Donna. He can feel his memories shift forward. Because he stands outside instead of going straight in, it happens slowly. It's probably worse that way.

Now he looks at Donna with new eyes. She can't stand the seventies, even when she's in them. He always just goes on with his life, or tries to. And because of that, they always fight.

He remembers a glass shattering against a wall—not on his head, but only by luck and because she can't throw worth a damn. Her hand jumps up to her cheek. He knows she is remembering a slap. He feels his face go hot with mingled shame and rage. With a sound like a strangled sob, she turns away and starts, half stumbling, down the steps.

He takes a reflexive step after her. It moves him far enough from his apartment for the bad times to fade a bit in his mind.

She stops, too. She looks at him from the stairs. She shakes her head. "That was a bad one," she says. "No wonder we don't hang out together all the times."

"No wonder," he says tonelessly. He feels beat up, hung over; too much has happened too fast. He is horny and angry and emotionally bruised, all at once. He walks down the stairs to Donna. She doesn't run or swing on him, which is something. Standing by her, he feels better. In the sixties, he usually feels better standing by her.

He takes a deep breath. "Let me go inside and turn the conditioner off."

"Are you sure you want to? I don't want you to mess up your place just for me."

"It won't be bad," he says, and hopes he isn't lying.

She squeezes his hand. "You're sweet. I'll try to make you glad you did."

The promise in that is enough to send him up the stairs two at a time. A couple of half-trotting steps to the walkway and he is in the apartment.

He was right. Doing it all at once is better than a little bit at a time, the way diving into a cold swimming pool gets you used to it faster than going in by easy stages. The memories come rushing back, of course. They always do. But in the fully conditioned mid-seventies of his apartment, they are older, mostly healed; they don't have the hurt they did before, when they were fresher.

He puts his hand on the chronostat, turns if off with a decisive twist of his wrist. Its hum dies. He's used to the background noise. He goes into the bedroom, opens the window to let outside air in faster. The mingling makes memories jump into focus again, but only for a moment: now they are going rather than coming.

When he walks back into the living room, the little calculator is gone from his coffee table. That's a good sign, he thinks. He glances at the chronostat needle. It's already down around seventy. He opens and closes the front door several times to bring in fresh air. The swirl is confusing, but only for a little while.

He looks at the needle again. Sixty-eight, he sees. That should be plenty good. Donna is still waiting on the stairs. "Come on in," he says.

"All right," she says. Now she takes the steps two at a time. She shows a lot of leg doing it.

"Wine?"

"Sure. Whatever you've got."

He opens the refrigerator. A half-gallon of Spañada is in there. He pours a couple of glasses, takes them into the living room.

"I like the poster," she says. It's a black-light KEEP ON TRUCKIN' poster, about the size of a baby billboard. When the conditioner is running, it isn't there. That doesn't matter to Tom if Donna likes it. He won't even miss the Chinese print that will replace it.

And then, as they have done a lot of times before, they head for the bedroom. Afterward, still naked, Tom wheels the TV in from out front. He plugs it in, spins the dial till he finds some news, then flops back onto the bed with Donna.

For a while, he doesn't pay much attention to the TV. Watching the flush fade from between Donna's breasts is much more interesting. He does hear that Minnesota is finally up into the thirties. "Not good, but better," he says, to show he has been following what's going on.

Donna nods; she really is watching. "Remember last winter, when it got below double zero and stayed there, and they had to try to get food to the markets with horses and buggies? People starved. In the United States, starved. I couldn't believe it."

"Terrible," Tom agrees. Then he has to start watching, too, because the weatherman is coming on.

As usual, the fellow is insanely cheerful. "The early seventies tomorrow through most of the metropolitan area," he says, whacking the map with his pointer, "rising into the mid- or late seventies in the valleys and the desert. Have a *fine* day, Los Angeles!" He whacks the map again.

Donna sucks in air between her teeth. "I'd better go," she says, catching Tom by surprise. She swings her feet onto the floor, turns her panties right side out, slides them up her legs.

"I'd hoped you'd spend the night," he says. He is trying to sound hurt but fears that the words have come out petulant instead.

Evidently not. Donna replies gently, "Tom, right now, I love you very much. But if I sleep with you tonight—and I mean sleep—and we wake up in the early seventies, what's going to happen?"

His scowl says he knows the answer to that. Donna's nod is sad, but she stands up and starts pulling on her pantyhose. Tom aches at the thought of having her go, and not just because he wants her again. Right now, he really loves her, too.

He says, "Tell you what. Suppose I set the conditioner for sixty-eight. Will you stay then?"

He has startled her. "Do you really want to?" she says. She doesn't sound as if she believes it, but she does get back onto the bed.

He wonders if he believes it himself. The place won't be the same in the late sixties. He'll miss that little calculator. There should be a slide rule around somewhere now, he thinks, but a slide rule won't help him keep his checkbook straight. And that's just the tip of the iceberg. The frozen pizza will taste more like cardboard and less like pizza in the sixties. But—

"Let's try it," he says. Better cardboard with Donna, he thinks, than mozzarella without.

He shuts the bedroom window, goes out front to adjust the chronostat. It doesn't kick in right away, since the place is already around sixty-eight, but moving the needle makes him think again about what he's doing. A bookcase is gone, he sees. He'll miss some of those books.

"Hell with it," he says out loud and heads for the bathroom. While he is brushing his teeth, he starts rummaging frantically through the drawers by the sink. The toothbrush is still in his mouth; fluoridated foam dribbles down his chin, so that he looks like a mad dog. He stops as suddenly as he started. He does have a spare toothbrush, rather to his surprise. Donna giggles when, with a flourish, he hands it to her.

"When are you working these days?" she asks when she comes back to bed. "If it's close to when you had this place before—"

"No," he says quickly. He understands what she means. If he spends his office time reliving fights that are fresh to him, this will never fly, no matter how well they get on when they are home together. "How about you?" he asks.

She laughs. "I probably wouldn't have gone into the mall if I hadn't heard the year conditioner had broken down. I like the sixties. I work in a little record store called Barefoot Sounds. It suits me."

"I can see that," he says, nodding. Donna will never be a pragmatist. The more she stays out of the eighties, the better off she'll be. He yawns, lies down beside her. "Let's go to bed."

She smiles a broad's smile at him—there's no other word for it. "We've already done that."

He picks up a pillow, makes as if to hit her with it. "To sleep, I mean."

"Okay." She sprawls across him, warm and soft, to turn off the light. She has, he knows, a gift for falling asleep right away. Sure enough, only a couple of minutes later, her voice is blurry as she asks, "Drive me to work in the morning?"

"Sure." He hesitates. With a name like Barefoot Sounds, her record store sounds like a thoroughly sixties place. "If the weather changes, will I be able to find it?"

The mattress shifts to her nod. "It's year-conditioned. No matter what the weather's like outside, there are always sixties refugees popping in. We do a pretty good business, as a matter of fact."

"Okay," he says again. A couple of minutes later, he can tell that she has dropped off. He takes longer to go to sleep himself. He hasn't shared a bed with a woman for a while. He is very conscious of her weight pressing down the bed, of the small noises her breathing makes, of her smell. To trust someone enough to sleep with him, he thinks, takes more faith in some ways than just to go to bed with him. Suddenly, he wants her even more than he did before.

He lies still in the darkness. He has never yet met a woman who is eager just after she wakes up. Besides, he thinks, she'll be here tomorrow.

He hopes . . . Weather in the early seventies tomorrow. Nasty weather for him and Donna.

He falls asleep worrying about it. Sometime around two in the morning, the year conditioner kicks in. He wakes with a start. Donna never stirs. He reaches over, softly puts his hand on the curve of her hip. She mutters something, rolls onto her stomach. He jerks his hand away. She doesn't wake up. He takes a long time to go back to sleep.

The alarm clock's buzz might as well be a bomb going off by his ear. He needs a loud one. The adrenaline rush keeps him going till his first cup of coffee. The only thing that wakes Donna is his bouncing out of bed. He has forgotten what a dedicated sleeper she is.

But she has two plates of eggs scrambled, toast buttered, and the coffee perking by the time his tie is knotted. "Now I know why I asked you to stay," he says. "I just eat corn flakes when I'm here by myself."

"Poor baby," she croons. He makes a face at her.

While he is stacking the dishes in the sink, he asks, "So where is this Barefoot Sounds of yours?"

"Down in Gardena, on Crenshaw. I hope I'm not going to make you late."

He looks at his watch, calculates in his head. "I ought to make it. I won't bother washing up now, though. I'll get 'em tonight. Shall I pick you up? What time do you get off?"

"Four-thirty."

He grunts. "I probably can't get up that way till maybe half past five."

"I'll stay inside," she promises. "That way, I'll be sure to be glad to see you."

She does have sense, he knows, no matter how she sometimes hides it. "Sounds like a good idea to me," he says.

Just how good it is he discovers the minute they walk out the door. It's in the seventies, all right: the weatherman had it right on the button. By the time Tom and Donna get to the bottom of the stairs, they aren't holding hands anymore.

He strides ahead of her, turns back to snap, "I don't have all day to get you where you're going, you know."

"Don't do me any favors." She puts her hands on her hips. "If you're in such a hurry, just tell me where the nearest bus stop is and take off. I'll manage fine."

"It's—" All that saves things is that he has no idea where the nearest bus stop is. Like a lot of people in L.A., he's helpless without a car. "Just come on," he says. In the seventies, she really does drive him crazy. The angry click of her heels on the walk tells him it's mutual.

He unlocks her door, goes around to unlock his, slides behind the wheel; he's not opening doors for her, not right now. He doesn't even look at her as she gets in. The engine roars to life when he turns the key, floors the gas pedal. He doesn't wait for it to warm up before he reaches for the year-conditioner switch. He has to change the setting; usually he keeps it in the eighties, to help him gear up for work.

The conditioner takes a while to make a difference; but little by little, the tense silence between Tom and Donna becomes friendlier. "My last car didn't have a year conditioner," he says.

She shakes her head. "I couldn't live like that."

He finds Barefoot Sounds without much trouble. It's at the back of a little shopping center where most of the stores are kept a lot newer. He shrugs. From what Donna says, the place pays the rent, and that's what counts. Besides, he likes sixties music.

"Maybe I'll stop in when I pick you up," he says.

"Sure, why not? I'll introduce you to Rick, the guy who runs the place.'' She leans over to kiss him, then gets out. He drives right off; he's left the motor running while he stops in the parking lot—he doesn't want the year conditioner to die.

But he doesn't like the look on Donna's face that he sees in the rearview mirror. The seventies are hard on them, and that's all there is to it. He hopes she does remember to wait for him in the store. If she stays outside, she'll be ready to spit in his eye by the time he gets there.

More likely, he thinks, she'll just up and leave.

If she does, she does; there's nothing he can do about it. He chews on that unsatisfying bit of philosophy all the way down the San Diego Freeway into Orange County.

When he gets out of the car, in the company lot, he hopes she *won't* be there in the afternoon. He hurries across the asphalt to the mirror-fronted office building, which is firmly in the eighties. A little more of this whipsawing and he won't be good for anything the rest of the day.

But he gains detachment even before he gets his computer booted up. As soon as he gets on line, he is too busy to worry about anything but his job. Now that the old front in the upper Midwest is finally breaking up, new orders come flooding in, and he has to integrate them into everything the system thinks it already knows.

He doesn't begin to get his head above water till lunchtime. Even then, he is too rushed to go out; he grabs a cheeseburger and a diet cola at the little in-house cafeteria. As he wolfs them down, Donna returns to the surface of his mind.

Being so far upyear gives him perspective on things. He knows that whenever the weather is in the early seventies, it'll be a dash from one year-conditioned place to another. Can he handle that? With eighties practicality, he realizes he'd better if he wants to keep her. He wonders what going from this long-distance indifference to a hot affair every night will do to him.

He also wonders what Donna is like in the eighties. He doubts he'll find out. She has made her choice, and this isn't it.

He has second thoughts again as he goes back out into the seventies at quitting time. But he has to go to his car anyhow, and as soon as it starts, he's all right again—he's left the year conditioner on. It's tough on his timing belt but good for his peace of mind.

Traffic is appalling. He's stoic about that. When the weather is in the eighties, things are even worse, with more cars on the road. When it drops into the fifties, the San Diego Freeway isn't there. Getting into town from Orange County on surface streets is a different kind of thrill.

He pulls into a parking space in front of Barefoot Sounds around 5:15. Not bad. Again he lets the year conditioner die with the engine without turning it off. He's trotting to the record store before the hum has altogether faded.

He's hardly out in the seventies long enough to remember to get hostile toward Donna. Then he's inside Barefoot Sounds and in the late sixties with a vengeance.

The place is wall-to-wall posters: a KEEP ON TRUCKIN' even gaudier than his, Peter Fonda on a motorcycle, Nixon so stoned his face is dribbling out between his fingers, Mickey and Minnie Mouse doing something obscene. Patchouli fills the air, thick enough to slice. And blasting out of the big speakers is "Love One Another," not the Youngbloods singing but a cover version: slower, more haunting, not one he hears much on the radio, no matter when he is. . . .

"My God!" Tom says. "That's H. P. Lovecraft!"

The fellow behind the cash register raises an eyebrow. He has frizzy brown hair and a Fu Manchu mustache. "I'm impressed," he says. "Half my regulars wouldn't know that one, and you're new here. Can I help you find something?"

"Only in a manner of speaking. I'm here to pick up Donna." Tom looks around. He doesn't see her. He starts worrying. There aren't many places to hide.

But the fellow—he must be the Rick she mentioned, Tom realizes—sticks his head behind a curtain, says, "Hon, your ride's here." *Hon?* Tom scowls until he notices that the guy is wearing a wedding ring. Then he relaxes—a little.

Donna comes out. The way her face lights up when she sees him makes him put his silly fears in the trash, where they belong. In the late sixties, he and Donna are good together. He whistles a couple of bars from the Doors song.

Rick cocks that eyebrow again. "You know your stuff. You should be coming in here all the time."

"Maybe I should. This is quite a place." Tom takes another look around. He rubs his chin, considering. "Who does your buying for you?"

"You're looking at him, my man," Rick says, laughing. He jabs himself in the chest with a thumb. "Why?"

"Nothing, really. Just a thought." Tom turns to Donna. "Are you ready to go?"

"And then some."

She's been waiting for him, Tom realizes. She can't be happy standing around while he chews the fat with her boss. "Sorry," he says. He nods at Rick. "Good to meet you."

"You, too." Rick pulls his wallet out of the hip pocket of his striped bell-bottoms. He extends a card, hands it to Tom. He may be a freak, but he's not running Barefoot Sounds to starve. "You ever get anywhere on that thought of yours, let me know, you hear?"

"I will." Tom sticks the card in his own wallet. Donna is at the door, tapping her foot. No matter how good he and she are, she is going to be one unhappy lady any second now. Maybe gallantry will help. With an extravagant bow, Tom holds the door open for her.

She steps through. "Took you long enough," she says. Her voice has an edge to it—she's outside, back in the early seventies. As he joins her, Tom feels his stomach start to churn.

This time, the tension breaks before it builds to a full-scale fight, thanks to Tom's car's being just a couple of steps away. They are inside and the year conditioner is going before they can do much more than start to glare at each other.

They both relax as it goes to work. Tom heads for his apartment. After a while, Donna asks, "What were you thinking about back there in the store?"

But Tom says, "Let it keep for now. It isn't ripe yet. Let's see how things go with us, then maybe I'll bring it up again."

"The curiosity will kill me." Donna doesn't push, though. In the seventies, she'd be all over him, which would only make him clam up harder. Luckily, she's thinking of something else when he pulls up in front of his building. The silence is guarded as they go up the stairs, but at least it is silence, and things are fine again once they're inside his place.

Come the weekend, Donna moves her stuff into his apartment. Without ever much talking about it, they fall into a routine that gets firmer day by day. Tom likes it. The only fly in the ointment, in fact, is his job. It's not the commute that bothers him. But he doesn't like not caring about Donna eight hours a day. He can deal with it, but he doesn't like it.

Finally, he digs out Rick's card and calls him. "You sure?"

Rick says when he's done talking. "The pay would be peanuts next to what you're pulling down in your eighties job."

"Get serious," Tom says. "Every twenty-dollar bill I have in my wallet there turns into a five here."

Rick is silent awhile, thinking it over. At last, he says, "I'd say I've got myself a new buyer." He hesitates. "You love her a lot, don't you? You'd have to, to do something like this."

"In the sixties, I love her a lot, and she's a sixties person. If I want to stay with her, I'd better be one, too. Hell," Tom laughs, "I'm getting good on my slide rule again."

Donna's smile stretches across her entire face the first day they go into Barefoot Sounds together to work. This time, she holds the door open for him. "Come on in," she says. "The weather's fine."

"Yes," he says. "It is." She follows him in. The door closes after them.

This is the one story I've written that my wife has never read. Some of you know what dealing with a colicky baby is like. Rachel, our second daughter, was one. Colicky babies can make you paranoid—you start to think they're wailing just to drive you crazy. To a writer, a paranoid thought like that can be the springboard for a story. But Laura won't look at it. Can't say I blame her.

CRYBABY

THIS TIME, THE STEAKS WERE RARE ENOUGH when it started.

Pete Flowers had a potholder in his hand. He was opening the broiler door. Doug's wail went through him like the sudden malignant whine of a dentist's drill. Pete's hand jerked against the hot metal.

"Shit," he snarled, snatching it away. He put a week's worth of glare into the two long strides that got him to the kitchen sink. "You said he was really down this time."

"He *was*," Mary insisted. "He nursed like a champ. He burped. He was dry—you changed him yourself. And he didn't even wiggle when I put him in the crib. He didn't, Pete."

"Shit," Pete Flowers said again, softly this time. He hadn't heard everything his wife said, not over the splash of cold water on his burned hand. Doug was still crying, though. There wasn't any place in the condo where he couldn't hear that. God knows I know it, too, he thought, reaching for a dish towel. He gingerly dried his hand.

He looked so grim when he stamped past the dining room table that alarm sprang into Mary's tired blue eyes. "Where are you going?"

"To get him, where else?" He started down the hall toward the room that, up until six weeks ago, had been his cherished study. Now the books were either in boxes or shoehorned into the master bedroom.

Not, he thought, that he had done much reading in Japanese history—or anything else that took longer to go through than *Bloom County*—lately. He'd had to go all the way up to the assistant dean for academic affairs at San Flavio State to get his sabbatical approved a year early. He'd fought the good fight gladly, eager to take a year off to help Mary with the baby. Now he wondered how good an idea it had been.

Doug's shrieks neared the pitch only dogs can hear. His father set his jaw so hard his teeth ground together. He turned on the light in the baby's room; even in Southern California, November twilight fades to darkness by six.

The baby's head was turned toward Pete. As usual, his frustrated anger met tough sledding when he looked at his son. Doug's hair—the first, incredibly fine growth of baby hair, now being rubbed away toward temporary baldness by his crib sheets—was even fairer than Mary's, but his eyes were already darkening from infant gray-blue toward Pete's own unspectacular brown.

He picked up Doug, slid a finger inside his Huggies. (Or was one of them just a Huggie—or even a Huggy? A fine point of language he'd never reached a firm conclusion about.)

Doug was dry, and still yelling. Pete didn't know whether to be pleased or not. He wouldn't have to change him, but at least he would have known what the kid's problem was if his finger had come out dripping with liquid poop.

He hoisted Doug up on his left shoulder, patted his back. "There, there," he crooned, "there, there." Maybe Doug would burp or fart or whatever he needed to do. He didn't sound gassy, though. Pete knew that cry. He wasn't drawing up his legs either. Pete sighed. Maybe Doug was yelling because he felt like yelling, too.

Mary, bless her heart, had the steaks on the table. She'd already cut hers into bite-sized pieces, so she could eat with one hand. She held out her arms. "I'll take him, Pete."

"Thanks." He got his hand behind Doug's head to cradle it, and hissed—it was the burned hand. He guided the baby into the crook of his wife's elbow. "Got him?"

"Yes. How's your hand?"

He looked at it. "Turning red. I'll live."

"Put some Cort-Aid on it."

"After dinner." He slathered A-1 Sauce on the steak, cut off a big bite. He made a dissatisfied noise, deep in his throat. "A little too done. He timed it just right."

"I'm sorry. I should have gotten up sooner."

"Never mind." Pete tried to sound as if he meant it. He hated overcooked beef. He ate his hamburgers rare too, which faintly revolted Mary. After five years of marriage, though, she had learned he fought change hard.

The steak tasted fine to her. She dropped a green bean on Doug. She was eating righthanded because she held him in her left arm, but even after forced intensive practice she wasn't good at it.

"He's calmed down, anyhow," she said, plucking the bean off Doug's THUMBSUCKERS ANONYMOUS T-shirt and sticking it in her mouth.

"Sure he has. Why not? His mission's accomplished—he's screwed up dinner."

Mary had a glass of Zinfandel halfway to her mouth. She put it down so hard a little splashed onto the tablecloth. "Oh, for God's sake, Pete," she said, her voice low and calm in the way that meant she'd be shouting if she weren't watching herself. "He's just a teeny tiny baby. He doesn't know what he's doing. All he knows is that something's bothering him."

"Usually he doesn't know what, though."

"Pete." This time she was a little louder: last warning.

"Yes, yes, yes." He gave in, settled down, and ate. But once lodged, the thought would not go away.

The first couple of weeks, of course, were chaos. Pete had thought he was ready. Looking back, he supposed he was, as ready as anyone could be who only knew about babies from hearsay. He started finding out how little that was even before Doug got home. Wrestling a car seat into place in the back of a two-door Toyota Tercel was an introduction of sorts.

But only of sorts. Doug had been born just past four in the morning, and seemed convinced night was day, and vice versa. That first dreadful night at home, he was awake—and yowling—almost all the time from one till five.

Even when he did catnap, it did Pete and Mary precious little good. They had the bassinet in their bedroom, and jumped every time Doug wriggled or breathed funny. Wriggling and breathing funny, Pete decided in a moment when he would have contemplated suicide had he been less tired, were about all newborns did. He soon revised that to include making frequent horrible messes.

Once was enough to teach him to keep a spare diaper over Doug's middle whenever he was changing him. "The fountains of Versailles," Mary called it; she was writing her dissertation on Voltaire. What Pete called it did not bear repeating, but then *he'd* had to wash his face.

The other thing Doug did was stay awake. Pawing through *The First Twelve Months of Life* one day, Pete protested, ''The book says he's supposed to sleep seventeen to twenty hours a day.'' Before the baby was born, that had sounded reasonable. It even sounded as if it left parents a few hours a day to live their own lives.

''I don't think he's read the book,'' Mary said wanly. ''Here, you take him for a while. My shoulder's getting sore from rocking him in my arms.''

Pete took Doug. The baby squirmed and yarped and dozed off. Pete carried him into his room (the bassinet was in there now, though Doug still looked small and lost in a crib), set him down. Doug sighed. His mouth made little *suck-suck* sounds. Pete backed away and started down the hall.

He'd got about halfway to the front room when Doug let out an ''Ooo-wah!'' behind him. He stiffened in outrage. Then his shoulders sagged. He turned around and went back to pick up the baby.

''This all comes with the territory,'' he said when he reappeared, as much to himself as to Mary. Doug was already back to sleep in his arms. He tried to put him down again. This time he did not even get out of the room.

It was Mary's turn to console him. ''It gets better.''

''Sure it does,'' he said, and wondered if he would live that long.

But it did, some. Doug began to sleep, if not more, at least at more consistent times. He was awake for longer stretches during the day and less during the night, though he still wanted to be fed every couple of hours around the clock. Mary's fair complexion made the circles under her eyes seem darker than they really were, or so Pete told himself. As for him, the two staples of his life were Visine and caffeine.

Doug learned to smile. At first the expression was hard to tell from the one he wore when he had gas, but it soon became unmistakably an outlet for pleasure and the baby's first real communication other than screaming. Pete cherished it for that. The sight of his face or Mary's could touch it off.

Doug also developed another expression, a way of looking at things out of the corner of his eye. It made him look absurdly wise and knowing, as if he had a secret and was doing his best not to let on. Pete loved it. He would even smile when Doug assumed it while being cuddled after a crying bout. "All right, you self-satisfied little beast, that's more like it," he would say.

Doug seemed to reserve that smug look for him. Mary saw it much less often.

However much Pete came to love his son, though, he never got used to the hour after hour of banshee wails that marked Doug's bad days. Calling them colic gave them a name, but not one that really helped. In the moments he could grab, Pete read about colic with desperate intensity, trying to find some clue to making Doug feel better, or at least shut up.

The more Pete read, the less he found he knew. Colic wasn't the digestive upset people used to think it was. At least, the babies who were having fits didn't show any unusual intestinal activity. Also, breastfed babies got it as often as babies who used bottles. Colicky babies put on weight just as fast as any others.

They made a hell of a lot more noise, though.

Pete noticed early on that Doug owned an exquisite sense of timing. A couple of times Mary drove down to the Seven-Eleven to tide them over on diapers. Pete did the big Saturday shopping; he welcomed the chance to get out of the condo.

Both times, Doug had been out like a light when Mary left on the diaper run. Once he made Pete forget to put chili powder in a recipe, which wasn't the same without it. The other time, he caught his father with his hand on his zipper. Pete was about to burst by the time Mary got back. By then Doug was quiet, and looking smug.

Sometimes he wouldn't be quiet, no matter what. Those were the worst. Evolution designed a baby's cry to be noticed, to make its parents want to fix whatever was wrong. Evolution did not design parents to listen to a squawking baby at close range for hours, not and keep their marbles too.

They tried everything they could think of. Pete put a cotton ball in his left ear while he was toting Doug around. Sometimes, when the din was very bad, he put cotton balls in both ears. They didn't block Doug's racket, or come close. They did blunt the edge of it. Out of some perverse mommy equivalent of machismo, Mary refused to have anything to do with earplugs.

In any case, they were only for Pete's sake, as he put it one frazzled middle of the night. Except on the days when nothing helped, two things helped with Doug. One was bouncing him while sitting on the edge of the mattress. The other was cranking up the rock on the stereo. The rhythmic thump of the bass seemed to soothe him. He especially like Led Zeppelin, which dismayed Pete and horrified Mary.

Bouncing and Led Zep or not, though, Doug kept his gift for interrupting his parents, and Pete in particular. He wished he'd never thought, even as a sour joke, that the baby was doing it on purpose. It made him notice just exactly how often Doug's crying sabotaged things he needed to do or, worse, wanted to do.

The baby started yowling out of the blue one morning, for instance, just when Pete was shaving that impossible spot above the center of his upper lip. His hand jumped. He didn't quite slice off his lip, but he gave it the old college try.

"I haven't needed that much styptic pencil since I was fifteen years old and just learning how," he grumbled as he poured himself a bowl of Special K.

"There's still some blood under your chin," Mary told him. She was holding Doug, who by this time had calmed down considerably. He turned his head to try to follow his father across the kitchen as Pete walked over to wet a paper towel and watched him out of the corner of his eye while he dabbed at himself.

Pete threw the crumpled towel in the trash. He scowled back at his son. "Pleased with yourself?" He didn't sound as if he was kidding, or as if he was talking to a baby. He sounded more like someone talking to a fellow who had just done him a dirty trick.

Mary caught his tone. "For heaven's sake, Pete, he's just a baby. He doesn't know what he's doing."

"Yeah, you said that before. But enough things have happened with this crazy kid that I swear I'm beginning to wonder."

Mary felt Doug's diaper. "I can tell you what's happened with this crazy kid. I can also tell you that you're going to change him, because if I don't take a leak you'll have to change me too. Here." She thrust Doug at him.

He grinned a lopsided grin. "I'd have more fun putting the powder on you." She made a face back over her shoulder at him as she hurried down the hall.

Doug somehow missed interfering with dinner that evening, which gave Pete hope for the future. The baby nursed vigorously just after eight and was sound asleep (better yet, *soundless* asleep) by nine. Mary levered herself out of the rocking chair with her free hand, carried him over to his father on the couch. "Give him a kiss and I'll put him in his crib."

Pete leaned forward to kiss Doug's fine sparse fair hair. It had a sweet, clean smell that only had a little to do with being just washed. Pete knew he could do his own hair with Suave baby shampoo from now till doomsday and it would never smell like that. Doug was fresher-baked than he, and that was all there was to it.

Mary toted Doug away. He hadn't stirred for the kiss. "Down. That was almost too easy to stand," she said when she came back.

"Tell me about it. If it were this easy all the time, I'd like having the little critter around more." Pete saw her face cloud, said quickly. "I didn't mean it like that. But he is a strain."

"That he is." Mary stretched. Something in her back crackled. "Ooh. Nice. Now, what shall I do with this rare and priceless gift of privacy at a civilized hour?" Pete had an idea about that, but before he could say anything she went on, "I know—I'll take a shower. I think the flies were homing on me instead of the garbage when I took it out this afternoon."

Pete waited till the blow drier stopped whirring in the bathroom. Then he threw open the door, grabbed Mary around the waist, and lifted her off her feet. She let out an indignant squawk as he carried her away. "What are you doing, you maniac? You'll hurt yourself! Put me down, Pete, right now!"

He did, on the bed. Through the shirt he was pulling over his head, he told her, "What better way to spend an early evening when we're both awake and someone else isn't?" He fumbled with the brass button on his Levi's.

"I can't think of one." Mary sat up. "Here, let me help you."

"Much more help like that," Pete said a moment later, "and you'll have to wash these jeans." He kicked them off.

"Ah. I'll stop, then." Mary lay back again. Pete joined her on the bed. After a minute, she laughed. "My milk's letting down."

As always, Pete marveled at how sweet it was. Babies, he thought, had things a lot better than calves. They also got their milk in much more attractive containers.

His kisses drifted down her belly. He raised an eyebrow. "Shall I commit a felony for you?"

"What are you talking about?" Her golden hair slid across bare shoulders as she shook her head.

"Thanks to the wisdom of our duly elected Assembly, and to our know-nothing governor who wants to be president—*and* with a big hand for the Supreme Court—this" (he stopped talking; Mary murmured with pleasure) "is illegal again. Fortunately, it's not immoral or fattening."

After some little while, Mary pushed Pete down flat on the bed. Her eyes were enormous in the dim light. "You shouldn't be the only criminal in the family," she said softly. Her voice was low and heavy. He could feel the warmth of her breath on him.

Doug started to cry.

"Oh, no," Mary said. Pete heard something odd in her voice: not only annoyance over being interrupted, but also concern at how he would take it.

He surprised both of them by laughing, and by meaning it. "What the hell," he said, climbing back into his jeans. "I'll change him, or whatever he needs. He ought to go back to sleep pretty soon, and then, my lovely dear, I shall return."

"I'll be waiting," Mary promised.

"Of course you will. Dressed like that, where would you go?"

Her snort followed him into Doug's room. What the hell, what the hell, he repeated to himself: the kid's only a baby, after all. He wondered how often he'd said that in the last couple of months. Enough that if he'd had a dollar for every time, he could have afforded a nanny and not needed to worry about any of this, that was for sure.

Which was a damn sight more than he could say for his sex life. A dollar for each time there wouldn't have bought him dinner for one at any place fancier than the local Sizzler.

He stopped worrying about it as he stooped to pick up Doug. The baby really did sound upset, and the nightlight showed Pete that he had somehow managed to twist himself at right angles to the way Mary always set him down.

"All right, sport, what's going on here?" Doug yelled louder than ever as Pete lifted him. His father's hands under his chest squeezed the air from him until Pete shifted him into the crook of his left elbow. Pete stuck his right hand into Doug's diaper. The baby was dry. Pete frowned, just a little. There went the most obvious reason for Doug's distress.

"Maybe you spit up," Pete muttered. Doug's chin was damp, but then Doug's chin was often damp. This was only drool, not spit-up sour milk. Pete ran his hand over the crib sheet. It was dry too. Not only that, Doug threw out his arms and shrieked when his father bent down.

"I'm not going to drop you," Pete told him, though for an

instant the prospect seemed tempting, if for no other reason than to get the little squawkbox away from his ear.

He felt Doug's forehead, to see if his son had a fever. Doug was cool. He stuck a finger in the baby's mouth, felt around to see if he was cutting a tooth. It was early, but still possible. It was possible, but not true.

"What's happening in there?" Mary asked from the master bedroom.

"Beats me." Pete remembered what he'd said at breakfast a couple of weeks before. "Maybe he's doing it on purpose."

He looked at Doug, who was still hollering—now probably in resentment at having something that wasn't a nipple shoved in his mouth. Then Doug met Pete's eye. He stopped crying for a moment, cocked his head to one side so he could peer up at his father out of the corner of his eye. It was his smug look, but something more was there, too. *Gotcha*, was what Pete thought.

"Why, you little sonofabitch!" he said.

He didn't realize he'd spoken out loud until Mary called, "What'd he do? Did he poop?"

Pete opened his mouth to answer, then left it hanging open. What was he going to tell her, that a nine-week-old baby had interrupted them because he was feeling mischievous? That he'd done it on purpose? She'd think he was crazy—he, Pete, not he, Doug.

If anyone else had told that to him, Pete thought, he wouldn't have believed it either. Doug started crying again. Now his face was just a baby face, eyes screwed shut, cheeks puffed out, mouth wide open. But Pete was sure of what he had seen. It was not an expression that belonged on the face of a baby too young to have teeth. The last time he'd seen it, when he was nineteen, his cousin Stan had just pulled a practical joke on him. He'd punched Stan.

"Pete?"

He had to say something. "I don't know what his problem is. He's just yelling and he won't shut up."

He heard Mary sigh. "I'm coming." She was just wearing jeans herself, which painfully reminded Pete of what wasn't happening. But she was only thinking about Doug now. "Here, let me have him."

Pete passed her the baby. He didn't stop crying when she took him. He didn't stop crying, in fact, until one in the morning. By then Pete and Mary had taken turns bouncing him till their legs were sore, and had danced him to rock 'n' roll until their next-door neighbor pounded on the living-room wall, something she'd never done before.

Pete was holding Doug when he finally gave up and fell asleep. Pete was no longer interested in sex; he was no longer interested in anything but collapse. He carried Doug down the hall.

The baby's eyes opened. Pete cringed. Before Doug came along, his father had never imagined that anything that weighed twelve pounds and had trouble holding up its head could make him cringe. Now he knew better. He tried without much hope to brace himself for the next round of howls.

They didn't come. Instead, Doug gave him that knowing sidelong look again, sighed, and went back to sleep.

"Why, you little sonofabitch," Pete whispered. "You *did* do that on purpose." Another thing he had not known was how angry it was possible to get at a baby.

Doug slept for almost twenty minutes.

Thinking back, Pete decided the real war between his son and him began that night. He was a large, grown man. Logically, all the weapons should have been on his side. He told himself that, a lot, as he toted Doug around and wished and wished and wished the wailing, wiggling little creature in his arms would be quiet.

Wishing did not do much good. Neither did logic. Doug was not equipped to understand logic. He was equipped to make noise, at a volume that would have put a stack of Marshall amps to shame.

Doug didn't seem out to drive *Mary* nuts. When it was just the two of them in the condo, he behaved like any other baby: sometimes he cried and sometimes he didn't. But she got the backwash of his feud with Pete. So did everyone else within half a mile, Pete thought.

Pete began to spend as much time as he could away from home. Trouble was, that wasn't really much. He wasn't the sort of person who got anything out of sitting in a bar for hours, soaking up beers. He was happier drinking at home: it was cheaper and the company (berserk bawling ghetto blaster excluded) better.

Tacking an extra ten minutes on a trip to the store or inventing an excuse to get away to the mall for half an hour just didn't do enough to help. Besides, Mary got stir-crazy too, all the more so when she was cooped up with Doug by herself. She started inventing excuses of her own.

Pete even called San Flavio State about ending his sabbatical early.

The department chairperson's laugh was not altogether kind. "Baby's not as much fun as you thought, Peter?" David Endicott turned serious. "It's not just that I'd look like a fool, having to go to the assistant dean irregularly to get her to undo something I'd gone to her to approve irregularly only six months ago. It really isn't; I hope you understand that. But we've already done the budget transfer, so we can't pay you till next September anyhow. This is the '80s, Peter. Soft money for that kind of thing just isn't there anymore."

"I know. Thanks anyhow, David." Pete hung up. He took off his glasses, bent his head and rubbed his eyes with the heels of his hands. He'd known what Endicott would tell him before he picked up the phone. That he'd called regardless didn't seem a good sign.

Doug started up again, though he'd only been asleep a little while. Mary hadn't heard Pete on the phone, but she heard Doug. "Get him, will you?" she called from the kitchen. "My hands are greasy."

"All right." Pete walked slowly into his son's bedroom. He slammed his closed fist against the wall, as hard as he could. Pain shot up his arm.

"What was that?" Mary exclaimed.

That was your husband, not hitting his kid. Pete tried the taste of the words in his mouth, tried hearing them with Mary's ears. They would never do. They would frighten her. They frightened him.

"It's that bitch next door again," he answered after a pause he hoped she did not notice, "pounding for Doug to be quiet." He could not remember the last time he had lied to her about anything important.

"Well, she can go to hell, too," Mary said indignantly. The tigress defending her young, Pete thought. No, he could not have said what he almost told her. He would have to bear his secret, and his secret shame, alone.

He picked up Doug, who was now yowling indignantly at the slight delay. He put his face close to the baby's. Those small, wide, darkening eyes met his. "Will you please for God's sake just shut up?" he whispered. He did not know if he was taking the name of the Lord in vain or making one of the few honest prayers he had ever made in his life.

Doug actually did quiet down pretty fast; Pete's arms were

automatically rocking him the way he liked—when he liked anything. His father was not reassured. Doug's face wore the smug expression he had come to know only too well.

"That wasn't too bad," Mary said when Pete toted the baby in a few minutes later. Doug was awake but not fussing. He tried to turn his head toward his mother's voice, and smiled in her direction. Mary smiled back; it was hard not to. Then she saw Pete's face. "Why so glum, hon?"

"Just tired, I guess." Pete knew he had shown weakness in the presence of the enemy. He also knew that was something else he could not tell his wife, not when the enemy was their son.

Mary could see what was going on, though, even if she did not understand it. When they went to bed that night, too worn for anything but whatever sleep Doug was going to let them have, she touched her husband's arm. "Pete, please don't take it so personally when Doug cries. I hate to watch you clamping your jaw when you carry him around. You act as though you think he deliberately sets out to provoke you."

"Sometimes I do wonder. His timing is awfully good." Pete kept his tone light on purpose. Mary could take his words as a routine complaint if she wanted . . . or she could ask just how serious he was. He was ready to cite chapter and verse to her, if she gave him half a chance.

"Pete." His heart sank. Her voice had that ring that sounds like patience but is really anything but. "He's just—"

"—a baby," Pete finished sourly.

"Well, he is." Mary was starting to sound angry. "Now let's go to sleep, shall we? We don't have time for this foolishness, not when Doug's liable to wake up any old time at all."

Pete was angry too, silently, frustratedly furious. It seemed to him that his wife had contradicted herself without so much as noticing. If Doug were "just a baby," they'd have some idea, at least, of when he'd be awake and when he'd be asleep. The only thing they were sure of now was that he'd pick the most inconvenient times possible.

That struck Pete as something nobody ought to find normal. Then something else struck him: fatigue, which laid him low as surely as if he had been sapped. For once, even Doug's howls failed to wake him. He never noticed Mary twice stumbling out of bed to nurse the baby. It was a splendid victory, and he did not know he'd won it.

* * *

The next few days made Pete wonder if he'd been wrong all along. Doug was amazingly civilized. He slept regular hours and was cheerful when he was awake. Pete paid him the ultimate compliment: "You wouldn't think it was the same baby."

Mary snorted but, he noticed, did not disagree.

The fragile hope Pete had nourished only made him hurt worse when it was dashed. His first stab at a Christmas list disintegrated in his mind when Doug let out a screech that should have burst from the iron throat of an insane calliope. Mary got to the baby before he did. He saw tears in her eyes. She'd had hopes, too.

"Hush, hush, hush," she murmured. She hugged Doug's little body against the softness of her breast, leaned his chin on her shoulder. She moved in the little dance steps that sometimes helped calm him. Nothing helped calm him today. Somehow Pete had thought it was going to be like that.

After a while, with an apprehensive look in her eye, Mary handed the baby to him and went into the kitchen to make dinner. Pete was fine with steaks and chops and hamburger, and had done most of the cooking since Doug was born. But Mary was a really good cook. She missed being in front of a stove; Doug's amiable spell had encouraged her to send her husband out for fancier food than he was up to making himself. Tonight she had something exotic and oriental planned for a pork roast.

That left Pete holding the baby. He carried Doug into the living room, turned on the stereo, and started going round and round the coffee table. The pile on the carpet was noticeably more beaten down there than anywhere else in the room.

"Hush, hush, hush, you little monster." Despite his words, his tone was a fair imitation of Mary's croon. He was determined not to let Doug get his goat—or not to let him know he had; listening to Doug at close range would have turned the back of Job's neck red. But Pete swayed and jiggled, as dedicated to calming his son as Doug was to driving him out of his tree.

He thought he was earning at least a draw. Doug's howls came further and further apart, and took on the rusty-hinge quality that showed the baby was getting tired. "Shh, shh," Pete sang. He turned his head. "How's dinner coming?"

"Getting there. How's he doing?"

"Not too bad." Pete glanced down at Doug. The baby's gaze met his with more directness and intelligence than ten-week-olds are supposed to show. Then Doug let out all the stops. Pete only *thought* he'd heard him cry before. He wished he'd been right.

He looked at Doug again. His son's face wasn't all screwed up, as baby's faces usually are when they pitch fits. Except for having his mouth open wide enough to let out all that horrible noise, Doug wasn't acting upset at all. He seemed . . . positively *smug*.

Rage filled Pete. "What sort of noise would you make if you really were hurting?" he growled. For a moment, the idea of dropping the kid just to find out looked awfully good. Almost without willing it, Pete felt his arm start to straighten to let go of Doug.

"Dinner," Mary called—shouted, rather, to be heard over the sound effects. "What was that you were saying to him?"

"Nothing." Saved by the bell, Pete thought. He wasn't sure whether he meant Doug or himself.

His legs felt very light as he carried Doug into the kitchen. He took a while to recognize the feeling, or rather to remember it. When he was a kid, they had felt that way whenever he was scared green and getting ready to run like hell. He was that scared again, but now he could not run.

He plopped Doug into his yellow plastic infant seat, setting him down with exaggerated care, as if to make up for his thoughts of moments before. He expected the baby to raise even more Cain at being put down, but Doug was mostly quiet while his parents ate. His few tentative yarps, though, sent worried jolts quivering through Pete. He wondered each time if this would be the one where the baby really let loose, and so he enjoyed the excellent pork roast less than he should have.

As he was filling the sink to soak the dishes, he wondered if Doug was beginning to learn subtlety to go with his brute-force hysterics. Babies learned things as they got older. Thinking about the sort of things Doug might like to learn filled Pete with dread.

In the two days that followed, Pete felt as if he were on a ship that had holed itself on submerged rocks: he sank slowly and on an even keel. The deck seemed stable and level under his feet, but he was going down all the same.

What made it even worse was that, as far as Mary could see, Doug was only a baby who cried too much. His outbursts didn't particularly interrupt her unless she was doing something with Pete, like eating lunch. He didn't yowl just to make her jump, or just to disrupt her train of thought.

And he didn't give that little aren't-I-clever-to-be-driving-you-bonkers stare out of the corner of his eye when she held him. By now, that expression infuriated Pete as much as Doug's crying. It was a constant reminder that his son was having sport at his expense. Sooner or later, Pete promised himself grimly, that would have to stop.

Had he been able to find boned chicken thighs on his last trip to Safeway, things might have turned out better. As it was, he'd brought home thighs with the bones still in. Mary had taken them out of the fridge to start defrosting early that afternoon, and was cutting the still partly frozen meat away from the bones. "This'll be good," she promised. "I'm just sorry you're stuck with Doug while I work on 'em."

"What?" Pete had heard maybe one word in three. Doug was squalling in his ear. Doug had been squalling in his ear for the past hour and a half, since he woke up from his latest nap. He wasn't hungry; he'd nursed for five minutes a while ago, and spit the nipple out. He wasn't wet, or poopy, or gassy, or warm, or cold, or anything. He was just ornery. Pete's tolerance for orneriness had worn very thin.

Mary turned away from the countertop to repeat herself. Doug yelled even louder, drowning her out again. He looked smugly up at his father. *What are you going to do about it?* his eyes seemed to say.

Pete heard the words in his head as plainly as if they were spoken aloud. "This," he answered, and threw the baby against the refrigerator.

The thud of the little body hitting the yellow-enameled metal door killed his fury like a bucket of icewater poured over a campfire. Horror replaced it. He took a step toward Doug, who for the moment was not crying at all.

"No!" Mary sprang at him. No linebacker could have done a better job of stopping him in his tracks. Linebackers, however, do not commonly carry knives. Rushing to defend Doug, Mary probably forgot she was still holding hers. It sliced a long furrow in Pete's sleeve, and in his arm.

The pain, and the sudden wet warmth of spilled blood, made him automatically grapple for the blade. He was bigger and stronger than Mary. He yanked it out of her hand. She fought back with more ferocity than he had dreamed was in her. They wrestled. She tripped him. They fell to the Solarion tile floor. He felt the knife go in.

There are not many places where a single knifethrust will kill at once. The soft flesh under the angle of the jaw is one of them.

"Mary?" Pete said. Even then, though, from the way she convulsed and suddenly stopped fighting him, he knew he would get no answer.

He pulled out the knife. His blood and Mary's were both on it, in a last terrible mingling. He sat on the floor of the kitchen, with Mary's body, and with Doug (Doug was crying again, and this time, by Christ, Pete knew why), and with the half-boned chicken thighs, and with the ruin of everything he had spent a lifetime building.

He looked at the knife again. It looked better to him now, better than whatever else lay ahead of him. He made sure he had a firm grip on it, drove it into his chest.

He took much longer dying than Mary, and hurt more than he had ever imagined he could, as his heart tried to beat around stainless steel. Consciousness finally faded. The last sound in his ears was Doug, crying.

Vicki Garreau fumbled with the car seat's catch as she took Doug out. Poor little fellow, she thought: he was too young to be coming home from the hospital for the second time, and to a new, unfamiliar home at that. Thinking about the baby made it easier not to think about what had happened to her sister and brother-in-law.

Doug squirmed and complained in Vicki's inexpert grasp. "Careful," her husband Jim said. He was hovering behind her, a big, thick-shouldered man with a coal-black handlebar mustache. "Don't hurt him."

"I'll try not to," she said. "He's just lucky to have only a cracked rib. Babies are tough little things, the doctor said."

"A good thing, too," Jim rumbled. The image of the dent in the refrigerator door would stay with him as long as he lived. He and Vicki had been trying to start a family of their own; after their nephew so suddenly and horribly became an orphan, they moved at once to start adoption proceedings.

"Shh. He's falling asleep again." Vicki carried him up the walk toward their house. As Jim hurried past her to open the door, she said softly, "If we hadn't lived a hundred and fifty miles away—" Try as she would, her mind, like his, kept coming back to Mary's kitchen.

Jim grunted and nodded. He opened the deadbolt, then the regular lock. He bent down to kiss his wife's hair as she brought the baby—their baby now, he thought—inside. She turned her head, managed a smile. He thought about how much she looked like her older sister, though her eyes were green, not blue.

She came out of the room that was now Doug's room a few minutes later. ''I was just standing there watching him. He's sleeping like a little angel.''

''Good. I put on a pot of coffee. After two and a half, three hours on the freeway, I need it.''

''I won't turn down a cup myself.''

The rich, dark smell filled the kitchen. Vicki got cups from the dish drainer. ''I'll pour.''

''Thanks.''

She handed him his, and was pouring her own when Doug began to cry. She wasn't expecting it. The smooth brown stream wavered. ''Ouch,'' she said. She popped a finger in her mouth. When she took it out, she was laughing. ''We'll just have to get used to that, won't we?''

Most of this story is set in the town where I grew up, at a time when I was about four years old. To help my memory along, I was lucky enough to have my father's 1953 road atlas, which showed me how much of the Los Angeles freeway system that we take for granted today didn't exist a little more than a generation ago.

What sticks in my mind most about writing "Hindsight" is the night I finished it. I wrote the last few paragraphs at my in-laws' house about 12:30 A.M. just after Christmas 1983. Laura was deathly ill from stomach flu and couldn't do anything much about it because she'd found out she was pregnant a couple of weeks before. We were all supposed to leave at three in the morning to visit her relatives in San Francisco and give them the news. I went alone and was a zombie all the way up Interstate 5. Laura flew in a day or two later, mostly recovered. It was a sleepy, busy, happy time.

HINDSIGHT

KATHERINE TAPPED ON THE STUDY DOOR. ''Mail's here.''

''Be out soon,'' Pete Lundquist called, not looking up from his typewriter. He flicked the carriage return lever. The paper advanced a double space. A small part of his mind noticed that the ribbon needed changing; it was nearer gray than black. All his conscious attention, though, was focused on the novelette he was working on.

Another couple of paragraphs got him to the end of a section and, by luck, to the end of a page at the same time. A good enough place to stop for a while, he decided. He rolled the story out of the big Underwood office machine, peeled off the carbons one by one and put them in their stacks, and set the original on top of the typewriter to come back to later.

He stretched till his bones creaked. He was tall enough that his fingertips missed the ceiling only by a few inches: a thin stick of a man, with angular, not quite handsome features, very blue eyes, and a shock of blond hair that no amount of Wildroot or Vitalis could flatten for long. In a couple of weeks he would turn thirty, something he tried not to remember.

95

"How's it going?" Katherine asked when he finally emerged. That was not just interest in the story for its own sake. When a free-lancer had trouble writing, steak turned to hamburger and hamburger to macaroni and cheese.

She relaxed, a little, as he said, "Not bad. I should be done in a couple of days, and get it out." He looked at her fondly. Physically they were total opposites; she was dark and inclined to plumpness, and he could rest his chin on the top of her head. But she had a good deal of the discipline that kept him steadily at the typewriter. With checks coming in on no schedule and for wildly varying amounts, she needed it.

"What's the good news today?" he asked.

"Not much." She displayed two envelopes and a magazine in a brown paper wrapper. "A gas bill, a check from *Interplanetary*—"

"The one should just about cover the other," he said sourly. *Interplanetary* paid late and not much and probably wasn't long for this world, but they had bought a short story he couldn't unload on any better market, so he had no real right to complain.

"—and the new *Astonishing*," Katherine finished.

"Aha!" he said. "Now I have the excuse I need for a break." She made a face at him; that just meant he would be busy later. She went into the kitchen to start dinner.

He lit a Chesterfield and sank into a shabby but comfortable overstuffed armchair with a sigh of contentment. It was a couple of minutes before four. He turned on the radio to catch the hourly news. The dial lit; he waited for the tubes to warm up and the sound to start.

He stripped off the *Astonishing*'s wrapper, turned to the table of contents. He didn't have anything in this month's issue, though he had been in the last one and would show up again in a couple of months. He saw with pleasure that there was a long novelette by Mark Gordian. He wondered what this one would be like. Gordian had mastered a number of different styles.

First things first, he thought. No one who read *Astonishing* put off the editorial. James McGregor could be—often tried to be—infuriating, but he was never dull.

As Pete read, he listened to the news with half an ear. Queen Elizabeth's coronation dominated it. The Korean truce talks at Panmunjom dragged on and on. A new political party had been formed in the Philippines, and was promising great things. "And in sports," the announcer went on, "both the Seals and the

Oaks fell further behind the Pacific Coast League-leading Hollywood Stars last night as—''

He was just turning to the Gordian story when the side door slammed. Not for the first time, he wondered how two small boys managed to sound like a platoon. ''What's going on there?'' he said, trying without much luck to sound stern.

''Daddy's out!'' Wayne shouted joyfully. The six-year-old sounded as if Pete had just been released from jail. He came charging into the living room and flung himself at his father's lap. His brother Carl, who was seven, was right behind. Pete barely saved the *Astonishing* from getting squashed.

''And what have you two been up to?'' he asked.

''Playing with Stevie next door,'' Carl answered. ''His cousin Philip is visiting him from Denver. He's nine. He can throw a curveball.''

''That's nice,'' Pete said. ''Go wash your hands. With soap.'' He got nervous whenever his boys made a new friend—who knew whether the kid might be bringing infantile paralysis with him? The polio season was just starting, but it was already worse than last year's, and there had been almost 60,000 cases in 1952.

Pete did not get back to the *Astonishing* until he was done drying the dinner dishes and putting them away. He threw on a cardigan sweater; northern California late spring evenings were nothing like the ones he had grown up with in Wisconsin. But neither were the winters, thank God.

He flipped to the Gordian story. It was called ''Reactions,'' which might mean anything. With Gordian, you never could tell—take the serial with the innocuous name ''Watergate,'' for instance. Critics—serious critics—talked about the book version in the same breath with *1984*. To Pete, though, it was science fiction at its best, straightforward extrapolation of how difficult government skulduggery would inevitably become when copy machines and recorders were everyday items.

It also made Joe McCarthy hopping mad, something else Pete approved of.

It was hard to see how the same author could also write ''Houston, We Have a Problem,'' a gripping tale of an early moon flight gone wrong, and *Tet Offensive*, a future war gone wronger. Barring the exotic hardware, that one looked disquietingly possible too, if you noticed the page-four stories about the fun the French were having trying to hold on to Indochina.

But Gordian—damn him!—didn't confine himself to the near future. ''Neutron Star'' had had all the astronomers who read science fiction buzzing a couple of years ago (and there were a lot of them). So did "Supernova," though Pete found the casual way computing machines were handled in that one even more exciting. It was a yarn he wished he'd written himself.

There were literally dozens more, not all in *Astonishing* by any means; *Galactic* and *Strangeness and Science Fantasy* had their share too. "All You Zombies" made every other time-travel story obsolete. "Sunjammer I" and "Sunjammer II" struck Pete as the prose equivalent of a jazz pianist improvising on a theme. And "Time Considered as a Helix of Semi-Precious Stones" was a literary firework that defied description.

Ever since Gordian started selling in 1949, he'd turned out even more words than Asimov, and not a bad story in the bunch. All things considered, he was the one writer who made Pete feel inadequate.

He settled in and began to read. By the end of the third page, he felt his hair trying to stand on end. He had not been so afraid since he'd driven a tank-destroyer through the crumbling wreck-age of the Third Reich. But that had been a simple fear, fear that a kid with a grenade or an old man with a *Panzerfaust* or some diehard in a Royal Tiger tank would make sure he never saw the States again. This—

Discipline or no, he got very little writing done that night.

He spent the next week in a fever of anticipation waiting for McGregor's reply to his letter. He'd sent it airmail, and stuck another red six-cent stamp on the self-addressed return envelope he enclosed with it. At the moment, answers worried him more than pennies.

When the note finally came, he gritted his teeth against the anticlimax. "Dear Pete," the *Astonishing* editor had written, "I'm very sorry that Gordian picked off an idea you thought was yours, but things like that happen all the time (you should see my slush pile!). I'm sure you still have enough fresh notions to keep you going. Let me see one of those. Best, Jim."

Pete threw the letter on the kitchen table. "He doesn't believe me," he said bitterly.

"Would you, on someone's word alone?" Katherine said. "I'm still not sure I do, and I've seen your outline for myself."

"I suppose you're right," Peter admitted. "I guess I just think of Jim McGregor as slightly more than human. Well, by Christ, I can show him."

He turned on his heel and hurried into the study. He ran a

fresh piece of paper into the typewriter. "Dear Jim," he wrote, "I realize I should have sent the enclosed with my first letter to you. I trust you will take my word that it was drafted some months ago. If you find it interesting, let me know. Yours, Pete Lundquist."

He looked at the letter for a moment, added a P.S.: "I don't know when I would have gotten around to writing from this skeleton. I have several ideas ahead of it, and one or two of them look like novels. But it would have happened eventually, I'm sure. You tell me what that story would have looked like."

This envelope was a lot fatter than the last one, but he sent it airmail too.

Three days later the telephone rang at 6:30 A.M. The unexpected noise made Pete cut himself shaving. Holding a piece of tissue to his chin, he got to the phone a split second ahead of his wife. Their eyes met in shared alarm; calls at odd hours generally spelled trouble.

"Mr. Peter Lundquist, please," the operator said.

"Speaking."

The woman's next words were a blessed relief: "I have a long-distance person-to-person call from a James McGregor in New York City."

"Yes, go ahead," Pete said, and mouthed to Katherine, "It's McGregor."

"Ho-ho! The game's afoot, Watson."

He waved her to silence. The editor's voice came on the line, raspy not just with distance but also from too many cigarettes: "That you, Pete?"

"I'm here." He had to stop himself from adding, "sir." So did most people who talked with McGregor.

"I'm only going to ask you once, and I expect a straight answer: Are you pulling my leg?"

Pete enjoyed a certain reputation as a practical joker, which at the moment he could have done without. "No," he said.

"All right, then. In a way, I was hoping you were. As is, how do you feel about meeting me in Los Angeles next week?"

"Why Los Angeles?" Pete was not at his best early in the morning, and the three-hour time difference from New York only made McGregor's advantage worse.

The *Astonishing* editor's sharp sniff showed he was holding on to his patience with both hands. "Because this Mark Gordian writes out of a post-office box in a town called Gardena. It took some work with a big atlas to find the place, but it's about fifteen miles south of L.A. I'd like to have a word with Gordian—don't you think you would too?''

Pete gulped. ''Put like that, I suppose I would. Uh, Jim . . . what do you think is going on?''

''I don't know.'' McGregor sounded angry at the admission. ''The first thing that occurs to me is telepathy, and I don't much fancy that for an explanation either.''

''Why not? If anyone's been urging more basic research in extrasensory perception lately, it's you.''

''Research, yes. But if Gordian picked this out of your brain, he stands to everyone else on Earth like the Empire State building to a girl's dollhouse. I edit science fiction; I never planned on living it.''

That Pete understood down to the ground. He had majored in engineering at college, and drew a very firm line between what was real and what wasn't. He shivered as the implications began to sink in. ''If Gordian's a telepath, how do we know he's not reading our minds right now?''

''We don't,'' McGregor said. ''And I have another question for you: if Gordian's a telepath, why is he reading *your* mind instead of Einstein's or Eisenhower's or Albert Schweitzer's? You'll be driving down to L.A., won't you?''

''I guess so,'' Pete said absently. He was still chewing on the more important query; in conversation as in his letters, McGregor had a gift for going right to the heart of an issue.

''Good. Pick me up at the airport, then. I'll be getting in at about a quarter past five on Friday evening—it's Trans World flight 107. If you've come up with any good answers, give 'em to me then.''

''All right,'' Pete said. He was talking to a dead line.

Pete left with first light Thursday morning. By starting early, he got into Los Angeles before dark. The ride south along U.S. 101 was both hot and dull. Radio stations faded in and out as he drove. A little above Santa Barbara, the road came down to the Pacific. It was pretty enough to tempt Pete to stay on the Coast Highway the rest of the way, but he went back to 101 when it jogged inland again below Ventura and ran east toward the San Fernando Valley.

Sepulveda Boulevard led him south through the Sepulveda Pass and into the more built-up part of Los Angeles. None of the famous freeways was anywhere close; the nearest one, the

Harbor, stopped just south of downtown, though his map showed its projected route all the way out to San Pedro.

He checked into a motel in a suburban district called West-chester, used the change from his ten-spot to buy a sandwich and Coke at the coffee shop down the street, then came back, took a shower, and went to sleep.

The six-lane tunnel that took Sepulveda under the airport's runways had only been open for a couple of months. Pete could see how much easier it made access to the facility. It had also allowed the runways to be lengthened.

The big silver DC-6 rolled to a stop about half an hour late. The enormous propellors spun themselves to silence. The peo-ple who filed off the plane looked weary, and no wonder; count-ing a forty-five-minute layover in St. Louis, they had been traveling for ten hours.

"Jim!" Pete called, striding forward to shake the editor's hand. As always, he was disappointed that James McGregor looked nothing like Kimball Kinnison. McGregor was in his early forties, of average height and build. His sandy crewcut was going gray above his ears, and his hair thinned at the tem-ples. When younger, his face had been beaky; now craggy was a better word. Only his eyes seemed lensman-keen, and even then one had to look sharply, for he wore heavy, dark-framed glasses.

"Good to see you," McGregor said. They had met several times at conventions and other gatherings, and Pete had dropped into the *Astonishing* office once while in New York on other business. They argued for two hours. Pete lost, over and over, but the experience gave him notions for three new stories, all of which McGregor bought.

"Let's get my luggage," the editor said, "and some food, and a drink, and then back to wherever you're staying. I have some things to show you, now."

"Okay," Pete said, but disappointedly, "if you don't want to go down to Gardena first."

"What for? All we have to go on is a post-office box number, and the post office is closed."

Pete shook his head in chagrin at not having thought of that, but McGregor was already going on: "Unless, of course, he has a phone number in the local book. Worth a try, don't you think?" They were passing a bank of telephones on the way to the bag-gage claim area; McGregor found a chained phone book for the right part of town, pawed through its dog-eared pages. "Gordan

. . . Gorden . . . Gordillo—so much for that. Well, we're no worse off."

"No," Pete said, still slightly stunned. The *Astonishing* editor could no more help throwing off ideas than a fissioning plutonium atom could help spitting neutrons, and the results were about as explosive.

Over dinner at the coffee shop near the motel, the talk had nothing to do with the mysterious Mark Gordian. Perhaps because he was tired, McGregor was full of sarcasm about the rioting in East Germany ("Which shows where the workers stand in the workers' paradise."), the unmanned Navaho guided bomber ("It'll be obsolete before it flies. Rockets are faster than jets."), and the way CBS and NBC has handled the televising of Queen Elizabeth's coronation ("Imagine sending P-51s to meet the British jet that brought the film to Canada. The RCAF has jets of their own, and got their film to the lab first and on the air first. Naturally—jets are faster than prop jobs.").

"It's still remarkable, having seen it the same day it happened," Pete insisted.

"Oh, no doubt. Me, though, I'll take one of Arthur Clarke's relay satellites, and see it the same minute it happens." The thing about McGregor, Pete thought, was that "good enough" would not do for him—he insisted on perfection. Sometimes he managed to wring it out of people, too.

Back at the motel, the editor unlocked the suitcase he had parked by the bed before going out to eat. He pulled out a fat manila folder. "What's in there?" Pete asked.

"A couple of manuscripts I've got from Gordian that I pulled out of the file. Look them over; I'd like to hear what you think of them." McGregor plainly had no intention of saying anything more for a bit; he sat in the motel room's shabby armchair puffing on an Old Gold while Pete sprawled full-length on the bed, reading.

" 'The Hole Man,' eh?" Pete said. "That's a nice piece of work—gloomy, but nice."

McGregor only nodded and waited.

Pete felt flustered, as if facing a one-man oral exam committee without having studied. He nervously stacked the pages the editor had given him.

His fingers caught wrongness his eyes had missed. "Funny paper," he remarked; all four edges were rough, as if they had been torn off from perforations. "I've heard of typing paper sold in a roll, so you can run it into your typewriter continuously and rip off each sheet as you finish, but that would have smooth sides.''

"So it would," McGregor said. "I don't understand this either, but I noticed it. Keep going."

After a few minutes, Pete said, "That's a high-quality ribbon he's using." He wasn't sure what made him notice that—probably a twinge of guilt at the decrepit state of his own.

"It's what they call a carbon film ribbon," McGregor explained. "They use them for legal documents and other things that might need to be photostatted. The things are hard to find and hideously expensive, because you can only go through them once. I've never had stories typed on them before submitted before, I can tell you that."

"You've been researching this," Pete said accusingly.

"Guilty as charged. I can also tell you that one of New York's better detectives looked at some of these pages and couldn't match the typeface to anything in his collection. He was so surprised he didn't charge me."

"Curiouser and curiouser."

"Isn't it? The gumshoe did notice something I flat-out missed. You're not spotting it, but it's pretty obvious when it gets pointed out to you."

Pete stared without result at the pages in front of him. "All right, I give up. What is it?"

"Look at the right margin."

"My God! It's justified!" Pete felt like kicking himself for not noticing that right away. Every typescript he'd ever seen had a ragged right margin, but the pages of "The Hole Man" were so consistent and seemed so natural the way they were that their strangeness slipped by him.

"Very good," the *Astonishing* editor said. "Again, there's a gadget that will pull off the same stunt, but it's hard to come by—and why on Earth would you bother? The result's pretty, sure, but more trouble than it's worth."

"I'd say so." Pete sat up on the bed and took out a cigarette—he needed something to calm his nerves. He tapped the end of the Chesterfield on the nightstand to tamp down the tobacco; filtertips struck him as vaguely effeminate, and made the smoke taste like sawdust anyway. After a couple of deep drags, he said, "Whatever Gordian is, I don't think he's a telepath."

McGregor peered at him over the tops of his glasses. "Why's that?"

"It's not so much all this." He waved at the papers beside

him. "This only helps confirm what I really decided on the drive down here—about 'Reactions,' I mean."

"How's that?"

"How would I put it? Something like this, maybe: there's more in the story you printed than I've thought of yet. The ideas, the world, even the names match, but the story has a depth of detail that I wouldn't begin to worry about until I actually started writing."

The editor steepled his fingertips. "And so? What conclusions do you draw?"

"Me? I'd rather not," Pete said, shaking his head. "I'd sooner believe in mind-reading."

For the first time, he saw McGregor angry at him. "If you reject the data, what do you work from then? A ouija board, or the entrails of a sheep?"

"That's not fair," Pete protested. He felt himself flushing. "The whole thing is impossible."

"It is? Then why are we in Los Angeles?"

Pete had no good answer to that. McGregor got up and swatted him on the shoulder. "Nothing we can do about it at the moment, anyway. Maybe things will clear up when we meet Gordian. For now, though, I'd just as soon go to bed. I'm still running on East Coast time."

"Fair enough," Pete said, but he was a long time falling asleep.

"This is part of the fourth largest city in the country?" McGregor said incredulously as Pete passed the airport going south on Sepulveda.

"Well, actually, no," Pete answered. "According to that map on your lap, this is the sovereign city of El Segundo." There were streets and houses on the west side of Sepulveda; most of the east side was simply a field, brown under the summer sun and full of tumbleweeds.

"Mostly oilwells, from what I can see of it."

"It does look that way." Pete turned left onto El Segundo Boulevard. He drove for about a mile before coming on more houses. Then, just west of Hawthorne High School, the Chevy bumped over the streetcar tracks.

"Signs of life," McGregor said. "A few, anyway."

About four miles later, Pete turned right on Vermont and headed south. The street was wide and looked as if it ought to be important, but it had a dirt center divider and there were good long stretches of field along it. It did, however, boast of supermarket, a liquor store across the street, and a couple of large, garish buildings that identified themselves as "clubs." "Wonder what those are," McGregor said.

"Poker parlors," Pete said, pleased as always when he knew something the *Astonishing* editor didn't (it didn't happen very often). "Under California law, draw poker's a game of skill, and it's local option whether to allow it or not. This Gardena makes a bundle off the taxes the clubs pay."

Gardena Boulevard, where the post office was, was as much of a business district as the little town had. There was a Rexall drugstore on the corner at Vermont, a small department store and a jeweler's a little farther west, and then a pink stucco Bank of America, its gold Old English lettering gleaming in the morning sun.

But even Gardena Boulevard had its share of houses, mostly white clapboard buildings that dated from well before the war. The post office was next to one of those, just west of a narrow street called Budlong. Pete pulled in front of it; there was plenty of room to park. "Now what?" he said as he killed the engine.

McGregor was wrestling with the road map; as Pete might have expected, his competence extended to refolding one of the damned things. He tossed it into the glove compartment. "Now," he said, "we go in and wait for Mr. Gordian to open box one forty-eight."

"And get ourselves thrown out by the postmaster when we hang around for six or eight hours looking for somebody who doesn't show up."

"Nonsense. Writers haunt mailboxes; it's part of the disease. As for the postmaster, leave him to me."

"I suppose I have to." They were already walking up the low, broad steps into the building.

But it proved just as the editor had predicted. When the gaunt fellow behind the counter asked, "Help you gents?" McGregor said, "Yes. Could you tell me what time you usually put mail in your boxes? We're supposed to meet someone here then."

The man accepted that as casually as McGregor has said it. "Usually about eleven," he answered. "You've got some time to use up."

"Any place we could get a cup of coffee?" Pete asked, not wanting to be entirely left out.

"There's a delicatessen down the block there," the man said. He pointed west. "Reckon they can help you."

The coffee at Giuliano's was scalding hot and strong enough to growl, but good. While Pete and McGregor were drinking it, a Japanese man wearing a suit and hat came in; a lot of the people on the street in Gardena were Orientals. The man bought half a pound of cotto salami, paid the clerk and thanked him, and walked out.

"Acculturation." McGregor chuckled. His gaze sharpened, as if coming into focus. "Hmm—seems to me you could do something with that. Suppose you had an alien race, now, just coming into contact with technologically superior Terrans—"

The resulting conversation had the deli clerk listening, popeyed, from behind his counter and Pete frantically scribbling notes. He barely remembered to look at his watch. "It's half-past ten," he said. "We'd better get back, in case they're early today."

The *Astonishing* editor got up (to the clerk's obvious disappointment), but was not a man easily derailed from his train of thought. "All very well," he said as they walked back toward the post office, "but what about the attitude of the aliens' priests? No matter how much Terran gadgets eased life for their people, wouldn't they see them as black magic? And how would that affect their society?"

"You could take different approaches to that," Pete said. "The priests might even be right, for their special set of circumstances."

"So they might. My God, there's no one right answer! What I want to see is a good, solid, internally consistent story that carries its underlying assumptions—whatever those are—as far as they can go."

A couple of people were already waiting by the post office boxes, and several more came in after Pete and McGregor. "They can't *all* be writers," Pete whispered behind his hand.

The editor rolled his eyes. "You'd be amazed."

At five after eleven a mailman with a fat bag and a jingling ring full of keys pushed through the small crowd and began filling the boxes. McGregor nudged Pete in the ribs, but he had also seen the envelopes going into number 148.

Pete looked round, wondering which (if any) of the men near him was the mysterious Mark Gordian. Surely not the bald little man in overalls; he looked as if he didn't read anything, let alone write. The fellow who looked like a doctor was more likely, or the muscular man wearing a loud tie.

He got a lesson on how much such speculation was worth

when the person who opened the box proved to be a freckled, redheaded woman with glasses. She might have been a couple of years younger than he was, and looked comfortably casual in a rust-colored blouse and green pedal pushers.

McGregor chuckled beside him. "I suppose there's no reason Gordian can't be married."

"I guess not," Pete agreed. He was taken aback all the same; he had used so much energy thinking about Mark Gordian the writer and Mark Gordian the enigma that Mark Gordian the person was outside his reckoning.

The woman paid no attention to him or McGregor. They followed her outside. She was opening the mail. One envelope plainly had a check in it; that went into her purse. After she opened another one, she said, "Oh, shit," crumpled up the sheet of paper inside, and threw it away. She did not seem angry, merely irritated; it was how a man would swear. Pete blinked.

Her car was parked a couple of spaces down from his Chevy. He frowned a little; she drove a cheap, ugly Volkswagen Bug. Having spent several months getting shot at by Germans, he did not care for the idea of buying automobiles from them.

She was unlocking the car door when he called, "Excuse me, are you Mrs. Gordian?"

For a second she did not react. Then she looked up in surprise. "I don't think I know you," she said, "but yes, I'm Miss Gordian." Pete felt stupid for not noticing she wore no ring, and only a little better because McGregor had missed it too.

The editor nodded to her in apology. He said, "You are related to Mark Gordian, aren't you?"

Her eyes narrowed. Pete thought she was going to drive away without answering, and got ready to dive into his car after her. Instead, though, she began to ask, "Who are—" She stopped. "You're James McGregor." It sounded like an accusation.

"Yes." He indicated Pete. "This is Peter Lundquist."

Her eyebrows shot up. "Why, so it is!" she exclaimed. It was as if she recognized him, and he was sure he had never seen her before. She hesitated again. "Why are you looking for Mark Gordian?"

Pete gave it to her in one word: " 'Reactions.' "

He could see it hit home. "Oh," she said, and kicked at the sidewalk. "Oh, shit." This time it sounded like resignation. "You were already working on it?"

His heart thuttered inside his chest. He forced himself to steadiness. "Yes."

"*Are* you related to Mark Gordian?" McGregor persisted.

One corner of her mouth quirked upward. "In a manner of speaking. I *am* Mark Gordian."

Pete had never seen the *Astonishing* editor with a foolish expression on his face, but suspected he bore a similar one on his own. McGregor's rally was a visible thing. "Fair enough, I suppose," he said. "There's E. Maine Hull, after all, and C. L. Moore, and I understand Andre Norton is a woman too. Pleased to meet you, 'Mark.' "

She was still studying the two of them. "I'm not nearly sure I'm pleased to meet you. Who else knows you're here?" It was a sharp challenge; Pete thought her close to bolting again.

"My wife, of course," the editor said, and Pete echoed him. McGregor added, "There's a detective back in New York who's interested in the typewriter you use."

"I daresay he would be." She chuckled without much humor. "No one else? Not the FBI or the CIA?"

Pete spread his hands. "What would we have to show them? They'd laugh themselves sick at us Buck Rogers types. And besides," he added with characteristic independence, "what business is it of theirs, anyway?"

"Yes, you would be one to say that, wouldn't you?" Again he had the feeling she knew a good deal about him. She nodded slowly, as if coming to a decision. "All right, follow me home if you like. If anyone is, you're entitled to an explanation." She did not wait for an answer, but stooped to get into the Volkswagen. Its raucous air-cooled engine roared to life.

About ten minutes later she pulled into the driveway of a freshly built tract house; the front lawn still had the half-threadbare look that tender new grass gives. Pete parked his Chevrolet across the street. She was locking her car while he and McGregor walked over.

She waved at the house. "Isn't it splendid? I've only been in about four months. Eleven thousand five hundred dollars and a four-and-a-half percent loan."

"Everything is too expensive these days," Pete said sympathetically.

She turned red and made a peculiar strangled noise that perplexed him until he saw she was trying not to laugh. "Never mind," she said. "Care for some lunch? I'm no great cook, but sandwiches are easy, and there's beer in the refrigerator."

"Sold," McGregor said at once. Pete nodded too.

"Come on, then."

For a reason Pete had trouble naming, the inside of her house disappointed him. It was pleasant enough, with Early American furniture, Raphael prints on the walls, and a number of well-filled bookcases—nothing out of the ordinary. Then he realized that was the problem. He had expected something strange, and did not know what to make of this blatant normality.

She led him and McGregor into the kitchen, slapped ham, dill pickle, and mustard on rye bread, used a churchkey to open three cans of Burgermeister. For a few minutes they were all busy eating. "That was good," Pete said, wiping his mouth. "Thanks, uh—your name isn't really Mark, is it?"

She smiled. "It's Michelle, as a matter of fact."

Almost at the same time, the two men got out their cigarettes and looked round for an ashtray. They did not see one. Michelle Gordian's smile disappeared. "I'd rather you didn't smoke in the house," she said, a trifle sharply. McGregor shrugged and put his pack away. So, reluctantly, did Pete; his nicotine habit was much stronger than the editor's.

Michelle put the few dishes in the sink, then said, "Why don't we go back into the living room? It's more comfortable there."

She waved them to the couch, sat down herself in a rocking chair facing them. She came to the point with a directness Pete was not used to in a woman: "Just what is it you think I am?"

He had to try twice before he got the words out: "A time-traveler." Speculating about the impossible was much easier than proposing it—that implied belief.

"Why?" She effortlessly controlled the conversation; for once even McGregor did not seem eager to break in. As much as anything else, that helped make Pete take the preposterous idea seriously.

He plowed ahead, outlining the strangeness he and the *Astonishing* editor had found. As he spoke, he knew how absurd he had to sound. He waited for Michelle to burst into laughter. But instead she was leaning forward in the rocker, following him intently. He thought of her for the first time as an attractive woman; interest brought her features to life.

When he had stumbled to a halt, she was silent for most of a minute. As had been true outside the post office, though, once she made up her mind she went with it all the way. "You're right, of course," she said briskly.

McGregor had been gathering himself while Pete was talking. "I'd like to see more proof than a peculiar typewriter and a story that corresponds too well to an outline," he said. "I've been burned before. And forgive me, but nothing here looks the least bit, ah, extratemporal. That goes for what I take to be your study, too, from what I saw of it from the kitchen.''

"I'm not that careless," Michelle said, "even if I obviously wasn't careful enough. I have neighbors and friends who visit me; what would they make of a disc drive or a VCR?''

Nonsense words and letters, Pete thought. McGregor's snort said he agreed with that judgment. He shook his head with sarcastic mock sadness. "So, of course, you have nothing to show us.''

Michelle Gordian's eyes sparked angrily. "I didn't say that," she snapped. She rummaged in her purse, took out a thin white plastic rectangle about the size of a driver's license, fiddled with it for a moment, and tossed it to her guests. "Go ahead—it's on. Just punch the numbers and functions and signs.''

There was an inch-long strip of silvery stuff at the top of the card, with an angular dark gray zero at the right edge. Pete pressed the 7, and almost dropped the card when, silently and without any fuss, the matching number took the zero's place. McGregor leaned over and punched the radical sign. The 7 disappeared in turn, to be instantly replaced by 2.6457513.

"That," the editor said softly, "is the most astounding thing I have ever seen in my life.''

Pete hardly heard him. He had used desktop electric calculators before, bulky machines half as big as a typewriter, was used to the whirr of their motors, the ratcheting thunk of turning gears and cams, the wait for everything to finish in a multidigit multiplication. But here for the asking, at the press not even of a button, was 2.6457513. He had met the future, and he was in love.

When Michelle held out her hand for the incredible little device, he did not want to give it back. All he could think of to say was, "If you're used to machines like this, how can you stand living in 1953?''

McGregor, as was his way, carried that thought a step further: "How many centuries in the future are you from?''

One of her carroty eyebrows rose. "I'm sorry to disappoint you, but only about thirty-five years." When the two men exclaimed in disbelief, she said, "Think of this, then: what would the best aeronautical engineer in the world have made of an F-86 jet fighter in 1918? The more technology grows, the more it can grow. You both know that.''

"Yes, but I never had my nose rubbed in it like this before," McGregor muttered.

Pete did not look at it that way. The idea of the future had drawn him long before he began writing about it. Now he had held a piece of it in his hand, had touched the warm palm and fingers of it with his own.

He had to know more. "What else can you show us?" he breathed. "What were those things you named, a 'VCR' and and a, uh, 'disc driver'? You must have them here, or you wouldn't have mentioned them."

"Disc drive," she corrected absently. "Yes, I have them. Whether you should see them or not—well, having come this far, I suppose you deserve to know the rest. Come on out to the garage with me."

She led them through the kitchen and service porch. As they walked down the steps into the backyard, she locked the door behind them. "Why bother?" Pete said. "We aren't going to be gone all that long, are we?"

She looked surprised, then sheepish. "Force of habit. Something else I brought with me from the 1980s, I'm afraid."

McGregor cleared his throat. "Which brings up another point. Pete asked how you live here; I'm more interested in why. And why so secretly? With what you know, why not give the United States the help we need against the Reds?"

Something changed in her face. She was younger than Pete, years younger than the editor, but living through her life in the future (My God—she wouldn't even be born yet! Pete thought) had left her more streetwise, more cynical than both of them together. His misgivings stirred again.

She said bleakly, "Why do you think the government deserves that kind of edge?"

"Why don't you?" McGregor demanded after a short, stunned pause. The hostile edge was back in his voice, and Pete did not blame him.

Michelle was unabashed. "For one thing, *Watergate* wasn't exactly fiction. All I did was change some names. Do you want to know who President Cavanaugh really is?" She paused for dramatic effect, then told them.

McGregor winced. "I will be damned," Pete said.

She continued inexorably, "Does the name Klaus Barbie mean anything to either of you?"

"The Butcher of Lyon," Pete exclaimed. "I went through there not long after the Nazis left. What about him?"

"He's living in South America now, because he was a resource to our intelligence agencies and we helped spirit him away from the French. Just about thirty years from now, he'll finally get captured and we'll get around to apologizing to France."

Pete started to say, "I don't believe it," but the words stuck in his throat.

"Shall I go on?" Michelle asked McGregor. "Or will you believe I have some reason for doing things like I am?"

"You have an unpleasant way of making your points," he said, but took the argument no further.

She unlocked the garage door, swung it up, turned on the light, and closed it behind the three of them. The front third of the garage held the same sort of stuff Pete's did: a couple of trashcans, a lawnmower, some gardening and hand tools, a pile of boxes filled with miscellaneous junk. The rest was walled off. A door had been cut in the wall; a stout deadbolt gleamed above the knob.

"This is where I do my real work," she said as she unbolted and unlocked it.

She reached for a light switch just to the side of the door. Pete was not sure what to expect—probably something like the inside of a flying saucer. It wasn't like that. The general impressions reminded him of his own working area: office furniture, lots of books and records. There was an amenity he wished he had thought of for himself—a small refrigerator—in one corner.

The more he looked, though, the stranger things got. The television set was no model he had seen before, and he did not know what the small box, full of knobs and buttons, attached to it was. The radio, record player, and speakers were similarly recognizable but not familiar, and seemed somehow naked out by themselves without a cabinet.

And the gadget on the desk had a keyboard, but if a typewriter had been its mother, she had been unfaithful with a TV set. Wires led to a couple of other unfamiliar machines—no, wait, there was paper in one of them. "No wonder your paper looks like that!" Pete said. "You've got little side-strips for the holes to mesh with the sprockets of the electric printer, and then you just peel them off. How clever!"

"That was the hardest thing to install," she remarked. "I don't want to say much about how I travel, but I can't bring anything back with me that I can't carry. These days I mostly stay here, anyway, unless I need something I can only get up-time. Happens I like it here.''

Pete walked over to the desk. There was a magazine on it, next to the keyboard-*cum*-screen. He did not recognize the title, or the emblem prominently displayed on the cover: a stylized rabbit's head in a bow tie. ''Gala 33rd Anniversary Issue!'' the magazine proclaimed. The date (seeing that gave him chills) let him make a quick subtraction.

''It's almost ready to begin.'' The connection with his own times was cheering, in a way. Then he noticed something else. ''This cost *five dollars*?'' he said in horror.

''It's not as awful as it sounds,'' Michelle reassured him. ''In terms of 1953 money, it's somewhere between a dollar and a dollar and a half.''

He frowned. Not even the postwar inflation had been as bad as that. Some things in the future looked to be mixed blessings after all.

He picked up the magazine. ''May I?''

''Go ahead,'' she said. There was something in her voice he could not quite read. She kept her face carefully blank as she went on, ''In some ways it will probably interest you more than it does me.''

The first few pages were mostly ads. The quality of the color reproduction surpassed anything 1953 could offer. Pete gaped at the lines of the cars. They were the most blatantly different element, though fashions had also changed, women's hairstyles were new, and mustaches and beards were common on men.

The magazine fell open naturally at the center. A very pretty girl smiled out at Pete. ''Ah, I see what you meant; it's like *Esquire*,'' he said, and opened the foldout.

He closed it in a hurry, scarlet to the roots of his hair. ''Where did you get this, this pornography?'' he stammered.

He turned even redder when he saw how hard she was trying not to laugh at him. ''By my standards, it isn't pornography; in fact, it's very mild, compared to some others,'' she said gently. ''And I bought it at the same place I got my little calculator—the Rexall's at the corner of Vermont and Gardena Boulevard.''

''You bought it yourself? You didn't have a man get it for you? I don't believe it. How could you show your face anywhere afterward?''

''Women do a lot of things in my time that they can't do here-and-now.'' She eyed him with disconcerting directness, smiled so that her lips parted very slightly. Did that mean what he thought it did? He was not sure he wanted to know. He had never seriously looked at another woman since he married Katherine, but there was no denying he felt drawn to Michelle Gordian now. He could not tell where his interest in her for her origin stopped and his interest in her as a person—and as a woman—began.

He was grateful when she changed the subject, and suspected her to be aware of it. She said, "Anyhow, the pictures weren't the reason I bought the magazine. It has a Clarke story in it that I want to use."

For a moment, all that did was to convince Pete that the publication wasn't obscene, at least in its own context: he could not imagine Arthur Clarke publishing in anything that was. Then the full meaning of her words hit him. "You're saying you've plagiarized all your work, then?" he asked coldly. "So that's why you came back here—to make an easy living off what other people have done." His liking for her flickered and blew out.

"It certainly looks that way," McGregor put in. Where exotic technology had lured Pete, with editor's instinct McGregor had been drawn to the bookshelves. Most of the volumes there were pocket books. Some of the writers' names were familiar, others not. The books were shelved alphabetically by author's last name; Pete's glance flicked to the L's. He was startled to see how much he had done—would have done?—will have done? He gave up on the right verb form.

In any case, McGregor was holding several books in his hand. He showed one to Pete. "You'll notice it's called *Neutron Star*," he said. "It also has 'At the Core' and 'The Handicapped' in it. Here's another one: *The Hugo Winners, Volume V*, with 'Not So You'd Notice.' I can go on for a while, if you like."

He looked at Michelle Gordian as at some particularly unpleasant insect, an expression Pete understood completely. He had always reckoned thieves of other people's work beneath contempt; that the authors of the stories stolen here could have no chance to prove these words their own only made it worse.

Pete could not even bring himself to respect the way Michelle stood up to the scorn he and McGregor directed at her. "Don't you want to hear my reason for doing what I'm doing?" she asked.

"Does it matter?" Pete ground out. He felt ashamed of his thoughts of a few minutes before.

"It's obvious anyway," McGregor said. "It's one of the oldest cliches in science fiction—the time-traveler using special knowledge to get rich. I never thought I'd see anyone actually do it, that's all.''

" 'Get rich?' '' Michelle echoed. It was her turn to flush now, but from anger rather than embarrassment. ''Not likely, at three cents a word and down. If money were what I wanted, there are easier ways than spending so much time in front of my word processor.'' Seeing their uncomprehending looks, she jabbed a thumb at the mutant typewriter.

Pete thought of his own troubles making ends meet, but her expostulation did nothing to move McGregor. ''What then?'' the editor snapped. ''Look at the name you've built for yourself here and now. Who are you up in your own time?''

He plainly thought the question rhetorical, but she answered it. ''An up-and-coming SF author, if you must know. You've been picking books off the shelves; why don't you get mine out?'' There were four of them, three novels and a collection of stories, published, Pete noticed, under her own name. She said, ''You can see I don't have to steal everything I do. That's come in handy, because some of what I've sold wouldn't be publishable in a science fiction magazine in the 1980s.''

Pete pointed to the magazine with the rabbit on the cover. ''After seeing *that*, I'd think you could get anything into print.''

She smiled. ''In that sense, you can, pretty much. But not everything I've written myself is science *fiction*, if you see what I mean.''

''Oh.'' Pete and McGregor looked at each other. The writer asked in a low voice, ''Which ones are real?''

''To hell with that.'' McGregor made an impatient gesture. He peered at Michelle over the top of his glasses. ''You're saying you have some reason besides the strictly personal for doing what you're doing.''

Relief showed on her face. ''Yes, I do.''

''It had better be a good one.''

''I think it is.''

The *Astonishing* editor waited, but she said nothing more. Finally he barked, ''Well?''

''Think it through for yourself,'' she said. Nothing could have been better calculated to engage his interest. ''You, too, Pete,'' she urged. ''You must have read a fair number of the stories I've had published—I won't call them mine if that offends you. What do they have in common?''

Not much, was Pete's first thought. They were too diverse— and no wonder, if they actually came from many different pens.

But McGregor saw what she was driving at. He was more used to considering a number of stories together than Pete. He said slowly, "If I had to pick any one thing, it would be the way your characters attack problems. They all have a knack for applying knowledge logically."

"Thanks," she said. "That's one of the main ideas I've been trying to get across." She turned to Pete, asked with seeming irrelevance, "You have school-age kids, don't you?"

"A couple of boys," he nodded. "Why?"

"How are they learning to read?"

He made a sour face. "About how you'd guess—this current idiocy of pictures and 'looking at the shape of the whole word,' whatever that means. It doesn't matter. When Carl turned four, I bought an old phonics reader at a secondhand bookstore and taught him myself, the right way; I did the same for his brother a year later. They're both near the top of their classes now."

"I'm sure they are. But what about the children whose parents didn't bother? How well are they going to do when they come across an unfamiliar word? You're a good SF writer—extrapolate. What happens when those kids grow up? What happens when some of them become teachers and try to teach *their* sons and daughters to read?"

Pete thought about that, and did not like the answer he came up with. "You're telling us that's how it's going to be?"

"I'm afraid I am. You can watch out for something called 'new math,' too, which is just as delightful as reading through pictures."

"Thirty-odd years isn't that long a time," McGregor protested. "When the Roman Empire fell in the west, it took generations for the decline in literacy to become as widespread as you're implying. And we're starting at a much higher level than the Romans ever reached."

"True enough," Michelle said, "but then, the Romans were carrying on as best they could, trying to preserve what they had with the barbarians at the gates."

She stopped there, letting the two men follow her train of thought for themselves. "You mean we don't?" Pete said. His fist clenched; the notion that the United States, having surmounted the Depression and World War II, put western Europe back on its feet, and contained the Reds in Korea, could suffer a loss of will, was enough to infuriate him.

As was so often true, James McGregor asked the question that needed asking. "What went—er, goes—wrong?"

"My hindsight isn't long enough to be sure," Michelle said, "but I can put my finger on a couple of things. One is education, as I said. Another is the hangover from the war in Vietnam."

"In where?" the editor said, but Pete's memory jogged back to his thoughts when he was about to read "Reactions." He exclaimed, "Oh, my God! 'Tet Offensive'!"

McGregor stared from one of them to the other. "You're not telling me that one's based on fact?" he demanded of Michelle. At her nod, he gave a rueful laugh. He said, "You know, when you sent it to me, I almost bounced it because it seemed too unlikely for the readers to believe. The only things that saved it were the gadgetry on the one hand and the fact that it was internally self-consistent on the other. No wonder, I guess." He was still shaking his head.

"No wonder at all," Michelle said. "The war is one of the reasons a magazine can cost five dollars. There wasn't—won't be—enough money to pay for guns and butter both, so the printing presses tried to make up the difference."

"That always happens," Pete said.

"Yes, but I think it was the least of the damage," Michelle replied. "What is it Heinlein says?—it doesn't matter if a hamburger costs ten dollars as long as there's plenty of hamburger. The harm done the country's institutions was worse."

"The riots and marches and such?" Pete asked; they had only been sketched in as background to the story, but they formed a constant counterpoint to the fighting that occupied center stage.

"Those are just the outward signs of what I mean," Michelle said. "To this day I'm not sure whether the war was right or wrong in itself, but it was certainly botched. People got very cynical about everything the government did (Watergate helped there too), and a lot of them automatically opposed it or thought it was stupid when it tried to do anything at all.

"And with contempt for the government went contempt for organization and standards of every sort. That aided and abetted the failure of education, I fear. And naturally, with the emphasis on the importance of the individual, anything that didn't produce immediate, obvious benefits had hard sledding. Even the space program had rough going—once weather satellites and communications satellites were in place, people took them for granted and didn't think about all the R&D it took to get them up in the first place. What can I tell you? The interest of the country just swung away from science and technology. There's no prettier way to put it than that.''

"That can't be strictly true," Pete protested. "What about all these things?" He waved at the television, the contraption wired to it, the—what had she called it?—word processor.

She pointed at them one at a time in turn, saying, "Made in Taiwan, made in Japan (nobody in the United States manufactures videocassette recorders—we can't compete), made in Japan . . . the microcomputer is American-built, but the Japanese models are just as good and getting better—and cheaper.''

Seeing their stricken expressions, she went on gently, "It's not all bad, up when I come from. Blacks—no, I'm sorry, Negroes is the polite word now—and women have many more opportunities than here-and-now, and a lot take advantage of them. Many people who would die or be crippled today can be saved.''

" 'Heart Transplant' will come true, then?" McGregor asked.

"Oh, yes, but it's just the most dramatic one of a whole range of new techniques. . . . What else? Well, we're still holding the line against the Russians. I expect we will, a while longer. That's not a bad thing; they're smoother then than they are now, but no nicer.''

"All very interesting, I'm sure," the editor said, "but it still doesn't answer the question we've had all along: why *are* you here?''

"I thought I was explaining that," she said. "I'm trying to change the future, of course." Her voice took on a fresh urgency, as if she were a lawyer trying to convince two magistrates of the justice of her case. "We missed coming so much further than we did by so little. The moon program petered out—''

That drew a grunt from McGregor and sent a wave of anguish through Pete. He did not want to believe it, but it fit horridly well with everything else Michelle had told them.

He pulled his attention back to what she was saying: "Compared to my time, education, interest, and (maybe most important) purpose are still strong here and now. I'm just trying to nudge things along a little bit, to get across the idea that the best way to solve a problem is to apply knowledge to it, as you said, Mr. McGregor. That's true both of my own stories and of the ones I've taken from other writers.''

"And you've also slipped some of your special knowledge into them," the editor said.

"Of course. An amazing number of the people who read SF are engineers and scientists themselves; that's more true now than it will be in my time. If they pick up a notion or two from one of my near-future pieces, and act on them now instead— you see what I'm driving at, I think. I've done my best to describe hardware and techniques as precisely as I could.''

"Using science fiction to save the world, eh?" McGregor said. "Much as I hate to say it, isn't that a trifle naive?"

"If ideas don't do the trick, what will?" Michelle retorted. The *Astonishing* editor grunted again.

A considerable silence fell before Pete nerved himself to ask, "Any luck?"

"I still have hope" was all she said. "Do you really want to find out more than that?"

"No, I suppose not," he said, and wondered if he meant it. He decided he did. Knowing what lay ahead was too much like losing his free will. He shuddered at the burden Michelle Gordian had taken on herself.

McGregor must have been thinking along the same lines, for he said to her, "What can I do to help?"

"The best thing would be to forget that this whole visit ever happened," she answered. "For God's sake, don't be any easier on my stories because of it. If they aren't worth reading, nobody'll care—or even find out—what's in them."

His grin was wolfish. "You needn't worry about that. If I start publishing stories that aren't worth reading, the magazine goes under and I either starve or have to start making an honest living for myself."

She made a face at him. "Fair enough." Stepping past Pete, she opened the door that led out to the mundane world of 1953.

"Excuse me." When they were walking back to the house, Pete took out his cigarettes, gratefully sucked in the harsh smoke. Seeing Michelle's expression of distaste, he quoted,

" 'Tobacco is a dirty weed.
It satisfies no normal need.
It makes you thin, it makes you lean,
It takes the hair right off your bean.
It's the worst darn stuff I've ever seen. I like it.' "

"The more fool you," she told him, but she waited until he had had enough and crushed the butt under his heel.

Once they were inside, McGregor said feelingly, "I hope no

one will argue with me when I say that calls for another drink. A very dry Martini, if you have the makings.''

"I'll wave the vermouth at it as I toss in the cherry," she promised. "Anything for you, Pete?''

"I wouldn't turn down another beer.''

She handed it to him, made the editor's drink and a gin and tonic for herself. She watched McGregor take a cautious sip. ''Is that all right?''

"I'll let you know when my eyes uncross," he wheezed, but the glass rapidly emptied.

After he was done, he seemed impatient to be gone. Pete thought he wanted to talk privately about the amazing day, but he said very little on the drive back to the motel. At last Pete said, ''What is it, Jim? I've never seen you knock back a drink so fast, and I've never heard you so quiet.''

"You didn't pay a lot of attention to the books back there, did you?''

"No, not really. Why?''

"I wish I hadn't.'' There was a long pause. "One of them was called *The James McGregor Memorial Anthology*.''

"*The*—oh, Jim!''

"Yeah. It's good to know I'll be well thought of, I suppose.''

Pete could only admire the editor's composure. Even a kidnapper facing the gas chamber could hope his sentence would be commuted; this one, though indefinite, was certain. Pete hesitated, then asked, "Did you, uh, look at the copyright date?''

"The hell I did!'' McGregor said, echoing Pete's feelings exactly: ''That's a chunk of the future I have no desire to know more about, thank you very much.''

"What will you do now?''

"What would you expect? Get a flight back to New York and go on with *Astonishing*, of course. There's certainly nothing I'd rather do.'' He fished his wallet out of his pocket, pawed through it. "Where's that Trans World reservation-and-ticket number? Oh, here it is—Michigan 8141. I'll have to give them a call when we get back to our digs.''

They were pulling into the motel parking lot when Pete said reflectively, ''Things aren't going to be as simple—or as good— up ahead as I'd hoped, from what Michelle says.''

The editor laughed at him. "Remember what de Camp put in the mouth of one of his characters? Something to the effect that a truthful traveler coming back from heaven would report its charm greatly overrated.''

"Well, maybe so. Still, I'm not sorry she's trying to bend the future a bit. Imagine reaching the moon and then cutting back on space exploration. It's crazy!"

"You get no arguments from me. If I thought you were wrong, I'd be calling the FBI now, not TWA." Pete turned off the ignition. They got out of the car. McGregor went on, "Let's get ourselves packed. Our wives will be missing us."

"So they will," Pete agreed, but he was disturbed to find himself thinking as much of Michelle Gordian as of Katherine.

The big propellors began to spin, slowly at first but then blurring toward invisibility. Even behind the steel and glass of the terminal, the roar of the radial engines sank into a man's bones. The airliner rolled west along the runway. It sprang into the air; the landing gear folded up into its belly.

Wishing McGregor well, Pete walked back through the terminal toward the parking lot off Century Boulevard. He passed the row of telephones in which the editor had searched in vain for "Mark" Gordian's number. He hesitated, took out a dime, and went over to an unused phone.

He dialed with a rising sense of trepidation. He heard three rings, four, five; he was about to hang up, more relieved than not, when his call got answered. "Hello?"

"Michelle?"

"Yes, this is Michelle Gordian. Who's calling, please?" She sounded out of breath; she had probably come running in from outside, he thought, to pick up the phone.

"This is Pete Lundquist, Michelle."

"How did you get my number?" she demanded, both anger and alarm in her voice.

"I saw it on your telephone yesterday," he said apologetically. "I have a good memory for such things."

"Oh." She seemed mollified, but only a little. "What is it you want, then?"

Not altogether sure of the answer to that himself, he decided to take her literally. "I've been thinking of the conversation we had yesterday, and—"

"—you decided you really want to know what's going to happen after all," she interrupted. Again he heard her full of the cynicism that appeared to come so easily to the future. She said, "You were smarter before, I promise you."

"I believe it," he said quickly. "It's just that—well, there I was in a room full of machines from your time, and every one of them turned off! I felt like Tantalus and the bunch of grapes. All I was going to ask was to see them work just once. Anything more than that I'll cheerfully stay ignorant of.''

The line was silent so long that he said, ''Hello?''

''I'm here,'' she answered. ''Well, why not? The worst part of living back here is the loneliness. My neighbors are friendly, but we have so little in common with one another, and I don't dare show them what I have in the garage. Either they wouldn't understand or they'd expose me. You're enough different that— tell you what. I was just going out to the garage to work on a story of my own when you called, and that'll probably keep me busy through the afternoon. Why don't you come over around nine tonight? Come straight out to the garage; I'll probably still be in there anyhow.''

''Nine o'clock,'' he repeated. ''I'll be there.'' He hung up. Everything is okay, he told himself fiercely; I'm only going to have a look at marvels I won't have the chance to see again. But the interior dialog would not stop: in that case, why are your palms so sweaty? came the next question. His response was to ignore it.

As things worked out, he was late; never having gone directly to Michelle Gordian's house, he lost his way a couple of times, and streetlights were few and far between. When he finally did arrive, he thought she had changed her mind and was going to meet him in the house: behind drawn drapes, the lights were on. But no one came to the door when he rang the bell. He went back around the house to the garage.

Michelle was at the word processor when he entered her sanctum. She waved without turning around, saying, ''With you in a couple of minutes. I'm working through a tough part, and it's taking longer than I thought it would. Sorry.''

He didn't answer. He was not sure she could hear him: a record was spinning on the turntable, and she was listening to it through a pair of earphones. Instead, he walked over to the green-glowing screen in front of which she was sitting. As he came up, she muttered an obscenity under her breath, punched a couple of keys. Pete stared—on the screen, a paragraph had disappeared. A letter at a time, a new version began taking shape.

''I want this gadget!'' he cried in honest envy, thinking of scissors and paste and snowdrifts of crumpled paper in his wastebasket.

She could hear—he saw her smile at him. ''I think that'll do it,'' she said. She hit different buttons. A light on the small rectangular box next to the screen came on; the box started chuckling to itself. ''Storing what I've written on the floppy disc,'' she explained, taking off the earphones. ''I'll print it out tomorrow.''

He must have looked like a small boy who had just lost his candy. ''Oh, you really were interested in the machines, then?'' she said.

He nodded, but felt his face grow hot at her ironic tone.

She waited until the disc drive had fallen silent, typed out a new command. Pete jumped as the printer started purring like a large mechanical cat. Paper rose at an astonishing rate. ''How fast does it type?'' he asked.

''About three hundred words a minute, I think,'' she said indifferently.

He peered into its works, exclaimed, ''It's printing left-to-right and right-to-left!''

''Why not? It's quicker that way. It's not as if it knows what it's doing, or anything like that. It's just a tool, like an automobile.''

''Yes, but I'm used to automobiles, and I'm not used to this.'' He changed the subject. ''Was the record you had on from your time or mine?''

''Mine, or at least you would say so. Actually, it's pretty old. It's from, uh''—she looked at the back of the cardboard sleeve—''1978.''

''That's new enough for me,'' he laughed. He took the record cover, turned it over. The design on the front was the same as that on the other side: a stylized street lined with geometric shapes running like a purple-pink bend sinister across a black background. '' 'Robin Trower. Caravan to Midnight,' '' he read. ''May I hear it?''

He was surprised when she hesitated. ''I don't know if I ought to do this to you,'' she said. ''It's only rock-and-roll, but I like it.''

''Only what?''

''Never mind. Popular music.''

''It's okay,'' he reassured her. ''I like Bach and Vivaldi, sure, but I can listen to Perry Como too.''

For some reason, that seemed to fluster her more. ''It's not—like Perry Como.''

''Is Robin Trower a girl singer, then, like Rosemary Clooney? That's all right.''

"He's an Englishman who plays electric guitar," Michelle said flatly.

"Oh." If she thought she was going to put him off, she was wrong. The idea of futuristic technology married to music only intrigued him more. "Sounds fascinating."

His determination made her throw her hands in the air. "All right. Don't say you weren't warned." She set the earphones on his head. They were padded with red sponge rubber, lighter and more comfortable than the ones radiomen had used during the war. "You might as well listen to the first side first," she said, flipping the record in her hands. He saw it flex, and guessed it was unbreakable. He wished some of the hard shellac platters he'd once owned had been.

Then the needle—housed in a more elaborate cartridge than current phonographs employed—was dropping. Pete heard it hiss on the opening grooves of the record, listened to the syncopated thump of drums. He just had time to realize that the sound was marvelously clear before the snarling whine of the guitar made him jump straight up. Then everything was happening at once—guitar, drums, and a singer who attacked his song like a man going after a snake with an axe.

Michelle had the volume up very high. Pete felt as if he were listening to a jet engine warming up in stereophonic sound (something he knew only from a few big movie theaters). "It's not like Perry Como at all," he said. He could hardly hear himself talk. He saw Michelle's lips move, but made nothing of her reply.

He had almost snatched the earphones off at the first stunning jolt, but he soon realized that this Robin Trower knew exactly what he was doing and had his unruly instrument under control. The music was so strange he could not tell whether he liked it or not, but he recognized talent when he heard it.

The song—it was called "My Love (Burning Love)," he saw on the sleeve—came to an appropriately fiery end. In the brief moment of silence between tracks, Michelle said, "The next one's quieter."

"Jesus, I hope so." He lifted off the earphones. "Too strong for my blood, I think," he said, adding reflectively, "That's what I'd call real zorch."

He was obscurely pleased that he had managed to puzzle her. "Real what?"

"It's what the young hepcats say when they mean something like 'strange and marvelous,' " he explained. "There's a bop-talking San Francisco disk jockey named Red Blanchard who's their hero up where I live. Bunch of crazy kids, the kind who dye their hair green or wear purple lipstick or red eyebrow pencil—what's so funny?''

"Nothing, really," she got out after a while. "*Plus ça change, plus c'est la même chose*, that's all." She studied him. "What would you like now?"

He hesitated but played safe. "If this is your record player, what can your TV do?"

She shrugged, turned it on. The picture filled the screen much more quickly than on the sets with which he was familiar, and it was very sharp, but the difference seemed of degree rather than of kind. He was disappointed. He must have shown it, for she said, "Remember, it can only give back the signal it's getting. However—" She went over to her desk, took out a plastic case a little larger than a fat paperback. "A videocassette," she said, loading it into the box attached to the television.

"Magnetic tape?" Pete asked, and at her startled nod he said smugly, "They were talking about it in *Time* last month."

"That'll teach me to show off. I ought to tell you this is old too. I've seen it a million times, but I never mind watching it again."

He did not answer. He was staring at the words flowing across the starry background: "A long time ago, in a galaxy far, far away . . ." The story background being laid out mattered much less to him than the fact that the lettering was glowing gold. There had been talk of color TV for years, but unexpectedly seeing one was something else again.

Michelle brought her desk chair over next to his. He felt about seventeen, at the movies with a date. The headlong action of the space opera he was watching only added to the feeling; it reminded him of a film made by splicing several months' worth of serials together.

Halfway through, he burst out, "My Lord, that's Alec Guinness!" The actor's snow-white beard brought home the inexorable passage of time even more starkly than the calculator card Michelle carried; Pete wondered what the years would do to *him*.

"What did you think?" she asked when the tape was done.

"The Hollywood word is 'colossal,' isn't it? The color, the trick photography—unbelievable. I almost hate to quibble about how thin the plot is."

"A man of taste." She sighed. "It's so much fun, though, I don't want to admit that you're right."

He glanced down at his watch. "It's almost one," he said in disbelief. "I ought to be getting back to the motel." He rose and stretched. "Thank you for a really marvelous time."

The hackneyed formality of the phrase made the evening seem more like a date than ever. Without much conscious thought, Pete put his arms around Michelle to try for a good-night kiss.

He got more than he bargained for. Her body molded itself to his; he could feel the soft firmness of her breasts against his chest. And the kiss, instead of the prim peck he had expected, left delighted thunder in his brain when he finally came up for air.

Michelle pulled back, just a little. "The hardest thing for me living back here, I think, is having a relationship," she said.

"A wh—a what?" he stammered, still half-stunned by the yielding warmth of her under his hands—but not too stunned to respond, another part of him noted clinically.

"Most men here and now treat a woman as if she were a child," Michelle said, "and even with the ones who might not, how can I get close? I have too much to hide. But you already know my secret, and you've been looking forward for years. It's a damned attractive combination." She swayed toward him again.

The directness of her approach, though, did more to put him off than to arouse him; he was used to the game being played another way. "Easy there," he said, disengaging.

"It was pure intellectual curiosity, then, that brought you back here tonight?" she said with stinging sarcasm. "Tell me that was all, but wipe the lipstick off first."

He could still taste it on his lips. "I can't tell you that," he admitted, knowing miserably that he was going to regret whatever happened next, either way.

An army buddy had once told him, "The hardest thing in the world is turning it down when it's there for the taking." "How do you know?" he'd asked—"Ever done it?" "Me? Hell, no—and don't that prove my point?" His buddy would not have had a second thought here.

His buddy, though, had not spent his entire adulthood building a life with one woman. Though it took all Pete's will, he turned toward the door of Michelle's study.

Her voice pursued him. "You run, and you don't even know what you're missing."

The promise in that almost stopped him again. From everything he had seen, her era was much looser than his. There were things he had never dared ask of Katherine. . . . But then, why had Michelle Gordian chosen to live in 1953 if not for its virtues, such as they were?

"I know what I have," he said quietly, and walked into the night.

Gardner Dozois and Susan Casper asked me for a Jack the Ripper story for an anthology they were putting together. It was, I think, only the second time I'd ever been asked, so I said yes right away. Then I had to come up with a story idea. I wasn't sure I could; up to that time, I'd just taken ideas as they came rather than aiming toward a specific subject. But I began to think about Jack, about how and why he might have done the insanely vicious things he did. Once I found an answer to that, the story almost wrote itself.

GENTLEMEN OF THE SHADE

THE GAS FLAME FLICKERED EVER SO SLIGHTLY within its mantle of pearly glass as Hignett opened the door to fetch us in our port and cheeses. All five of us were in the lounge that Friday evening, an uncommon occasion in the annals of the Sanguine Club and one calling therefore for a measure of celebration.

As always, the cheeses went untouched, yet Hignett will insist on setting them out; as well reverse the phases of the moon as expect an English butler to change his habits. But some of us quite favor port, I among them. I have great relish for the fashion in which it makes the sweet blood sing through my veins.

Bowing, Hignett took his leave of us. I poured the tawny port with my own hand. For the toast to the Queen, all of us raised glasses to our lips, as is but fitting. Then, following our custom, we toasted the Club as well, after which those of us who care not for such drink may in honor decline further potations.

Yet whether or not we imbibe, the company of our own kind is precious to us, for we are so few even in London, the greatest city the world has known. Thus it was that we all paid close heed when young Martin said, "I saw in the streets last evening one I reckon will make a sixth for us."

"By Jove!" said Titus. He is the eldest of us, and swears that oath from force of habit. "How long has it been since you joined us, Martin, dear chap?"

"Myself?" Martin rubbed the mustache he has lately taken

to wearing. "I don't recollect, exactly. It has been some goodish while, hasn't it?"

"Six!" I exclaimed, suddenly finding new significance in the number. "Then two of us can be away and still leave enough for the whist table!"

Amidst general laughter, Titus said, "Ah, Jerome, this unwholesome passion of yours for the pasteboards does truly make me believe you to have Hoyle's blood in you."

"Surely not, after so long," I replied, which occasioned fresh mirth. I sighed in mock heaviness. "Ah, well, I fear me even so we may go without a game as often as not. But tell us more of the new one, Martin, so as to permit me to indulge my idle fancy."

"You will understand I was upon my own occasions, and so not able to make proper enquiry of him," Martin said, "but there can be little doubt of the matter. Like calls to like, as we all know."

"He noted you, then?" Arnold asked, rising to refill his goblet.

"Oh, I should certainly think so. He stared at me for some moments before proceeding down Buck's Row."

"Buck's Row, is it?" said Titus with an indulgent chuckle. "Out chasing the Whitechapel tarts again like a proper young buck, were you?"

"No denying they're easy to come by there," Martin returned. In that he was, of course, not in error. Every one of us in the Club, I am certain, has resorted to the unfortunate "widows" of Whitechapel to slake his lusts when no finer opportunity presented itself.

"A pity you did not think to have him join you, so you could hunt together," remarked Arnold.

The shadow of a frown passed across Martin's countenance. "I had intended to do so, my friend, yet something, I know not what, stayed my hand. I felt somehow the invitation would be unwelcome to him."

"Indeed!" Titus rumbled indignantly. "If this individual spurns the friendship of an honored member"—"You honor me, sir," Martin broke in. "Not at all, sir," our Senior replied, before resuming—"an honored member, as I say, of what is, if I may speak with pardonable pride, perhaps the most exclusive club in London, why then, this individual appears to me to be no gentleman, and hence not an appropriate aspirant for membership under any circumstances."

Norton had not taken part in the discussion up to this time, contenting himself with sitting close to the fire and observing the play of the flames. As always when he did choose to speak, his words were to the point. "Nonsense, Titus," he said. "Martin put it well: like calls to like."

"You think we shall encounter him again, then, under circumstances more apt to let us judge his suitability?"

"I am certain of it," Norton replied, nor in the end did he prove mistaken. I often think him the wisest of us all.

The evening passed most pleasantly, as do all our weekly gatherings. Our practice is to meet until midnight, and then to adjourn to seek the less cerebral pleasures the night affords. By the end of August, the sun does not rise until near on five of the clock, granting us no small opportunity to do as we would under the comforting blanket of night.

For myself, I chose to wander the Whitechapel streets. Past midnight, many London districts lay quiet as the crypt. Not so Whitechapel, which like so much of the dissolute East End of the city knows night from day no more than good from evil. The narrow winding streets that change their names from block to block have always their share of traffic. I sought them for that, as I have many times before, but also, I will not deny, in the hope that I might encounter the personage whom Martin had previously met.

That I did not. I supposed him to have sated himself the night before, and so to be in no need of such peregrinations now—here again, as events transpired, I was not in error. Yet this produced in me only the mildest of disappointments for, as I have said, I had other reasons for frequenting Whitechapel.

The clocks were just striking two when I saw coming toward me down Flower and Dean Street a likely-seeming wench. Most of the few lamps that such a small, dingy lane merits were long since out, so she was nearly upon me before realizing I was there. She drew back in startlement, fearing, I suppose, me to be some footpad, but then decided from my topper, clawhammer, and brocaded waistcoat that such was not the case.

"Begging your pardon, guv'nor," she said, smiling now, "but you did give me 'arf a turn, springing from the shadows like that." She smelled of sweat and beer and sausage.

I bowed myself nearly double, saying, "It is I who must apologize to you, my dear, for frightening so lovely a creature." This is the way the game is played, as it has been from time immemorial.

"Don't you talk posh, now!" she exclaimed. She put her hands on her hips, looking saucily up at me. She was a fine strong trollop, with rounded haunches and a shelflike bosom that she thrust my way; plainly she profited better from her whoring than so many of the skinny lasses who peddle their wares in Whitechapel. Her voice turned crooning, coaxing. "Only sixpence, sir, for a night to remember always."

Her price was more than that of the usual Whitechapel tart, but had I been other than I, I daresay I should have found her worth the difference. As it was, I hesitated only long enough to find the proper coin and press it into her hand. She peered down through the gloom to ensure I had not cheated her, then pressed her warm, firm body against me. "What's your pleasure, love?" she murmured in my ear, her tongue teasing at it between words.

When I led her to a wall in deeper darkness, she gave forth a tiny sigh, having I suppose hoped to ply her trade at leisure in a bed. She hiked up her skirts willingly enough, though, and her mouth sought mine with practiced art. Her hands fumbled at my trouser buttons while my teeth nibbled her lower lip.

" 'Ave a care," she protested, twisting in my embrace. "I'd not like for you to make me bleed." Then she sighed again, a sound different from that which had gone before, and stood stock-still and silent as one made into a statue. Her skirts rustled to the ground once more. I bent my head to her white neck and began to feed.

Were it not for the amnesic and anaesthetic agent contained within our spittle, I do not doubt that humans should have hounded us vampires to extinction a long age ago. Even as is, they remain uneasily aware of our existence, though less so, I own to my relief, in this teeming faceless metropolis of London where no one knows his neighbor, or cares to, than in the hidden faraway mountains and valleys whence our kind sprang and where folk memory and fear run back forever.

When I had drunk my fill, I passed my tongue over the twin wounds I had inflicted, whereupon they healed with the same rapidity as does my own flesh. The whore stirred then. What her dreams were I cannot say, but they must have been sweet, for she declared roundly, "Ah, sir, you can do me any time, and for free if you're hard up." Greater praise can no courtesan give. She seemed not a whit perplexed at the absence of any spunk of mine dribbling down her fat thighs; doubtless she had coupled with another recently enough beforehand so as not to miss it.

She entreated me for another round, but I begged off, claiming adequate satisfaction, as was indeed the case. We went our separate ways, each well pleased with the other.

She had just turned down Osborn Street toward Christ Church and I was about to enter on Commercial Street when I spied one who had to be he whom Martin had previously encountered. His jaunty stride and erect carriage proclaimed him recently to have fed, and fed well, yet somehow I found myself also aware of Titus's stricture, delivered sight unseen, that here was no gentleman. I could find no concrete reason for this feeling, and was about to dismiss it as a vagary of my own when he also became aware of my presence.

His grin was mirthless; while his cold eyes still held me, he slowly ran his tongue over his lips, as if to say he was fain to drink from my veins. My shock and revulsion must have appeared on my features, for his smile grew wider yet. He bowed so perfectly as to make perfection itself a mockery, then disappeared.

I know not how else to put it. We have of course sometimes the ability briefly to cloud a mere man's mind, but I had never thought, never imagined the occasion could arise, to turn this power upon my own kind. Only the trick's surprise, I think, lent it success, but success, at least a moment's worth, it undeniably had. By the time I recovered full use of my faculties, the crass japester was gone.

I felt angry enough, nearly, to go in pursuit of him. Yet the sun would rise at five, and my flat lay in Knightsbridge, no small distance away. Reluctantly I turned my step toward the Aldgate Station. As well I did; the train was late, and morning twilight already painting the eastern horizon with bright colors when I neared home.

The streets by then were filling with the legions of wagons London requires for her daily revictualing. Newsboys stood on every corner hawking their papers. I spent a penny and tucked one away for later reading, time having grown too short for me to linger.

My landlady is of a blessedly incurious nature; so long as the rent is promptly paid and an appearance of quiet and order maintained, she does not wonder at one of her tenants not being seen abroad by day. All of us of the Sanguine Club have digs of this sort: another advantage of the metropolis over lesser towns, where folk of such mercenary nature are in shorter supply. Did they not exist, we should be reduced to squalid, hole-and-corner ways of sheltering ourselves from the sun, ways in ill-accord with the style we find pleasing once night has fallen.

The setting of the sun having restored my vitality, I glanced through the paper I had purchased before. The headlines screamed of a particularly grisly murder done in Whitechapel in the small hours of the previous day. Being who and what I am, such does not easily oppress me, but the details of the killing—for the paper proved to be of the lurid sort—did give me more than momentary pause.

I soon dismissed them from my mind, however, being engaged in going up and down in the city in search of profit. Men with whom I deal often enough for them to note my nocturnal habit ask no more questions on it than my landlady, seeing therein the chance to mulct me by virtue of my ignorance of the day's events. At times they even find their efforts crowned with success, but, if I may be excused for boasting, infrequently. I have matched myself against their kind too long now to be easily fooled. Most of the losses I suffer are self-inflicted.

I could be, I suppose, a Croesus or a Crassus, but to what end? The truly rich become conspicuous by virtue of their wealth, and such prominence is a luxury, perhaps the one luxury, I cannot afford. My road to safety lies in drawing no attention to myself.

At the next gathering of the club, that being Friday the seventh, only four of us were in attendance, Martin having either business similar to mine or the need to replenish himself at one of the multitudinous springs of life abounding in the city. By then the Whitechapel slaying was old news, and occasioned no conversation; none of us, full of the wisdom long years bring though we are, yet saw the danger from that direction.

We spoke instead of the new one. I added the tale of my brief encounter to what Martin had related at the previous meeting, and found I was not the only one to have seen the subject of our discussion. So also had Titus and Norton, both in the East End.

Neither appeared to have formed a favorable impression of the newcomer, though as was true with Martin and myself, neither had passed words with him. Said our Senior, "He may eventually make a sixth for us, but no denying he has a rougher manner than do those whose good company now serves to warm these rooms."

Norton being Norton was more plainspoken: "Like calls to like, as I said last week, and I wish it didn't."

Of those present, only Arnold had not yet set eyes on the stranger. He now enquired, "What in him engenders such aversion?"

To that none of the rest of us could easily reply, the more so as nothing substantial backed our hesitancy. At last Norton said, "He strikes me as the sort who, were he hungry, would feed on Hignett."

"On our own servant? I should sooner starve!"

"So should we all, Arnold, so should we all," Titus said soothingly, for the shock in our fellow's voice was quite apparent. Norton and I gave our vigorous agreement. Some things are not done.

We decided it more prudent for a time not to seek out the newcomer. If he showed any greater desire than heretofore for intercourse with us, he could without undue difficulty contrive to make his path cross one of ours. If not, loss of his society seemed a hardship under which we could bear up with equanimity.

Having settled that, as we thought, to our satisfaction, we adjourned at my urging to cards, over which we passed the balance of the meeting, Arnold and I losing three guineas each to Norton and Titus. There are mortals, and not a few of them too, with better card sense than Arnold's. Once we broke up, I hunted in Mayfair with good enough luck and went home.

Upon arising on the evening of the eighth, my first concern was a paper, as I had not purchased one before retiring and as the newsboys were crying them with a fervor warning that something of which I should not be ignorant had passed during the hours of my undead sleep. And so it proved: at some time near 5:30 that morning, about when I was going up to bed, the Whitechapel killer had slain again, as hideously as before, the very least of his atrocities being the cutting of his victim's throat so savagely as almost to sever her head from her body.

Every one of the entrepreneurs with whom I had dealings that evening mentioned of his own accord the murders. An awful fascination lay beneath their ejaculations of horror. I had no trouble understanding it. A madman who kills once is frightening, but one who kills twice is far more than doubly so, the second slaying portending who could say how many more to come.

This fear, not surprisingly, was all the worse among those whom the killer had marked for his own. Few tarts walked the streets the next several evenings, and such as did often went in pairs to afford themselves at least what pitiful protection numbers gave. I had a lean time of it, in which misfortune, as I learned at the next meeting of the Club, I was not alone. For the first time in some years we had not even a quorum, three of our five being absent, presumably in search of sustenance. The gathering, if by that name I may dignify an occasion on which only Arnold and I were present, was the worst I remember, and ended early, something hitherto unknown among us. Nor did my business affairs prosper in the nights that followed. I have seldom known a less pleasant period.

At length, despite our resolutions to the contrary, I felt compelled to visit the new one's haunts in the East End. I suspect I was not the first of us driven to this step. Twelve hundred drabs walk the brown-fogged streets of Whitechapel, and hunger works in them no less than in me. Fear of the knife that may come fades to insignificance when set against the rumbling of the belly that never leaves.

I did then eventually manage to gain nourishment, but only after a search long and inconvenient enough to leave me rather out of temper despite my success. Not to put too fine a point on it, I should have chosen another time to make the acquaintance of our new associate. The choice proved not to be mine to make: he hailed me as I was walking toward St. Mary's Station on Whitechapel Road.

Something in the timbre of his voice spoke to me, though I had not heard it before; even as I turned, I knew who he was. He hurried up to me and pumped my hand. We must have made a curious spectacle for those few people who witnessed our meeting. Like all members of the Sanguine Club, I dress to suit my station; moreover, formal attire with its stark blacks and whites fits my temperament, and I have been told I look well in it.

My new companion, by contrast, wore a checkered suit of cut and pattern so bold as to be more appropriate for the comedic stage than even for a swell in the streets of Whitechapel. Of his tie I will say nothing save that it made the suit stodgy by comparison. His boots were patent leather, with mother-of-pearl buttons. On his head perched a low-crowned billycock hat as evil as the rest of the rig.

I should not have been surprised to smell on his breath whiskey or more likely gin (the favored drink of Whitechapel), but must confess I could not. "Hullo, old chap," he said, his accent exactly   would expect from the clothes. "You must be one o' the toffs I've seen now and again. The name's Jack, and pleased t'meetcher.''

Still a bit nonplused at such heartiness where before he had kept his distance, I rather coolly returned my own name.

"Pleased t'meetcher," he said again, as if once were not enough. Now that he stood close by, I had the chance to study him as well as his villainous apparel. He was taller than I, and of younger seeming (though among us, I know, this is of smaller signification than is the case with mankind), with greasy side-whiskers like, you will I pray forgive me, a pimp's.

Having repeated himself, he appeared to have shot his conversational bolt, for he stood waiting for some response from me. "Do you by any chance play whist?" I asked, lacking any better query.

He threw back his head and laughed loud and long. "Blimey, no! I've better games than that, yes I do.'' He set a finger by the side of his nose and winked with a familiarity he had no right to assume.

"What are those?" I asked, seeing he expected it of me. In truth I heartily wished the encounter over. We have long made it a point to extend the privileges of the Sanguine Club to all our kind in London, but despite ancient custom I would willingly have withheld them from this Jack, whose vulgarity disbarred him from our class.

This thought must have been plain on my face, as he laughed again, less good-naturedly than before. "Why, the ones wiv dear Pollie and Annie, of course.''

The names so casually thrown out meant nothing to me for a moment. When at last I did make the connection, I took it to be no more than a joke of taste similar to the rest of his character. "Claiming yourself to be Leather Apron, sir, or whatever else the papers call that killer, is not a jest I find amusing.''

"Jest, is it?" He drew himself up, offended. "I wasn't jokin' wiv yer. Ah, Annie, she screamed once, but too late." His eyes lit in, I saw, fond memory. That more than anything else convinced me he spoke the truth.

I wished then the sign of the cross were not forbidden me. Still, I fought to believe my fear mistaken. "You cannot mean that!" I cried. "The second killing, by all accounts, was done in broad daylight, and—" I forbore to state the obvious, that none of our kind may endure Old Sol.

"Oh, it were daylight, right enough, but the sun not up. I 'ad just time to do 'er proper, then nip into my 'idin' place on

'Anbury Street. The bobbies, they never found me,'' he added with scorn in his voice for the earnest bumbling humans who sought to track him down. However much I found the thought repugnant, I saw he was truly one of us in that, his sentiment differing perhaps in degree from our own, but not in kind.

I observed also once more the relish with which he spoke of the slaying, and of his hairsbreadth escape from destruction; the sun is a greater danger to us than ever Scotland Yard will be. Still, we of the Sanguine Club have survived and flourished as we have in London by making it a point never to draw undue attention to ourselves. Being helpless by day, we are hideously vulnerable should a determined foe ever set himself against us. I said as much to Jack, most vehemently, but saw at once I was making no impression upon him.

''Aren't you the toffee-nose, now?'' he said. ''I didn't ask for no by-your-leave, and don't need one of you neither. You bloody fool, they're only people, and I'll deal wiv 'em just as I please. Go on; tell me you've not done likewise.''

To that I could make no immediate reply. I have fed innumerable times from victims who would have recoiled in loathing if in full possession of their senses. Nor am I myself guiltless of killing; few if any among us are. Yet with reflection, I think I may say I have never slain wantonly, for the mere sport of it. Such conduct must inevitably debase one who employs it, and in Jack I could not help noting the signs of that defilement. Having no regard for our prey, he would end with the same emptiness of feeling for his fellows (a process I thought already well advanced, by his rudeness toward me) and for himself. I have seen madness so many times among humanity, but never thought to detect it in one of my own.

All this is, however, as I say, the product of rumination considerably after the fact. At the time I found myself so very unnerved as to fasten on utter trivialities as if they were matters of great importance. I asked, then, not that he give over his cruel sport, but rather where he had come by the apron that gave him his sobriquet in the newspapers.

He answered without hesitation: ''Across the lane from where I done the first one is Barber's 'Orse Slaughter 'Ouse—I filched it there, just after I 'ad me bit o' fun. Fancy the fools thinkin' it 'as some meanin' to it.'' His amusement confirmed what I had already marked, that he found humanity so far beneath him that it existed but for him to do with as he wished.

Again I expostulated with him, urging him to turn from his course of slaughter.

"Bloody 'ell I will," he said coarsely. " 'Oo's to make me, any road? The bobbies? They couldn't catch the clap in an 'orehouse."

At last I began to grow angry myself, rather than merely appalled, as I had been up to this point. "If necessary, my associates and I shall prevent you. If you risked only yourself, I would say do as you please and be damned to you, but your antics threaten all of us, for if by some mischance you are captured you expose not only your own presence alone but reveal that of your kind as well. We have been comfortable in London for long years; we should not care to have to abandon it suddenly and seek to establish ourselves elsewhere on short notice."

I saw this warning, at least, hit home; Jack might despise mankind, but could scarcely ignore the threat his fellows might pose to him. "You've no right to order me about so," he said sullenly, his hands curling into fists.

"The right to self-preservation knows no bounds," I returned. "I am willing to let what is done stay done; we can hardly, after all, yield you up to the constabulary without showing them also what you are. But no more, Jack. You will have us to reckon with if you kill again."

For an instant I thought he would strike me, such was the ferocity suffusing his features. I resolved he should not relish the attempt if he made it. But he did not, contenting himself instead with turning his back and wordlessly taking himself off in the rudest fashion imaginable. I went on to the station and then to my home.

At the next meeting of the Club I discovered I had not been the only one to encounter Jack and hear his boasts. So also had Norton, who, I was pleased to learn, had issued a warning near identical to mine. If anything, he was blunter than I; Norton, as I have remarked, is not given to mincing words. Our actions met with general approbation, Martin being the only one to express serious doubt at what we had done.

As the youngest among us (he has been a member fewer than two hundred years), Martin is, I fear, rather more given than the rest of us to the passing intellectual vagaries of the mass of humanity, and has lately been much taken with what they call psychology. He said, "Perhaps this Jack acts as he does because he has been deprived of the company of his own kind, and would be more inclined toward sociability in the world as a whole if his day-to-day existence included commerce with his fellows.''

This I found a dubious proposition; having met Jack, I thought him vicious to the core, and not likely to reform merely through the good agency of the Club. Norton confined himself to a single snort, but the fashion in which he rolled his eyes was eloquent.

Titus and Arnold, however, with less acquaintance of the newcomer, eagerly embraced Martin's suggestion: the prospect of adding another to our number after so long proved irresistible to them. After some little argument, I began to wonder myself if I had not been too harsh a judge of Jack, nor did Norton protest overmuch when it was decided to tender an invitation to the Club to him for the following Friday, that is to say September twenty-first.

I remarked on Norton's reticence as we broke up, and was rewarded with a glance redolent of cynicism. ''They'll find out,'' he said, and vanished into the night.

It was with a curious mingling of anticipation and apprehension that I entered the premises of the Club for our next meeting, an exhilarating mixture whose like I had not known since the bad nights when all of mankind was superstitious enough to make our kind's every moment a risk. Titus was there before me, his features communicating the same excitement I felt. At that I knew surprise afresh, Titus having seen everything under the moon: he derives his name, after all, from that of the Roman Augustus in whose reign he was born.

''He'll come?'' I asked.

''So Martin tells me,'' replied our Senior.

And indeed it was not long before good Hignett appeared at the lounge door to announce the arrival of our guest. Being the perfect butler, he breathes discretion no less than air, yet I could hear no hint of approval in his voice. What tone he would have taken had he known more of Jack I can only imagine. Even now his eye lingered doubtfully on the newcomer, whose garments were as gaudy as the ones in which I had first met him, and which contrasted most strikingly with the sober raiment we of the Sanguine Club commonly prefer.

After leaving the port and the inevitable cheeses, Hignett retired to grant us our privacy. We spent some moments taking the measure of the stranger in our midst, while he, I should think, likewise took ours. He addressed us first, commenting, ''What a grim lot o' sobersides y'are.''

''Your plumage is certainly brighter than ours, but beneath it we are much the same," said Martin, still proceeding along the lines he had proposed at our previous session.

"Oh, balls," Jack retorted; he still behaved as though on the Whitechapel streets rather than in one of the more refined salons London boasts. Norton and I exchanged a knowing glance. Titus's raised eyebrow was eloquent as a shout.

Martin, however, remained as yet undaunted, and persisted, "But we are. The differences between you and us, whatever they may be, are as nothing when set against the difference between the lot of us on the one hand and those among whom we dwell on the other."

"Why ape 'em so, then?" asked Jack, dismissing with a sneer our crystal and plate, the overstuffed chintz chairs in which we sat, our carpets and our paneling of carved and polished oak, our gaslight which yields an illumination more like that of the sun (or so say those who can compare the two) than any previously created, in short all the amenities that serve to make the Sanguine Club the pleasant haven it is. His scorn at last made an impression upon Martin, who knew not how to respond.

"Why should we not like our comforts, sir?" Titus, as I have found in the course of our long association, is rarely at a loss for words. He continued, "We have been in straitened circumstances more often than I can readily recall, and more than I for one should care to. Let me remind you, no one compels you to share in this against your will."

"An' a good thing, too—I'd sooner drink 'orseblood from Barber's, I would, than 'ave a digs like this. Blimey, next you'll be joinin' the bleedin' Church o' Hengland."

"Now you see here!" Arnold, half-rising from his seat in anger, spoke for all of us. Horseblood is an expedient upon which I have not had to rely since the Black Death five-and-a-half centuries ago made men both too scarce and too wary to be easily approached. To this night I shudder at the memory of the taste, as do all those of us whom mischance has at one time or another reduced to such a condition. I almost found it more shocking than the notion of entering a church.

Yet Jack displayed no remorse, which indeed, as should by this point be apparent, played no part in his character. "Get on!" he said. "You might as well be people your own selves, way you carry on. They ain't but our cattle, and don't deserve better from us than they give their beasts."

"If what Jerome and Norton say is true, you give them rather worse than that," Titus said.

Jack's grin was broad and insolent. "Aye, well, we all have our sports. I like making 'em die monstrous well, better even than feeding off 'em." He drew from his belt a long sharp blade, and lowered his eyes so as to study the gleaming, polished steel. Did our reflections appear in mirrors, I should have said he was examining his features in the metal.

"But you must not act so," Titus expostulated. "Can you not grasp that your slayings endanger not you alone, but all of us? These cattle, as you call them, possess the ability to turn upon their predators and hunt us down. They must never suspect themselves to be prey."

"You talk like this bugger 'ere," said Jack, pointing in my direction. "I were wrong, guv'nor, an' own to it—it's not men the lot of yez are, it's so many old women. An' as for Jack, 'e does as 'e pleases, an' any as don't fancy it can go play wiv themselves for all 'e cares."

"Several of us have warned you of the consequences of persisting in your folly," said Titus in a voice like that of a magistrate passing sentence. "Let me say now that you may consider that warning to come from the Sanguine Club as a whole." He looked from one of us to the next, and found no dissent to his pronouncement, even Martin by this time having come to realize our now unwelcome guest was not amenable to reason.

"You try an' stop me and I'll give yer what Pollie an' Annie got," Jack shouted in a perfect transport of fury, brandishing the weapon with which he had so brutally let the life from the two poor jades. We were, however, many to his one, and not taken by surprise as had been his earlier victims. Norton seized the knife that sat among Hignett's despised cheeses. Of the rest of us, several, myself included, carried blades of our own, if not so vicious as the one Jack bore.

Balked thus even of exciting terror, Jack foully cursed us all and fled, being as I suspected too great a coward to attack without the odds all in his favor. He slammed the door behind him with violence to make my goblet of port spring from the endtable where it sat and hurtle to the floor. Only the quickness of my kind enabled me to save it from destruction and thus earn, though he would never know of it, Hignett's gratitude.

The crash of Jack's abrupt departure was still ringing in our ears when Martin most graciously turned to me and said, "You and Norton appear to have been correct; my apologies for doubting you."

"We shall have to watch him," Titus said. "I fear he will pay no heed to our advice."

"We shall also have to keep watch over Whitechapel as a whole, from this time forth," Arnold said. "He may escape our close surveillance, yet be deterred by observing our vigilance throughout the district."

"We must make the attempt, commencing this very night," Titus declared, again with no disagreement. "That is a mad dog loose on the streets of London, mad enough, I fear, to enable even the purblind humans of Scotland Yard eventually to run him to earth."

"Which will also endanger us," I put in.

"Precisely. If, however, we prevent his slaying again, the hue and cry over this pair of killings will eventually subside. As we are all gathered here now, let us agree on a rotation that will permit at least three of us to patrol Whitechapel each night, and" (here Titus paused to utter a heavy sigh) "all of us on our Fridays. Preservation here must take precedence over sociability."

There was some grumbling at that, but not much; one thing our years confer upon us is the ability to see what must be done. Hignett evinced signs of distress when we summoned him from downstairs long before the time usually appointed, and more upon being informed we should not be reconvening for some indefinite period. Not even the promise that his pay would continue heartened him to any great extent; he had grown used to our routine, and naturally resented any interruption thereof.

Having decided to patrol Whitechapel, we walked west along the south bank of the Thames past the Tower of London and the edifice that will upon its completion be known as Tower Bridge (and which would, were it complete, offer us more convenient access to the northeastern part of the city) to London Bridge and up Gracechurch Street to Fenchurch Street and Whitechapel. Once there, we separated, to cover as much ground as our limited numbers permitted.

Jack had by this time gained a considerable lead upon us; we could but hope he had worked no mischief while we were coming to the decision to pursue him. Yet the evening was still relatively young, and both of his previous atrocities had taken place in later hours, the second, indeed, so close to sunrise as to seem to me to display a heedlessness to danger suitable only to a lunatic among our kind.

I prowled the lanes near Spitalfields Market, not far from

where I had first set eyes on Jack after supping off the young whore, as I have already related. I should not have been sorry to encounter her there once more, since, I having in a manner of speaking made her acquaintance, she would not have shied from my approach, as did several ladies of the evening, and I was, if not yet ravenous, certainly growing hungry.

It must have been nearing three when I spied Jack in Crispin Street, between Dorset and Brushfield. He was coming up behind a tart when I hailed him; they both turned at the sound of my voice. "Ah, cousin Jack, how are you these days?" I called cheerily, pretending not to have noticed her. In my most solicitous tones, I continued, "The pox troubles you less, I hope?"

"Piss off!" he snarled. The damage to his cause, however, was done, for the whore speedily took herself elsewhere. He shook his fist at me. "You'll pay for that, you bugger. I only wanted a bit of a taste from 'er."

"Starve," I said coldly, our enmity now open and undisguised. Would that keeping him from his prey might have forced that fate upon him, but we do not perish so easily. Still, the hunger for blood grows maddening if long unsatisfied, and I relished his suffering hardly less than he the twin effusions of gore he had visited upon Whitechapel.

He slunk away; I followed. He employed all the tricks of our kind to throw me off his track. Against a man they would surely have succeeded, but I was ready for them and am in any case no man, though here I found myself in the curious position of defending humanity against one of my own kind gone bad. He failed to escape me. Indeed, as we went down Old Montague Street, Arnold fell in with us, and he and I kept double vigil on Jack till the sky began to grow light.

The weakness of our plan then became apparent, for Arnold and I found ourselves compelled to withdraw to our own domiciles in distant parts of the city to protect ourselves against the imminent arrival of the sun, while Jack, who evidently quartered himself in or around Whitechapel, was at liberty to carry out whatever outrage he could for some little while before finding it necessary to seek shelter. A similar period of freedom would be his after every sunset, as we would have to travel from our homes to the East End and locate him afresh each night. Still, I reflected as I made my way out of the slums toward Knightsbridge, in the early hours of the evening people swarmed through the streets, making the privacy and leisure required for his crimes hard to come by. That gave me some small reason, at least, to hope.

Yet I must confess that when nightfall restored my vitality I departed from my flat with no little trepidation, fearing to learn of some new work of savagery during the morning twilight. The newsboys were, however, using other means to cry their papers, and I knew relief. The concern of getting through each night was new to me, and rather invigorating; it granted a bit of insight into the sort of existence mortals must lead.

That was not one of the nights assigned me to wander through Whitechapel, nor on my next couple of tours of duty there did I set eyes on Jack. The newspapers made no mention of fresh East End horrors though, so the Sanguine Club was performing as well as Titus could have wished.

Our Senior, however, greeted me with grim and troubled countenance as we met on Fenchurch Street early in the evening of the twenty-seventh, preparatory to our nightly Whitechapel vigil. He drew from his waistcoat pocket an envelope which he handed to me, saying, "The scoundrel grows bolder. I stopped by the Club briefly last night to pay my respects to Hignett, and found this waiting there for us."

The note the envelope contained was to the point, viz.: "You dear chums aren't as clever as you think. You won't catch me if I don't want that. And remember, you haven't found my address but I know where this place is. Give me trouble—not that you really can—and the peelers will too. Yours, Jack the Ripper."

"The Ripper, is it?" My lip curled at the grotesque sobriquet, and also at the tone of the missive and the threat it conveyed. Titus perfectly understood my sentiments, having no doubt worked through during the course of the previous night the thought process now mine.

He said, "We shall have to consider harsher measures than we have contemplated up to this point. A menace to the Club is a menace to us all, individually and severally."

I nodded my affirmation. Yet to suppress Jack we had first to find him, which proved less easy than heretofore. Norton and I met in the morning twilight of the twenty-eighth at St. Mary's Station without either one of us having set eyes on him. "He may be staying indoors for fear of our response to his note," I said, having first informed Norton of the letter's contents.

My dour colleague gloomily shook his head. "He fears nothing, else he would not have sent it in the first place." Norton paused a while in silent thought—an attitude not uncommon for him—then continued, "My guess is, he is merely deciding what new atrocity to use to draw attention to himself." I did not care for this conclusion but, in view of Jack's already demonstrated proclivities, hardly found myself in position to contradict it.

The night of Saturday the twenty-ninth found me in the East End once more. Most of the previous evening, when under happier circumstances the Sanguine Club would have met, I spent beating down a most stubborn man over the price of a shipment of copra, and was sorely tempted to sink teeth into his neck afterward to repay him for the vexation and delay he caused me. I had not thought the transaction would take above an hour, but the wretch haggled over every farthing. Titus was most annoyed at my failure to join our prearranged patrol, and I counted myself fortunate that Jack again absented himself as well.

Early in the evening I thought I caught a glimpse of Jack by London Hospital as I was coming down Mount Street from Whitechapel Road, but though I hastened up and down Oxford Street, and Philpot and Turner which come off it, I could find no certain trace. Full of vague misgivings, I turned west onto Commercial Road.

Midnight passed, and I still had no idea of my quarry's whereabouts. I had by chance encountered both Martin and Arnold, who shared the night with me, and learned of their equal lack of success. "I believe he must still be in hiding, in the hope of waiting us out," Arnold said.

"If so," I replied, "he is in yet another way a fool. Does he think us mortals, to grow bored after days or weeks and let down our guard?"

The answer to that soon became all too clear. At one or so a great outcry arose on Berner Street, scarcely a hundred yards from Commercial Road where I had walked but a short while before. As soon as I heard the words "Leather Apron," I knew Jack had chosen to strike again in defiance not only of human London, but also of the Sanguine Club, and also that he had succeeded in evading us, making good on the boast in his recent note.

I started to rush toward the scene of this latest crime, but had not gone far before I checked myself. I reasoned that Jack could scarcely strike again in or close to such a crowd, if that was his desire, but would take advantage of the confusion this murder engendered, and of the natural attraction of the constabulary in the area to it. It was Norton's reasoning that made me fear Jack would not be content with a single slaying, but might well look at once for a fresh victim to demonstrate everyone's impotence in bringing him to heel.

My instinct proved accurate, yet I was unfortunately not in time to prevent Jack's next gruesome crime; that I came so close only served to frustrate me more thoroughly than abject failure would have done. I was trotting west along Fenchurch Street, about to turn down Jewry Street to go past the Fenchurch Street Station, as the hour approached twenty of two, when suddenly there came to my nose the thick rich scent of fresh-spilled blood.

Being who I am, that savory aroma draws me irresistibly, and I am by the nature of things more sensitive to it by far than is a man, or even, I should say, a hound. Normally it would have afforded me only pleasure, but now I felt alarm as well, realizing that the large quantity required to produce the odor in the intensity with which I perceived it could only have come from the sort of wounds Jack delighted in inflicting.

I followed my nose up Mitre Street to a courtyard off the roadway, where, as I had feared, lay the body of a woman. Despite the sweetness of the blood-tang rising intoxicatingly from her and from the great pool of gore on the paving, I confess with shame to drawing back in horror, for not only had she been eviscerated, but her throat was slashed, her features mutilated almost beyond identity, and part of one earlobe nearly severed from her head.

I had time to learn no more than that, or to feed past the briefest sampling, for I heard coming up Mitre Street the firm, uncompromising tread likely in that part of the city to belong only to a bobby, footpads and whores being more circumspect and men of good conscience in short supply. I withdrew from the court, thankful for my ability to move with silence and not to draw the eye if I did not wish it. Hardly a minute later, the blast of a police whistle pierced the night as humanity discovered this latest piece of Jack's handiwork.

As I once more walked Mitre Street, I discovered the odor of blood to be diminishing less rapidly than I should have expected. Looking down, I discovered a drop on the pavement. I stooped to taste of it; I could not doubt its likeness to that which I had just tried. A bit further along the street was another. I hastened down this track, hoping also to discover one of my fellows to lend me assistance in overpowering Jack. As if in answer to my wish, up came Martin from a sidestreet, drawn like me by the pull of blood. Together we hastened after Jack.

The drippings from his hand or knife soon ceased, yet the

alluring aroma still lingering in the air granted us a trail we could have followed blindfolded. I wondered how Jack hoped to escape pursuers of our sort, but soon found he knew the East End better than did Martin or myself, and was able to turn that knowledge to his advantage.

On Goldstone Street, in front of the common stairs leading to Numbers 108 to 119, stood a public sink. It was full of water, water which my nose at once informed me to be tinctured with blood: here Jack had paused to rinse from this hands the traces of his recent deeds. Martin found also a bit of bloodstained black cloth similar to that of a garment the latest unfortunate victim had worn.

At the base of the sink, close by the piece of fabric, lay a lump of chalk. I picked it up and tossed it in the air idly once or twice, then, thinking back on Jewry Street where I had been when first I detected Jack's newest abomination, was seized by inspiration. The Jews of London form a grouping larger than we of the Sanguine Club, yet hardly less despised than we would become were Jack's insanity finally to expose our identity to the general populace. How better, thought I, to distract suspicion from us than by casting it upon others themselves in low repute? Above the sink, then, I chalked, "The Jewes are the men who will not be blamed for nothing," a message ambiguous enough, or so I hoped, to excite attention without offering any definite information. And when Martin would have removed the blood-stained cloth, I prevailed on him to replace it, to draw the eyes and thoughts of the constabulary to my scrawled note.

Martin and I then attempted to resume our pursuit, but unsuccessfully. In washing himself and, I believe, cleansing his blade on the rag from his victim's apron, he removed the lingering effluvium by which we had followed him, and forced us to rely once more on chance to bring us into proximity to him. Chance did not prove kind, even when we separated in order to cover more ground than would have been possible in tandem. Just as he had bragged, Jack had slain again (and slain twice!), eluding all attempts to stay his hand.

I was mightily cast down in spirit as I traveled homeward in the morning twilight. Nor did the clamor in the papers the next evening and during the nights that followed serve to assuage my anxiety. "Revolting and mysterious," "horrible," and "ghastly" were among the epithets they applied to the slayings; "Whitechapel horrors," shrieked *The Illustrated Police News*. It was, however, a subhead in that same paper which truly gave me cause for concern: it spoke of the latest "victim of the White-chapel Fiend," a designation whose aptness I knew only too well, and one which I could only hope would not be literally construed.

Titus must also have seen that paper and drawn the same conclusion as had I. When I came to myself on the evening of the second I found in my postbox a note in his classic hand. "Henceforward we must all fare forth nightly," he wrote, "to prevent a repetition of these latest acts of depravity. We owe this duty not only to ourselves but to our flock, lest they suffer flaying rather than the judicious shearing we administer."

Put so, the plea was impossible to withstand. All of us prowled the sordid streets of Whitechapel the next few nights, and en-countered one another frequently. Of Jack, however, we found no sign; once more he chose to hide himself in his lair. Yet none of us, now, was reassured on that account, and when he did briefly sally forth he worked as much mischief, almost, without spilling a drop of blood as he had with his knife.

We failed to apprehend him in his forays, but their results soon became apparent. The lunatic, it transpired, had not merely written to us of the Sanguine Club, but also, in his arrogance, to the papers and the police! They, with wisdom unusual in humans, had suppressed his earliest missive, sent around the same time as the one to us, perhaps being uncertain as to its authenticity, but he sent another note after the horrid morning of the thirtieth, boasting of what he termed his "Double Event." As the police had not yet announced the murders, not even men could doubt its genuineness.

Once more the press went mad, filled with lurid rehashes and speculations, some claiming the Ripper (for so he had styled himself also in his public letters) to be a man seeking to stamp out the vice of prostitution (presumably by extirpating those who plied the trade), others taking varying psychological tacks which intrigued our faddish Martin with their crackbrained ingenuity and left the rest of us sourly amused, still others alleging Jack a deranged *shochet*.

"Your work takes credit there, Jerome," Titus remarked to me as we chanced upon each other one evening not far from the place where Jack's last victim had died. "A madman of a ritual slaughterer fits the particulars of the case well."

"The Jews always make convenient scapegoats," I replied.

"How true," Titus murmured, and again I was reminded of the Caesar for whom he had been named.

Other, darker conjectures also saw print, though, ones I could not view without trepidation. For those Jack himself was responsible, due to a bit of sport he had had with the police after his second killing. After slaying Annie Chapman, he had torn two rings from her fingers and set them with some pennies and a pair of new-minted farthings at her feet. This he had wasted time to do, I thought with a frisson of dread, as the sun was on the point of rising and ending his amusements forever! It naturally brought to mind black, sorcerous rituals of unknown but doubtless vile purpose, and thoughts of sorcery and of matters in any way unmundane were the last things I desired to see inculcated in the folk of London.

I did my best to set aside my worries. For all Jack's dark skill, murder no longer came easy in Whitechapel. Aside from us of the Sanguine Club, the constabulary increased their patrols in the district, while a certain Mr. George Lusk established a Whitechapel Vigilance Committee whose membership also went back and forth through the area.

Neither constables nor committee members, I noted during my own wanderings, refrained from enjoying the occasional streetwalker, but the women themselves took more pleasure from those encounters than they should have from a meeting with Jack. The same also holds true for the whores we of the Club engaged. As I have previously noted, the wounds we inflicted healed quickly, the only aftereffect being perhaps a temporary lassitude if one of us fed overdeep because of unusual hunger.

Jack may have taken a hiatus from slaughter, but remained intent on baiting those who so futilely pursued him. October was not yet a week old when he showed his scorn for the Whitechapel Vigilance Committee by means of a macabre gift to its founder: he sent Mr. Lusk, in a neatly wrapped cardboard box, half the kidney of his latest victim, with a mocking note enclosed.

"He will be the ruin of us all," I said gloomily to Martin upon the papers' disclosure of this new ghoulery. "Would you had never set eyes on him."

"With that I cannot take issue," replied my colleague, "yet this lapse, however revolting humans may find it—and I confess," he added with a fastidious shudder, "to being repelled myself at the prospect of eating a piece from a woman's kidney— however revolting, I say, it does not add to any fears directed toward us, for none of our kind would do such a deed, not even Jack, I should say."

"One never knows, where he is concerned," I said, and Martin's only response was a glum nod.

As October wore on, more letters came to the papers and police, each one setting off a new flurry of alarm. Some of these may indeed have been written by Jack; others, I suspect, sprang from the pens of men hardly less mad than he, and fully as eager for notoriety. Men have so little time to make their mark that such activity is in them at least faintly comprehensible, but for Jack, with years beyond limit before him, I offer no explanation past simple viciousness. In his instance, that was more than adequate.

Still, despite sensations such as I have described, the month progressed with fresh slayings. Once I dashed a couple of furlongs down Old Montague Street into Baker's Row, drawn as on the night of the Double Event by the scent of blood, but discovered only a stabbed man of middle years with his pockets turned out: a matter in which the police were certain to take an interest, but not one, I was confident, that concerned me.

My business affairs suffered somewhat during this period, but not to any irreparable extent; at bottom they were sound, and not liable to sudden disruption. I thought I would miss the weekly society of the Sanguine Club to a greater degree than proved to be the case. The truth is that we of the Club saw more of one another in our wanderings through Whitechapel than we had at our meetings.

October passed into November, the nights growing longer but less pleasant, being now more liable to chill and to wet fogs. These minor discomforts aside, winter long has been our kind's favorite season of the year, especially since coming to this northern latitude where around the December solstice we may be out and about seventeen hours of the twenty-four, and fifteen even in the mid-autumnal times to which my narrative now has come. Yet with Jack abroad, the increased period of darkness seemed this year no boon, as I was only capable of viewing it as a greater opportunity for him to sally forth on another murderous jaunt.

On the evening of the eighth, then, I reached Whitechapel before the clocks struck five. By the time they chimed for six, I had already encountered in the narrow, gridless streets Norton, Arnold, and Titus. We tipped our hats each to the other as we passed. I saw Martin for the first time that night shortly after six. We were complete, as ready as we might be should the chance present itself.

The night gave at the outset no reason for supposing it likely to prove different from any other. I wandered up toward Bish-opsgate Station, having learned that the whore who was Jack's latest victim had been released from there not long before her last, fatal encounter. "Ta-ta, old cock, I'll see you again soon!" she had called drunkenly to the gaoler, a prediction that, unfor-tunately for her, was quickly proven inaccurate.

Wherever Jack prowled, if indeed he was on the loose at that hour, I found no trace of him. Seeing that so many prostitutes passed through the station, I made it a point to hang about: Jack might well seek in those environs an easy target. Whores indeed I saw in plenty thereabouts but, as I say, no sign of Jack. When the clocks struck twelve, ushering in a new day, I gave it up and went to hunt elsewhere.

Walking down Dorset Street near twelve-thirty, I heard a woman with an Irish lilt to her voice singing in a room on one of the courtyards there. I paused a moment to listen; such good spirits are rarely to be found in Whitechapel. Then I continued east, going by London Hospital and the Jews' Cemetery, my route in fact passing the opening of Buck's Row onto Brady Street, close to the site of Jack's first killing.

That area proved no more profitable than had been my prior wanderings of the night—no more profitable, indeed, than the whole of the past five weeks' exertions on the part of the San-guine Club. True, I am more patient than a man, but even pa-tience such as mine desires some reward, some hint that it is not employed in pursuit of an *ignis fatuus*. As I lacked any such hint, it was with downcast mien that I turned my steps westward once more.

My nostrils began to twitch before I had any conscious aware-ness of the fact. I was on Wentworth Street between Commercial and Goulston, when at last my head went suddenly up and back, as I have seen a wolf's do on taking a scent. Blood was in the air, and had been for some little while. Yet like a wolf which scents its prey at a distance, I had to cast about to find the precise source of the odor.

In this search I was unsurprised to encounter Norton, who was coming down Flower and Dean Street toward Commercial. His features bore the same abstracted set I knew appeared on my own. "Odd sort of trail," he said without preamble, as is his way.

"It is." I tested the air again. "The source lies north of us still, I am certain, but more precise than that I cannot be. It is not like the spoor I took from Jack's last pleasantry."

"A *man* could have followed that, from what you said of it," Norton snorted, and though he spoke in jest I do not think him far wrong. He continued, "Let us hunt together."

I agreed at once, and we proceeded side by side up Commercial (which in the dark and quiet of the small hours belied its name) to a corner where, after deliberation, we turned west onto White Street rather than east on Fashion. Well that we did, for hurrying in our direction from Bishopsgate came Titus. His strides, unlike our own, had nothing of doubt to them. Being our Senior, he is well-supplied with hunters' lore.

"Well met!" he cried on recognizing us. "This way! We have him, unless I miss my guess!" Practically at a run, he swept us north along Crispin Street to Dorset, the very ground I had patrolled not long before.

The scent trail was stronger now, but remained curiously diffuse. "How do you track with such confidence?" I asked.

"That is much blood, escaping but slowly to the outside air," Titus replied. "I think our quarry has taken his atrocious games indoors, in hopes of thwarting us. He has been—you will, I pray, pardon the play on words—too sanguine in his expectations."

His proposed explanation so precisely fit the spoor we were following that I felt within me the surge of hope I recently described as lacking. A much-battered signboard on the street read "Miller's Court"; it was the one from which I had earlier heard song. A light burned in Number 13. From that door, too, welled the scent which had drawn us; now that we had come so close, its source could not be mistaken.

As our tacit leader, Titus grasped the doorknob, Norton and I standing behind him to prevent Jack from bursting past and fleeing. Jack evidently had anticipated no disturbances, for the door was not locked. On Titus's opening it, the blood smell came forth as strongly as ever I have known it, save only on the battlefield.

The scene I glimpsed over Titus's shoulder will remain with me through all my nights. Our approach had taken Jack unawares, he being so intent on his pleasure that the world beyond the squalid little room was of no import to him. A picture-nail in his hand, he stared at us in frozen shock from his place by the wall.

Both my eyes and nose, though, drew me away from him to the naked flesh on the bed. I use that appellative in preference to body, for with leisure at his disposal Jack gained the opportunity to exercise his twisted ingenuity to a far greater and more grisly extent than he had on the streets of Whitechapel. The chamber more closely resembled an abattoir than a lodging.

By her skin, such of it as was not covered with blood, the poor wretch whose abode this presumably had been was younger than the previous objects of his depravity. Whether she was fairer as well I cannot say, as he had repeatedly slashed her face and sliced off her nose and ears to set them on a bedside table. The only relief for her was that she could have known none of this, as her throat was cut; it gaped at me like a second, speechless mouth.

Nor had Jack contented himself with working those mutilations. Along with her nose and ears on that table lay her heart, her kidneys (another offering, perhaps, to George Lusk), and her breasts, his gory handprints upon them. He had gutted her as well.

Not even those horrors were the worst. When we interrupted him, Jack was engaged in hanging bits of the woman's flesh on the wall, as if they were engravings the effect of whose placement he was examining.

The tableau that held us all could not have endured above a few seconds. Jack first recovered the power of motion, and waved in invitation to the blood-drenched sheets. "Plenty there for the lot o' yez," said he, grinning.

So overpowering was the aroma hanging in the room that my tongue of itself ran across my lips, and my head swung toward that scarlet swamp. So, I saw, did Titus's. Norton, fortunately, was made of sterner stuff, and was not taken by surprise when Jack tried to spring past us. Their grapple recalled to our senses the Senior and myself, and I seized Jack's wrist as he tried to take hold of his already much-used knife, which, had it found one of our hearts, could have slain us as certainly as if we were mortal.

In point of fact, Jack did score Norton's arm with the blade before Titus rapped his hand against the floor and sent the weapon skittering away. Norton cursed at the pain of the cut, but only for a moment, as it healed almost at once. The struggle, being three against one, did not last long after that. Having subdued Jack and stuffed a silk handkerchief in his mouth to prevent his crying out, we dragged him from the dingy cubicle out into Mitre Court.

Just then, likely drawn by the fresh outpouring of the blood scent from the newly opened door of Number 13, into the court rushed Martin, and the stout fellow had with him a length of rope for use in the event that Jack should be captured, an eventuality for which he, perhaps inspirited by youthful optimism, was more prepared than were we his elders. We quickly trussed our quarry and hauled him away to obtain more certain privacy in which to decide his fate.

We were coming out of Mitre Court onto Dorset Street when I exclaimed, "The knife!"

"What of it? Let it be," Titus said. Norton grunted in agreement.

On most occasions, the one's experience and the other's sagacity would have been plenty to persuade me to accede to their wishes, but everything connected with Jack, it seemed, was out of the ordinary. I shook my head, saying, "That blade has fleshed itself in you, Norton. Men in laboratories are all too clever these days; who knows what examination of the weapon might reveal to them?"

Martin supported me, and my other two colleagues saw the force of my concern: why stop Jack if we gave ourselves away through the mute testimony of the knife? I dashed into Number 13 once more, found the blade, and tucked it into the waistband of my trousers. I found coherent thought in that blood-charged atmosphere next to impossible, but realized it would be wise to screen the horrid and pathetic corpse on the bed from view. Accordingly, I shut the door and dragged up a heavy bureau to secure it, only then realizing I was still inside myself.

Feeling very much a fool, I climbed to the top of the chest of drawers, broke out a pane of glass, and awkwardly scrambled down outside. I hurried to catch up to my comrades, who were conveying Jack along Commercial Street. As he was most unwilling, this would have attracted undue attention from passersby, save that we do not draw men's notice unless we wish it.

We turned off onto Thrawl Street and there, in the shelter of a recessed doorway, held a low-voiced discussion. "He must perish; there is no help for it," Martin declared. To this statement none of us dissented. Jack glared mute hatred at us all.

"How then?" said I. I drew forth Jack's own knife. "Shall I drive this into his breast now, and put an end to it?" The plan had a certain poetic aptness I found appealing.

Martin nodded approvingly, but Titus, to my surprise, demurred. He explained, "Had I not observed this latest outrage, Jerome, I should have no complaint. But having seen it, my judgment is that the punishment you propose errs in the excessive mercy it would grant."

"What then?" I cast about for some harsher fate, but arrived only at the obvious. "Shall we leave him, bound, for the sun to find?" I have never seen the effects of sunlight on the flesh of our kind, of course; had I been in position to observe it, I should not now be able to report our conversation. Yet instinctively we know what we risk. It is said to be spectacularly pyrotechnic.

Jack's writhings increased when he heard my proposal. He had dared the sun to kill for his own satisfaction, but showed no relish for facing it without choice. Our Senior coldly stared down at him. "You deserve worse."

"So he does," Norton said. "However much the sun may pain him, it will only be for a little while. He ought instead to have eternity to contemplate his failings."

"How do you propose to accomplish that?" asked Martin. "Shall we store him away in the basement of the Sanguine Club? Watch him as we will, one day he may effect his escape and endanger us all over again."

"I'd not intended that," replied Norton.

"What then?" Titus and I demanded together.

"I say we take him to the Tower Bridge now building, and brick him up in one of its towers. Then every evening he will awaken to feel the traffic pounding close by, yet be powerless to free himself from his little crypt. He will get rather hungry, bye and bye."

The image evoked by Norton's words made the small hairs prickle up at the nape of my neck. To remain forever in a tiny, black, airless chamber, to feel hunger grow and grow and grow, and not to be able even to perish . . . were he not already mad, such incarceration would speedily render Jack so.

"Ah, most fitting indeed," Titus said in admiration. Martin and I both nodded; Norton's ingenuity was a fitting match for that which Jack had displayed. Lifting the miscreant, we set off for the bridge, which lay only a couple of furlongs to the south of us. Our untiring strength served us well as we bore Jack thither. His constant struggles might have exhausted a party of men, or at the least persuaded them to knock him over the head.

Although we draw little notice from mortals when we do not wish it, the night watchman spied our approach and turned his lantern on us. " 'Ere, wot's this?" he cried, seeing Jack's helpless figure in our arms.

We were, however, prepared for this eventuality. Martin sprang forward, to sink his teeth into the watchman's hand. At once the fellow, under the influence of our comrade's spittle, grew calm and quiet. Titus, Norton, and I pressed onto the unfinished span of the bridge and into its northern tower, Martin staying behind to murmur in the watchman's ear and guide his dreams so he should remember nothing out of the ordinary.

The other three of us fell to with a will. The bricklayers had left the tools of their trade when they went home for the night. "Do you suppose they will notice their labor is further advanced than when they left it?" I asked, slapping a brick into place.

Titus brought up a fresh hod of mortar. "I doubt they will complain of it, if they should," he said, with the slightest hint of chuckle in his voice, and I could not argue with him in that.

Norton paused a moment from his labor to stir Jack with his foot. "Nor will this one complain, not while the sun's in the sky. And by the time it sets tomorrow, they'll have built well past him." He was right in that; already the tower stood higher than the nearby Tower of London from which the bridge derives its name. Norton continued, "After that, he can shout as he pleases, and think on what he's done to merit his new home."

Soon, what with our unstinting effort, Jack's receptacle was ready to receive him. We lifted him high, set him inside, and bricked him up. I thought I heard him whimpering behind his gag, but he made no sound loud enough to penetrate the masonry surrounding him. That was also massive enough to keep him from forcing his way out, bound as he was, while the cement joining the bricks remained unset. He would eventually succeed in scraping through the ropes that held him, but not before daybreak . . . and the next night would be too late.

"There," said Norton when we had finished, "is a job well done."

Nodding, we went back to reclaim Martin, who left off charming the night watchman. That worthy stirred as he came back to himself. He touched his grizzled forelock. "You chaps 'ave a good evenin' now," he said respectfully as we walked past him. We were none too soon, for the sky had already begun to pale toward morning.

"Well, my comrades, I shall see you this evening," Titus said as we prepared to go our separate ways. I am embarrassed to confess that I, along with the rest of us, stared at him in some puzzlement over the import of his words. Had we not just vanquished Jack? Seeing our confusion, he burst out laughing: "Have you forgotten, friends, it will be Club night?" As a matter of fact, we had, having given the day of the week but scant regard in our unceasing pursuit of Jack.

On boarding my train at St. Mary's Station, I found myself in the same car as Arnold, who as luck would have it had spent the entire night in the eastern portion of Whitechapel, which accounted for his nose failing to catch the spoor that led the rest of us to Jack; he had entered the train at Whitechapel Station, half a mile east of my own boarding point. He fortunately took in good part my heckling over his absence.

After so long away, our return to the comforts of the Sanguine Club proved doubly delightful, and stout Hignett's welcome flattering in the extreme. Almost I found myself tempted to try eating cheese for his sake, no matter that it should render me ill, our kind not being suited to digest it.

Despite the desire I and, no doubt, the rest of us felt to take the opportunity to begin to return to order our interrupted affairs, all of us were present that evening to symbolize the formal renewal of our weekly fellowship. We drank to the Queen and to the Club, and also all drank again to an unusual third toast proposed by Titus: "To the eternal restoration of our security!" Indeed, at that we raised a cheer and flung our goblets into the fireplace. A merrier gathering of the Club I cannot recall.

And yet now, in afterthought, I wonder how permanent our settlement of these past months' horrors shall prove. I was not yet in London when Peter of Colechurch erected Old London Bridge seven centuries ago, but recall well the massive reconstruction undertaken by Charles Lebelye, as that was but a hundred thirty years gone by; and there are still men alive who remember the building of New London Bridge in its place by John Rennie, Jr., from the plans of his father six decades ago.

Who can be certain Tower Bridge will not someday have a similar fate befall it, and release Jack once more into the world, madder and more savage even than before? As the French say, *"Tout passe, tout casse, tout lasse"*—everything passes, everything perishes, everything palls. We of the Sanguine Club, to whom the proverb does not apply, know its truth better than most. Still, even by our standards, Jack surely will not find freedom soon. If and when he should, that, I daresay, will be time for our concern.

Lest unwary readers reckon this story the product of a diseased mind, they should know it is the product of two. My longtime friend Kevin R. Sandes must bear his full share of responsibility for its contents; so must the Anheuser-Busch Corporation. I don't normally compose surrounded by potables. This once, it seemed to work.

THE BORING BEAST

AN EXCERPT, O PRINCE, FROM AN ANCIENT chronicle:

A brisk westerly breeze drove the galley *Wasteful* into the port of Zamorazamaria. At the *Wasteful*'s helm stood Condom, the Trojan, one massive fist clamped round the wheel. The other clutched a skin of wine. Six feet and a span in height, he would have been taller yet had the fickle gods favored him with a forehead. Only a leather kilt hid his bronze skin and bulging thews from the sun. His hide was crisscrossed with scars, all too many of them self-inflicted.

A sudden roll spoiled his aim, spilling wine over his face and down his lantern jaw. Muttering an oath, he groped for a rag—and the ship's ram crunched into the side of a beamy merchantman tied up at a Zamorazamarian quay.

Condom took in the situation with one fuddled glance. "Back oars!" he bellowed. The ram pulled free, and the merchantman, a six-foot hole torn in her flank, promptly began to sink. Her crew scrambled like fleas on a drowning dog, cursing and screaming and diving over the side.

"What's going on here?" shrilled Captain Mince, emerging from his cabin. "How is a person to sleep with this crashing about? Why, I was thrown clear out of my hammock, and I ripped my new culottes." He fingered the pink silk regretfully. The cries of the foundering ship's sailors drew his gaze. "Condom, how clumsy of you!" he exclaimed, slapping the barbarian's muscly buttocks.

"Captain, I told you I'd break your arm if you did that again."

"You know I despise rough trade. Let's see if we can't give these dears some help, shall we?"

158

While Mince bickered with the dripping, furious merchants, his crew, Condom among them, roared into the dives and bordels of the decaying harbor district. The Trojan got hopelessly lost in the twisting back streets of Zamorazamaria. He put his faith in his innate barbarian instincts. Stepping up to the first man he saw, he wrapped an overmuscled arm round the fellow's neck and growled, "Tell me where the nearest grogshop is before I tear your head off!"

The man's mouth moved soundlessly. His hands scrabbled at Condom's flexors. The mighty warrior loosed his grip a trifle. Gasping, the man wheezed, "The Lusty Widow is two doors down. Its name is spelled out right in front."

Condom could not read six different languages. "Thanks, bud!" he said, giving his benefactor a slap on the back that sent him reeling into the curbside offal. Condom swaggered down the street until, with the keen-honed senses of the barbarian, his nose caught the sweet scent of beer.

Shaking his square-cut mane of black hair from his dull blue eyes, he strode into the tavern and threw himself into a chair. It collapsed. He picked himself up, only to face the irate proprietress bearing down on him with a bludgeon. She had time for one quick curse before Condom, whose sense of chivalry was rude indeed, decked her with a right. He snarled, "I want beer and I want quiet. After three bloody months cruising with Captain Mince, I *need* beer!"

She crawled away to fetch it. Condom settled back in a new, stronger chair for some serious drinking. Little did he suspect (which was true most of the time) that he was being watched from afar. Know, O Prince, that in long-ago Zamorazamaria lived the infamous necromancer, wizard, and unholy priest Sloth-Amok. He dwelt in his dark Tower of the Bat like a spider in its web, controlling the lives and destinies of the port city's inhabitants.

Sloth-Amok was a tall, dingy man, with scaly shoulders and aloof, toadlike features. From warty skull to webbed feet, his skin was a deep, venomous green. His bulbous eyes peered into a scrying-cauldron of cold split pea soup. "Heh-heh." He chuckled, flicking a fly from his eyebrow with his long pink tongue. He turned to his familiar, whose name was Gulp, saying, " 'Tis a pity one so stupid as Condom, the Trojan, must die, but die he shall, for I have read in the guano of a thousand starlings that he is the only man alive who might thwart my schemes."

His familiar leered evilly and slobbered, "Can I help, master? Does master want poor ugly Gulp to help?"

"Indeed you may, good Gulp. And I know how." The wizard strode to a table across the chamber; it was there that he conducted his most fiendish experiments. The wooden surface was strewn with eye of newt, toe of frog, wing of bat, ring of bat, rope of bat, mobile of bat, and other exotica. The sorcerer produced a bowl filled with puffy-looking purple stuff. "This is it, Gulp!"

" 'It,' master?"

"Yes, it! You bear in your gnarled paws the downfall of Condom, the Trojan."

"It seems no more than a common plum duff, your malignity."

"You are wrong, good Gulp, for there is nothing common about it. You gaze upon a masterpiece of inventive sorcery: the world's first exploding plum duff!"

Gulp blinked, swallowed nervously. "An exploding plum duff? Will it work, master?"

"Do you doubt me, worm in the pomegranate of life? Of course it will work. Never has it failed me."

"But, master, you said this was the first—"

"Never mind what I said, dolt of a familiar. We must now prepare your steed." Sloth-Amok's lithe, webbed fingers moved in the intricate passes of a spell he alone knew. Gulp cowered, terrified by the abyssal forces the great sorcerer so easily overcame. There was a puff of smoke, a reek of tuna, and a thirty-foot flying fish lay flopping on the stone floor of Sloth-Amok's chamber.

Gulp gulped. "Master, are you sure—"

"Quick, fool," Sloth-Amok cried, pressing the deadly pudding into his familiar's sweaty palm. "Look not a gift fish in the mouth. Ere it perish, mount and fly to the Lusty Widow!"

Condom was still swilling swinishly when Gulp, wearing a fearful expression and loud pantaloons, slunk into the tavern. Outside in the street his mount was gasping its last. Condom looked up muzzily. "Hey," he said. "You look familiar."

"I am."

"Have a beer."

Gulp set his murderous yummy under Condom's chair while the Trojan drank, then drained his own tankard and fled. A cry of dismay floated into the grogshop when he found his charger covered by a wriggling carpet of starving dockside cats. He scuttled down the street and back toward Sloth-Amok's lair.

He had not been gone long when Condom discovered the plum duff. "Blow my nose!" he exclaimed. "This must be a gift from the gods!" Not pausing to think twice (or even once), he downed the entire bowlful. He sat back with a contented sigh and raised his jack to his lips, but, before he could swallow, Sloth-Amok's hideous plan went into effect. The plum duff exploded.

Now, during his tour aboard the *Wasteful*, Condom had acquired a cast-iron stomach (in fact, he had won it at dice). Thus the Trojan, instead of spattering off the walls of the Lusty Widow, but felt his innards give a tremendous jerk.

Trembling, he leaped to his feet. He opened his mouth to gasp for air, but found himself belching instead. The deep bass roar echoed through the city. Birds fell from the sky, stunned by the concussion. And Condom, internal tremor satisfied, thumped his chest, sat down, and drank more beer.

Sloth-Amok had seen everything in his vat of soup. He shrieked with rage and danced about his chamber, ripping warts from his forehead and hurling them to the floor. The scrying-cauldron erupted, splattering split peas over his second-best robe. "What's this," he cackled, peering into the seething mass. "By the earwax of Hiram, god of small puddles, Condom shall not escape me!"

The Trojan was still feeling the aftereffects of his cataclysmic belch when a mysterious figure sat down beside him, its form and features hidden by a dark robe and hood. With the inborn suspicion of the barbarian, Condom growled, "Hey, you got another one of them plum duffs like the last fellow brung? It was good!"

A soft, serious voice answered him: "Of plum duffs I know nothing, good sir. I seek a mighty warrior, yclept Condom, the Trojan. Know you such a man?"

His low brow furrowed, as if in thought. "I heard the name somewheres. . . . Wait a minute! That's me!"

"Truly? Then you must come with me, and quickly, for my mistress is in desperate peril!"

"Where's that? I don't know my way past the docks too good."

The stranger swept back the hood of the robe. She proved to be a beautiful maiden, her fine features twisted in an exasperated pout. She rose, saying, "Come with me, great hero. My mistress, the princess Zamaria, has great need for aid only a champion like yourself can provide."

"Zamaria, huh?" Lustful thoughts ran through Condom's head like pigs through a wallow: if this was a serving-wench, the princess had to be even more luscious. "Sure thing, honey. Take me to her." He fumbled at his purse (a gift from Captain Mince), but the maiden impatiently drew a gold bracelet from her arm and tossed it on the table.

In his sanctum Sloth-Amok laughed to himself. He hurried to a book of lore, riffling its pages to the cantrip he had in mind. Once sure it was within his capacity, he slammed the book shut and began the spell.

Quickly mixing philosopher's stone (kidney, he thought, would be better than gall), tongue of toad, parsley, sage, rosemary, and a pinch of potent garfunkel root, he simmered them at medium heat for two minutes, tossed in a maraschino cherry, and cried out words of power. His magic done, he sank back on a bed of nails, exulting, "At last! Now the Trojan twit is done forever!"

A pit suddenly yawned beneath Condom. Princess Zamaria's maidservant sprang back with a shriek of horror, but the stalwart Trojan, unfazed at this terrifying apparition, stooped and picked it up. "Geez, this musta come from a sleepy peach," he said, chucking it into the gutter.

Baring his unbrushed teeth in an agony of frustrated fury, Sloth-Amok threw a year's supply of freeze-dried dragon blood, two sorcerous tomes, and a slightly used dwarf into his furnace. Little millipedes scurried from his leggings.

The serving-maid and Condom entered the royal palace through a secret doorway opening in the middle of a crumbling, ivy-covered wall. She led the Trojan through what seemed like miles of dank halls. His feet hurt; had he had any idea how to get out of the palace, he would have given the whole adventure up as a bad job. At last they came to a broad oaken door. The maid shut it in his face, ordering him to wait. Sulkily, he composed himself to obey.

She reappeared a few moments later. "You may come with me," she said.

The barbarian was more than willing to comply, for she had doffed her concealing mantle for a long blue gown that barely covered her breasts and clung provocatively to her rounded haunches. But when he tried to clasp her to his furry bosom, she evaded him with an ease bespeaking long practice and an oiled skin.

She led him to a jewel-encrusted door and bade him enter.

"These are the private chambers of her majesty, Princess Zamaria. A court function prevents her from being present. Still, within are all the implements you will require to succor Zamorazamaria in her hour of need." Condom's own implement was making his kilt rise; he tugged it back into place and entered the Princess Zamaria's boudoir.

Flickering lamps illuminated a chamber of unbelievable magnificence. The walls were covered with tapestries depicting men, women, and a variety of animals writhing in fantastic variations on the act of love. A huge round bed, piled high with pillows, silks, and furs, stood in the center of the room. The Trojan leaped onto it. "By Crumb, this is the life!" He leered at Zamaria's maid. "Now, my little oyster, what can I do to—uh, *for*—you?"

"O Condom, you must be the shield and protector of my mistress!" she cried. "Only you can save Zamorazamaria from utter ruin. The foul necromancer Sloth-Amok"—("Bigot!" sneered the wizard, who was watching all in his magical kettle)—"has the princess's fiancé, Elagabalus, in captivity, and is demanding her hand from her father, King Philiboustros. His limitless supplies of gold, created by the black arts, have corrupted everyone who might otherwise have braved a rescue. . . ." What fools these mortals be! Sloth-Amok thought. Making gold was easy; bullion cubes dropped into boiling water sufficed for all his needs. "Condom, you must save Elagabalus from Sloth-Amok's evil clutches. Any reward the kingdom can offer will be yours!"

"What do I hafta do?" he panted, lecherous visions still dancing in his head.

She did not seem to notice his burning gaze. "Were Elagabalus but free of the Tower of the Bat, he and Zamaria could wed and save the kingdom from the sorcerer's wicked domination. The omens have shown you to be the only man with a prayer of rescuing him, if you but will."

"I will! I will!"

"Truly, it is a task only a fool or a hero would undertake with so little hesitation," she said, giving him the benefit of the doubt. "The Tower of the Bat is easy to enter, but hard to leave.

"We have, indeed, only the dying babbles of men who have pressed beyond the outworks, but it is known that in the topmost pinnacle of the Tower of the Bat squats the invincible Boring Beast, which must be slain ere Elagabalus is saved. Will you aid Zamorazamaria in her hour of need, O Condom? It must be now, for if Elagabalus is not freed, King Philiboustros will give my mistress's hand to Sloth-Amok tomorrow.''

The princess's hand did not much interest Condom, but if she was anything like her maidservant, he had a good healthy yen for her adjacent giblets. Still, there was that damned danger. He paused a while for thought; his reasoning advanced with the sluglike pace that marks the barbarian. ''I'll do it!'' he said at last.

The serving-maid's lips parted in the first smile he had won from her. She bent down and, wincing, kissed him passionately. ''Gracious Condom!'' she said, skipping back before he could pin her to the bed. ''There is not a moment to lose if the kingdom is to be saved. Listen closely, for I have here a charm to aid you. . . .''

An hour later Condom was crouched before the frowning gate of Sloth-Amok's fortress. He was frowning himself, trying to remember what the charm was for.

After ascending the feared Thirteen Steps (these were made from the skulls and bones of virgins over the age of seventy-three, a story in itself), Condom at last confronted the Tower of the Bat. Having searched in vain for a knocker (he kept thinking of Zamaria's wench), he smote the door with his huge fist.

Only silence answered.

He drew his mighty axe and began to chop away at the iron-bound wood. Suddenly, a small panel above the door flew open. One of Gulp's beady little eyes peered through. ''What are you doing, you idiot? Can't you read the sign?''

Condom squinted up at Gulp. ''I don't see no sign.''

''Under your feet, cretin.''

Condom looked down. '' 'Welcome'?'' he guessed.

''No, lackwit. It says, 'Go away!' is what it says. So go away!'' Gulp slammed the panel shut, leaving the barbarian with a perplexed scowl on his face. He muttered something impolite and resumed his assault on the door.

Gulp reappeared. ''No one home!'' he snapped, and vanished.

''Why didn't you say so in the first place?'' Condom grumbled peevishly. He started down the dolorous stairway, but paused and turned back. ''I don't care if you're there or not. Here I come!''

Chips flew as the axe smashed into the rock-hard timbers. ''What do you think you're doing, you overthewed oaf?'' Gulp cried. "Who in the seventeen distinct and different hells do you think you are?"

"I'm, uh, Condom, the Trojan, and if you don't get out of my way, I'll chop pieces off you, too." With a last brutal stroke, the barbarian reduced the entranceway to the Tower of the Bat to a pile of fagots. Gulp fled, screeching in dismay.

The Trojan climbed the Tower's gloomy stair to its end, only to find himself in a place any man in full possession of his faculties would have paid his soul as ransom to avoid: the chamber of the Boring Beast.

Know, O peerless Prince, that though the Beast is long vanished from this world, his progeny live on: the dealer who at great length extols the virtues of a worthless slave, the mage full of praise for his latest worthless nostrum, or your minister of finance. But the Boring Beast, O Prince, surpassed these in its capacity for ennui to the same degree as Your Radiance surpasses his humble servant, myself. For the dread Beast was wont to drone on and on over this and that, saying nothing whatever at such inordinate length as to freeze the ardor of the doughtiest warriors—and these brave men and bold, and not to be despised in battle, and men who always fought at the fore and never gave way . . . I crave pardon, O Prince, for even the thought of the Boring Beast conjures up its image. Suffice to say, any fool caught in its spell could no more escape than bird from mesmerizing snake. And into its dominion the Trojan now thrust himself.

At first he had no notion of aught amiss; the chamber he entered seemed deserted, save for a pile of gray furs in one corner. Condom paid the drab heap scant heed. Nor did he dwell on the row of still bodies before it, once-mighty men now no more than mummified skin stretched drum-tight over dry bones. The spell of the Beast had held them enthralled until they perished.

And now its colorless voice threatened the Trojan with the same desiccation. The Beast was talking, it seemed, of the state of its bowels, but so dull were its words that little meaning came to him, only a monotonous drone that made his mouth sag open in a huge yawn. In his chamber, Sloth-Amok peered, chuckling, into the scrying-kettle as he watched the Boring Beast ensorcel the barbarian.

Condom's eyelids began to droop; so, unbeknownst to him, did those of Sloth-Amok. The great sorcerer had never before witnessed the Beast toying with a victim, and found himself quite unable to resist the field of tedium it projected. With a soft snore, he fell face-first into the split peas.

As fate would have it, Condom put up a stronger resistance to Elagabalus's dreary guardian. He had forgotten the charm he had been given, small white tablets created specifically against this menace by the renegade mage Amphet-Amun. But his own resources were not so meager as might be thought. For one thing, he had often hunted wild bores through the forests of his native land. For another, he had the true barbarian distrust of speeches; as he himself had trouble stringing more than three words together, he naturally found listening to anyone else's long-winded talk unpleasant. Stifling a yawn, he moved toward the Boring Beast, languidly raising his axe. "Will you for Crumb's sake shut up?" he growled.

The Beast did not yet understand that its soporific techniques were failing. "Now I have always found that a brew of salt water and radishes makes a good cathartic," it informed him confidentially.

"Enough!" Condom roared. His gleaming blade bit deep into the Boring Beast's flabby gray flesh. Its cry of agony, this once, produced no ennui; not since the day it had bored its eggshell open had it been so rudely beset. Again and again Condom smote the insipid monster. At last his axe pierced its bladder of boredom. Pent-up anesthetic gases hissed free. The Beast fell with a final low, inane wail; within moments Condom swooned beside it.

When he woke, his head ached abominably, both from the aftereffects of the gases which had sustained the Beast and from the onset of a devastating hangover. He rose, groaning; even the dim light of the Beast's chamber seemed far too bright. And from the door behind the monster's corpse came insistent pounding and a voice whose words were muffled by the thick wood of the portal.

Condom wished the noise would go away, but whoever was making it kept right on. He also raised his voice, so the Trojan finally understood what he was saying: "Who has come to rescue Elagabalus?"

With a will, the barbarian took his axe to the door. He tried to ignore the racket he was making. As soon as he had hacked through the stout timbers, a pale hand snaked through the hole to turn the outer knob, which, the Trojan discovered, had not been locked. The door swung open and Elagabalus stepped out.

He was a tall, slim young man, dressed in fine silks now

soiled from having been worn for days on end. Also of silk was the cloth over his eyes, for he was blind. "Good sir," he said, extending his hand in Condom's general direction, "I congratulate you, though I know you not. Any warrior stout enough to vanquish the Boring Beast must be a hero indeed. Know, sir hero, that you have saved Elagabalus, prince of Hypodermia and the intended husband of Zamorazamaria's fairest princess." He paused, waiting for his rescuer to introduce himself.

Condom's care for such social graces, however, was minimal. "Come on!" he shouted, grabbing the blind prince's arm with such sudden force that Elagabalus all but fell. Elagabalus perforce followed the Trojan as he began stumbling down the stairs toward freedom.

In another part of the Tower of the Bat, Gulp sidled into Sloth-Amok's private quarters, to find the dreaded wizard snoring into his split peas. "Wake up, your maleficence!" he exclaimed.

"Wuzzat?" Sloth-Amok's head rose from the scrying-cauldron. He flicked his face nearly clean with a few quick strokes of his batrachian tongue. As full consciousness returned, he peered into the vat of soup, confidently expecting to find Condom as inert as he himself had been a moment before.

Instead he saw the barbarian and Elagabalus dashing down the Thirteen Steps. "To the palace!" Elagabalus cried, the taste of liberty lighting his aristocratic features.

Sloth-Amok cursed Condom so vilely that Gulp's toenails curled. Froggy eyes bulging, the wizard plowed through his library for a spell hideous enough to wreak proper vengeance on the Trojan.

The sentries at the palace gate stared at the mismatched pair blundering toward them. "Mithrandir!" their captain swore, not sure whose fantasy he was in. He hefted his spear threateningly.

Elagabalus's quick ear, though, recognized the officer's voice. "Do you not know me, Faex?" he said. "It is I, Elagabalus, saved for Zamaria from the foul clutches of Sloth-Amok."

Faex looked the blind prince over. "Well, damn me if you're not," he said. "This is great news." He turned to one of his troopers. "Clunes, move your buns; fetch the princess here at once. Tell her past all hope her fiancé is rescued!"

Sloth-Amok found the volume he was seeking, the great *Treasury* of s'te-goR. He riffled through its baleful pages, at last coming to the section he needed. Raising the book above his head, he cried out, "1014.7!" in a voice like thunder.

A horde of demons, fiends, devils, satans, devas [*Zoroas-*

trian], shedus [*Biblical*], gyres [*Scot.*], bad or evil spirits, un-
clean spirits, hellions [*colloq.*]; cacodemons, incubi, succubi;
jinnis or jinnees, genies, genii, jinniyehs [*fem.*]; evil genii; af-
reets, barghests [even Sloth-Amok was unclear about what barghests were, O Prince, but he had summoned them, and they
came], flibbertigibbets, trolls; ogres, ogresses; ghouls, lamiai,
and Harpies vomited from the bowels of the Tower of the Bat.
The Tower groaned, suffering from a bad case of mixed metaphor; the horde, yeeping, gibbering, roaring, and making whatever noise barghests make, stormed through the streets of
Zamorazamaria after Condom. The townsfolk who saw them
disappeared, most of them permanently.

Horns blared inside the palace, trumpeting a royal fanfare.
Peering into the entrance hall, Condom saw the princess'
serving-maid hurrying toward him, amazed delight on her face.
His heart, among other things, leaped. He opened his arms and
lumbered forward. ''Hey, sweets, look, I done it, see? I done
it!''

She sidestepped with a dancer's adroitness, went gracefully
to one knee before Elagabalus. ''Welcome, your highness, in
the name of my mistress, Princess Zamaria.'' She glanced behind her. ''She comes to greet you even as I speak.''

The guardsmen bowed low, eyes on the polished marble floor.
Condom, untroubled by effete civilized notions like politeness,
gaped at the mountain of flesh wallowing toward him. Zamaria
waddled, she wobbled, she wheezed; her vast rolls of fat shook
like the gelatin that dances round a cold ham. And like a five-
pound sausage stuffed into a three-pound skin, her huge bulk
was shoehorned into a cloth-of-gold gown that clung mercilessly
to every curve.

''My darling!'' she cried to her fiancé, her voice harsh as a
raven's caw. Condom spoke with the rude frankness that marks
the barbarian. ''By Crumb, buddy, it's a good thing you're
blind,'' he told Elagabalus. ''If you could see, you'd run miles,
and I ain't kidding.''

All heads snapped his way, then, as if drawn by some irresistible fascination, swung toward the Princess Zamaria. Her
finger stabbed at the Trojan. ''Kill him!'' she screeched. ''Kill
him, kill him, *kill him*!''

''Shit!'' said Condom, and Faex leaped at him with a vicious
spearthrust. But the Trojan, with no thoughts to slow his reflexes, sprang to one side and brought down both hands, club-
fashion, on the back of the captain's neck. Faex smashed to the

ground, pike flying from nerveless fingers. And Condom, still acting on instinct, seized Zamaria's maidservant, slung her over his shoulder, and dashed down the street, a hundred guardsmen pouring after him.

If they had carried bows, he would have been pincushioned, but they had swords and pikes, and had to close with him to finish him off. Breath sobbing in his throat and the serving-wench in his ear, he reeled round a corner, the guards just a few strides behind. Then the Trojan, with a grunt of fright, whirled and dashed back the way he had come, straight toward the startled palace guards. But they had no chance to hack him down, for hard on his heels was the slavering spawn of Sloth-Amok's conjuration.

Both sides forgot Condom, their common quarry, as they smashed together. "Demons, fiends, devils, satans!" a soldier shrieked. He would have gone through the whole catalog, but a deva killed him. Another guardsman, quicker-witted, exorcised a whole squadron of jinnees with a bottle of vermouth. Three flibbertigibbets danced maniacally up one side of a trooper and down the other. They were not much use as far as fighting went, but spread chaos far and wide.

A cursing guardsman slashed at the monster in front of him. "What *is* that thing?" panted one of his squadmates, who had just unstrung a Harpy.

"A barghest," the soldier said—someone, at least, knew one when he saw one.

"Well, buy it a drink, then!" the other shouted. A lamia tore out his throat a moment later, and there was nobody to say he did not deserve it.

Caught in the center of the maelstrom, Condom kicked and pounded his way toward the edge. In the struggle for survival, none of the combatants paid him any special heed. He had almost won free when an ogre loomed before him. Zamaria's serving-maid swooned as it extended a misshapen, gore-dripping paw toward the Trojan. It roared, "Say, you look like a cousin of mine. You from Darfurdadarbeda?"

"Nah, my folks ain't from that far out in the Styx," Condom said.

"Oh. Sorry, bud. You still look like her, though." With a berserk bellow of rage, the ogre returned to the fray.

Condom sprang onto a stallion that was tied nearby to help the plot along, dug his heels into its side, and galloped for the city gates. A few angry shouts rose behind him, but guardsmen and creatures were still locked in fatal embrace (save, perhaps, for those troopers clutching succubi). The sounds of fighting faded in the distance.

The gate guards did not hinder the Trojan's flight. Burly barbarians with gorgeous, half-clad wenches draped over their saddlebows were two a copper in those days, if the tales that come down from them are to be believed.

The maidservant was awake and squirming when Condom reined the blowing stallion to a halt. The city was far away. The road ran through a glade of quiet, almost unearthly beauty. Tall, slim pines stood silhouetted against the flaming sky of sunset; thrush and warbler sang day's last sleepy songs. And to one side stretched a broad expanse of soft emerald grass.

With a slow smile, Condom dismounted from the great horse. The maid's waist was supple under his fingers as he helped her descend. He laid a hand on her arm, gently guiding her toward the inviting meadow. Her warm flesh was smooth as silk.

She kicked him in the crotch.

He was still writhing on the ground when she clambered aboard the stallion, wheeled it about, and trotted back toward Zamorazamaria. After a while he could sit up. He tried to laugh gustily and think thoughts full of primitive nobility, thoughts on meeting misfortune with stoic equanimity and on the instability of fortune, but his groin hurt and he was none too good at thinking anyhow. He crawled off into the woods and was sick instead.

Twice now, I've used ideas that originally appeared as bits of background in one story to give me another. My novel *Noninterference* (Del Rey, 1988) sprang from a bit of background business in a novelette that never sold. And something in another story of mine ("Herbig-Haro," my first sale to Stan Schmidt at *Analog*) seemed worth expanding into a story of its own. "The Road Not Taken" is the result: a first-contact story, but not of the usual sort.

THE ROAD NOT TAKEN

CAPTAIN TOGRAM WAS USING THE CHAMBER-pot when the *Indomitable* broke out of hyperdrive. As happened all too often, nausea surged through the Roxolan officer. He raised the pot and was abruptly sick into it.

When the spasm was done, he set the thundermug down and wiped his streaming eyes with the soft, gray-brown fur of his forearm. "The gods curse it!" he burst out. "Why don't the shipmasters warn us when they do that?" Several of his troopers echoed him more pungently.

At that moment, a runner appeared in the doorway. "We're back in normal space," the youth squeaked, before dashing on to the next chamber. Jeers and oaths followed him: "No shit!" "Thanks for the news!" "Tell the steerers—they might not have got the word!"

Togram sighed and scratched his muzzle in annoyance at his own irritability. As an officer, he was supposed to set an example for his soldiers. He was junior enough to take such responsibilities seriously, but had had enough service to realize he should never expect too much from anyone more than a couple of notches above him. High ranks went to those with ancient blood or fresh money.

Sighing again, he stowed the chamberpot in its niche. The metal cover he slid over it did little to relieve the stench. After sixteen days in space, the *Indomitable* reeked of ordure, stale food, and staler bodies. It was no better in any other ship of the Roxolan fleet, or any other. Travel between the stars was simply like that. Stinks and darkness were part of the price the soldiers paid to make the kingdom grow.

Togram picked up a lantern and shook it to rouse the glow-mites inside. They flashed silver in alarm. Some races, the captain knew, lit their ships with torches or candles, but glowmites used less air, even if they could only shine intermittently.

Ever the careful soldier, Togram checked his weapons while the light lasted. He always kept all four of his pistols loaded and ready to use; when landing operations began, one pair would go on his belt, the other in his boot tops. He was more worried about his sword. The perpetually moist air aboard ship was not good for the blade. Sure enough, he found a spot of rust to scour away.

As he polished the rapier, he wondered what the new system would be like. He prayed for it to have a habitable planet. The air in the *Indomitable* might be too foul to breathe by the time the ship could get back to the nearest Roxolan-held planet. That was one of the risks starfarers took. It was not a major one—small yellow suns usually shepherded a life-bearing world or two—but it was there.

He wished he hadn't let himself think about it; like an aching fang, the worry, once there, would not go away. He got up from his pile of bedding to see how the steerers were doing.

As usual with them, both Ransisc and his apprentice Olgren were complaining about the poor quality of the glass through which they trained their spyglasses. "You ought to stop whining," Togram said, squinting in from the doorway. "At least you have light to see by." After seeing so long by glowmite lantern, he had to wait for his eyes to adjust to the harsh raw sunlight flooding the observation chamber before he could go in.

Olgren's ears went back in annoyance. Ransisc was older and calmer. He set his hand on his apprentice's arm. "If you rise to all of Togram's jibes, you'll have time for nothing else—he's been a troublemaker since he came out of the egg. Isn't that right, Togram?"

"Whatever you say." Togram liked the white-muzzled senior steerer. Unlike most of his breed, Ransisc did not act as if he believed his important job made him something special in the gods' scheme of things.

Olgren stiffened suddenly; the tip of his stumpy tail twitched. "This one's a world!" he exclaimed.

"Let's see," Ransisc said. Olgren moved away from his spyglass. The two steerers had been examining bright stars one by one, looking for those that would show discs and prove themselves actually to be planets.

"It's a world," Ransisc said at length, "but not one for us—those yellow, banded planets always have poisonous air, and too much of it." Seeing Olgren's dejection, he added, "It's not a total loss—if we look along a line from that planet to its sun, we should find others fairly soon."

"Try that one," Togram said, pointing toward a ruddy star that looked brighter than most of the others he could see.

Olgren muttered something haughty about knowing his business better than any amateur, but Ransisc said sharply, "The captain has seen more worlds from space than you, sirrah. Suppose you do as he asks." Ears drooping dejectedly, Olgren obeyed.

Then his pique vanished. "A planet with green patches!" he shouted.

Ransisc had been aiming his spyglass at a different part of the sky, but that brought him hurrying over. He shoved his apprentice aside, fiddled with the spyglass's focus, peered long at the magnified image. Olgren was hopping from one foot to the other, his muddy brown fur puffed out with impatience to hear the verdict.

"Maybe," the senior steerer said, and Olgren's face lit, but it fell again as Ransisc continued, "I don't see anything that looks like open water. If we find nothing better, I say we try it, but let's search a while longer."

"You've just made a *luof* very happy," Togram said. Ransisc chuckled. The Roxolani brought the little creatures along to test new planets' air. If a *luof* could breathe it in the airlock of a flyer, it would also be safe for the animal's masters.

The steerers growled in irritation as several stars in a row stubbornly stayed mere points of light. Then Ransisc stiffened at his spyglass. "Here it is," he said softly. "*This* is what we want. Come here, Olgren."

"Oh my, yes," the apprentice said a moment later.

"Go report it to Warmaster Slevon, and ask him if his devices have picked up any hyperdrive vibrations except for the fleet's." As Olgren hurried away, Ransisc beckoned Togram over. "See for yourself."

The captain of foot bent over the eyepiece. Against the black of space, the world in the spyglass field looked achingly like Roxolan: deep ocean blue, covered with swirls of white cloud.

A good-sized moon hung nearby. Both were in approximately half-phase, being nearer their star than was the *Indomitable*.

"Did you spy any land?" Togram asked.

"Look near the top of the image, below the ice cap," Ransisc said. "Those browns and greens aren't colors water usually takes. If we want any world in this system, you're looking at it now."

They took turns examining the distant planet and trying to sketch its features until Olgren came back. "Well?" Togram said, though he saw the apprentice's ears were high and cheerful.

"Not a hyperdrive emanation but ours in the whole system!" Olgren grinned. Ransisc and Togram both pounded him on the back, as if he were the cause of the good news and not just its bearer.

The captain's smile was even wider than Olgren's. This was going to be an easy one, which, as a professional soldier, he thoroughly approved of. If no one hereabouts could build a hyperdrive, either the system had no intelligent life at all or its inhabitants were still primitives, ignorant of gunpowder, fliers, and other aspects of warfare as it was practiced among the stars.

He rubbed his hands. He could hardly wait for landfall.

Buck Herzog was bored. After four months in space, with five and a half more staring him in the face, it was hardly surprising. Earth was a bright star behind the *Ares III*, with Luna a dimmer companion; Mars glowed ahead.

"It's your exercise period, Buck," Art Snyder called. Of the five-person crew, he was probably the most officious.

"All right, Pancho." Herzog sighed. He pushed himself over to the bicycle and began pumping away, at first languidly, then harder. The work helped keep calcium in his bones in spite of free-fall. Besides, it was something to do.

Melissa Ott was listening to the news from home. "Fernando Valenzuela died last night," she said.

"Who?" Snyder was not a baseball fan.

Herzog was, and a Californian to boot. "I saw him at an Old-Timers' game once, and I remember my dad and my grandfather always talking about him," he said. "How old was he, Mel?"

"Seventy-nine," she answered.

"He always was too heavy," Herzog said sadly.

"Jesus Christ!"

Herzog blinked. No one on the *Ares III* had sounded that

excited since liftoff from the American space station. Melissa was staring at the radar screen. "Freddie!" she yelled.

Frederica Lindstrom, the ship's electronics expert, had just gotten out of the cramped shower space. She dove for the control board, still trailing a stream of water droplets. She did not bother with a towel; modesty aboard the *Ares III* had long since vanished.

Melissa's shout even made Claude Jonnard stick his head out of the little biology lab where he spent most of his time. "What's wrong?" he called from the hatchway.

"Radar's gone to hell," Melissa told him.

"What do you mean, gone to hell?" Jonnard demanded indignantly. He was one of those annoying people who think quantitatively all the time, and think everyone else does, too.

"There are about a hundred, maybe a hundred fifty, objects on the screen that have no right to be there," answered Frederica Lindstrom, who had a milder case of the same disease. "Range appears to be a couple of million kilometers."

"They weren't there a minute ago, either," Melissa said. "I hollered when they showed up."

As Frederica fiddled with the radar and the computer, Herzog stayed on the exercise bike, feeling singularly useless: what good is a geologist millions of kilometers away from rocks? He wouldn't even get his name in the history books—no one remembers the crew of the third expedition to anywhere.

Frederica finished her checks. "I can't find anything wrong," she said, sounding angry at herself and the equipment both.

"Time to get on the horn to Earth, Freddie," Art Snyder said. "If I'm going to land this beast, I can't have the radar telling me lies."

Melissa was already talking into the microphone. "Houston, this is *Ares III*. We have a problem—"

Even at light-speed, there were a good many minutes of waiting. They crawled past, one by one. Everyone jumped when the speaker crackled to life. "*Ares III*, this is Houston Control. Ladies and gentlemen, I don't quite know how to tell you this, but we see them too."

The communicator kept talking, but no one was listening to her anymore. Herzog felt his scalp tingle as his hair, in primitive reflex, tried to stand on end. Awe filled him. He had never thought he would live to see humanity contact another race. "Call them, Mel," he said urgently.

She hesitated. "I don't know, Buck. Maybe we should let Houston handle this."

"Screw Houston," he said, surprised at his own vehemence. "By the time the bureaucrats down there figure out what to do, we'll be coming down on Mars. We're the people on the spot. Are you going to throw away the most important moment in the history of the species?"

Melissa looked from one of her crewmates to the next. Whatever she saw in their faces must have satisfied her, for she shifted the aim of the antenna and began to speak: "This is the spacecraft *Ares III*, calling the unknown ships. Welcome from the people of Earth." She turned off the transmitter for a moment. "How many languages do we have?"

The call went out in Russian, Mandarin, Japanese, French, German, Spanish, even Latin. ("Who knows the last time they may have visited?" Frederica said when Snyder gave her an odd look.)

If the wait for a reply from Earth had been long, this one was infinitely worse. The delay stretched far, far past the fifteen-second speed-of-light round trip. "Even if they don't speak any of our languages, shouldn't they say *something*?" Melissa demanded of the air. It did not answer, nor did the aliens.

Then, one at a time, the strange ships began darting away sunward, toward Earth. "My God, the acceleration!" Snyder said. "Those are no rockets!" He looked suddenly sheepish. "I don't suppose starships would have rockets, would they?"

The *Ares III* lay alone again in its part of space, pursuing its Hohmann orbit inexorably toward Mars. Buck Herzog wanted to cry.

As was their practice, the ships of the Roxolan fleet gathered above the pole of the new planet's hemisphere with the most land. Because everyone would be coming to the same spot, the doctrine made visual rendezvous easy. Soon only four ships were unaccounted for. A scoutship hurried around to the other pole, found them, and brought them back.

"Always some water-lovers every trip." Togram chuckled to the steerers as he brought them the news. He took all the chances he could to go to their dome, not just for the sunlight but also because, unlike many soldiers, he was interested in planets for their own sake. With any head for figures, he might have tried to become a steerer himself.

He had a decent hand with quill and paper, so Ransisc and

Olgren were willing to let him spell them at the spyglass and add to the sketchmaps they were making of the world below.

"Funny sort of planet," he remarked. "I've never seen one with so many forest fires or volcanoes or whatever they are on the dark side."

"I still think they're cities," Olgren said, with a defiant glance at Ransisc.

"They're too big and too bright," the senior steerer said patiently; the argument, plainly, had been going on for some time.

"This is your first trip offplanet, isn't it, Olgren?" Togram asked.

"Well, what if it is?"

"Only that you don't have enough perspective. Egelloc on Roxolan has almost a million people, and from space it's next to invisible at night. It's nowhere near as bright as those lights, either. Remember, this is a primitive planet. I admit it looks like there's intelligent life down there, but how could a race that hasn't even stumbled across the hyperdrive build cities ten times as great as Egelloc?"

"I don't know," Olgren said sulkily. "But from what little I can see by moonlight, those lights look to be in good spots for cities—on coasts, or along rivers, or whatever."

Ransisc sighed. "What are we going to do with him, Togram? He's so sure he knows everything, he won't listen to reason. Were you like that when you were young?"

"Till my clanfathers beat it out of me, anyway. No need getting all excited, though. Soon enough the flyers will go down with their *luofi*, and then we'll know." He swallowed a snort of laughter, then sobered abruptly, hoping he hadn't been as gullible as Olgren when he was young.

"I have one of the alien vessels on radar," the SR-81 pilot reported. "It's down to 80,000 meters and still descending." He was at his own plane's operational ceiling, barely half as high as the ship entering atmosphere.

"For God's sake, hold your fire," ground control ordered. The command had been dinned into him before he took off, but the brass were not about to let him forget. He did not really blame them. One trigger-happy idiot could ruin humanity forever.

"I'm beginning to get a visual image," he said, glancing at the head-up display projected in front of him. A moment later he added, "It's one damn funny-looking ship, I can tell you that already. Where are the wings?"

"We're picking up the image now too," the ground-control officer said. "They must use the same principle for their in-atmosphere machines as they do for their spacecraft: some sort of antigravity that gives them both lift and drive capability."

The alien ship kept ignoring the SR-81, just as all the aliens had ignored every terrestrial signal beamed at them. The craft continued its slow descent, while the SR-81 pilot circled below, hoping he would not have to go down to the aerial tanker to refuel.

"One question answered," he called to the ground. "It's a warplane." No craft whose purpose was peaceful would have had those glaring eyes and that snarling, fang-filled mouth painted on its belly. Some USAF ground-attack aircraft carried similar markings.

At last the alien reached the level at which the SR-81 was loitering. The pilot called the ground again. "Permission to pass in front of the aircraft?" he asked. "Maybe everybody's asleep in there and I can wake 'em up."

After a long silence, ground control gave grudging assent. "No hostile gestures," the controller warned.

"What do you think I'm going to do, flip him the finger?" the pilot muttered, but his radio was off. Acceleration pushed him back in his seat as he guided the SR-81 into a long, slow turn that would carry it about half a kilometer in front of the vessel from the spacefleet.

His airplane's camera gave him a brief glimpse of the alien pilot, who was sitting behind a small, dirty windscreen.

The being from the stars saw him, too. Of that there was no doubt. The alien jinked like a startled fawn, performing maneuvers that would have smeared the SR-81 pilot against the walls of his pressure cabin—if his aircraft could have matched them in the first place.

"I'm giving pursuit!" he shouted. Ground control screamed at him, but he was the man on the spot. The surge from his afterburner made the pressure he had felt before a love pat by comparison.

Better streamlining made his plane faster than the craft from the starships, but that did not do him much good. Every time its pilot caught sight of him, the alien ship danced away with effortless ease. The SR-81 pilot felt like a man trying to kill a butterfly with a hatchet.

To add to his frustration, his fuel warning light came on. In any case, his aircraft was designed for the thin atmosphere at the edge of space, not the increasingly denser air through which the alien flew. He swore, but he had to pull away.

As his SR-81 gulped kerosene from the tanker, he could not help wondering what would have happened if he'd turned a missile loose. There were a couple of times he'd had a perfect shot. That was one thought he kept firmly to himself. What his superiors would do if they knew about it was too gruesome to contemplate.

The troopers crowded round Togram as he came back from the officers' conclave. "What's the word, captain?" "Did the *luof* live?" "What's it like down there?"

"The *luof* lived, boys!" Togram said with a broad smile.

His company raised a cheer that echoed deafeningly in the barracks room. "We're going down!" they whooped. Ears stood high in excitement. Some soldiers waved plumed hats in the fetid air. Others, of a bent more like their captain's, went over to their pallets and began seeing to their weapons.

"How tough are they going to be, sir?" a gray-furred veteran named Ilingua asked as Togram went by. "I hear the flier pilot saw some funny things."

Togram's smile got wider. "By the heavens and hells, Ilingua, haven't you done this often enough before to know better than to pay heed to rumors you hear before planetfall?"

"I hope so, sir," Ilingua said, "but these are so strange I thought there might be something to them." When Togram did not answer, the trooper shook his head at his own foolishness and shook up a lantern so he could examine his dagger's edge.

As inconspicuously as he could, the captain let out a sigh. He did not know what to believe himself, and he had listened to the pilot's report. How could the locals have flying machines when they did not know contragravity? Togram had heard of a race that used hot-air balloons before it discovered the better way of doing things, but no balloon could have reached the altitude the locals' flier had achieved, and no balloon could have changed direction, as the pilot had violently insisted this craft had done.

Assume he was wrong, as he had to be. But how was one to take his account of towns as big as the ones whose possibility Ransisc had ridiculed, of a world so populous there was precious little open space? And lantern signals from other ships showed their scout pilots were reporting the same wild improbabilities.

Well, in the long run it would not matter if this race was numerous as *reffo* at a picnic. There would simply be that many more subjects here for Roxolan.

"This is a terrible waste," Billy Cox said to anyone who would listen as he slung his duffel bag over his shoulder and tramped out to the waiting truck. "We should be meeting the starpeople with open arms, not with a show of force."

"You tell 'em, Professor." Sergeant Santos Amoros chuckled from behind him. "Me, I'd sooner stay on my butt in a nice, air-conditioned barracks than face L.A. summer smog and sun any old day. Damn shame you're just a Spec-1. If you was president, you could give the orders any way you wanted, instead o' takin' 'em."

Cox didn't think that was very fair either. He'd been just a few units short of his M.A. in poli-sci when the big buildup after the second Syrian crisis sucked him into the army.

He had to fold his lanky length like a jackknife to get under the olive-drab canopy of the truck and down into the passenger compartment. The seats were too hard and too close together. Jamming people into the vehicle counted for more than their comfort while they were there. Typical military thinking, Cox thought disparagingly.

The truck filled. The big diesel rumbled to life. A black soldier dug out a deck of cards and bet anyone that he could turn twenty-five cards into five pat poker hands. A couple of greenhorns took him up on it. Cox had found out the expensive way that it was a sucker bet. The black man was grinning as he offered the deck to one of his marks to shuffle.

Riffff! The ripple of the pasteboards was authoritative enough to make everybody in the truck turn his head. "Where'd you learn to handle cards like that, man?" demanded the black soldier, whose name was Jim but whom everyone called Junior.

"Dealing blackjack in Vegas." *Riffff!*

"Hey, Junior," Cox called, "all of a sudden I want ten bucks of your action."

"Up yours too, pal," Junior said, glumly watching the cards move as if they had lives of their own.

The truck rolled northward, part of a convoy of trucks, MICVs, and light tanks that stretched for miles. An entire regiment was heading into Los Angeles, to be billeted by companies in different parts of the sprawling city. Cox approved of that; it made it less likely that he would personally come face-to-face with any of the aliens.

"Sandy," he said to Amoros, who was squeezed in next to him, "even if I'm wrong and the aliens aren't friendly, what the hell good will hand weapons do? It'd be like taking on an elephant with a safety pin."

"Professor, like I told you already, they don't pay me to think, or you neither. Just as well, too. I'm gonna do what the lieutenant tells me, and you're gonna do what I tell you, and everything is gonna be fine, right?"

"Sure," Cox said, because Sandy, while he wasn't a bad guy, was a sergeant. All the same, the Neo-Armalite between Cox's boots seemed very futile, and his helmet and body armor as thin and gauzy as a stripper's negligee.

The sky outside the steerers' dome began to go from black to deep blue as the *Indomitable* entered atmosphere. "There," Olgren said, pointing. "That's where we'll land."

"Can't see much from this height," Togram remarked.

"Let him use your spyglass, Olgren," Ransisc said. "He'll be going back to his company soon."

Togram grunted; that was more than a comment—it was also a hint. Even so, he was happy to peer through the eyepiece. The ground seemed to leap toward him. There was a moment of disorientation as he adjusted to the inverted image, which put the ocean on the wrong side of the field of view. But he was not interested in sightseeing. He wanted to learn what his soldiers and rest of the troops aboard the *Indomitable* would have to do to carve out a beachhead and hold it against the locals.

"There's a spot that looks promising," he said. "The greenery there in the midst of the buildings in the eastern—no, the western—part of the city. That should give us a clear landing zone, a good campground, and a base for landing reinforcements."

"Let's see what you're talking about," Ransisc said, elbowing him aside. "Hmm, yes, I see the stretch you mean. That might not be bad. Olgren, come look at this. Can you find it again in the Warmaster's spyglass? All right then, go point it out to him. Suggest it as our setdown point."

The apprentice hurried away. Ransisc bent over the eyepiece again. "Hmm," he repeated. "They build tall down there, don't they?"

"I thought so," Togram said. "And there's a lot of traffic on those roads. They've spent a fortune cobblestoning them all, too; I didn't see any dust kicked up.''

"This should be a rich conquest," Ransisc said.

Something swift, metallic, and predator-lean flashed past the observation window. "By the gods, they do have fliers, don't they?" Togram said. In spite of the pilots' claims, deep down he hadn't believed it until he saw it for himself.

He noticed Ransisc's ears twitching impatiently, and realized he really had spent too much time in the observation room. He picked up his glowmite lantern and went back to his troopers.

A couple of them gave him a resentful look for being away so long, but he cheered them up by passing on as much as he could about their landing site. Common soldiers loved nothing better than inside information. They second-guessed their superiors without it, but the game was even more fun when they had some idea of what they were talking about.

A runner appeared in the doorway. "Captain Togram, your company will planet from airlock three."

"Three," Togram acknowledged, and the runner trotted off to pass orders to other ground troop leaders. The captain put his plumed hat on his head (the plume was scarlet, so his company could recognize him in combat), checked his pistols one last time, and ordered his troopers to follow him.

The reeking darkness was as oppressive in front of the inner airlock door as anywhere else aboard the *Indomitable*, but somehow easier to bear. Soon the doors would swing open and he would feel fresh breezes riffling his fur, taste sweet clean air, enjoy sunlight for more than a few precious units at a stretch. Soon he would measure himself against these new beings in combat.

He felt the slightest of jolts as the *Indomitable*'s fliers launched themselves from the mother ship. There would be no *luofi* aboard them this time, but rather musketeers to terrorize the natives with fire from above, and jars of gunpowder to be touched off and dropped. The Roxolani always strove to make as savage a first impression as they could. Terror doubled their effective numbers.

Another jolt came, different from the one before. They were down.

A shadow spread across the UCLA campus. Craning his neck, Junior said, "Will you look at the size of the mother!" He had been saying that for the last five minutes, as the starship slowly descended.

Each time, Billy Cox could only nod, his mouth dry, his hands clutching the plastic grip and cool metal barrel of his rifle. The Neo-Armalite seemed totally impotent against the huge bulk floating so arrogantly downward. The alien flying machines around it were as minnows beside a whale, while they in turn dwarfed the USAF planes circling at a greater distance. The roar of their jets assailed the ears of the nervous troops and civilians on the ground. The aliens' engines were eerily silent.

The starship landed in the open quad between New Royce, New Haines, New Kinsey, and New Powell Halls. It towered higher than any of the two-story red brick buildings, each a reconstruction of one overthrown in the earthquake of 2034. Cox heard saplings splinter under the weight of the alien craft. He wondered what it would have done to the big trees that had fallen five years ago along with the famous old halls.

"All right, they've landed. Let's move on up," Lieutenant Shotton ordered. He could not quite keep the wobble out of his voice, but he trotted south toward the starship. His platoon followed him past Dickson Art Center, past New Bunche Hall. Not so long ago, Billy Cox had walked this campus barefoot. Now his boots thudded on concrete.

The platoon deployed in front of Dodd Hall, looking west toward the spacecraft. A little breeze toyed with the leaves of the young, hopeful trees planted to replace the stalwarts lost to the quake.

"Take as much cover as you can," Lieutenant Shotton ordered quietly. The platoon scrambled into flowerbeds, snuggled down behind thin tree trunks. Out on Hilgard Avenue, diesels roared as armored fighting vehicles took positions with good lines of fire.

It was all such a waste, Cox thought bitterly. The thing to do was to make friends with the aliens, not to assume automatically they were dangerous.

Something, at least, was being done along those lines. A delegation came out of Murphy Hall and slowly walked behind a white flag from the administration building toward the starship. At the head of the delegation was the mayor of Los Angeles; the President and governor were busy elsewhere. Billy Cox would have given anything to be part of the delegation instead of sprawled here on his belly in the grass. If only the

aliens had waited until he was fifty or so, had given him a chance
to get established—

Sergeant Amoros nudged him with an elbow. "Look there,
man. Something's happening—"

Amoros was right. Several hatchways which had been shut
were swinging open, allowing Earth's air to mingle with the
ship's.

The westerly breeze picked up. Cox's nose twitched. He could
not name all the exotic odors wafting his way, but he recognized
sewage and garbage when he smelled them. "God, what a
stink!" he said.

"By the gods, what a stink!" Togram exclaimed. When the
outer airlock doors went down, he had expected real fresh air
to replace the stale, overused gases inside the *Indomitable*. This
stuff smelled like smoky peat fires, or lamps whose wicks hadn't
quite been extinguished. And it stung! He felt the nictitating
membranes flick across his eyes to protect them.

"Deploy!" he ordered, leading his company forward. This
was the tricky part. If the locals had nerve enough, they could
hit the Roxolani just as the latter were coming out of their ship,
and cause all sorts of trouble. Most races without hyperdrive,
though, were too overawed by the arrival of travelers from the
stars to try anything like that. And if they didn't do it fast, it
would be too late.

They weren't doing it here. Togram saw a few locals, but they
were keeping a respectful distance. He wasn't sure how many
there were. Their mottled skins—or was that clothing?—made
them hard to notice and count. But they were plainly warriors,
both by the way they acted and by the weapons they bore.

His own company went into its familiar two-line formation,
the first crouching, the second standing and aiming their muskets over the heads of the troops in front.

"Ah, there we go," Togram said happily. The bunch approaching behind the white banner had to be the local nobles.
The mottling, the captain saw, was clothing, for these beings
wore entirely different garments, somber except for strange, narrow neckcloths. They were taller and skinnier than Roxolani,
with muzzleless faces.

"Ilingua!" Togram called. The veteran trooper led the right
flank squad of the company.

"Sir!"

"Your troops, quarter-right face. At the command, pick off

the leaders there. That will demoralize the rest,'' Togram said, quoting standard doctrine.

"Slowmatches ready!" Togram said. The Roxolani lowered the smoldering cords to the touchholes of their muskets. "Take your aim!" The guns moved, very slightly. "Fire!"

"Teddy bears!" Sandy Amoros exclaimed. The same thought had leaped into Cox's mind. The beings emerging from the spaceship were round, brown, and furry, with long noses and big ears. Teddy bears, however, did not normally carry weapons. They also, Cox thought, did not commonly live in a place that smelled like sewage. Of course, it might have been perfume to them. But if it was, they and Earthpeople were going to have trouble getting along.

He watched the Teddy bears as they took their positions. Somehow their positioning did not suggest that they were forming an honor guard for the mayor and his party. Yet it did look familiar to Cox, although he could not quite figure out why.

Then he had it. If he had been anywhere but at UCLA, he would not have made the connection. But he remembered a course he had taken on the rise of the European nation-states in the sixteenth century, and on the importance of the professional, disciplined armies the kings had created. Those early armies had performed evolutions like this one.

It was a funny coincidence. He was about to mention it to his sergeant when the world blew up.

Flames spurted from the aliens' guns. Great gouts of smoke puffed into the sky. Something that sounded like an angry wasp buzzed past Cox's ear. He heard shouts and shrieks from either side. Most of the mayor's delegation was down, some motionless, others thrashing.

There was a crash from the starship, and another one an instant later as a roundshout smashed into the brickwork of Dodd Hall. A chip stung Cox in the back of the neck. The breeze brought him the smell of fireworks, one he had not smelled for years.

"Reload!" Togram yelled. "Another volley, then at 'em with the bayonet!" His troopers worked frantically, measuring powder charges and ramming round bullets home.

* * *

"So that's how they wanna play!" Amoros shouted. "Nail their hides to the wall!" The tip of his little finger had been shot away. He did not seem to know it.

Cox's Neo-Armalite was already barking, spitting a stream of hot brass cartridges, slamming against his shoulder. He rammed in clip after clip, playing the rifle like a hose. If one bullet didn't bite, the next would.

Others from the platoon were also firing. Cox heard bursts of automatic weapons fire from different parts of the campus, too, and the deeper blasts of rocket-propelled grenades and field artillery. Smoke not of the aliens' making began to envelop their ship and the soldiers around it.

One or two shots came back at the platoon, and then a few more, but so few that Cox, in stunned disbelief, shouted to his sergeant, "This isn't fair!"

"Fuck 'em!" Amoros shouted back. "They wanna throw their weight around, they take their chances. Only good thing they did was knock over the mayor. Always did hate that old crackpot."

The harsh *tac-tac-tac* did not sound like any gunfire Togram had heard. The shots came too close together, making a horrible sheet of noise. And if the locals were shooting back at his troopers, where were the thick, choking clouds of gunpowder smoke over their position?

He did not know the answer to that. What he did know was that his company was going down like grain before a scythe. Here a soldier was hit by three bullets at once and fell awkwardly, as if his body could not tell in which direction to twist. There another had the top of his head gruesomely removed.

The volley the captain had screamed for was stillborn. Perhaps a squad's worth of soldiers moved toward the locals, the sun glinting bravely off their long, polished bayonets. None of them got more than a half-sixteen of paces before falling.

Ilingua looked at Togram, horror in his eyes, his ears flat against his head. The captain knew his were the same. "What are they doing to us?" Ilingua howled.

Togram could only shake his head helplessly. He dove behind a corpse, fired one of his pistols at the enemy. There was still a chance, he thought—how would these demonic aliens stand up under their first air attack?

A flier swooped toward the locals. Musketeers blasted away from firing ports, drew back to reload.

"Take that, you whoresons!" Togram shouted. He did not,

however, raise his fist in the air. That, he had already learned, was dangerous.

"Incoming aircraft!" Sergeant Amoros roared. His squad, those not already prone, flung themselves on their faces. Cox heard shouts of pain through the combat din as men were wounded.

The Cottonmouth crew launched their shoulder-fired AA missile at the alien flying machine. The pilot must have had reflexes like a cat's. He sidestepped his machine in midair; no plane built on Earth could have matched that performance. The Cottonmouth shot harmlessly past.

The flier dropped what looked like a load of crockery. The ground jumped as the bombs exploded. Cursing, deafened, Billy Cox stopped worrying whether the fight was fair.

But the flier pilot had not seen the F-29 fighter on his tail. The USAF plane released two missiles from point-blank range, less than a mile. The infrared-seeker found no target and blew itself up, but the missile that homed on radar streaked straight toward the flier. The explosion made Cox bury his face in the ground and clap his hands over his ears.

So this is war, he thought: I can't see, I can barely hear, and my side is winning. What must it be like for the losers?

Hope died in Togram's hearts when the first flier fell victim to the locals' aircraft. The rest of the *Indomitable*'s machines did not last much longer. They could evade, but had even less ability to hit back than the Roxolan ground forces. And they were hideously vulnerable when attacked in their pilots' blind spots, from below or behind.

One of the starship's cannon managed to fire again, and quickly drew a response from the traveling fortresses Togram got glimpses of as they took their positions in the streets outside this parklike area.

When the first shell struck, the luckless captain thought for an instant that it was another gun going off aboard the *Indomitable*. The sound of the explosion was nothing like the crash a solid shot made when it smacked into a target. A fragment of hot metal buried itself in the ground by Togram's hand. That made him think a cannon had blown up, but more explosions on the ship's superstructure and fountains of dirt flying up from misses showed it was just more from the locals' fiendish arsenal.

Something large and hard struck the captain in the back of the neck. The world spiraled down into blackness.

"Cease fire!" The order reached the field artillery first, then the infantry units at the very front line. Billy Cox pushed up his cuff to look at his watch, stared in disbelief. The whole firefight had lasted less than twenty minutes.

He looked around. Lieutenant Shotton was getting up from behind an ornamental palm. "Let's see what we have," he said. His rifle still at the ready, he began to walk slowly toward the starship. It was hardly more than a smoking ruin. For that matter, neither were the buildings around it. The damage to their predecessors had been worse in the big quake, but not much.

Alien corpses littered the lawn. The blood splashing the bright green grass was crimson as any man's. Cox bent to pick up a pistol. The weapon was beautifully made, with scenes of combat carved into the grayish wood of the stock. But he recognized it as a single-shot piece, a small-arm obsolete for at least two centuries. He shook his head in wonderment.

Sergeant Amoros lifted a conical object from where it had fallen beside a dead alien. "What the hell is this?" he demanded.

Again Cox had the feeling of being caught up in something he did not understand. "It's a powderhorn," he said.

"Like in the movies? Pioneers and all that good shit?"

"The very same."

"Damn," Amoros said feelingly. Cox nodded in agreement.

Along with the rest of the platoon, they moved closer to the wrecked ship. Most of the aliens had died still in the two neat rows from which they had opened fire on the soldiers.

Here, behind another corpse, lay the body of the scarlet-plumed officer who had given the order to begin that horrifyingly uneven encounter. Then, startling Cox, the alien moaned and stirred, just as might a human starting to come to. "Grab him; he's a live one!" Cox exclaimed.

Several men jumped on the reviving alien, who was too groggy to fight back. Soldiers began peering into the holes torn in the starship, and even going inside. There they were still wary; the ship was so incredibly much bigger than any human spacecraft that there were surely survivors despite the shellacking it had taken.

As always happens, the men did not get to enjoy such pleasures long. The fighting had been over for only minutes when the first team of experts came thuttering in by helicopter, saw common soldiers in their private preserve, and made horrified noises. The experts also promptly relieved the platoon of its prisoner.

Sergeant Amoros watched resentfully as they took the alien away. "You must've known it would happen, Sandy," Cox consoled him. "We do the dirty work and the brass takes over once things get cleaned up again."

"Yeah, but wouldn't it be wonderful if just once it was the other way round?" Amoros laughed without humor. "You don't need to tell me: fat friggin' chance."

When Togram woke up on his back, he knew something was wrong. Roxolani always slept prone. For a moment he wondered how he had got to where he was . . . too much water-of-life the night before? His pounding head made that a good possibility.

Then memory came flooding back. Those damnable locals with their sorcerous weapons! Had his people rallied and beaten back the enemy after all? He vowed to light votive lamps to Edieva, mistress of battles, for the rest of his life if that was true.

The room he was in began to register. Nothing was familiar, from the bed he lay on to the light in the ceiling that glowed bright as sunshine and neither smoked nor flickered. No, he did not think the Roxolani had won their fight.

Fear settled like ice in his vitals. He knew how his own race treated prisoners, had heard spacers' stories of even worse things among other folk. He shuddered to think of the refined tortures a race as ferocious as his captors could invent.

He got shakily to his feet. By the end of the bed he found his hat, some smoked meat obviously taken from the *Indomitable*, and a translucent jug made of something that was neither leather nor glass nor baked clay nor metal. Whatever it was, it was too soft and flexible to make a weapon.

The jar had water in it: *not* water from the *Indomitable*. That was already beginning to taste stale. This was cool and fresh and so pure as to have no taste whatever, water so fine he had only found its like in a couple of mountain springs.

The door opened on noiseless hinges. In came two of the locals. One was small and wore a white coat—a female, if those chest projections were breasts. The other was dressed in the same clothes the local warriors had worn, though those offered no camouflage here. That one carried what was plainly a rifle and, the gods curse him, looked extremely alert.

To Togram's surprise, the female took charge. The other local was merely a bodyguard. Some spoiled princess, curious about these outsiders, the captain thought. Well, he was happier about treating with her than meeting the local executioner.

She sat down, waved for him also to take a seat. He tried a chair, found it uncomfortable—too low in the back, not built for his wide rump and short legs. He sat on the floor instead.

She set a small box on the table by the chair. Togram pointed at it. "What's that?" he asked.

He thought she had not understood—no blame to her for that; she had none of his language. She was playing with the box, pushing a button here, a button there. Then his ears went back and his hackles rose, for the box said, "What's that?" in Roxolani. After a moment he realized it was speaking in his own voice. He swore and made a sign against witchcraft.

She said something, fooled with the box again. This time it echoed her. She pointed at it. " 'Recorder,' " she said. She paused expectantly.

What was she waiting for, the Roxolanic name for that thing? "I've never seen one of those in my life, and I hope I never do again," he said. She scratched her head. When she made the gadget again repeat what he had said, only the thought of the soldier with the gun kept him from flinging it against the wall.

Despite that contretemps, they did eventually make progress on the language. Togram had picked up snatches of a good many tongues in the course of his adventurous life; that was one reason he had made captain in spite of low birth and paltry connections. And the female—Togram heard her name as Hildachesta—had a gift for them, as well as the box that never forgot.

"Why did your people attack us?" she asked one day, when she had come far enough in Roxolanic to be able to frame the question.

He knew he was being interrogated, no matter how polite she sounded. He had played that game with prisoners himself. His ears twitched in a shrug. He had always believed in giving straight answers; that was one reason he was only a captain. He said, "To take what you grow and make and use it for ourselves. Why would anyone want to conquer anyone else?"

"Why indeed?" she murmured, and was silent a little while; his forthright reply seemed to have closed off a line of questioning. She tried again: "How are your people able to walk—I mean, travel—faster than light, when the rest of your arts are so simple?''

His fur bristled with indignation. "They are not! We make gunpowder, we cast iron and smelt steel, we have spyglasses to help our steerers guide us from star to star. We are no savages huddling in caves or shooting at each other with bows and arrows.''

His speech, of course, was not that neat or simple. He had to backtrack, to use elaborate circumlocutions, to playact to make Hildachesta understand. She scratched her head in the gesture of puzzlement he had come to recognize. She said, "We have known all these things you mention for hundreds of years, but we did not think anyone could walk—damn, I keep saying that instead of 'travel'—faster than light. How did your people learn to do that?''

"We discovered it for ourselves," he said proudly. "We did not have to learn it from some other starfaring race, as many folk do.''

"But *how* did you discover it?" she persisted.

"How do I know? I'm a soldier; what do I care for such things? Who knows who invented gunpowder or found out about using bellows in a smithy to get the fire hot enough to melt iron? These things happen, that's all.''

She broke off the questions early that day.

"It's humiliating," Hilda Chester said. "If these fool aliens had waited a few more years before they came, we likely would have blown ourselves to kingdom come without ever knowing there was more real estate around. Christ, from what the Roxolani say, races that scarcely know how to work iron fly starships and never think twice about it.''

"Except when the starships don't get home," Charlie Ebbets answered. His tie was in his pocket and his collar open against Pasadena's fierce summer heat, although the Caltech Atheneum was efficiently air-conditioned. Along with so many other engineers and scientists, he depended on linguists like Hilda Chester for a link to the aliens.

"I don't quite understand it myself," she said. "Apart from the hyperdrive and contragravity, the Roxolani are backward, almost primitive. And the other species out there must be the same, or someone would have overrun them long since.''

Ebbets said, "Once you see it, the drive is amazingly simple. The research crews say anybody could have stumbled over the principle at almost any time in our history. The best guess is that most races did come across it, and once they did, why, all their creative energy would naturally go into refining and improving it.''

"But we missed it," Hilda said slowly, "and so our technology developed in a different way."

"That's right. That's why the Roxolani don't know anything about controlled electricity, to say nothing of atomics. And the thing is, as well as we can tell so far, the hyperdrive and contragravity don't have the ancillary applications the electromagnetic spectrum does. All they do is move things from here to there in a hurry."

"That should be enough at the moment," Hilda said. Ebbets nodded. There were almost nine billion people jammed onto the Earth, half of them hungry. Now, suddenly, there were places for them to go and a means to get them there.

"I think," Ebbets said musingly, "we're going to be an awful surprise to the peoples out there."

It took Hilda a second to see what he was driving at. "If that's a joke, it's not funny. It's been a hundred years since the last war of conquest."

"Sure—they've gotten too expensive and too dangerous. But what kind of fight could the Roxolani or anyone else at their level of technology put up against us? The Aztecs and Incas were plenty brave. How much good did it do them against the Spaniards?"

"I hope we've gotten smarter in the last five hundred years," Hilda said. All the same, she left her sandwich half-eaten. She found she was not hungry any more.

"Ransisc!" Togram exclaimed as the senior steerer limped into his cubicle. Ransisc was thinner than he had been a few moons before, aboard the misnamed *Indomitable*. His fur had grown out white around several scars Togram did not remember.

His air of amused detachment had not changed, though. "Tougher than bullets, are you, or didn't the humans think you were worth killing?"

"The latter, I suspect. With their firepower, why should they worry about one soldier more or less?" Togram said bitterly. "I didn't know you were still alive, either."

"Through no fault of my own, I assure you," Ransisc said. "Olgren, next to me—" His voice broke off. It was not possible to be detached about everything.

"What are you doing here?" the captain asked. "Not that I'm not glad to see you, but you're the first Roxolan face I've set eyes on since—" It was his turn to hesitate.

"Since we landed." Togram nodded in relief at the steerer's circumlocution. Ransisc went on, "I've seen several others before you. I suspect we're being allowed to get together so the humans can listen to us talking with each other."

"How could they do that?" Togram asked, then answered his own question. "Oh, the recorders, of course." He perforce used the English word. "Well, we'll fix that."

He dropped into Oyag, the most widely spoken language on a planet the Roxolani had conquered fifty years before. "What's going to happen to us, Ransisc?"

"Back on Roxolan, they'll have realized something's gone wrong by now," the steerer answered in the same tongue.

That did nothing to cheer Togram. "There are so many ways to lose ships," he said gloomily. "And even if the High Warmaster does send another fleet after us, it won't have any more luck than we did. These gods-accursed humans have too many war-machines." He paused and took a long, moody pull at a bottle of vodka. The flavored liquors the locals brewed made him sick, but vodka he liked. "How is it they have all these machines and we don't, or any race we know of? They must be wizards, selling their souls to the demons for knowledge."

Ransisc's nose twitched in disagreement. "I asked one of their savants the same question. He gave me back a poem by a human named Hail or Snow or something of that sort. It was about someone who stood at a fork in the road and ended up taking the less-used track. That's what the humans did. Most races find the hyperdrive and go traveling. The humans never did, and so their search for knowledge went in a different direction."

"Didn't it!" Togram shuddered at the recollection of that brief, terrible combat. "Guns that spit dozens of bullets without reloading, cannon mounted on armored platforms that move by themselves, rockets that follow their targets by themselves . . . And there are the things we didn't see, the ones the humans only talk about—the bombs that can blow up a whole city, each one by itself."

"I don't know if I believe that," Ransisc said.

"I do. They sound afraid when they speak of them."

"Well, maybe. But it's not just the weapons they have. It's the machines that let them see and talk to one another from far away; the machines that do their reckoning for them; their recorders and everything that has to do with them. From what they say of their medicine, I'm almost tempted to believe you and think they are wizards—they actually know what causes their diseases, and how to cure or even prevent them. And their farming: this planet is far more crowded than any I've seen or heard of, but it grows enough for all these humans."

Togram sadly waggled his ears. "It seems so unfair. All that they got, just by not stumbling onto the hyperdrive."

"They have it now," Ransisc reminded him. "Thanks to us."

The Roxolani looked at each other, appalled. They spoke together: "What have we done?"

The next two short fantasies both have their roots in medieval literature. "The Castle of the Sparrowhawk" is based on a tale told by that champion teller of tales, Sir John Mandeville, in his *Travels*— a volume I heartily recommend to anyone who enjoys marvels, whether real, imagined, or—best of all—real and imagined so commingled that the one is impossible to tell from the other.

THE CASTLE OF THE SPARROWHAWK

SIR JOHN MANDEVILLE HEARD THE TALE OF the castle of the sparrowhawk, but only from afar, and imperfectly. If a man could keep that sparrowhawk, which dwelt in the topmost tower of the castle, awake for seven days and nights, he would win whatever earthly thing might be his heart's desire. So much Mandeville knew.

But he lied when he put that castle in Armenia. Armenia, surely, was a strange and exotic land to his readers in England or France or Italy, but the castle of the sparrowhawk lay beyond the fields we know. How could it be otherwise, when even Mandeville tells us a lady of Faerie kept that sparrowhawk?

Perhaps we may excuse him after all, though, for the tale as he learned it did involve an Armenian prince—Mandeville calls him a king, to make the story grander, but only the truth here. Natural enough, then, for him to set that castle there. Natural, but wrong.

You might think Prince Rupen of Etchmiadzin had no need to go searching for the castle of the sparrowhawk. He was young. He was strong, in principality and in person. He was brave, and even beginning to be wise. His face, a handsome face in the half-eagle, half-lion way so many Armenians have, was more apt to be seen in a smile than a scowl.

Yet despite his smiles, he was not happy, not lastingly so. He felt that nothing he owned was his by right. His principality he had from his father, and his face and form as well. Even his bravery and the beginnings of wisdom had been inculcated in him.

"What would I have been had I been born an ugly, palsied pig-farmer?" he cried one day in a fit of self-doubt.

"Someone other than yourself," his vizier answered sensibly.

But that did not satisfy him. He was, after all, only *beginning* to be wise.

In the east, the line between the fields we know and those beyond is not drawn so firmly as in our mundane corner of the world. Too, in the tortuous mountains of Armenia, who knows what fields lie three valleys over? And so, when Rupen, armed with no more than determination—and a crossbow, in case of dragons—set out to seek the castle of the sparrowhawk, he was not surprised that one day he found it.

But for a certain feline grace, the grooms and servants of the castle were hardly different from those he had left behind at Etchmiadzin. They tended his horse, fed him ground lamb and pine nuts, and gave him wine spiced with cinnamon. He drank deeply and flung himself on the featherbed to which they led him. To hold the sparrowhawk wakeful seven days and nights, he would have to go without sleep himself. He stored it away now, like a woodchuck fattening itself for winter.

No one disturbed his rest; he was allowed to emerge from his chamber when he would. After he had eaten again, the seneschal of the castle asked leave to have speech with him. The mark of Faerie lay more heavily on that man than on his underlings. In the fields we know, his mien and bearing would have suited a sovereign, not a bailiff. So would his robes, of sea-green samite shot through with silver threads and decked with pearls.

Said he to Rupen, "Is it your will to essay the ordeal of the sparrowhawk?"

"It is," the prince replied.

The seneschal bowed. "You have come, no doubt, seeking the reward success will bring. My duty is to inform you of the cost of failure; word thereof somehow does not travel so widely. If the bird sleep, you forfeit more than your life. Your soul is lost as well. The prayers of your priests do not reach here to save it."

Rupen believed him absolutely. The churches of Armenia with their conical domes had never seemed more distant. For all that, he said, "I will go on."

The seneschal bowed again. "Be it so, then. Honor to your courage. I will take you to the lady Olissa. Come."

There were one hundred and forty-four steps on the spiral

stair that led to the sparrowhawk's eyrie. Prince Rupen counted
them one by one as he climbed behind the seneschal. His heart
pounded and his breath came short by the time they reached the
top. The seneschal was unchanged; he might have been a falcon
himself, by the ease with which he took the stairs.

The door at the head of the stairway was of some golden wood
Rupen did not know. Light streamed into the gloomy stairwell
when the seneschal opened it, briefly dazzling Rupen. As his
eyes took its measure, he saw a broad expanse of enameled blue
sky, a single perch, and standing beside it one who had to be
Olissa.

"Are you of a sudden afraid, then?" the seneschal asked
when Rupen hung back. "You may yet withdraw, the only pen-
alty being that never again shall you find your way hither."

"Afraid?" Rupen murmured, as from far away. "No, I am
not afraid." But still he stayed in the antechamber; to take a
step might have meant pulling his eyes away from Olissa for an
instant, and he could not have borne it.

Her hair stormed in bright waves to her waist, the color of the
new-risen sun. Her skin was like snow faintly tinged with ripe
apples. The curves of her body bade fair to bring tears to his
eyes. So, for another reason, did the sculpted lines of her chin,
her cheeks, the tiny curve of her ear where it peeped from among
fiery ringlets. He thought how the pagan Greeks would have
slain themselves in despair of capturing her in stone.

Her eyes? Like the sea, they were never the same shade twice.

He stood until she extended a slim hand his way. Then indeed
he moved forward, as iron will toward a lodestone. When she
spoke, he learned what the sound was that silver bells sought.
"Knowing the danger," she asked, "you still wish to undertake
the ordeal?"

He could only nod.

"Honor to your courage." Olissa echoed the seneschal; it
was the first thing that recalled him to Rupen's mind since he
set eyes on her. Then the man of Faerie was again forgotten as
she went on, "I will have provender fetched here; you must
undertake the test alone with the sparrowhawk."

The thought that she would leave filled him with despair. But
when she asked him, "Will you drink wine at meat?" he had
to think of a reply, if only not to appear a fool before her.

"No, bring me water or milk, if you would," he said. He
would not have chosen them in Armenia, but he feared no flux

here. He felt bound to explain, "Come the seventh day, I shall be drowsy enough without the grape."

"A man of sense as well as bravery. It shall be as you wish, or even better."

Already Rupen heard servants on the stairs, though no sign he could detect had summoned them. Along with the flaky loaves and smoked meats, they set down ewers the fragrance of whose contents made his nose twitch.

"Fruit nectars," Olissa said. "Does it please you?"

He bowed his thanks. Against the liquid elegance of the seneschal, his courtesy seemed a miserable clumsy thing, but he gave it as a man will give a copper when he has no gold to spend.

She nodded to him, and he felt as if the Emperor of Byzantium and the Great Khan had prostrated themselves at his feet. Saying, "Perhaps we shall meet again in seven days, you and I," she stepped past him to join the seneschal in the antechamber at the head of the stairs.

The door of the golden wood was swinging shut when Rupen blurted out a final thought: "If no one is here to watch me, how will you know if I fail?"

He had hoped for a last word from Olissa, but it was the seneschal who answered him. "We shall know, never fear," he said, and the iron promise in his voice sent a snake of dread slithering through Rupen's bowels. Soundlessly, the door closed.

With the glory of Olissa gone, Rupen turned to the sparrowhawk for the first time. It stared back at him with fierce topaz eyes, and screeched shrilly. He had flown hawks, and knew what that cry meant. "Hungry, are you? I was not sure the birds of Faerie had to eat."

Among the supplies the castle servants had brought was a large, low, earthen pot with a lid of openweave wickerwork. Small scuttling sounds came from it. When Rupen lifted the lid, he found mice, brown, white, and gray, scrambling about inside. He reached in, caught one and killed it, and offered it to the sparrowhawk. The bird ate greedily. It called for more, though the tip of the mouse's tail still dangled from its beak.

Rupen shook his head. "A stuffed belly makes for restfulness. We'll both stay a bit empty through this week." The sparrowhawk glared as if it understood. Perhaps, he thought, it did.

As dusk fell, it tucked its head under a wing. He clapped his hands. The sparrowhawk hissed at him. He lit a torch and set it in its sconce. It burned with the clean, sweet smell of sandal-wood.

That night, drowsiness did not trouble Rupen, who was sustained by imaginings of Olissa. He felt fresh as just-fallen snow when dawn streaked the eastern sky with carmine and gold. The sparrowhawk, by then, was too furious with him to think of sleep.

Noon was not long past when he fed it another mouse. Soon after, the first yawn crept out of hiding and stretched itself in his throat. He strangled it, but felt others stirring to take its place. Presently they would thrive.

To hold them back, he began to sing. He sang every song he knew, and sang them all once again when he was through. The din sufficed to keep the sparrowhawk awake through most of the night. Eventually, though, it grew used to the sound of his voice, and began to close its eyes. Seeing that, he fell silent, which served as well as a thunderclap. The bird started up wildly; its bright stare had hatred in it.

That was how the second day passed.

Prince Rupen stumbled through the third and fourth days as if drunk. He laughed hoarsely at nothing, and kept dropping the chunks of bread he cut for supper. He was too tired to notice they had not gone stale, as they would have in the fields we know. The sparrowhawk began to sway on its perch. Some of the luster was gone from its bright plumage.

On the fifth day, it took Rupen a very long time to catch the bird its mouse. The mice were wide awake. When at last he had the furry little creature, he started to pop it into his own mouth. Only the sparrowhawk's shriek of protest recalled him to himself, for a little while.

He remembered nothing whatsoever of the sixth day.

Sometime in the middle of the last night, he decided he wanted to die. He lurched over to the edge of the eyrie's floor and looked longingly at the castle courtyard far below. The thought of forfeiting his soul for failing the ordeal did not check him, nor did the certainty that suicides suffered the same fate. But he lacked the energy to take the step that would have sent him tumbling down.

He did not remember why he kept snapping his fingers in the sparrowhawk's face. The bird, by then, lacked the spirit even to bite at him. Its eyes might have been dull yellow glass now, not topaz. Both of them had forgotten the mice.

The sun came up. Rupen stared at it until the pain penetrated the fog between his eyes and his brain. Tears streamed down his cheeks, and continued to flow long after the pain was past. He had no idea why he wept, or how to stop.

Nor did the sound of footsteps on the stairs convey to him a meaning. Yet when the door swung open, he somehow contrived a bow to the lady Olissa.

She curtseyed in return, as lovely as she had been a week before. "Rest now, bold prince," she murmured. "You have won."

The seneschal sprang out from behind her to ease Rupen to the slates of the floor, his first snores already begun. Olissa paid the man no attention, but crooned to the sparrowhawk, "And thou, little warrior, rest thyself as well." The bird gave what would have been a chirp had its voice been sweeter, and pushed its head into the white palm of her hand like a lovesick cat. Then it too slept.

The seneschal said, "To look at him lying there, this mortal now has in his possession his heart's desire."

"Ah, but he will not reckon it so when he wakes," Olissa replied.

The sun sliding fingers under his eyelids roused Rupen. He sprang up in horror, certain he was doomed. Ice formed round his heart to see the perch he had so long guarded empty.

Olissa's laugh, a sound like springtime, made him whirl. "Fear not," she said. "You have slept the day around. The ordeal is behind you, and you have only to claim your reward."

"You did come to me, then," Rupen said, amazed. "I thought surely it was a dream."

"No dream," she said. "What would you?"

He was not yet ready for that question. "The sparrow-hawk—?" he asked.

His concern won a smile from her. "It is a bird of Faerie, and recovers itself more quickly than those you may have known. Already it is on the wing, hunting mice it does not have to scream for."

Rupen flushed to be reminded of his vagaries during the trial. That reminded him of his present sadly draggled state. "As part of my reward, may I ask for a great hot tub and the loan of fresh clothing?"

"It shall be as you desire; you are not the first to make that request. While you bathe, think on what else you would have. I shall come to your bedchamber in an hour's time, to hear you."

The soaps and scents of Faerie, finer and more delicate than the ones we know, washed the last lingering exhaustion from his bones. His borrowed silks clung to him like a second skin. As he combed his hair and thick curly beard, he noticed the mirror on the wall above the tub was not befogged by steam. He wished he could take that secret back with him to Etchmiadzin.

He started when the soft knock came at the bedchamber door. At the first touch of the latch, the door opened as silently as all the others in the castle of the sparrowhawk. The lady Olissa stepped in. As if it were a well-trained dog, the door swung shut behind her.

She watched him a moment with her sea-colored eyes. "Ask for any earthly thing you may desire, for you have nobly acquitted yourself in the task set you."

Had it been the seneschal granting him that boon, Rupen would have answered differently. But he was a young man, and quite refreshed, so he said, "Of earthly things, Etchmiadzin fills all my wants. Therefore—" His resolve faltered, and he hesitated, but at last he did go on, all in a rush: "—I ask of you no more than that you share this bed with me here for a night and a day. I could desire nothing more."

Still her eyes reminded him of the sea, the sea at storm. Almost he quailed before her anger, and was steadied only by the thought that she would despise him for his fear.

She said, "Beware, mortal. I am no earthly thing, but of the Faerie realm. Choose you another benison, one suited to your station."

"Am I not a prince?" Rupen cried. He was only beginning to be wise. "In truth, I would ask for nothing else."

"For the last time, can I not dissuade you from this folly?"

"No," he said.

"Be it so, then," she said with a wintry sigh, "but with this gift you demand of me I shall give you another, such as you deserve for your presumption. Etchmiadzin will not so delight you on your return; you will come to know war and need and loss. And ten years hence I charge you to think upon this day and what you have earned here now."

Her words fell on deaf ears, for as she spoke she was loosing the stays of her gown and letting it fall to the floor. Rupen had imagined how she might be. Now he saw what a poor, paltry, niggling thing his imagination was. Then he touched her, and that was past all imagining.

* * *

Afterward, riding back to Etchmiadzin, he wished he had asked for a year. On the other hand, half an hour might have served as well, or as poorly. Anything less than forever was not enough.

He returned by the road he had taken into Faerie, but somehow he did not enter the fields we know where he had left them. Yet he was still in Armenia, only a few days' journey from his principality. He had half looked for a greater vengeance.

Then he found his border closed against him, and his onetime vizier holding the throne of his ancestors. "If a prince go haring into Faerie rather than look after his own land, he does not deserve to rule," the usurper had told the nobles, and most said aye and swore him allegiance.

But not all. Prince Rupen soon mustered a band of warriors and undertook to regain by force what had once been his by right. Fighting and siege and murder engulfed the land of Etchmiadzin that had been so fair. By his own hand Rupen slew a cousin who had been a dear friend. He watched comrades of old die in his service, or live on maimed.

And in the end it did not avail. Etchmiadzin remained lost. By the time he admitted that in his heart, Rupen had lived the soldier's life so long that he found any other savorless. From a nest high in the hills—to its sorrow, Armenia has many of them—he and his swooped down into the valleys to seize what they might.

Sometimes Rupen was nearly as rich as a bandit chief as he had been in the castle of Etchmiadzin. More often he went hungry. There were white scars on his arms, and along his ribs, and a great gash on his cheek and forehead that was only partly hidden by the leather patch covering the ruin of his left eyesocket.

He seldom thought of Faerie. Few even of the hard-bitten crew who rode with him had the nerve to bring up his journey to the castle of the sparrowhawk. After a while, most of those who had known of it were dead.

Then one day, as the lady Olissa had decreed, full memory came flooding back, and he knew in astonishment that a decade had passed. He thought of the tiny space of time he had spent in her arms, of his life as a prince before, and the long years of misfortune that came after. He thought of what he had become: ladder-ribbed, huddled close to a tiny fire in a drafty hut, drinking sour wine.

He thought of Olissa again. Not even the folk of Faerie see

all the future, exactly as it will be. "I'd do it over again, just the same way," he said out loud.

One or two of his men looked up. The rest kept on with what they were doing.

A couple of things came together in "The Summer Garden." One is its model—it springs from a tale in Boccaccio's *Decameron*. The other was my falling in love, just about the time when I wrote the piece, with a woman who did not fall in love with me. These things happen. One of the advantages of being a writer is having the chance to work them out on paper.

A different version of this story appeared in the February 1982 *Fantasy Book* as "The Summer's Garden." The editor liked the idea but did not approve of its high, almost Dunsanian style and demanded a complete rewrite. He also introduced sundry other changes, most of them, I think, gratuitous. For better or worse, this is the way I think "The Summer Garden" ought to read.

THE SUMMER GARDEN

IN THE EMPIRE OF KAR V'SHEM, IN THE TOWN of Sennar, through which flow the laughing waters of the River Veprel, there lived the merchant Ansovald. A warm, good-hearted man, he had grown nearly rich from his trade in the furs and honey that the River Veprel brought down from the fabled North, and his home was in the finest quarter of the city, not too far from the marketplace but not too close to the church. With him dwelt his wife Dianora, the delight of his life. Her skin was fairer than the whitest linen, her eyes more green than the verdant jade which now and then appeared from out of the trackless East, her hair the blue-black of the midnight sky, and her nature . . . ah, with her nature we press close to the heart of the matter, for she was of that rare breed who can bear to give hurt to no living creature.

Being such as one, it is only natural that Dianora shared with her dear husband some years of wedded bliss. Nor should it surprise us to learn that her beauty and warmth attracted the notice of others in the town of Sennar beside the merchant Ansovald. Toward these she was, as was her way, unfailingly kind, but, as she truly loved her husband, unfailingly unavailable. One by one, some sooner, some later, they came to understand this and troubled her no more. All save Rand.

Now Rand was a belted knight, a veteran of wars and san-guinary single conflicts, yet withal a poet and dreamer as well. The experiences of his life had forged in him a singleness of purpose not easily matched in all the Empire of Kar V'Shem, let alone the sleepy town of Sennar. Thus when his sonnets fell on deaf ears and his gifts were discreetly returned, he did not grow downhearted—as had so many before him—but paid court to Dianora with greater vigor than before, reckoning the prize he sought all the more valuable for its difficulty of attainment.

The lady was unwilling simply to tell him to be gone; she did not wish to wound his feelings, recognizing his manly qualities even if they tempted her not. Instead, through a maidservant she sent him a message, as follows: "Know that to prove your deep love for me, you must produce in dead of winter a garden full of summer's fruits and flowers. Then I shall be yours to com-mand, but until and unless this be done, you must cease impor-tuning me." Confidently expecting that Rand would find the assigned task as difficult as she deemed it, she banished the knight from her thoughts, glad she had found a way to dismiss him without harshness and certain he would not pester her again.

But no sooner had her servant delivered the note and departed than Rand struck scarred fist against strong palm and spoke. "I shall do it," he vowed, though there was none to hear him. The arduousness of the task did not daunt him as the lady Dianora had hoped; in his wanderings he had seen more marvels than she had ever imagined, she who had never strayed more than a mile or two beyond the sheltering walls of the town of Sennar.

Undaunted Rand may have been, but also uncertain as to how to proceed, for he himself had no notion of how such a wonder as that required of him might be produced. How could one call into being the fragrance and beauty of a summer garden in a world all drear with cold and ice? All the savants and sages to whom he put the question owned themselves baffled. And so for a year and more he remained thwarted, until the mage Portolis took it in his mind to visit Sennar.

When he learned of the arrival of so famous a thaumaturge as Portolis, Rand wasted no time in making his acquaintance and setting forth the problem which had so long tormented him. After he had spoken, Portolis scanned his face. Rand would sooner have faced some men's swords than the wizard's eyes, for they were gray and hard as the granite ramparts of the moun-tains of Rincia, behind which the sun god sought his bed each day. But it ill-behooved a belted knight to show any trace of fear, and so Rand sat unflinching.

At length the wizard nodded slowly. "I can do this thing," he said, "yet the price of its success may be more than you would willingly pay."

Quoth Rand, "For the love of my lady Dianora no price could be too great."

The knight thought he saw a glint of irony kindle for a moment in the terrible eyes of Portolis, but it faded so quickly he could not be sure. "Are you certain of this?" the wizard asked. Rand had been gripped by his obsession for long and long, and could do nothing else but nod. "Be it so, then," Portolis said. "My fee—which must be paid in advance, as the components of this spell are quite costly—is seven thousand seven hundred seven and seventy kraybecks of gold."

Rand blanched, for after paying so great a sum he would be left in poverty. But his resolve was firm and his voice steady as he answered, "I shall deliver it to you on the morrow."

"Next week will suffice," the wizard said idly. "It is still some time before Midwinter Day, at which time, the gods willing, I shall do as you have requested."

As events transpired, the knight was glad Portolis had not required payment on the following day: to meet the magician's price he was compelled to mortgage both mansion and lands. He dismissed servant after servant, no longer able to afford their keep, until at last he was left with but one retainer, a stolid old fellow named Fant. Together they dwelt miserably in one small room of Rand's palatial home, for the knight lacked the wherewithal to heat the entire building. Rand bore his self-inflicted pauperhood proudly, for his heart, if not his body, was warmed by visions of Dianora in his arms; what, if anything, Fant did for like sustenance, it never occurred to Rand to inquire.

Unmoved by the slide of his client into penury, the wizard's preparations for his spell proceeded apace. More than once he left the town of Sennar for some days, arousing fear in the heart of Rand that he was being deluded by some traveling mountebank. But he always returned, and he expressed grave satisfaction whenever the knight queried his progress.

Midwinter Day, when at length it came, dawned clear and cold, the pale sun seeming wan and weak in a steel-blue sky. The entire surround of the town of Sennar was white and still. Even the laughing River Veprel, whose scurrying waters had long defied the icy hand of winter, lay prisoned under a palm-thick sheet of ice. An unsmiling 'prentice of the mage Portolis called upon Rand and Fant to repair to a certain spot by the banks of the river, where, he said, all was ready for the effort, saving only their presence.

Seen from without, the walls of Sennar lost for Rand the aspect of comfort and reassurance they had always before possessed. A warrior born, he had misread Dianora's relegation as challenge, and to his infatuate mind the fortifications formed the perfect metaphor for her heart. In this belief he was most sincere and, poor soul, most mistaken, for the woman's only thought had been to spare him pain.

Vermilion ribbon delineated the area in which the conjuration was to take place. Inside, pentacles had been scribed in snow. Marching around them in intricate goemetric patterns, half a dozen chanting acolytes swung thuribles, charging the frosty air with pungent incenses.

Alone and still in the center of this stir stood Portolis. The north wind frisked playfully through gray tendrils of his beard, but there was nothing of play in his proud hawk face as he greeted Rand. "I ask you once more, sir knight," said he, "if you wish me to proceed?"

"Did I not, would I have beggared myself for you?" Rand demanded harshly. The mage looked him full in the face, then curtly bowed. So loud was Rand's heart pounding in his breast, he was surprised Portolis made no remark on it.

The wizard raised his arms. The acolytes froze, silent in their places, as if seized of a sudden by winter. Through the thunder in his veins Rand heard the wind's thin whisper die, as if the very universe held its breath. His voice ringing like a deep-toned bronzen bell, Portolis began the spell over which he had labored long, his pale fingers flying through its intricate passes like things independently alive.

Rand had never thought on what it might be like to be in the midst of an unfolding miracle. A glow like the distillation of a thousand sunrises suffused the air, conjoined with a scent like that of attar of roses but a thousand times more sweet, a thousand times more delicate, a scent to penetrate to the root of the heart and set it winging free. Portolis's voice was the perfect backdrop to the bedazzlement of Rand's senses, for though he knew not the tongue in which the wizard sang, he felt tears of joy course down his cheeks and fall hot and steaming in the snow.

Snow? As the mists of the enchantment faded, Rand looked down to find his boots no longer coated with rime but cushioned by a carpet of greenest grass. He cried out in wonder and delight: within Portolis's scarlet-lined square, summer reigned. Looking spent and drawn, the wizard leaned against a veritable apple tree full of ruddy fruit. A blue butterfly wheeled round his head; startled perhaps by a blink, perhaps by nothing at all, it darted away, out beyond the confines of his magic, and fell, an azure icicle, to the snow.

The knight all but thought himself still bemused, for hard by the apple tree was one laden with plump pears, next to that a fragrant-leafed orange tree, and beside it bearers of peaches, apricots, and purple figs, soft and deliciously ripe. The perfumes of fruit and trees mingled with those of the flowers clustering round them: roses red as maidens' lips (and Rand's heart throbbed, to think of Dianora), others yellow as the sun, tulips like bells of flame, lilies of every size, shape, and hue, and wild tropic blooms that the knight, traveled though he was, could never have hoped to name.

Filled with awe, Rand touched the smooth, gray-brown bark of the fig, and stroked a parchmentlike leaf. He nipped off a tiny piece between thumb and forefinger and watched, entranced, as beads of white sap formed to seal off the injury he had worked. He questioned his senses no longer. Everything round him was too real, too detailed, to be a mere vision, even one produced by so gifted a warlock as Portolis.

Forethoughtfully having brought along a wicker basket, the knight now filled it with the choicest products of the wondrous summer garden. He handed it to his servant, bidding him repair to the town of Sennar, present it to the lady Dianora as token of the knight's true love, and lead her back to the paradise whose creation Rand had caused.

So intent was Rand on watching his servant near the gates of Sennar that he failed to hear Portolis come up beside him. "So," the wizard said, his voice a tattered ghost of itself, "you have your garden and soon shall have your woman, if that be your desire. Will you then be content?"

"Again and again you ask me this, as if to say it will not be so," Rand cried angrily. "Why do you hound me? I have spent all my substance to gain my lady's submission and love. Once achieved, how could they not fill me with delight?"

The wizard did not reply.

As Fant came up to the gates, their guardsmen, in recognition of the marvel of which he was a part, grounded their spears, doffed conical helms, and bowed low in salute until he was past. "Well, well," he said to himself. "This consorting with magicians is not such a bad thing, no matter what I may have thought in the past. When has a poor servant ever before been greeted like a baron? No, like a prince or better!" And with a fine indolent wave to its warders, he entered the town of Sennar.

When he reached the home of Ansovald the merchant, Fant was greeted with some surprise by the maidservant who had delivered Dianora's message to his master. Recognizing him at once, she said, "You've not come this way in some time. What can I do for you now?" Before an answer could cross his lips, she went on, "Don't stand there and let all the warm out; it's rare cold today. Come in and toast your bones by the fire."

"I'm glad to do that," he replied, and spent the next several minutes savoring the delicious heat. Then, recalling his mission, he handed the maid his basket, saying, "My master bids me deliver this token to your lady and escort her back to the spot where he awaits her."

"Does he indeed?" she said with a toss of her head. "The cheek of the man!" Now, as it happened, she was altogether ignorant of the content of the message she had delivered to Rand so long ago, though she could scarcely have been unaware of his feelings toward her mistress. She commented, "It will take more than a hamper of fruit to change my lady's mind about your knight, I warrant."

Fant shrugged. "That's not for me to say, nor you either," he answered. "Could I ask for a mug of hot wine? I'm chilled clean to the marrow."

"You're as bad as your master." The maid sniffed, but she put some over the fire to heat. While Fant waited with ill-concealed eagerness, she took up the basket and carried it upstairs to the lady Dianora.

The lady had been weaving, and was not sorry to be interrupted. "What have you there for me?" she asked, seeing the basket but not yet understanding what it contained. Her maid repeated Fant's message, punctuated with condemnations of Rand's arrogance and his servant's insolence, and departed, leaving Dianora alone to struggle with her conscience.

She was flattered and complimented beyond all measure by Rand's devotion to the cause of winning her, and she knew full well what his adherence to that cause had cost him, for his sudden and inexplicable slide into poverty had for weeks been one of the paramount topics of conversation in the town of Sennar.

But despite his evident adoration, her heart was in her husband's keeping only, and she no more desired to lie with the knight in love than she had when she made her rash promise so long ago. Yet that promise had been freely given, extorted or coerced from her in no way, and how with honor could she now refuse to keep it? To do so would work far more grievous hurt on Rand than even the coldest and most summary rejection a year and a half ago. Bitterly she repented of her imprudent words, but that repentance no more effaced them than a sparrow's shadow made to disappear the Rincian granite whereon it fell.

When her servant returned to take her reply to Fant, she found she had none to give.

It was not much later that the merchant Ansovald, according to his custom, returned from the marketplace to lunch with his wife. Though she did what she could to conceal her distress, Ansovald soon noticed it and asked what troubled her. With a great show of indignation, she denied that anything was wrong. This deceived the merchant not at all but alarmed him no little, for if in their years of marriage he had come to rely upon anything, it was his wife's candor.

Therefore he persisted, and ere long had the entire story from her, though toward its end she was in tears. When he had heard everything, he was silent for a long time. His fingers curled his beard into ringlets, as was his unconscious custom while deep in thought. He had long known Dianora had admirers other than himself, and the notion did not much upset him; indeed, in his secret heart he was rather proud of it, as reflecting favorably upon his own manhood. Whether or not she occasionally succumbed to temptation mattered less to him than it might to other men, for he was fully assured of both her love and her discretion, and was sure she would do no injury to himself or to their union. Furthermore, he knew her pledge to Rand had been made not in expectation of its eventual fulfillment, but in the hope that it would, without wounding the knight, make him realize that his attentions were superfluous.

All of which considerations were now wide of the mark, as Rand had, by whatever means, met the conditions imposed upon him. Ansovald felt nothing but admiration for his perseverance and ingenuity, however unfortunate he found their target. Moreover, as a reputable merchant, he was a man to whom agreements of any sort were sacred trusts, to be carried out by all parties to the best of their ability.

Accordingly, once he had relieved his wife's fears and kissed

her tears away, he told her, "I see but one thing which can in
honor be done. You must indeed go to Rand, explain to him the
motive behind your promise, and pray him not to hold you to
it."

The lady Dianora nodded; this was the same conclusion she
herself had reached. However . . . "And if he insist?"

Ansovald sighed; he did not much care for the position toward which his logic inexorably led him. "If he must have that
which he has sought so long and so hard, I see no easy way to
say him nay this once. You need have no fear of me because of
it; I will think none the worse of you, happen what may. A
woman's faithfulness lies in her heart, not between her thighs."

Barely believing her ears, Dianora marveled at her husband's
forbearance. Ansovald's words were nothing less than heresy in
that time and place, where most men would forthwith have sent
away their wives at the faintest hint of scandal.

The merchant rose from the table, belting his long marten-
fur coat round his ample middle. He stooped to kiss his wife
once more, saying gruffly, "Go on with you, now. Soonest begun, soonest done." And then he was gone, hurrying back to
his stall in the marketplace without the slightest trace of concern
in face or step.

Far longer than he had expected or hoped did Rand wait in
the summer garden for his beloved. He spoke no more to the
mage Portolis, having less and less liking for him as hour succeeded hour and the wan sun began to wester. Had the sorcerer
known even before the outset of his project its inherent futility,
and carried on for his enrichment alone, or perhaps to make the
knight a laughingstock? If so, thought Rand, he might well rue
it, sorcerer or no: cold steel was proof against most magics.

Such were the shapes of his gloomy reflections, when suddenly his heart gave a great leap: that was surely Fant coming
out through the gate of Sennar, and with him Dianora! The
knight's features, so long dour, lit with delight, and when he
shot a quick glance toward Portolis he spied a flush of interest
livening the wizard's sallow and exhausted features. Ha! Rand
thought: I have won, even against the old fool's prognostica-
tions.

Without giving Rand a word, a nod, any acknowledgment of
his presence, Dianora walked through the summer garden, now
bending to test a flower's fragrance, now rising to touch a leaf,
to test the ripeness of a dangling fruit. When her inspection was

complete, she squared her shoulders beneath their mantling furs and stood at last before him.

"My love!" he cried, taking both her hands in his. It was all he could do to keep from clasping her to him then and there, so often had this moment been prefigured in his thoughts and dreams. "You are mine at last!"

Her emerald gaze was sorrow-filled, but she answered him firmly. "I am yours this day, if that be your will; such was my pledge to you. But you must know I am not your love, nor have I ever been. My heart lies only with my husband, the merchant Ansovald, as it has always. Do you not see, my lord Rand, that your love for me is as out of season as is this garden in the midst of a world of snow?"

Her words pierced Rand's exultation to the marrow, and he stood for a moment bereft of speech, like a man sore wounded and only just aware of it. "But you are here—" he began, and then faltered into silence once more.

"Yes, I am here," she said, and Rand knew the bitterness in her voice was directed as much against herself as at him. "Sir knight, why could you not understand I meant but to discourage you without doing you harm, not to spur you on? If you must have your way with me, be it so, but I yield myself solely from faith to my foolish promise, not from love of you."

And now, too late, the knight understood Portolis's warnings and the trap he had laid for himself. In his passion he had failed to distinguish between satisfying his body's lust and the love of the heart within it. He had indeed won Dianora's submission, but he had no hope—had never had a hope—of winning the love that would make that submission something more than a few moments of meaningless sensual pleasure. He freed her hands; his own, like dead things, fell to his sides. "Go," he said, his voice betraying little of the anguish he felt. "I release you from your pledge. I have yet to bed a woman unwilling, and would scarcely start with so fine a one as you, who would suffer me for your word's sake alone. Go," he repeated, but now his grief made of the word a ghastly whisper.

Her gratitude he endured with soldier's courage, but as Fant escorted her back to her home in Sennar, the knight swung round to face Portolis with fierce accusation. "You foresaw this!"

But the mage shook his head. "Not so," he said gravely. "That all might not turn out as you had wished, yes, I saw that, but needed scant magic to do so. It was pikestaff plain your love was not returned, else what need had you of me? Yet who could have foretold such generosity and greatness of soul as was displayed by the lady Dianora in freely offering that which she had no reason to give but to honor a word she had thought unfulfillable, or by yourself in willingly abandoning a goal you had unswervingly sought and beggared yourself to achieve? I own I am baffled as to how to comport myself in the face of such unselfishness. For your heart I have no salve save the healing hand of time, but out of gratitude for what you have taught me of magnanimity, you shall find when you return to your home the seven thousand seven hundred seven and seventy kraybecks of gold you devoted to this enterprise. I think, Sir Rand, you shall prosper to the end of your days.''

The knight tried to decline this unexpected boon, but the mage Portolis was insistent, maintaining that any lesser action would leave him meanspirited in his own eyes. Not much later he departed the town of Sennar, never to return, but his magic stayed on. Forever after, the garden he had brought into being was sere and bare in summer, but bore abundantly when everywhere else frost held sway.

Nor was he a mean prophet, as Rand soon became one of the wealthiest men in the town of Sennar. His name became known all through the Empire of Kar V'Shem, for there was no work of philanthropy in which he failed to play a major role. In time he took a wife, and it is not to be doubted he loved her very much indeed. But until the end of his long and illustrious life, each year's Midwinter Day found him in Portolis's enchanted garden: the fruits thereof were out of season, but no denying they were sweet.

Alternate history stories are not really about the alternate worlds in which their authors set them. They're about our own world, as seen through the funhouse mirror of a changed past. They're thought experiments, testing the parameters of ideas in frameworks different from our own. "The Last Article" is an example of the type: a confrontation of extremes which, in our world, never met—and just as well, too.

THE LAST ARTICLE

Nonviolence is the first article of my faith. It is also the last article of my creed.

—Mohandas Gandhi

The one means that wins the easiest victory over reason: terror and force.

—Adolf Hitler, *Mein Kampf*

THE TANK RUMBLED DOWN THE RAJPATH, past the ruins of the Memorial Arch, toward the India Gate. The gateway arch was still standing, although it had taken a couple of shell hits in the fighting before New Delhi fell. The Union Jack fluttered above it.

British troops lined both sides of the Rajpath, watching silently as the tank rolled past them. Their khaki uniforms were filthy and torn; many wore bandages. They had the weary, past-caring stares of beaten men, though the Army of India had fought until flesh and munitions gave out.

The India Gate drew near. A military band, smartened up for the occasion, began to play as the tank went past. The bagpipes sounded thin and lost in the hot, humid air.

A single man stood waiting in the shadow of the Gate. Field Marshal Walther Model leaned down into the cupola of the Panzer IV. "No one can match the British at ceremonies of this sort," he said to his aide.

Major Dieter Lasch laughed, a bit unkindly. "They've had

214

enough practice, sir,'' he answered, raising his voice to be heard over the flatulent roar of the tank's engine.

"What is that tune?" the field marshal asked. "Does it have a meaning?"

"It's called 'The World Turned Upside Down,' " said Lasch, who had been involved with his British opposite number in planning the formal surrender. "Lord Cornwallis's army musicians played it when he yielded to the Americans at Yorktown."

"Ah, the Americans." Model was for a moment so lost in his own thoughts that his monocle threatened to slip from his right eye. He screwed it back in. The single lens was the only thing he shared with the clichéd image of a high German officer. He was no lean, hawk-faced Prussian. But his rounded features were unyielding, and his stocky body sustained the energy of his will better than the thin, dyspeptic frames of so many aristocrats. "The Americans," he repeated. "Well, that will be the next step, won't it? But enough. One thing at a time."

The panzer stopped. The driver switched off the engine. The sudden quiet was startling. Model leaped nimbly down. He had been leaping down from tanks for eight years now, since his days as a staff officer for the IV Corps in the Polish campaign.

The man in the shadows stepped forward, saluted. Flashbulbs lit his long, tired face as German photographers recorded the moment for history. The Englishman ignored cameras and cameramen alike. "Field Marshal Model," he said politely. He might have been about to discuss the weather.

Model admired his sangfroid. "Field Marshal Auchinleck," he replied, returning the salute and giving Auchinleck a last few seconds to remain his equal. Then he came back to the matter at hand. "Field Marshal, have you signed the instrument of surrender of the British Army of India to the forces of the Reich?"

"I have," Auchinleck replied. He reached into the left blouse pocket of his battledress, removed a folded sheet of paper. Before handing it to Model, though, he said, "I should like to request your permission to make a brief statement at this time."

"Of course, sir. You may say what you like, at whatever length you like." In victory, Model could afford to be magnanimous. He had even granted Marshal Zhukov leave to speak in the Soviet capitulation at Kuibishev, before the marshal was taken out and shot.

"I thank you." Auchinleck stiffly dipped his head. "I will say, then, that I find the terms I have been forced to accept to be cruelly hard on the brave men who have served under my command.''

''That is your privilege, sir.'' But Model's round face was no longer kindly, and his voice had iron in it as he replied, ''I must remind you, however, that my treating with you at all under the rules of war is an act of mercy for which Berlin may yet reprimand me. When Britain surrendered in 1941, all Imperial forces were also ordered to lay down their arms. I daresay you did not expect us to come so far, but I would be within my rights in reckoning you no more than so many bandits.''

A slow flush darkened Auchinleck's cheeks. ''We gave you a bloody good run, for bandits.''

''So you did.'' Model remained polite. He did not say he would ten times rather fight straight-up battles than deal with the partisans who to this day harassed the Germans and their allies in occupied Russia. ''Have you anything further to add?''

''No, sir, I do not.'' Auchinleck gave the German the signed surrender, handed him his sidearm. Model put the pistol in the empty holster he wore for the occasion. It did not fit well; the holster was made for a Walther P38, not this man-killing brute of a Webley and Scott. That mattered little, though—the ceremony was almost over.

Auchinleck and Model exchanged salutes for the last time. The British field marshal stepped away. A German lieutenant came up to lead him into captivity.

Major Lasch waved his left hand. The Union Jack came down from the flagpole on the India Gate. The swastika rose to replace it.

Lasch tapped discreetly on the door, stuck his head into the field marshal's office. ''That Indian politician is here for his appointment with you, sir.''

''Oh, yes. Very well, Dieter, send him in.'' Model had been dealing with Indian politicians even before the British surrender, and with hordes of them now that resistance was over. He had no more liking for the breed than for Russian politicians, or even German ones. No matter what pious principles they spouted, his experience was that they were all out for their own good first.

The small, frail brown man the aide showed in made him wonder. The Indian's emaciated frame and the plain white cotton loincloth that was his only garment contrasted starkly with the Victorian splendor of the Viceregal Palace from which Model was administering the Reich's new conquest. "Sit down, *Herr* Gandhi," the field marshal urged.

"I thank you very much, sir." As he took his seat, Gandhi seemed a child in an adult's chair: it was much too wide for him, and its soft, overstuffed cushions hardly sagged under his meager weight. But his eyes, Model saw, were not a child's eyes. They peered with disconcerting keenness through his wire-framed spectacles as he said, "I have come to enquire when we may expect German troops to depart from our country."

Model leaned forward, frowning. For a moment he thought he had misunderstood Gandhi's Gujarati-flavored English. When he was sure he had not, he said, "Do you think perhaps we have come all this way as tourists?"

"Indeed I do not." Gandhi's voice was sharp with disapproval. "Tourists do not leave so many dead behind them."

Model's temper kindled. "No, tourists do not pay such a high price for the journey. Having come regardless of that cost, I assure you we shall stay."

"I am very sorry, sir; I cannot permit it."

"*You* cannot?" Again, Model had to concentrate to keep his monocle from falling out. He had heard arrogance from politicians before, but this scrawny old devil surpassed belief. "Do you forget I can call my aide and have you shot behind this building? You would not be the first, I assure you."

"Yes, I know that," Gandhi said sadly. "If you have that fate in mind for me, I am an old man. I will not run."

Combat had taught Model a hard indifference to the prospect of injury or death. He saw the older man possessed something of the same sort, however he had acquired it. A moment later, he realized his threat had not only failed to frighten Gandhi, but had actually amused him. Disconcerted, the field marshal said, "Have you any serious issues to address?"

"Only the one I named just now. We are a nation of more than three hundred million; it is no more just for Germany to rule us than for the British."

Model shrugged. "If we are able to, we will. We have the strength to hold what we have conquered, I assure you."

"Where there is no right, there can be no strength," Gandhi said. "We will not permit you to hold us in bondage."

"Do you think to threaten me?" Model growled. In fact, though, the Indian's audacity surprised him. Most of the locals had fallen over themselves, fawning on their new masters. Here, at least, was a man out of the ordinary.

Gandhi was still shaking his head, although Model saw he had still not frightened him—a man out of the ordinary indeed, thought the field marshal, who respected courage when he found it. "I make no threats, sir, but I will do what I believe to be right."

"Most noble," Model said, but to his annoyance the words came out sincere rather than with the sardonic edge he had intended. He had heard such canting phrases before, from Englishmen, from Russians, yes, and from Germans as well. Somehow, though, this Gandhi struck him as one who always meant exactly what he said. He rubbed his chin, considering how to handle such an intransigent.

A large green fly came buzzing into the office. Model's air of detachment vanished the moment he heard that malignant whine. He sprang from his seat, swatted at the fly. He missed. The insect flew around a while longer, then settled on the arm of Gandhi's chair. "Kill it," Model told him. "Last week one of those accursed things bit me on the neck, and I still have the lump to prove it."

Gandhi brought his hand down, but several inches from the fly. Frightened, it took off. Gandhi rose. He was surprisingly nimble for a man nearing eighty. He chivvied the fly out of the office, ignoring Model, who watched his performance in openmouthed wonder.

"I hope it will not trouble you again," Gandhi said, returning as calmly as if he had done nothing out of the ordinary. "I am one of those who practice *ahimsa*: I will do no injury to any living thing."

Model remembered the fall of Moscow, and the smell of burning bodies filling the chilly autumn air. He remembered machine guns knocking down Cossack cavalry before they could close, and the screams of the wounded horses, more heartrending than any woman's. He knew of other things too, things he had not seen for himself and of which he had no desire to learn more.

"*Herr* Gandhi," he said, "how do you propose to bend to your will someone who opposes you, if you will not use force for the purpose?"

"I have never said I will not use force, sir." Gandhi's smile invited the field marshal to enjoy with him the distinction he was making. "I will not use violence. If my people refuse to cooperate in any way with yours, how can you compel them?

What choice will you have but to grant us leave to do as we will?''

Without the intelligence estimates he had read, Model would have dismissed the Indian as a madman. No madman, though, could have caused the British so much trouble. But perhaps the decadent Raj simply had not made him afraid. Model tried again. ''You understand that what you have said is treason against the Reich,'' he said harshly.

Gandhi bowed in his seat. ''You may, of course, do what you will with me. My spirit will in any case survive among my people.''

Model felt his face heat. Few men were immune to fear. Just his luck, he thought sourly, to have run into one of them. ''I warn you, *Herr* Gandhi, to obey the authority of the officials of the Reich, or it will be the worse for you.''

''I will do what I believe to be right, and nothing else. If you Germans exert yourselves toward the freeing of India, joyfully will I work with you. If not, then I regret we must be foes.''

The field marshal gave him one last chance to see reason. ''Were it you and I alone, there might be some doubt as to what would happen.'' Not much, he thought, not when Gandhi was twenty-odd years older and thin enough to break like a stick. He fought down the irrelevance, went on, ''But where, *Herr* Gandhi, is your *Wehrmacht*?''

Of all things, he had least expected to amuse the Indian again. Yet Gandhi's eyes unmistakably twinkled behind the lenses of his spectacles. ''Field Marshal, I have an army too.''

Model's patience, never of the most enduring sort, wore thin all at once. ''Get out!'' he snapped.

Gandhi stood, bowed, and departed. Major Lasch stuck his head into the office. The field marshal's glare drove him out again in a hurry.

''Well?'' Jawaharlal Nehru paced back and forth. Tall, slim, and saturnine, he towered over Gandhi without dominating him. ''Dare we use the same policies against the Germans that we employed against the English?''

''If we wish our land free, dare we do otherwise?'' Gandhi replied. ''They will not grant our wish of their own volition. Model struck me as a man not much differed from various British leaders whom we have succeeded in vexing in the past.'' He smiled at the memory of what passive resistance had done to officials charged with combating it.

"Very well, *Satyagraha* it is." But Nehru was not smiling. He had less humor than his older colleague.

Gandhi teased him gently: "Do you fear another spell in prison, then?" Both men had spent time behind bars during the war, until the British released them in a last, vain effort to rally the support of the Indian people to the Raj.

"You know better." Nehru refused to be drawn, and persisted, "The rumors that come out of Europe frighten me."

"Do you tell me you take them seriously?" Gandhi shook his head in surprise and a little reproof. "Each side in any war will always paint its opponents as blackly as it can."

"I hope you are right, and that that is all. Still, I confess I would feel more at ease with what we plan to do if you found me one Jew, officer or other rank, in the army now occupying us."

"You would be hard-pressed to find any among the forces they defeated. The British have little love for Jews either."

"Yes, but I daresay it could be done. With the Germans, they are banned by law. The English would never make such a rule. And while the laws are vile enough, I think of the tales that man Wiesenthal told, the one who came here, the gods know how, across Russia and Persia from Poland."

"Those I do not believe," Gandhi said firmly. "No nation could act in that way and hope to survive. Where could men be found to carry out such horrors."

"Azad Hind," Nehru said, quoting the "Free India" motto of the locals who had fought on the German side.

But Gandhi shook his head. "They are only soldiers, doing as soldiers have always done. Wiesenthal's claims are for an entirely different order of bestiality, one which could not exist without destroying the fabric of the state that gave it birth."

"I hope very much you are right," Nehru said.

Walther Model slammed the door behind him hard enough to make his aide, whose desk faced away from the field marshal's office, jump in alarm. "Enough of this twaddle for one day," Model said. "I need schnapps, to get the taste of these Indians out of my mouth. Come along if you care to, Dieter."

"Thank you, sir." Major Lasch threw down his pen, eagerly got to his feet. "I sometimes think conquering India was easier than ruling it will be."

Model rolled his eyes. "I *know* it was. I would ten times rather be planning a new campaign than sitting here bogged down in pettifogging details. The sooner Berlin sends me people trained in colonial administration, the happier I will be.''

The bar might have been taken from an English pub. It was dark, quiet, and paneled in walnut; a dartboard still hung on the wall. But a German sergeant in field-gray stood behind the bar and, despite the lazily turning ceiling fan, the temperature was close to thirty-five Celsius. The one might have been possible in occupied London, the other not.

Model knocked back his first shot at a gulp. He sipped his second more slowly, savoring it. Warmth spread through him, warmth that had nothing to do with the heat of the evening. He leaned back in his chair, steepled his fingers. ''A long day,'' he said.

''Yes, sir,'' Lasch agreed. ''After the effrontery of that Gandhi, any day would seem a long one. I've rarely seen you so angry.'' Considering Model's temper, that was no small statement.

''Ah, yes, Gandhi.'' Model's tone was reflective rather than irate; Lasch looked at him curiously. The field marshal said, ''For my money, he's worth a dozen of the ordinary sort.''

''Sir?'' The aide no longer tried to hide his surprise.

''He is an honest man. He tells me what he thinks, and he will stick by that. I may kill him—I may have to kill him—but he and I will both know why, and I will not change his mind.'' Model took another sip of schnapps. He hesitated, as if unsure whether to go on. At last he did. ''Do you know, Dieter, after he left I had a vision.''

''Sir?'' Now Lasch sounded alarmed.

The field marshal might have read his aide's thoughts. He chuckled wryly. ''No, no, I am not about to swear off eating beefsteak and wear sandals instead of my boots, that I promise. But I saw myself as a Roman procurator, listening to the rantings of some early Christian priest.''

Lasch raised an eyebrow. Such musings were unlike Model, who was usually direct to the point of bluntness and altogether materialistic—assets in the makeup of a general officer. The major cautiously sounded these unexpected depths: ''How do you suppose the Roman felt, facing that kind of man?''

''Bloody confused, I suspect,'' Model said, which sounded more like him. ''And because he and his comrades did not know how to handle such fanatics, you and I are Christians today, Dieter.''

"So we are." The major rubbed his chin. "Is that a bad thing?"

Model laughed and finished his drink. "From your point of view or mine, no. But I doubt that old Roman would agree with us, any more than Gandhi agrees with me over what will happen next here. But then, I have two advantages over the dead procurator." He raised his finger; the sergeant hurried over to fill his glass.

At Lasch's nod, the young man also poured more schnapps for him. The major drank, then said, "I should hope so. We are more civilized, more sophisticated, than the Romans ever dreamed of being."

But Model was still in that fey mood. "Are we? My procurator was such a sophisticate that he tolerated anything, and never saw the danger in a foe who would not do the same. Our Christian God, though, is a jealous god, who puts up with no rivals. And one who is a National Socialist serves also the *Volk*, to whom he owes sole loyalty. I am immune to Gandhi's virus in a way the Roman was not to the Christian's."

"Yes, that makes sense," Lasch agreed after a moment. "I had not thought of it in that way, but I see it is so. And what is our other advantage over the Roman procurator?"

Suddenly the field marshal looked hard and cold, much the way he had looked leading the tanks of Third Panzer against the Kremlin compound. "The machine gun," he said.

The rising sun's rays made the sandstone of the Red Fort seem even more the color of blood. Gandhi frowned and turned his back on the fortress, not caring for that thought. Even at dawn, the air was warm and muggy.

"I wish you were not here," Nehru told him. The younger man lifted his trademark fore-and-aft cap, scratched his graying hair, and glanced at the crowd growing around them. "The Germans' orders forbid assemblies, and they will hold you responsible for this gathering."

"I am, am I not?" Gandhi replied. "Would you have me send my followers into a danger I do not care to face myself? How would I presume to lead them afterward?"

"A general does not fight in the front ranks," Nehru came back. "If you are lost to our cause, will we be able to go on?"

"If not, then surely the cause is not worthy, yes? Now let us be going."

Nehru threw his hands in the air. Gandhi nodded, satisfied,

and worked his way toward the head of the crowd. Men and women stepped aside to let him through. Still shaking his head, Nehru followed.

The crowd slowly began to march east up Chandni Chauk, the Street of Silversmiths. Some of the fancy shops had been wrecked in the fighting, more looted afterward. But others were opening up, their owners as happy to take German money as they had been to serve the British before.

One of the proprietors, a man who had managed to stay plump even through the past year of hardship, came rushing out of his shop when he saw the procession go by. He ran to the head of the march and spotted Nehru, whose height and elegant dress singled him out.

"Are you out of your mind?" the silversmith shouted. "The Germans have banned assemblies. If they see you, something dreadful will happen."

"Is it not dreadful that they take away the liberty which properly belongs to us?" Gandhi asked. The silversmith spun round. His eyes grew wide when he recognized the man who was speaking to him. Gandhi went on, "Not only is it dreadful, it is wrong. And so we do not recognize the Germans' right to ban anything we may choose to do. Join us, will you?"

"Great-souled one, I—I—" the silversmith spluttered. Then his glance slid past Gandhi. "The Germans!" he squeaked. He turned and ran.

Gandhi led the procession toward the approaching squad. The Germans stamped down Chandni Chauk as if they expected the people in front of them to melt from their path. Their gear, Gandhi thought, was not that much different from what British soldiers wore: ankle boots, shorts, and open-necked tunics. But their coal-scuttle helmets gave them a look of sullen, beetle-browed ferocity the British tin hat did not convey. Even for a man of Gandhi's equanimity it was daunting, as no doubt it was intended to be.

"Hello, my friends," he said. "Do any of you speak English?"

"I speak it, a little," one of them replied. His shoulder straps had the twin pips of a sergeant-major; he was the squad-leader, then. He hefted his rifle, not menacingly, Gandhi thought, but to emphasize what he was saying. "Go to your homes back. This coming together is *verboten*."

"I am sorry, but I must refuse to obey your order," Gandhi said. "We are walking peacefully on our own street in our own city. We will harm no one, no matter what; this I promise you. But walk we will, as we wish." He repeated himself until he was sure the sergeant-major understood.

The German spoke to his comrades in his own language. One of the soldiers raised his gun and with a nasty smile pointed it at Gandhi. He nodded politely. The German blinked to see him unafraid. The sergeant-major slapped the rifle down. One of his men had a field telephone on his back. The sergeant-major cranked it, waited for a reply, spoke urgently into it.

Nehru caught Gandhi's eye. His dark, tired gaze was full of worry. Somehow that nettled Gandhi more than the Germans' arrogance in ordering about his people. He began to walk forward again. The marchers followed him, flowing around the German squad like water flowing round a boulder.

The soldier who had pointed his rifle at Gandhi shouted in alarm. He brought up the weapon again. The sergeant-major barked at him. Reluctantly, he lowered it.

"A sensible man," Gandhi said to Nehru. "He sees we do no injury to him or his, and so does none to us."

"Sadly, though, not everyone is so sensible," the younger man replied, "as witness his lance-corporal there. And even a sensible man may not be well-inclined to us. You notice he is still on the telephone."

The phone on Field Marshal Model's desk jangled. He jumped and swore; he had left orders he was to be disturbed only for an emergency. He had to find time to work. He picked up the phone. "This had better be good," he growled without preamble.

He listened, swore again, slammed the receiver down. "Lasch!" he shouted.

It was his aide's turn to jump. "Sir?"

"Don't just sit there on your fat arse," the field marshal said unfairly. "Call out my car and driver, and quickly. Then belt on your sidearm and come along. The Indians are doing something stupid. Oh, yes, order out a platoon and have them come after us. Up on Chandni Chauk, the trouble is."

Lasch called for the car and the troops, then hurried after Model. "A riot?" he asked as he caught up.

"No, no." Model moved his stumpy frame along so fast that the taller Lasch had to trot beside him. "Some of Gandhi's tricks, damn him."

The field marshal's Mercedes was waiting when he and his

aide hurried out of the viceregal palace. "Chandni Chauk,"
Model snapped as the driver held the door open for him. After
that he sat in furious silence as the powerful car roared up Irwin
Road, round a third of Connaught Circle, and north on Chelms-
ford Road past the bombed-out railway station until, for no reason Model could see, the street's name changed to Qutb Road.

A little later, the driver said, "Some kind of disturbance up
ahead, sir."

"Disturbance?" Lasch echoed, leaning forward to peer
through the windscreen. "It's a whole damned regiment's worth
of Indians coming at us. Don't they know better than that? And
what the devil," he added, his voice rising, "are so many of
our men doing ambling along beside them? Don't they know
they're supposed to break up this sort of thing?" In his indignation, he did not notice he was repeating himself.

"I suspect they don't," Model said dryly. "Gandhi, I gather,
can have that effect on people who aren't ready for his peculiar
brand of stubbornness. That, however, does not include me."
He tapped the driver on the shoulder. "Pull up about two hundred meters in front of the first rank of them, Joachim."

"Yes, sir."

Even before the car had stopped moving, Model jumped out
of it. Lasch, hand on his pistol, was close behind, protesting,
"What if one of those fanatics has a gun?"

"Then Colonel-General Weidling assumes command, and a
lot of Indians end up dead." Model strode toward Gandhi, ignoring the German troops who were drawing themselves to stiff,
horrified attention at the sight of his field marshal's uniform. He
would deal with them later. For the moment, Gandhi was more
important.

He had stopped—which meant the rest of the marchers did
too—and was waiting politely for Model to approach. The German commandant was not impressed. He thought Gandhi sincere and could not doubt his courage, but none of that mattered
at all. He said harshly, "You were warned against this sort of
behavior."

Gandhi looked him in the eye. They were very much of a
height. "And I told you, I do not recognize your right to give
such orders. This is our country, not yours, and if some of us
choose to walk on our streets, we will do so."

From behind Gandhi, Nehru's glance flicked worriedly from
one of the antagonists to the other. Model noticed him only
peripherally; if he was already afraid, he could be handled

whenever necessary. Gandhi was a tougher nut. The field marshal waved at the crowd behind the old man. "You are responsible for all these people. If harm comes to them, you will be to blame."

"Why should harm come to them. They are not soldiers. They do not attack your men. I told that to one of your sergeants, and he understood it, and refrained from hindering us. Surely you, sir, an educated, cultured man, can see that what I say is self-evident truth."

Model turned his head to speak to his aide in German: "If we did not have Goebbels, this would be the one for his job." He shuddered to think of the propaganda victory Gandhi would win if he got away with flouting German ordinances. The whole countryside would be boiling with partisans in a week. And he had already managed to hoodwink some Germans into letting him do it!

Then Gandhi surprised him again. *"Ich danke Ihnen, Herr Generalfeldmarschall, aber das glaube ich kein Kompliment zu sein,"* he said in slow but clear German: "I thank you, field marshal, but I believe that to be no compliment."

Having to hold his monocle in place helped Model keep his face straight. "Take it however you like," he said. "Get these people off the street, or they and you will face the consequences. We will do what you force us to."

"I force you to nothing. As for these people who follow, each does so of his or her own free will. We are free, and will show it, not by violence, but through firmness in truth."

Now Model listened with only half an ear. He had kept Gandhi talking long enough for the platoon he had ordered out to arrive. Half a dozen SdKfz 251 armored personnel carriers came clanking up. The men piled out of them. "Give me a firing line, three ranks deep," Model shouted. As the troopers scrambled to obey, he waved the halftracks into position behind them, all but blocking Qutb Road. The halftracks' commanders swiveled the machine guns at the front of the vehicles' troop compartments so they bore on the Indians.

Gandhi watched these preparations as calmly as if they had nothing to do with him. Again Model had to admire his calm. His followers were less able to keep fear from their faces. Very few, though, used the pause to slip away. Gandhi's discipline was a long way from the military sort, but effective all the same.

"Tell them to disperse now, and we can still get away without bloodshed," the field marshal said.

"We will shed no one's blood, sir. But we will continue on our pleasant journey. Moving carefully, we will, I think, be able to get between your large lorries there." Gandhi turned to wave his people forward once more.

"You insolent—" Rage choked Model, which was as well, for it kept him from cursing Gandhi like a fishwife. To give him time to master his temper, he plucked his monocle from his eye and began polishing the lens with a silk handkerchief. He replaced the monocle, started to jam the handkerchief back into his trouser pocket, then suddenly had a better idea.

"Come, Lasch," he said, and started toward the waiting German troops. About halfway to them, he dropped the handkerchief on the ground. He spoke in loud, simple German so his men and Gandhi could both follow: "If any Indians come past this spot, I wash my hands of them."

He might have known Gandhi would have a comeback ready. "That is what Pilate said also, you will recall, sir."

"Pilate washed his hands to evade responsibility," the field marshal answered steadily; he was in control of himself again. "I accept it: I am responsible to my Führer and to the *Oberkommando-Wehrmacht* for maintaining the Reich's control over India, and will do what I see fit to carry out that obligation."

For the first time since they had come to know each other, Gandhi looked sad. "I too, sir, have my responsibilities." He bowed slightly to Model.

Lasch chose that moment to whisper in his commander's ear: "Sir, what of our men over there? Had you planned to leave them in the line of fire?"

The field marshal frowned. He had planned to do just that; the wretches deserved no better, for being taken in by Gandhi. But Lasch had a point. The platoon might balk at shooting countrymen, if it came to that. "You men," Model said sourly, jabbing his marshal's baton at them, "fall in behind the armored personnel carriers, at once."

The Germans' boots pounded on the macadam as they dashed to obey. They were still all right, then, with a clear order in front of them. Something, Model thought, but not much.

He had also worried that the Indians would take advantage of the moment of confusion to press forward, but they did not. Gandhi and Nehru and a couple of other men were arguing among themselves. Model nodded once. Some of them knew he was in earnest, then. And Gandhi's followers' discipline, as the field marshal had thought a few minutes ago, was not of the military sort. He could not simply issue an order and know his will would be done.

"I issue no orders," Gandhi said. "Let each man follow his conscience as he will—what else is freedom?"

"They will follow *you* if you go forward, great-souled one," Nehru replied, "and that German, I fear, means to carry out his threat. Will you throw your life away, and those of your countrymen?"

"I will not throw my life away," Gandhi said, but before the men around him could relax he went on, "I will gladly give it, if freedom requires that. I am but one man. If I fall, others will surely carry on; perhaps the memory of me will serve to make them more steadfast."

He stepped forward.

"Oh, damnation," Nehru said softly, and followed.

For all his vigor, Gandhi was far from young. Nehru did not need to nod to the marchers close by him; of their own accord, they hurried ahead of the man who had led them for so long, forming with their bodies a barrier between him and the German guns.

He tried to go faster. "Stop! Leave me my place! What are you doing?" he cried, though in his heart he understood only too well.

"This once, they will not listen to you," Nehru said.

"But they must!" Gandhi peered through eyes dimmed now by tears as well as age. "Where is that stupid handkerchief? We must be almost to it!"

"For the last time, I warn you to halt!" Model shouted. The Indians still came on. The sound of their feet, sandal-clad or bare, was like a growing murmur on the pavement, very different from the clatter of German boots. "Fools!" the field marshal muttered under his breath. He turned to his men. "Take your aim!"

The advance slowed when the rifles came up; of that Model was certain. For a moment he thought that ultimate threat would be enough to bring the marchers to their senses. But then they advanced again. The Polish cavalry had shown that same reckless bravery, charging with lances and sabers and carbines against the German tanks. Model wondered whether the inhabitants of the *Reichsgeneralgouvernement* of Poland thought the gallantry worthwhile.

A man stepped on the field marshal's handkerchief. "Fire!" Model said.

A second passed, two. Nothing happened. Model scowled at his men. Gandhi's deviltry had got into them; sneaky as a Jew, he was turning the appearance of weakness into a strange kind of strength. But then trained discipline paid its dividend. One finger tightened on a Mauser trigger. A single shot rang out. As if it were a signal that recalled the other men to their duty, they too began to fire. From the armored personnel carriers, the machine guns started their deadly chatter. Model heard screams above the gunfire.

The volley smashed into the front ranks of marchers at close range. Men fell. Others ran, or tried to, only to be held by the power of the stream still advancing behind them. Once begun, the Germans methodically poured fire into the column of Indians. The march dissolved into a panic-stricken mob.

Gandhi still tried to press forward. A fleeing wounded man smashed into him, splashing him with blood and knocking him to the ground. Nehru and another man immediately lay down on top of him.

"Let me up! Let me up!" he shouted.

"No," Nehru screamed in his ear. "With shooting like this, you are in the safest spot you can be. We need you, and need you alive. Now we have martyrs around whom to rally our cause."

"Now we have dead husbands and wives, fathers and mothers. Who will tend to their loved ones?"

Gandhi had no time for more protest. Nehru and the other man hauled him to his feet and dragged him away. Soon they were among their people, all running now from the German guns. A bullet struck the back of the unknown man who was helping Gandhi escape. Gandhi heard the slap of the impact, felt the man jerk. Then the strong grip on him loosened as the man fell.

He tried to tear free from Nehru. Before he could, another Indian laid hold of him. Even at that horrid moment, he felt the irony of his predicament. All his life he had championed individual liberty, and here his own followers were robbing him of his. In other circumstances, it might have been funny.

"In here!" Nehru shouted. Several people had already broken down the door to a shop and, Gandhi saw a moment later, the rear exit as well. Then he was hustled into the alley behind the shop, and through a maze of lanes which reminded him the old Delhi, unlike its British-designed sister city, was an Indian town through and through.

At last the nameless man with Gandhi and Nehru knocked on the back door of a tearoom. The woman who opened it gasped to recognize her unexpected guests, then pressed her hands together in front of her and stepped aside to let them in. "You will be safe here," the man said, "at least for a while. Now I must see to my own family."

"From the bottom of our hearts, we thank you," Nehru replied as the fellow hurried away. Gandhi said nothing. He was winded, battered, and filled with anguish at the failure of the march and at the suffering it had brought to so many marchers and to their kinsfolk.

The woman sat the two fugitive leaders at a small table in the kitchen, served them tea and cakes. "I will leave you now, best ones," she said quietly, "lest those out front wonder why I neglect them for so long."

Gandhi left the cake on his plate. He sipped the tea. Its warmth began to restore him physically, but the wound in his spirit would never heal. "The Armritsar massacre pales beside this," he said, setting down the empty cup. "There the British panicked and opened fire. This had nothing of panic about it. Model told me what he would do, and he did it." He shook his head, still hardly believing what he had just been through.

"So he did." Nehru had gobbled his cake like a starving wolf, and ate his companion's when he saw Gandhi did not want it. His once-immaculate white jacket and pants were torn, filthy, and blood-spattered; his cap sat awry on his head. But his eyes, usually so somber, were lit with a fierce glow. "And by his brutality, he has delivered himself into our hands. No one now can imagine the Germans have anything but their own interests at heart. We will gain followers all over the country. After this, not a wheel will turn in India."

"Yes, I will declare the *Satyagraha* campaign," Gandhi said. "Noncooperation will show how we reject foreign rule, and will cost the Germans dear because they will not be able to exploit us. The combination of nonviolence and determined spirit will surely shame them into granting us our liberty."

"There—you see." Encouraged by his mentor's rally, Nehru

rose and came round the table to embrace the older man. "We will triumph yet."

"So we will," Gandhi said, and sighed heavily. He had pursued India's freedom for half his long life, and this change of masters was a setback he had not truly planned for, even after England and Russia fell. The British were finally beginning to listen to him when the Germans swept them aside. Now he had to begin anew. He sighed again. "It will cost our poor people dear, though."

"Cease firing," Model said. Few good targets were left on Qutb Road; almost all the Indians in the procession were down or had run from the guns.

Even after the bullets stopped, the street was far from silent. Most of the people the German platoon had shot were alive and shrieking: as if he needed more proof, the Russian campaign had taught the field marshal how hard human beings were to kill outright.

Still, the din distressed him, and evidently Lasch as well. "We ought to put them out of their misery," the major said.

"So we should." Model had a happy inspiration. "And I know just how. Come with me."

The two men turned their backs on the carnage and walked around the row of armored personnel carriers. As they passed the lieutenant commanding the platoon, Model nodded to him and said, "Well done."

The lieutenant saluted. "Thank you, sir." The soldiers in earshot nodded at one another: nothing bucked up the odds of getting promoted like performing under the commander's eye.

The Germans behind the armored vehicles were not so proud of themselves. They were the ones who had let the march get this big and come this far in the first place. Model slapped his boot with his field marshal's baton. "You all deserve courts-martial," he said coldly, glaring at them. "You know the orders concerning native assemblies, you there you were tagging along, more like sheepdogs than soldiers." He spat in disgust.

"But, sir—" began one of them—a sergeant-major, Model saw. He subsided in a hurry when Model's gaze swung his way.

"Speak," the field marshal urged. "Enlighten me—tell me what possessed you to act in the disgraceful way you did. Was it some evil spirit, perhaps? This country abounds with them, if you listen to the natives—as you all too obviously have been."

The sergeant-major flushed under Model's sarcasm, but finally burst out, "Sir, it didn't look to me as if they were up to any harm, that's all. The old man heading them up swore they were peaceful, and he looked too feeble to be anything but, if you take my meaning."

Model's smile had all the warmth of a Moscow December night. "And so in your wisdom you set aside the commands you had received. The results of that wisdom you hear now." The field marshal briefly let himself listen to the cries of the wounded, a sound the war had taught him to screen out. "Now then, come with me, yes, you, sergeant-major, and the rest of your shirkers too, or those of you who wish to avoid a court."

As he had known they would, they all trooped after him. "There is your handiwork," he said, pointing to the shambles in the street. His voice hardened. "You are responsible for those people lying there—had you acted as you should, you would have broken up that march long before it ever got so far or so large. Now the least you can do is give those people their release." He set hands on hips, waited.

No one moved. "Sir?" the sergeant-major said faintly. He seemed to have become the group's spokesman.

Model made an impatient gesture. "Go on, finish them. A bullet in the back of the head will quiet them once and for all."

"In cold blood, sir?" The sergeant-major had not wanted to understand him before. Now he had no choice.

The field marshal was inexorable. "They—and you—disobeyed the Reich's commands. They made themselves liable to capital punishment the moment they gathered. You at least have the chance to atone, by carrying out this just sentence."

"I don't think I can," the sergeant-major muttered.

He was probably just talking to himself, but Model gave him no chance to change his mind. He turned to the lieutenant of the platoon that had broken the march. "Place this man under arrest." After the sergeant-major had been seized, Model turned his chill, monocled stare at the rest of the reluctant soldiers. "Any others?"

Two more men let themselves be arrested rather than draw their weapons. The field marshal nodded to the others. "Carry out your orders." He had an afterthought. "If you find Gandhi or Nehru out there, bring them to me alive."

The Germans moved out hesitantly. They were no *Einsatzkommandos*, and not used to this kind of work. Some looked away as they administered the first *coup de grâce*; one missed as a result, and had his bullet ricochet off the pavement and almost

hit a comrade. But as the soldiers worked their way up Qutb
Road they became quicker, more confident, and more competent. War was like that, Model thought. So soon one became
used to what had been unimaginable.

After a while the flat cracks died away, but from lack of targets rather than reluctance. A few at a time, the soldiers returned
to Model. "No sign of the two leaders?" he asked. They all
shook their heads.

"Very well—dismissed. And obey your orders like good Germans henceforward."

"No further reprisals?" Lasch asked as the relieved troopers
hurried away.

"No, let them go. They carried out their part of the bargain,
and I will meet mine. I am a fair man, after all, Dieter."

"Very well, sir."

Gandhi listened with undisguised dismay as the shopkeeper
babbled out his tale of horror. "This is madness!" he cried.

"I doubt Field Marshal Model, for his part, understands the
principle of *ahimsa*," Nehru put in. Neither Gandhi nor he knew
exactly where they were: a safe house somewhere not far from
the center of Delhi was the best guess he could make. The men
who brought the shopkeeper were masked. What one did not
know, one could not tell the Germans if captured.

"Neither do you," the older man replied, which was true;
Nehru had a more pragmatic nature than Gandhi. Gandhi went
on, "Rather more to the point, neither do the British. And
Model, to speak to, seemed no different from any high-ranking
British military man. His specialty has made him harsh and
rigid, but he is not stupid and does not appear unusually cruel."

"Just a simple soldier, doing his job." Nehru's irony was
palpable.

"He must have gone insane," Gandhi said; it was the only
explanation that made even the slightest sense of the massacre
of the wounded. "Undoubtedly he will be censured when news
of this atrocity reaches Berlin, as General Dyer was by the British after Armritsar."

"Such is to be hoped." But again Nehru did not sound hopeful.

"How could it be otherwise, after such an appalling action?
What government, what leaders could fail to be filled with hu-
miliation and remorse at it?"

* * *

Model strode into the mess. The officers stood and raised their glasses in salute. "Sit, sit," the field marshal growled, using gruffness to hide his pleasure.

An Indian servant brought him a fair imitation of roast beef and Yorkshire pudding: better than they were eating in London these days, he thought. The servant was silent and unsmiling, but Model would only have noticed more about him had he been otherwise. Servants were supposed to assume a cloak of invisibility.

When the meal was done, Model took out his cigar-case. The *Waffen-SS* officer on his left produced a lighter. Model leaned forward, puffed a cigar into life. "My thanks, *Brigadeführer*," the field marshal said. He had little use for SS titles of rank, but brigade-commander was at least recognizably close to brigadier.

"Sir, it is my great pleasure," Jürgen Stroop declared. "You could not have handled things better. A lesson for the Indians—less than they deserve, too" (he also took no notice of the servant) "and a good one for your men as well. We train ours harshly too."

Model nodded. He knew about SS training methods. No one denied the daring of the *Waffen-SS* divisions. No one (except the SS) denied that the *Wehrmacht* had better officers.

Stroop drank. "A lesson," he repeated in a pedantic tone that went oddly with the SS's reputation for aggressiveness. "Force is the only thing the racially inferior can understand. Why, when I was in Warsaw—"

That had been four or five years ago, Model suddenly recalled. Stroop had been a *Brigadeführer* then too, if memory served; no wonder he was still one now, even after all the hard fighting since. He was lucky not to be a buck private. Imagine letting a pack of desperate, starving Jews chew up the finest troops in the world.

And imagine, afterward, submitting a 75-page operations report bound in leather and grandiosely called *The Warsaw Ghetto Is No More*. And imagine, with all that, having the crust to boast about it afterward. No wonder the man sounded like a pompous ass. He *was* a pompous ass, and an inept butcher to boot. Model had done enough butchery before today's work—anyone who fought in Russia learned all about butchery—but he had never botched it.

He did not revel in it, either. He wished Stroop would shut up. He thought about telling the *Brigadeführer* he would sooner have been listening to Gandhi. The look on the fellow's face, he thought, would be worth it. But no. One could never be sure who was listening. Better safe.

The shortwave set crackled to life. It was in a secret cellar, a tiny dark hot room lit only by the glow of its dial and by the red end of the cigarette in its owner's mouth. The Germans had made not turning in a radio a capital crime. Of course, Gandhi thought, harboring him was also a capital crime. That weighed on his conscience. But the man knew the risk he was taking.

The fellow (Gandhi knew him only as Lal) fiddled with the controls. "Usually we listen to the Americans," he said. "There is some hope of truth from them. But tonight you want to hear Berlin."

"Yes," Gandhi said. "I must learn what action is to be taken against Model."

"If any," Nehru added. He was once again impeccably attired in white, which made him the most easily visible object in the cellar.

"We have argued this before," Gandhi said tiredly. "No government can uphold the author of a cold-blooded slaughter of wounded men and women. The world would cry out in abhorrence."

Lal said, "That government controls too much of the world already." He adjusted the tuning knob again. After a burst of static, the strains of a Strauss waltz filled the little room. Lal grunted in satisfaction. "We are a little early yet."

After a few minutes, the incongruously sweet music died away. "This is Radio Berlin's English-language channel," an announcer declared. "In a moment, the news program." Another German tune rang out: the Horst Wessel Song. Gandhi's nostrils flared with distaste.

A new voice came over the air. "Good day. This is William Joyce." The nasal Oxonian accent was that of the archetypical British aristocrat, now vanished from India as well as England. It was the accent that flavored Gandhi's own English, and Nehru's as well. In fact, Gandhi had heard, Joyce was a New York-born rabblerouser of Irish blood who also happened to be a passionately sincere Nazi. The combination struck the Indian as distressing.

"What did the English used to call him?" Nehru murmured. "Lord Haw-Haw?"

Gandhi waved his friend to silence. Joyce was reading the

news, or what the Propaganda Ministry in Berlin wanted to present to English-speakers as the news.

Most of it was on the dull side: a trade agreement between Manchukuo, Japanese-dominated China, and Japanese-dominated Siberia; advances by German-supported French troops against American-supported French troops in a war by proxy in the African jungles. Slightly more interesting was the German warning about American interference in the East Asia Co-Prosperity Sphere.

One day soon, Gandhi thought sadly, the two mighty powers of the Old World would turn on the one great nation that stood between them. He feared the outcome. Thinking herself secure behind ocean barriers, the United States had stayed out of the European war. Now the war was bigger than Europe, and the oceans barriers no longer, but highways for her foes.

Lord Haw-Haw droned on and on. He gloated over the fate of rebels hunted down in Scotland: they were publicly hanged. Nehru leaned forward. "Now," he guessed. Gandhi nodded.

But the commentator passed on to unlikely sounding boasts about the prosperity of Europe under the New Order. Against his will, Gandhi felt anger rise in him. Were Indians too insignificant to the Reich even to be mentioned?

More music came from the radio: the first bars of the other German anthem, "Deutschland über Alles." William Joyce said solemnly, "And now, a special announcement from the Ministry for Administration of Acquired Territories. *Reichsminister* Reinhard Heydrich commends Field Marshal Walther Model's heroic suppression of insurrection in India, and warns that his leniency will not be repeated."

"Leniency!" Nehru and Gandhi burst out together, the latter making it into as much of a curse as he allowed himself.

As if explaining to them, the voice on the radio went on, "Henceforward, hostages will be taken at the slightest sound of disorder, and will be executed forthwith if it continues. Field Marshal Model has also placed a reward of 50,000 rupees on the capture of the criminal revolutionary Gandhi, and 25,000 on the capture of his henchman Nehru."

"Deutschland über Alles" rang out again, to signal the end of the announcement. Joyce went on to the next piece of news. "Turn that off," Nehru said after a moment. Lal obeyed, plunging the cellar into complete darkness. Nehru surprised Gandhi by laughing. "I have never before been the henchman of a criminal revolutionary."

The older man might as well not have heard him. "They commended him," he said. "Commended!" Disbelief put the full tally of his years in his voice, which usually sounded much stronger and younger.

"What will you do?" Lal asked quietly. A match flared, dazzling in the dark, as he lit another cigarette.

"They shall not govern India in this fashion," Gandhi snapped. "Not a soul will cooperate with them from now on. We outnumber them a thousand to one; what can they accomplish without us? We shall use that to full advantage."

"I hope the price is not more than the people can pay," Nehru said.

"The British shot us down too, and we were on our way toward prevailing," Gandhi said stoutly. As he would not have a few days before, though, he added, "So do I."

Field Marshal Model scowled and yawned at the same time. The pot of tea that should have been on his desk was nowhere to be found. His stomach growled. A plate of rolls should have been beside the teapot.

"How am I supposed to get anything done without breakfast?" he asked rhetorically (no one was in the office to hear him complain). Rhetorical complaint was not enough to satisfy him. "Lasch!" he shouted.

"Sir?" The aide came rushing in.

Model jerked his chin at the empty space on his desk where the silver tray full of good things should have been. "What's become of what's-his-name? Naoroji, that's it. If he's home with a hangover, he could have had the courtesy to let us know."

"I will enquire with the liaison officer for native personnel, sir, and also have the kitchen staff send you up something to eat." Lasch picked up a telephone, spoke into it. The longer he talked, the less happy he looked. When he turned back to the field marshal, his expression was a good match for the stony one Model often wore. He said, "None of the locals has shown up for work today, sir."

"What? None?" Model's frown made his monocle dig into his cheek. He hesitated. "I will feel better if you tell me some new hideous malady has broken out among them."

Lasch spoke with the liaison officer again. He shook his head. "Nothing like that, sir, or at least," he corrected himself with the caution that made him a good aide, "nothing Captain Wechsler knows about."

Model's phone rang again. It startled him; he jumped. *"Bitte?"* he growled into the mouthpiece, embarrassed at starting even though only Lasch had seen. He listened. Then he growled again, in good earnest this time. He slammed the phone down. "That was our railway officer. Hardly any natives are coming in to the station."

The phone rang again. *"Bitte?"* This time it was a swearword. Model snarled, cutting off whatever the man on the other end was saying, and hung up. "The damned clerks are staying out too," he shouted at Lasch, as if it were the major's fault. "I know what's wrong with the blasted locals, by God—an overdose of Gandhi, that's what."

"We should have shot him down in that riot he led," Lasch said angrily.

"Not for lack of effort that we didn't," Model said. Now that he saw where his trouble was coming from, he began thinking like a General Staff-trained officer again. That discipline went deep in him. His voice was cool and musing as he corrected his aide: "It was no riot, Dieter. That man is a skilled agitator. Armed with no more than words, he gave the British fits. Remember that the Führer started out as an agitator too."

"Ah, but the Führer wasn't above breaking heads to back up what he said." Lasch smiled reminiscently, and raised a fist. He was a Munich man, and wore on his sleeve the hashmark that showed Party membership before 1933.

But the field marshal said, "You think Gandhi doesn't? His way is to break them from the inside out, to make his foes doubt themselves. Those soldiers who took courts rather than obey their commanding officer had their heads broken, wouldn't you say? Think of him as a Russian tank commander, say, rather than as a political agitator. He is fighting us every bit as much as as much as the Russians did."

Lasch thought about it. Plainly, he did not like it. "A coward's way of fighting."

"The weak cannot use the weapons of the strong." Model shrugged. "He does what he can, and skillfully. But I can make his backers doubt themselves, too; see if I don't."

"Sir?"

"We'll start with the railway workers. They are the most essential to have back on the job, yes? Get a list of names. Cross off every twentieth one. Send a squad to each of those homes, haul the slackers out, and shoot them in the street. If the survivors don't report tomorrow, do it again. Keep at it every day until they go back to work or no workers are left."

"Yes, sir." Lasch hesitated. At last he asked, "Are you sure, sir?"

"Have you a better idea, Dieter? We have a dozen divisions here; Gandhi has the whole subcontinent. I have to convince them in a hurry that obeying me is a better idea than obeying him. Obeying is what counts. I don't care a *pfennig* as to whether they love me. *Oderint, dum metuant.*"

"Sir?" The major had no Latin.

" 'Let them hate, so long as they fear.' "

"Ah," Lasch said. "Yes, I like that." He fingered his chin as he thought. "In aid of which, the Muslims hereabouts like the Hindus none too well. I daresay we could use them to help hunt Gandhi down."

"Now that *I* like," Model said. "Most of our Indian Legion lads are Muslims. They will know people, or know people who know people. And"—the field marshal chuckled cynically—"the reward will do no harm, either. Now get those orders out, and ring up Legion-Colonel Sadar. We'll get those feelers in motion—and if they pay off, you'll probably have earned yourself a new pip on your shoulderboards."

"Thank you very much, sir!"

"My pleasure. As I say, you'll have earned it. So long as things go as they should, I am a very easy man to get along with. Even Gandhi could, if he wanted to. He will end up having caused a lot of people to be killed because he does not."

"Yes, sir," Lasch agreed. "If only he would see that, since we have won India from the British, we will not turn around and tamely yield it to those who could not claim it for themselves."

"You're turning into a political philosopher now, Dieter?"

"Ha! Not likely." But the major looked pleased as he picked up the phone.

"My dear friend, my ally, my teacher, we are losing," Nehru said as the messenger scuttled away from this latest in a series of what were hopefully called safe houses. "Day by day, more people return to their jobs."

Gandhi shook his head, slowly, as if the motion caused him physical pain. "But they must not. Each one who cooperates with the Germans sets back the day of his own freedom."

"Each one who fails to ends up dead," Nehru said dryly. "Most men lack your courage, great-souled one. To them, that carries more weight than the other. Some are willing to resist, but would rather take up arms than the restraint of *Satyagraha*."

"If they take up arms, they will be defeated. The British could not beat the Germans with guns and tanks and planes; how shall we? Besides, if we shoot a German here and there, we give them the excuse they need to strike at us. When one of their lieutenants was waylaid last month, their bombers leveled a village in reprisal. Against those who fight through nonviolence, they have no such justification."

"They do not seem to need one, either," Nehru pointed out.

Before Gandhi could reply to that, a man burst into the hovel where they were hiding. "You must flee!" he cried. "The Germans have found this place! They are coming. Out with me, quick! I have a cart waiting."

Nehru snatched up the canvas bag in which he carried his few belongings. For a man used to being something of a dandy, the haggard life of a fugitive came hard. Gandhi had never wanted much. Now that he had nothing, that did not disturb him. He rose calmly, followed the man who had come to warn them.

"Hurry!" the fellow shouted as they scrambled into his ox-cart while the hump-backed cattle watched indifferently with their liquid brown eyes. When Gandhi and Nehru were lying in the cart, the man piled blankets and straw mats over them. He scrambled up to take the reins, saying, "*Inshallah*, we shall be safely away from here before the platoon arrives." He flicked a switch over the backs of the cattle. They lowed indignantly. The cart rattled away.

Lying in the sweltering semi-darkness under the concealment the man had draped on him, Gandhi peered through chinks, trying to figure out where in Delhi he was going next. He had played the game more than once these last few weeks, though he knew doctrine said he should not. The less he knew, the less he could reveal. Unlike most men, though, he was confident he could not be made to talk against his will.

"We are using the technique the American Poe called the 'purloined letter,' I see," he remarked to Nehru. "We will be close by the German barracks. They will not think to look for us there."

The younger man frowned. "I did not know we had safe houses there," he said. Then he relaxed, as well as he could when folded into too small a space. "Of course, I do not pretend to know everything there is to know about such matters. It would be dangerous if I did."

"I was thinking much the same myself, though with me as subject of the sentence." Gandhi laughed quietly. "Try as we will, we always have ourselves at the center of things, don't we?"

He had to raise his voice to finish. An armored personnel carrier came rumbling and rattling toward them, getting louder as it approached. The silence when the driver suddenly killed the engine was a startling contrast to the previous racket. Then there was noise again, as soldiers shouted in German.

"What are they saying?" Nehru asked.

"Hush," Gandhi said absently, not from ill manners, but out of the concentration he needed to follow German at all. After a moment he resumed, "They are swearing at a black-bearded man, asking why he flagged them down."

"Why would anyone flag down German sol—" Nehru began, then stopped in abrupt dismay. The fellow who had burst into their hiding-place wore a bushy black beard. "We had better get out of—" Again Nehru broke off in midsentence, this time because the oxcart driver was throwing off the coverings that concealed his two passengers.

Nehru started to get to his feet so he could try to scramble out and run. Too late—a rifle barrel that looked wide as a tunnel was shoved in his face as a German came dashing up to the cart. The big curved magazine said the gun was one of the automatic assault rifles that had wreaked such havoc among the British infantry. A burst would turn a man into bloody hash. Nehru sank back in despair.

Gandhi, less spry than his friend, had only sat up in the bottom of the cart. "Good day, gentlemen," he said to the Germans peering down at him. His tone took no notice of their weapons.

"Down." The word was in such gutturally accented Hindi that Gandhi hardly understood it, but the accompanying gesture with a rifle was unmistakable.

Face a mask of misery, Nehru got out of the cart. A German helped Gandhi descend. *"Danke,"* he said. The soldier nodded gruffly. He pointed the the barrel of his rifle—toward the armored personnel carrier.

"My rupees!" the black-bearded man shouted.

Nehru turned on him, so quickly he almost got shot for it. "Your thirty pieces of silver, you mean," he cried.

"Ah, a British education," Gandhi murmured. No one was listening to him.

"My rupees," the man repeated. He did not understand

Nehru; so often, Gandhi thought sadly, that was at the root of everything.

"You'll get them," promised the sergeant leading the German squad. Gandhi wondered if he was telling the truth. Probably so, he decided. The British had had centuries to build a network of Indian clients. Here but a matter of months, the Germans would need all they could find.

"In." The soldier with a few words of Hindi nodded to the back of the armored personnel carrier. Up close, the vehicle took on a war-battered individuality its kind had lacked when they were just big, intimidating shapes rumbling down the highway. It was bullet-scarred and patched in a couple of places, with sheets of steel crudely welded on.

Inside, the jagged lips of the bullet holes had been hammered down so they did not gouge a man's back. The carrier smelled of leather, sweat, tobacco, smokeless powder, and exhaust fumes. It was crowded, all the more so with the two Indians added to its usual contingent. The motor's roar when it started up challenged even Gandhi's equanimity.

Not, he thought with uncharacteristic bitterness, that that equanimity had done him much good.

"They are here, sir," Lasch told Model, then, at the field marshal's blank look, amplified: "Gandhi and Nehru."

Model's eyebrow came down toward his monocle. "I won't bother with Nehru. Now that we have him, take him out and give him a noodle"—army slang for a bullet in the back of the neck—"but don't waste my time over him. Gandhi, now, is interesting. Fetch him in."

"Yes, sir." The major sighed. Model smiled. Lasch did not find Gandhi interesting. Lasch would never carry a field marshal's baton, not if he lived to be ninety.

Model waved away the soldiers who escorted Gandhi into his office. Either of them could have broken the little Indian like a stick. "Have a care," Gandhi said. "If I am the desperate criminal bandit you have styled me, I may overpower you and escape."

"If you do, you will have earned it," Model retorted. "Sit, if you care to."

"Thank you." Gandhi sat. "They took Jawaharlal away. Why have you summoned me instead?"

"To talk for a while, before you join him." Model saw that Gandhi knew what he meant, and that the old man remained unafraid. Not that that would change anything, Model thought, although he respected his opponent's courage the more for his keeping it in the last extremity.

"I will talk, in the hope of persuading you to have mercy on my people. For myself I ask nothing."

Model shrugged. "I was as merciful as the circumstances of war allowed, until you began your campaign against us. Since then, I have done what I needed to restore order. When it returns, I may be milder again."

"You seem a decent man," Gandhi said, puzzlement in his voice. "How can you so callously massacre people who have done you no harm?"

"I never would have, had you not urged them to folly."

"Seeking freedom is not folly."

"It is when you cannot gain it—and you cannot. Already your people are losing their stomach for—what do you call it? Passive resistance? A silly notion. A passive resister simply ends up dead, with no chance to hit back at his foe."

That hit a nerve, Model thought. Gandhi's voice was less detached as he answered, "*Satyagraha* strikes the oppressor's soul, not his body. You must be without honor or conscience, to fail to feel your victim's anguish."

Nettled in turn, the field marshal snapped, "I have honor. I follow the oath of obedience I swore with the army to the Führer and through him to the Reich. I need consider nothing past that."

Now Gandhi's calm was gone. "But he is a madman! What has he done to the Jews of Europe?"

"Removed them," Model said matter-of-factly; *Einsatzgruppe* B had followed Army Group Central to Moscow and beyond. "They were capitalists or Bolsheviks, and either way enemies of the Reich. When an enemy falls into a man's hands, what else is there to do but destroy him, lest he revive to turn the tables one day?"

Gandhi had buried his face in his hands. Without looking at Model, he said, "Make him a friend."

"Even the British knew better than that, or they would not have held India as long as they did," the field marshal snorted. "They must have begun to forget, though, or your movement would have got what it deserves long ago. You first made the mistake of confusing us with them long ago, by the way." He touched a fat dossier on his desk.

"When was that?" Gandhi asked indifferently. The man was

beaten now, Model thought with a touch of pride: he had succeeded where a generation of degenerate, decadent Englishmen had failed. Of course, the field marshal told himself, he had beaten the British too.

He opened the dossier, riffled through it. "Here we are," he said, nodding in satisfaction. "It was after *Kristallnacht*, eh, in 1938, when you urged the German Jews to play at the same game of passive resistance you were using here. Had they been fools enough to try it, we would have thanked you, you know: it would have let us bag the enemies of the Reich all the more easily."

"Yes, I made a mistake," Gandhi said. Now he was looking at the field marshal, looking at him with such fierceness that for a moment Model thought he would attack him despite advanced age and effete philosophy. But Gandhi only continued sorrowfully, "I made the mistake of thinking I faced a regime ruled by conscience, one that could at the very least be shamed into doing that which is right."

Model refused to be baited. "We do what is right for our *Volk*, for our Reich. We are meant to rule, and rule we do—as you see." The field marshal tapped the dossier again. "You could be sentenced to death for this earlier meddling in the affairs of the Fatherland, you know, even without these later acts of insane defiance you have caused."

"History will judge us," Gandhi warned as the field marshal rose to have him taken away.

Model smiled then. "Winners write history." He watched the two strapping German guards lead the old man off. "A very good morning's work," the field marshal told Lasch when Gandhi was gone. "What's on the menu for lunch?"

"Blood sausage and sauerkraut, I believe."

"Ah, good. Something to look forward to." Model sat down. He went back to work.

I was shooting the breeze with a friend of mine one day when he said, "Why don't you put me in one of your stories?" So I did—sort of. I don't write mainstream fiction very often. I don't sell it very often, either; this story makes once. Thanks, Bob.

THE GIRL WHO TOOK LESSONS

KAREN VAUGHAN LOOKED AT HER WATCH. "OH my goodness, I'm late," she exclaimed, for all the world like the White Rabbit. Her fork clattered on her plate as she got up from the table. Two quick strides took her to her husband. She pecked him on the cheek. "I've got to run, Mike. Have fun with the dishes. See you a little past ten."

He was still eating. By the time he'd swallowed the bite of chicken breast he'd been chewing, Karen was almost out the door. "What is it tonight?" he called after her. "The cake-decorating class?"

She frowned at him for forgetting. "No, that's Tuesdays. Tonight it's law for non-lawyers."

"Oh, that's right. Sorry." The apology, he feared, went for naught; Karen's heels were already clicking on the stairs as she headed for the garage. Sighing, he finished dinner. He didn't feel especially guilty about not being able to keep track of all his wife's classes. He wondered how she managed herself.

He squirted Ivory Liquid on a sponge, attacked the dishes in the sink. When they were done, he settled into the rocking chair with the latest Tom Clancy thriller. His hobbies were books and tropical fish, both of which kept him close to the condo. After spending the first couple of years of their marriage wondering just what Karen's hobbies were, he'd decided her main one was taking lessons. Nothing that had happened since made him want to change his mind.

Horseback riding, French cuisine, spreadsheets—what it was didn't matter, Mike thought in the couple of minutes before the novel completely engrossed him. If UCLA Extension or a local junior college or anybody else offered a course that piqued her interest, Karen would sign up for it. Once in a while, she'd sign him up too. He'd learned to waltz that way. He didn't suppose it had done him any lasting harm.

Tonight's chicken breasts, sautéed in a white wine sauce with fresh basil, garlic, and onions, were a legacy of the French cooking class. That was one that had left behind some lasting good. So had the spreadsheet course, which helped Karen get a promotion at the accounting firm she worked for. But she hadn't even looked at the epée in the hall closet for at least three years.

Mike shrugged. If taking lessons was what she enjoyed, that was all right with him. They could afford it, and he'd come to look forward to his frequent early evening privacy. Then he started turning pages in his page-turner, and the barking thunder of assault rifles made him stop worrying about his wife's classes.

He jumped at the noise of her key in the deadbolt. By the time she got in, though, he was back to the real world. He got up and gave her a hug. "How'd it go?"

"All right, I guess. We're going to get a quiz next week, he said. God knows when I'll have time to study." She said that whenever she had any kind of test coming up. She always did fine.

While she was talking, she hung her suit jacket in the hall closet. Then she walked down the hall to the bathroom, shedding more clothes as she went. By the time she got to the shower door, she was naked.

As he always did, Mike followed appreciatively, picking up after her. He liked to look at her. She was a natural blonde, and not a pound—well, not five pounds—heavier than the day they got married. He wished he could say the same.

He took off his own clothes while she was getting clean, scratched at the thick black hair on his chest and stomach. He sighed. Yes, he was an increasingly well-fed bear these days.

"Your turn," Karen said, emerging pink and glowing.

She was wearing a teddy instead of pajamas when he came back into the bedroom. "Hi, there," he said, grinning. After a decade of living together, a lot of their communication went on without words. She turned off the light as he hurried toward the bed.

Afterward, drifting toward sleep, he had a thought that had occurred to him before: she made love like an accountant. He'd never said that to her, for fear of hurting her feelings, but he meant it as a compliment. She was competent and orderly in bed as out, and if there were few surprises there were also few disappointments. "No, indeed," he muttered.

"What?" Karen asked. Only a long, slow breath answered her.

Their days went on in that regular fashion, except for the occasional Tuesday when Karen came home with bits of icing in her hair. But the magnificent chocolate cake she did up for Mike's birthday showed she had really got something out of that class.

Then, out of the blue, her firm decided to send her back to Chicago for three weeks. "We just got a big multinational for a client," she explained to Mike, "and fighting off a takeover bid has left their taxes screwed up like you wouldn't believe."

"And your people want *you* to go help straighten things out?" he said. "That's a feather in your cap."

"I'll just be part of a team, you know."

"All the same."

"I know," she said, "but three weeks! All my classes will go to hell. And," she added, as if suddenly remembering, "I'll miss you."

Typical, thought Mike, to get mentioned after the precious classes. But he wasn't too annoyed. He knew Karen was like that. "I'll miss you too," he said, and meant it; they hadn't been apart for more than a couple of days at a time since they'd been married.

Next Monday morning, he made one of love's ultimate sacrifices—he took a half-day off from his engineering job to drive her to LAX through rush-hour traffic. They kissed in the unloading zone till the fellow in the car in back of them leaned on his horn. Then Karen scooped her bags out of the trunk and dashed into the terminal.

While she was away, Mike did a lot of the clichéd things men do when apart from their wives. He worked late several times; going home seemed less attractive without anyone to go home to. He rediscovered all the reasons why he didn't like fast food or frozen entrées. He got horny and rented *Behind the Green Door*, only to find out few things were lonelier than watching a dirty movie by himself.

He talked with Karen every two or three days. Sometimes he'd call, sometimes she would. She called one of the nights he stayed late at the office and, when he called her the next day, accused him of having been out with a floozie. " 'Bimbo' is the eighties word," he told her. They both laughed.

Just when he was eagerly looking forward to having her home, she let him know she'd have to stay another two weeks. "I'm sorry,'' she said, ''but the situation here is so complicated that if we don't straighten it out now once and for all, we'll have to keep messing with it for the next five years.''

''What am I supposed to do, pitch a fit?'' He felt like it. ''I'll see you in two weeks.'' From his tone of voice, she might have been talking about the twenty-first century—and the late twenty-first century, at that.

However much they tried not to, the days crawled by. Another clichéd thing for a man to do is hug his wife silly when she finally gets off her plane. Mike did it.

''Well,'' Karen said, once she had her breath back. ''Hello.''

He looked at his watch. ''Come on,'' he said, herding her toward the baggage claim. ''I made reservations at the Szechuan place we go to, assuming your flight would be an hour late. And since you were only forty minutes late—''

''—we have a chance to get stuck on the freeway instead,'' Karen finished for him. ''Sounds good. Let's do it.''

''No, I told you, we'll have dinner first,'' he said. She snorted.

The world—even traffic—was a lot easier to handle after spicy pork and a couple of cold Tsingtao beers. Mike said so, adding, ''The good company doesn't hurt, either.'' Karen was looking out the window. She didn't seem to have heard him.

When they got back to the condo, she frowned for a few seconds. Then her face cleared. She pointed to Mike's fish tanks. ''I've been gone too long. I hear all the pumps and filters and things bubbling away. I'll have to get used to screening them out again.''

''You've been gone too long.'' Mike set down her suitcases. He hugged her again. ''That says it all.'' His right hand cupped her left buttock. ''Almost, all anyway.''

She drew away from him. ''Let me get cleaned up first. I've been in cars and a plane and airports all day long, and I feel really grubby.''

''Sure.'' They walked to the bedroom together. He took off his clothes while she was getting out of hers. He flopped down on the bed. ''After five weeks, I can probably just about stand waiting another fifteen minutes.''

''Okay,'' she said. She went into the bathroom. He listened to the shower running, then to the blow dryer's electric whine. When she came back, one of her eyebrows quirked. ''From the look of you, I'd say you could just barely wait.''

She got down on the bed beside him. After a while, Mike noticed long abstinence wasn't the only thing cranking his excitement to a pitch he hadn't felt since their honeymoon and maybe not then. Every time, every place she touched him, her caress seemed a sugared flame. And he had all he could do not to explode the instant she took him in her mouth. Snakes wished for tongues like that, he thought dizzily.

When at last he entered her, it was like sliding into heated honey. Again he thought he would come at once. But her smooth yet irresistible motion urged him on and on and on to a peak of pleasure he had never imagined, and then to a place past that. Like a thunderclap, his climax left him stunned.

"My God," he gasped, stunned still, "you've been taking lessons!"

From only a few inches away, he watched her face change. For a moment, he did not know what the change meant. Of all the expressions she might put on, calculation was the last he expected right now. Then she answered him. "Yes," she said, "I have. . . ."

The law for non-lawyers course did not go to waste. A couple of months later, she did their divorce herself.

ABOUT THE AUTHOR

Harry Turtledove is that rarity, a lifelong southern Californian. He is married and has three young daughters. After flunking out of Caltech, he earned a degree in Byzantine history and has taught at UCLA, Cal State Fullerton and Cal State Los Angeles. Academic jobs being few and precarious, however, his primary work since leaving school has been as a technical writer. He has had fantasy and science fiction published in *Isaac Asimov's, Amazing, Analog, Playboy,* and *Fantasy Book*. His hobbies include baseball, chess, and beer.